Acknowledgements

I have more people to thank than I can easily count, starting with my wife, Moneeka, without whose support none of the rest of this would have happened.

Then there's my alpha reading group: Jonathan, Rich, Greg, Allison, Dylin, Yih-hsien, Aurika, and Mom, who contributed immeasurably to early drafts. My professional mentors, Ande and Maurice who gave me much needed early advice. The gang at INKubators who helped polish pieces of this when I couldn't see how.

My developmental editor, Theodora Bryant of Book Editing Associates, whom I frustrated to no end (she says "No" to that; my story was fun to edit, and I am an excellent client). Chris McGrath, cover artist extraordinaire, whose work inspired me, along with Stephanie Yang who reminded me how important good graphic design really is, and who tirelessly helped me make choices I am ill equipped to make. Deranged Doctor studios for the first edition cover as well as spectacular marketing materials.

My web and marketing guru, Marc Greenwald, who designed jcmberne.com and did a wonderful job.

My online teachers: Brandon Sanderson and the cast of Writing Excuses, and Mur Lafferty of I Should Be Writing, all of whom were there for me and asked for nothing in return (at least in part because they have no idea who I am).

And last, my Facebook community, who brought me so much encouragement and support.

Wistful Ascending

Turn One of the Hybrid Helix

JCM Berne

The Gnost House

ISBN-13: 978-1-7349170-1-7

Cover image by Chris McGrath Cover graphics by Stephanie Yang

Contents

Prologue   1

1. Twelve Days Earlier   7

2. Biting Hands   17

3. Barks and Bites   28

4. Curiosity Kills   36

5. What's in a Name?   45

6. Lust at First Sight   54

7. Good Mourning to You   65

8. Rhymes with Fine   75

9. Chemistry With an Engineer   82

10. Legend of the Decipede   88

11. Tempting Fate   97

12. Told You So   106

13. You Might Find It   117

14. The Blue-Skinned Sommelier   122

15. Needle in a Shipstack   132

16. Bliss   141

17. Unpleasant Mysteries   150

18. Papa Bear Jokes   159

19. Tall, Pale, and (Mostly) Handsome   166

20. Levels of Intimidation   175

21. Earth Toys   187

22. Getting Things   200

23. The Dreadnought   209

24. Iron Squid   219

25. Devil Doctor   226

26. Deep History   237

27. Ramifications   249

28. Everything's a Nail   261

29. Ask a Soldier Back to War   269

30. Shockwaves   279

31. The Inquisition   290

32. Broken Point   304

33. Things are Still Nails   318

34. Already Dead   330

35. Breaking Hearts   341

36. Back to Work   353

37. Just After the Prologue   366

38. It's a Trap   376

Epilogue   388

Prologue

Beginning of The End

Rohan's helmet whined with the heavy demand as he drew in a painful, choppy breath.

"Rex, I know it's called a punchline, but you don't have to actually hit me—"

The enormous Hybrid drove a ham-sized fist deep into the soft tissue just below Rohan's sternum.

Mom said if I left Earth I'd die on some nameless moon. Looks like today is my chance to prove her right.

"Before we finish, I just want to say, 'Thank you.'" Rex's teeth gleamed between snarl-locked lips.

"For . . . what?" Rohan's voice was no more than a wheeze.

"I've wanted to do this for years, but I never thought you'd give me an excuse."

"You should have had . . . a little more faith. Give me enough time . . . and I can give anybody a reason . . . to try to kill me."

Rex struck again, a few centimeters lower, his hand sinking wrist-deep in Rohan's belly. The smaller man twisted and thrashed as the acid taste of bile rose in his throat. His heart pounded as he remembered how awful it was to vomit inside a sealed facemask.

He was trapped. Two of the select few people in the galaxy stronger than him held his arms in unbreakable grips. He was submerged thigh-deep in moonstone they had temporarily liquified. A contained gravity field that would have ground most people's bones into paste immobilized his spine.

If I just relax right now, the weight of my head might snap my neck. At least it would be fast. Given all the things I've done, that's probably what I deserve. Maybe more than I deserve.

A woman's voice came over the comm system. "Rex, ease off. If he pukes and chokes to death right now, we won't have a full revenge. And we won't have any answers."

She was hairless, with skin so black that human eyes couldn't quite focus on it. Her small ears lay flat to her skull. Two wide eyes shone like an owl's above her half-mask.

I know her. What was her code name again?

Rex raised a hand as if to slap her, then lowered it slowly. "We don't need answers. We're not investigators, not scientists." The sneer echoed through his tone. "Our way is to act. That's what you two forget, and why I've always been ranked higher."

Rohan coughed. Blood flecked the inside of his mask. "You're ranked higher because . . . the Fathers like the fact that you refuse . . . to think for yourself. It's not . . . respect."

Rohan *felt* Rex's anger surge. The big Hybrid hit him again.

Mom also said I didn't know when to keep my mouth shut. Ten years later and I still don't.

"Rex, I mean it. Calm down."

"Don't interfere, Clear Eyes. Unless you want to be next."

She flinched in response.

That's the Rex I remember. Why even try to persuade when physical threats are an option?

Rohan turned to her, and croaked, "Thanks for trying."

"Don't thank me. You're still going to die on this moon."

"Die? Can't we . . . talk this out?" He paused to draw in more air. "I'd much prefer to die . . . on a different moon. Maybe one with a name? Just to prove my mom wrong."

She turned to The Dwarf, who gripped Rohan's other arm. "Does he always babble this way? Does he doubt that his death is imminent?"

The Dwarf's gravelly sigh was audible over the comms. "He is always like this. When the danger is great his chattering only worsens." His fingers, the color and texture of fine Italian marble, held Rohan's right arm.

Rohan coughed again. The gravitational pressure was squeezing blood into his lungs. "The jokes are my secret weapon. My puns will get so bad . . . you'll let me go just to avoid them."

Rex pulled his arm back as if to deliver another blow, but paused mid-swing, his narrow-set eyes focusing on Clear Eyes. "You said you want answers? To what? We know what he did, and we know he has to die for it. What else is there to say?"

The Dwarf nodded. "Rex is right. Just kill him and get it over with. This brings me no joy."

"Listen, both of you. We know what he did, but not why, and most definitely not how." She tightened her grip uncomfortably. "Don't you think we need to know?"

The Dwarf sighed. "What difference will it make?"

No imagination, these guys. No curiosity, either. It hurts my pride to die at the hands of such a simple-minded pair. Clear Eyes is the only one with two functioning neurons to rub together.

Rex nodded. "He has to die. That's what matters."

"I am not disputing that. His fate is sealed." She swiveled her gaze between the others. "But that information would help us, going forward."

The big Hybrid's long blond hair swung through space as he shook his head. "You're overthinking. He won't willingly answer your questions, and even if he did, what would you really gain? Just a parade of facts spewed out to confuse you."

Rohan drew in a long, slow breath. *That's it. I might deserve to die, but Rex certainly doesn't deserve the satisfaction of being the one to kill me. I have to at least try to escape.*

With an effort of will he *pulled* energy up through the base of his tailbone in twin sparking, spiraling columns. They arced around his spine, winding around vertebrae and up to the base of his skull. A connection was made: a metaphysical circuit snapping shut. The Power coalesced and solidified, flooding out through his body.

His head cleared, his lungs relaxed, and even at fifty gravities, his weight was no longer a burden.

With all the strength he could muster, he jerked his body savagely to the left.

The jolt was sudden and violent enough to pull The Dwarf off balance. The stone-skinned man stumbled into Rohan, who immediately arced his upper body back to the right. His head cracked down into The Dwarf's face.

Think twice next time you multiply gravity around someone who's standing over you. "My mother's people call that karma."

The Dwarf fell backward, stunned, releasing his grip. Rohan's weight returned to normal as the stone around his boots loosened.

One problem solved.

Rohan *sent* a pulse of energy through his legs, pulverizing the puddle of stone holding him in place. He *grabbed* the pool of shards and *pulled* them up in a swirl, forming a quick cyclone of razor-edged pieces.

Rex, roughly humanoid but the size of a small grizzly bear, moved toward Rohan with a fist cocked back at his shoulder for a big overhand right. Rohan *willed* the storm of stone right at the giant, forcing Rex to flinch back and raise both arms to protect his facemask.

Big as you are, you still need that mask to breathe.

Clear Eyes held his left bicep. She jerked him toward her, pulling him off balance, and aimed a vicious knee at his gut.

He twisted, taking the blow on his side. Rohan ignored the cracking of a rib and twisted away, moving with the pull, and snapped a quick kick at the knee of her supporting leg.

"I thought you were too smart to take orders from Rex."

"Shut up."

"Your banter needs work. Did they take Witty Repartee 201 off the Academy curriculum?"

She *lifted* a meter off the ground, reached up with her free arm, and dropped an elbow toward his face.

He raised his right arm in time to deflect the blow. Then he *rose* and pulled her in with his left while punching her in the side.

She wouldn't let go.

They twisted and tumbled together, each tossing violent punches and snapping kicks at the other in a flurry so fast it resembled a pair of mating hummingbirds more than a fistfight.

Rohan torqued and pulled and shoved, fighting for a superior position; fighting to free his arm from her iron grip.

Her eyes gleamed denial. "You've never beaten me in training. You're certainly not going to manage it now, injured, while holding off Rex."

She's not wrong. "I don't see what I have to lose by trying."

Rex's jackhammer blows were rendering the stone pieces into powder. Rohan couldn't manipulate dust, not well enough to use it as a weapon. He tried to spot another source of loose stone nearby; failed.

He paid for his lack of focus when Clear Eyes locked his arm out and hyperextended the elbow, tearing soft tissue inside the joint with an agonizing pop. He fought through the pain and landed a solid punch on her face, loosening her grip just enough to ignite a spark of hope. He twisted his shoulder, fighting wildly to escape.

Before he could get free, a potent sinking feeling overwhelmed his gut as the gravity increased again, crushing him to the ground with a heavy jolt and a fresh cloud of moon dust.

Damn. Hoped The Dwarf would stay stunned longer.

A fast hook from Rex snapped his head around.

The hard surface of the moon liquified under Rohan's feet and he sank down, deep enough for stone to lick at his thighs. The Dwarf stepped up and grabbed his free arm, easily fending off Rohan's halfhearted defensive jabs.

Rex gripped Rohan's shoulders in baseball-glove-sized hands and propped him upright.

Rohan looked into the larger man's facemask and saw ice-cold eyes over a humorless smile.

"I know I should say I won't enjoy this, but it would be a lie." Rex pulled his right arm back, arching his entire body like a bow drawn by invisible hands.

Rohan watched dully as Rex's fist hurtled toward his face. "Things were going so well just a few days ago."

The impact sparked a flash of lightning inside Rohan's head, chased by a quick sunset into darkness.

1

Twelve Days Earlier

R ohan strolled casually along the wide residential boulevard that ran down the middle of the southern arm of the station. Children were playing aimlessly nearby, kicking balls back and forth in a game with no apparent rules.

He let out a long breath, turning his mind away from a vague feeling of disappointment. There had been a time when crowds of people would gather just to glimpse him walking by. He had moved to the station in part to get away from that celebrity, but he was discovering that anonymity had its own drawbacks. Like the loneliness he could somehow feel while walking through crowds of people on a space station filled with millions of sentient beings.

Don't forget, that loneliness is the price you're paying for a life where you haven't seen the inside of a regen tank in six months.

The comm link affixed to the skin behind his ear chirped.

"Tow Chief, please report to work early today. And by 'early,' I mean immediately."

He recognized the voice. Security Chief Wei Li. Not the person who usually coordinated his schedule; also, not technically his boss.

A red ball rolled to a stop at his feet. Rohan sighed and bent to pick it up. He tapped the spot on the back of his jaw that activated the comm link's microphone. "I'm not due for another two hours. How do you know I don't have a date?"

"Do you?"

He sighed. "No."

"Would you like a moment to check your social calendar? Perhaps you have an engagement that slipped your mind, teeming as it is with thoughts of the wide variety of social appointments with which you are confronted."

"No, there's nothing. As usual. I can come out."

His plan hadn't extended further than walking the corridors of the station and listening to songs over his comm. Songs he could already sing along with, despite being in a language he barely spoke.

A Lukhor child, neatly dressed in yellow pants and a red shirt, twin antennae standing at attention, came up and held his hands out for the ball.

Rohan tossed it over.

The boulevard was fifty meters wide, a rolling canyon with a clear diamond shell separating and protecting it from the cold vacuum of space. Walls of shops, living quarters, and offices in stone and wood rose up ten stories on either side. The air was cool, not as dry as expected, and the grass underfoot felt thick and crunchy.

This was the only station he'd ever seen with enough open area that people could actually live out their lives without succumbing to space sickness. Where kids had enough room to kick balls around.

The boy, both antennae twitching as he spoke, shook his head. "Those colors are terrible on you, mister. Brown skin against purple and yellow? You should get a new tailor. Ask for something in forest green or orange. Think about bright red, if you're cool enough to pull it off. Nah, not the red."

Rohan smiled. He was wearing a close-fitting jumpsuit. The yellow was somewhere between neon and actively fluorescent, with accents in a metallic purple rumored to cause an assortment of mental illnesses if a human stared at it too long. The material was thick and soft against his skin. The design was functional, not aesthetic.

The boy's reaction wasn't a surprise. Lukhor, as a species, were fashion-conscious. It obviously started young.

"Not my choice, buddy. It's the station uniform. Which you should know. I guess you're new here?"

The boy nodded. A voice called out and the boy turned and ran back to his parent.

Rohan's comm chirped again.

"The need is urgent, Rohan. One of the wormholes just opened. A ship has come through and is heading this way." Wei Li's tone was even, despite the enormity of her words.

"You mean one of the dormant wormholes? That haven't opened in ten thousand years?"

"I would have to do some research to determine the exact number."

"I thought . . . Never mind. Aren't the other ends of those wormholes supposed to lie outside of known space?"

"Seeing as we do not know where the other ends are located, by definition they are outside of known space, yes."

"So, we're talking about a first contact here? A new species? Or at least a new civilization?"

"That is Wistful's belief."

"Okay, that's super-interesting. But are you sure I'm the one you should be assigning to this particular task?"

"I am not, Tow Chief Rohan. However, Wistful is."

"Oh. All right, I'm coming. Where does she want me? Just head out into space or report for some kind of briefing?" He was concentrating as he spoke, trying to remember if he'd ever been trained in protocols for first contact situations. There had been a lot of training.

"Exit immediately to intercept. I am transmitting directions to your mask. You'll be briefed en route."

That voice was Wistful's. Unsurprisingly, the station had taken a direct interest in whatever was coming out of that wormhole.

"On my way."

Rohan looked around quickly, taking in the assortment of station residents walking to or from their jobs, children playing, and a scattering of tourists gawking at the views of the planet above them. He looked up, checking that the way was clear.

He *lifted* off the ground, accelerating rapidly toward the diamond lid high above the street. Just before striking it he turned, carving a right angle in the air, and continued up the corridor, his back skimming the roof, centimeters from the hard vacuum beyond it.

He flew station-north, toward the center section of the cross-shaped station, where he knew a rarely used airlock was waiting for him. He pulled his mask out of its pocket in his hood and over his face as he slipped into the open airlock. The mask was made of the same diamond-based material as the roof over the station; its air supply hissed awake as soon as the lining sealed to his face.

The airlock had cycled fully within seconds. He pulled himself through the outer door and into space, leaving the gravitational field generated by the station and floating away from the airlock.

Lines appeared, projected onto the inner surface of his mask, illuminating a flight path away from Wistful.

He flew a tight orbit around the station, leaving the nearby planet and the system's central star, Toth, behind him. It was a struggle to turn his attention away from the beauty of the station, coated in sparkling diamond and lit up by Toth and an array of vast floating mirrors.

Once clear of the station and the scattering of shuttles flying close to it, he punched up his speed.

On a planet his velocity was limited by how much drag he could overcome. In an Earth-like atmosphere he could reach his top speed in seconds. In open space, he could approach the speed of light, given enough time to accelerate. And a reason to go that fast.

Wistful's voice came over his comms. "Full acceleration, please. The ship is not responding to hails. It might be in need of assistance. Or deterrence." Her voice was flat, typical of an artificial intelligence, her tone failing to convey the urgency her words probably warranted.

"Copy." With an effort of will he *pushed* harder, increasing his acceleration by an order of magnitude.

"What am I supposed to be doing once I reach this ship?"

Wei Li answered. "First, attempt to establish communication. Offer any possible assistance, but as always, it is conditional upon the ship adhering to normal procedures."

"Meaning they have to agree to power down before approaching Wistful."

"Yes."

"And if they won't?"

"Do whatever you believe is required."

He sighed. "Copy."

He was halfway to the system's edge when his mask's display indicated he needed to slow down. He decelerated according to instructions, following a course that would bring him to a low velocity relative to the ship.

Rohan began probing the ship with both thoughts and comms the moment he saw it. No response. It was as useful as probing an asteroid.

"Wistful, I don't recognize this ship design. And she still won't talk to me."

Wei Li answered. "She isn't answering us, either, and I can detect no sign of life from the ship itself. She might be . . . dead? Perhaps something about the wormhole?"

If Wei Li couldn't *sense* her aura, the ship was most likely dead. Wei Li was one of the most sensitive empaths Rohan had ever met.

Had the wormhole killed the ship?

He put the idea aside. He wasn't smart enough to even guess at how dangerous it was to navigate a long-dead wormhole. That discussion was best left to the physicists. Or the mystics.

"I'll try to get her attention the old-fashioned way. Maybe there's a crew on board that will talk to me. Have you guys tried radio, maybe? Or lasers? Whatever people use. Maybe something low tech. Semaphore. Send someone out here with flags."

"We're trying everything within reason, from tachyons to radio. Wistful is helping us dig comm equipment out of storage lockers that haven't been opened since before your species developed language. We're testing each as quickly as we can."

The comm link dinged. Wei Li had nothing more to say.

Rohan flew closer to the alien ship.

The hull was a standard, highly reflective, white. Most civilizations built ships easy to see as a default—unless they specifically wanted ships that weren't.

The bulk of the ship fit into a vast teardrop shape, a common configuration for anything that was atmosphere-capable. It was distorted by three bulging spheres, two at the sides like bullish shoulders, and the last attached solidly to the tail of the teardrop.

The spheres looked like gravity bootstrap drives. Fairly common, as they were the cheapest and most efficient drives available and required no tech beyond basic artificial gravity. Also, a purely technical drive, which fit with it being a dead ship.

He felt a small frisson of anxiety as he got closer than was considered polite. He had little choice, as long as the ship wouldn't answer him.

Markings littered the hull he could recognize as writing but not decipher. He got closer still and saw blisters and discs marring the ship; probably sensors and docking ports. Closer yet, and he could make out scars etched into the outer layer that looked freshly repaired, unpainted metal gleaming jagged lines across the hull.

This ship has been through a firefight. Recently.

Rohan circled, hoping to find something like a porthole. He needed to contact someone inside.

He slowed as he neared the blunt end of the teardrop. "I'm approaching the front of the ship."

He coasted to a slow drift, close enough to touch the hull. He focused on the surface and floated along, braced for some reaction. Most ships would fire on anybody getting so close without an invitation.

Wei Li's voice spoke into his ear. "Anything?"

"Not yet. Wait . . . here's something."

He saw a break in the white of the hull: a strip of material, wide and thin, set flush into the hull, not reflecting any light.

A window.

Rohan floated across to the window, gently, arms held in front of him with hands open, like a child approaching to pet a stray cat.

Glare made it hard to see in. There was no visible reaction from the ship as he approached, so he put his hands on the hull and pressed his visor up against it.

With his hands cupped around his head he finally got a look inside the ship.

"It's a bridge. A command deck or observation deck or something. There's a big chair in the middle; I'd guess a captain's chair? And desks around it, all with a view of the window, and screens and switches and stuff." His voice trailed off.

Wistful spoke to him. "Are there crew, Rohan? What species?"

He laughed. "I was going to say they're like nothing I've seen before, but that's not really true. There are twelve of them, all staring at me."

"What species, Rohan?" Wei Li, less patient than Wistful, asked him.

"I think they're bears. Like, straight up. Earth bears."

The creatures in the room were tall, much taller than humans, and covered in heavy brown or black fur. Their jaws were long and filled with fearsome teeth, all uncomfortably exposed, because they stood with their mouths wide open and stared at him through the window.

Rohan fought back an involuntary quiver of fear. He supposed fearing bears was encoded somewhere deep inside the human half of his DNA.

He moved a couple of meters to his left. Their heads swiveled to follow him as he moved. A couple of them turned away, closing their jaws shut and tapping at their desks, as if using instruments to verify what they were seeing. Maybe they weren't used to people flying through space with no more protection than a facemask and a jumpsuit.

"Are you still trying to radio these guys? Because they are definitely aware of us."

Wei Li answered. "Still no response on any frequency we're monitoring."

"All right. I'll try to get inside. Maybe I can get them to, you know, talk-talk."

He rapped on the window. The nearest creatures jumped back at the sound. At least they weren't deaf.

He moved up so his full body was inside the viewing angle of the window. He showed his hands first, drawing attention to them.

Then he pointed to himself, tapping his own chest vigorously. Then he pointed through the window, to an open spot of floor near the front of the room.

"Can I use your bathroom?" He didn't mime that thought.

He repeated the motions, then pressed his face to the window again. One of the smaller of the creatures, its fur marked with gray streaks that Rohan assumed indicated advanced age, stepped forward. It waved at him, then pointed to its lower right.

Rohan nodded and flew in the indicated direction. A hole opened up in the hull.

Weapons port or airlock, he figured he'd find out pretty quickly.

He got lucky. "I'm inside. Can I breathe in here?"

"Checking. Pressure's within tolerances." His mask had quite a few sensors built into the edges, and Wistful could monitor them remotely. "Breathable for humanoids Class A through D."

"Great, thanks. Unmasking."

The inner door of the airlock opened as he slipped his mask off his face and dropped it over his back and into his hood.

Rohan took a deep breath. The air was slightly warmer than station standard, thickly humid, and smelled like summer day at a poorly maintained zoo.

First lesson: Space bears were not sticklers for personal hygiene.

Two of the bear creatures were standing outside the airlock. They were dressed in a dark-red material, shiny like leather and stiff enough to hold its shape; armor or the base of a space suit. Both were pointing large tubes of metal at him.

He briefly considered taking the guns away and doing rude things with them.

Instead, Rohan raised his hands. "Don't shoot. I come in peace."

The bears looked at each other quizzically, then turned back to him. One gestured toward the bridge.

He walked, hands still raised. He wasn't sure what to do. Should he try to appear *more* threatening? Make them afraid? Or be nice, go for cute and cuddly?

As a lance in the il'Drach Imperial Fleet he had been trained to lead with fear, to default to a show of force in almost every situation. He'd lived and breathed intimidation and violence daily for ten years.

I'm here, and not on the deck of a Fleet warship, because I decided that's not how I want to do things anymore.

The two guards led him to the bridge. The gray-streaked one walked over. Based on its relative size and build Rohan guessed it was a female. Though small for a space bear, she was still a foot taller than him and, at a guess, a hundred kilos heavier.

He smiled. Not too wide. Not all sentients viewed a baring of teeth as an inherently friendly gesture.

He cleared his throat and prepared to speak the Fire Speech. He was out of practice, but he doubted the bears could understand Drachna or English or the other local languages he knew.

He was rusty. He spoke slowly, enunciating carefully.

"Hello. I am Tow Chief Second Class Rohan, acting representative of the independent space station, Wistful." He pointed out the window in the general direction of the Wistful.

The bears all stepped away as he spoke, glancing wildly about.

The gray-streaked female spoke first. "How is it that we fly through the Eye, which has been closed for thousands of years, and the first being we meet can speak our language?"

Second lesson: Space bears were not sticklers for etiquette.

"Actually, funny thing. I don't. Speak your language, that is. It's kind of a trick, called the Fire Speech. Imagine every language is just a shadow cast on a wall by a fire. Someone taught me to speak like the fire."

The female tilted her head. *She seems dubious. Always hard to read the body language of a new species.*

"I do not understand."

"To tell the truth, I don't either. But it works."

She looked to the larger bear to her left, a gigantic creature with heavy scarring around his muzzle and a glowing red orb where his right eye should have been. He shrugged his huge, powerful-looking shoulders.

The female shook her head and turned back to Rohan. "I still don't understand, but that's not relevant right now. I am <roaring sound>, of the people of <another roaring sound>. I am the captain of this ship. We are looking for refuge. Food, water, air, rest. We have had a long journey. We would be most grateful for any aid you could offer."

Third lesson: Space bears could put theoretical concerns aside when there were practical matters to attend to. It was a good sign as far as Rohan was concerned.

"Okay, small problem there. I can't reproduce those sounds, either your name or that of your people. I don't think I have the right facial structure for it. I'll just say you are the Ursans, and you're going to be Ursula. Congratulations."

The Ursan tilted her head. "Why those words?"

"You look just like bears. They're a . . . creature from my homeworld." The Ursans muttered among themselves in unhappy tones. "Er, to be more specific, they're an apex predator species, and people of my race are terrified of them. We use stories of bears to scare our young ones when they misbehave."

The female nodded. "Then we will be happy to be known as Ursans."

"Great. You are welcome to dock at Wistful, and we can talk about providing whatever help you need. But you'll have to turn off your drives. No ship is allowed to approach the station under power."

The Ursans looked unhappy again. The large one-eyed Ursan surged forward two steps. "Let me kill him now for his insolence! How dare he suggest we turn off our drives!"

"Calm down <unintelligible roar that was probably a name>. Let him explain. We don't know their ways." She turned to Rohan. "This is a surrender? Turn off the drives. Is that what you are . . . demanding? Asking?"

Rohan spread his hands. "No, no, nothing like that. Not surrender. It's just standard procedure for anyone visiting. Respected guests, traders, anyone. Even Imperial warships power down when approaching Wistful. Otherwise, when you dock, one mistake firing the drives could tear the station in half. No offense."

2

Biting Hands

The one-eyed Ursan backed off. Rohan couldn't keep the name-roars straight. Ursula he could remember, but he wasn't going to make up real names for them all. He would have to use nicknames. Maybe Angry Bear for this one.

That works.

Ursula let out a heavy breath, somewhere between a sigh and a bark. "We can agree to powering down, since it is your way and we are in great need. But how will we approach?"

"Does your ship have an anchor point?"

Ursula shrugged. "I don't understand that term." She turned to some of her crew, who held their own paws up in confusion.

"Huh." Did they not have anchor points on their ships? "The place on your structure strong enough to bear the force of pulling the ship around. That's for me—I'm a tow chief. Second Class. I fly over, you power down, I pull your ship safely into a berth. When you're ready to leave, I pull you out."

"You mean you bring a ship to pull us into berth?"

Fourth lesson: These space bears were from really, really far away.

"No, no. Just me. With my hands." He held up his hands to illustrate.

Angry Bear growled at them. "He is mocking us!"

One of the other Ursans spoke up. "Ma'am, the superstructure where the main body connects to the aft drive should be able to handle that kind of stress."

Ursula nodded. "Explain to him."

The engineer looked at Rohan. "The sphere at the back of the ship is the aft drive. Where it meets the main body of the ship. We might have to peel back some hull to expose a, er, handhold. Shouldn't take long."

Rohan thought. "Sounds good. If you can do that now, I'll get clearance." He tapped his mask to show what he meant. "And then I can bring you in. We will start figuring out what you guys eat, what you need, medical stuff, all of that. You'll love it; Wistful is a wonderful place."

Angry Bear growled at him. "We are not meant to live on a space station. We will pause there, but we mean for the planet beyond."

Rohan shook his head. "You can't land on the planet, sorry. We can talk about all that stuff."

Angry Bear looked ready to growl and yell some more, but he reined himself in, spun around, and stormed off the bridge.

Ursula looked at Rohan. "The planet is forbidden to us? Why?"

"Not so much forbidden, but the native fauna are really dangerous. Nothing can survive on the surface for any length of time."

"Do not underestimate the toughness of our people."

Rohan shrugged. *Pick your battles.* "I'm just trying to look out for you."

Ursula nodded. "My engineers will begin work on the hull."

Rohan nodded back and turned away. He spoke more softly, a tone meant for his microphone and not the Ursans, and switched to Drachna. "I assume you guys got all of that."

Wistful answered. "It would be best if they could be dissuaded from visiting the planet."

Wei Li spoke shortly after her. "The question is, how best to do that? Forbidding them might just make them dig in their heels. Or hooves. Do they have heels, Rohan?"

Rohan looked down. "Their boots have heels. I could ask to see their feet, but given the smell in here I don't think asking anyone to take boots off is a good idea. Let me get a feel for them."

Rohan turned to Ursula. "I'd love to hear your story, if you're willing to tell it. Why you came here, what your people are like. Anything you can share about the worlds you came from."

"Tow Chief Second Class Rohan, are you trying to mate with me?"

Rohan stifled a laugh. "No, ma'am, no, I'm not. At least not at the moment."

She peppered him with questions while her crew scuttled away, busy with the ship alterations. "Who rules this sector of space?"

Rohan scratched his beard. "Most of this sector is under the control of the il'Drach Empire. The only exceptions are places the il'Drach haven't bothered to conquer yet. Places out of the way with few or no interesting resources. Like Toth, this system. With no habitable planets the il'Drach just don't bother. They leave it, and Wistful, alone."

She nodded. "They must be a most fierce, heavily-furred people, these il'Drach. Not like your kind."

"Well, you'll probably never meet a pureblood il'Drach in person. They mostly act through representatives." *Like me.*

"Are they cruel overlords, then, these il'Drach?"

He paused. *How do I explain the il'Drach?* "I don't know if I'd say that. They're mostly hands-off; let the planets do their own thing. They don't care about religious practices, or even economic structures. But they're capricious. Whole planets have been wiped out, down to the last microbe, by the il'Drach, with no explanation given. Not often, but still."

Her eyes widened. "And there is no resistance to their rule?"

"People try, but it never lasts. If you go far enough you will find independent systems at the edges, but they're only independent because, like I said, the il'Drach haven't gotten to them yet."

"I see. How far are we from our home system?"

"I honestly have no idea. I'm sure there are people working on that."

"Are most sentient species in this sector so small and hairless?"

"Compared to your people, I'd say so."

"Does this station have enough room for two thousand Ursans?"

"She has two million residents and I'd say she's at least half empty. Room is the least of our concerns."

He answered the rest of her questions as best he could until her engineers were finished modifying their ship for towing.

Wei Li spoke into his ear. "Wistful confirms: Drives are powered down."

Rohan excused himself and returned to the airlock. He was back in space within thirty seconds.

He circled to the rear of the teardrop and found the point where the hull had been pulled away from the ship's frame. He flew in and found a juncture where silvery structural elements fused together and flowed into the bootstrap drive.

If the ship had been designed to fly under the power of that single drive, then it should be able to take the same force when generated by his hands.

He gently put both hands over the anchor point. It was hot to the touch, lumpy with fresh welds. He summoned a smooth flow of Power into his body and *shoved*.

The ship moved.

"Wistful, we have acceleration. Where am I taking her?"

"Nose her in under port East 7A. She has a hatch at the top that we can mate to."

"Copy."

Wistful wasn't visible to the naked eye from that distance. Toth, a medium-sized yellow sun very similar to Sol, lay ahead, and the planet Toth 3 was a blip in front of it.

Rohan *pushed* the Ursan ship, gently propelling it toward Wistful.

After a while the station emerged from the surrounding darkness, a sparkling jewel between them and Toth 3, broad solar arrays fanning out on all sides.

Rohan reversed his grip and *pulled*, slowing the Ursan ship for their approach.

Wistful's eastern spur had a series of docking ports with flexible links that could mate with nonstandard ships. They were rarely used, because they were rarely needed. Whatever could be said about the drawbacks of the il'Drach Empire, it had enforced standards in areas like docking port configurations, messaging systems, and currencies that made people's lives generally easier.

Rohan listened to Earth songs while he flew. Ten years away from Earth and exposure to a hundred civilizations and he still loved music from home more than any other.

Wistful grew from a shapeless sparkle into a defined cross; a central ball with four thin arms spreading out, long and delicate.

As they approached more details came into focus. The center was a fat teardrop, hundreds of meters across, oriented as if it were falling toward the planet. That teardrop was studded with ports, struts, sensor arrays, and a multitude of rectangular decks jutting out at odd angles.

The four arms projected from the teardrop at perfect right angles to one another. They were thin and straight, their even lines disturbed only by the dozens of ships docked at various points along their length. Each arm fattened toward its tip, giving extra room for hydroponics farms, ranches, and fish tanks.

Rohan gently guided her into a spot below East 7A. He felt a small surge of pride as the massive vessel slipped into place. While any half-blooded il'Drach could simply drag ships through space, towing them safely into a berth required delicacy and skill. It had taken him two months of practice before Wistful would trust him to do the job independently.

He disengaged and watched as a docking cradle extended from the station and locked onto the Ursan ship.

"Wistful, any more ships need a tow? If not, I'm going to grab a shower and eat something. I missed breakfast."

Wei Li answered. "Please go inside the docking area first."

"Why?" It was an honest question. He was a tow chief, not security or diplomatic staff.

"We don't fully trust the peaceful intentions of these Ursans." The "we" clearly meant her and Wistful.

"Really? They seemed pleasant enough. But if you want . . ." Wistful had ages of experience in these matters. She might be wrong, but she wasn't paranoid or stupid.

"We do. Plus, they know you already. Having a familiar face on the station might ease their transition."

"Okay, I'll go in. But I'm adding 'First Contact Specialist' to my CV."

"If I knew what a CV was, I might object. In any case, I'll meet you there."

"Copy."

Rohan scratched at his face around the edges of his mask. His beard had grown into that medium-length where it was full enough to be itchy and unkempt-looking, but too short to stay in a nice beard shape. One thing he missed about the Imperial Fleet was its barbers.

"To your left, Rohan, and behind the blue turret." He imagined he heard laughter, or at least mockery, in Wistful's tone.

"Thanks, Wistful. I'm not used to finding the airlocks on this arm."

She didn't answer.

The outer airlock door was cycling open as he reached it. He had his mask off and secured in his hood before the airlock finished pressurizing.

The airlock opened into the lowest level of the station, full of maintenance machinery and equipment for moving heavy cargo off of, and onto, ships.

He nodded to a pair of lavender-skinned Kratics wearing ship's livery and welding something behind a displaced wall panel. He checked the wall markings to find the way to the main corridor and followed.

He was quickly glad he hadn't placed a bet with Wei Li over the peaceful disposition of the Ursans. A roar was echoing through the corridor's metal walls, loud enough to be heard over a storm of shouts and screaming.

"Bring me that flying plant-eater who dared demand the surrender of the *Pride of Ursa*! I will be picking my teeth with his bones while the captain of this station comes to capitulate to us! And be fast; the longer I wait the more of you will find homes in my belly!" Angry Bear was earning his nickname.

"Wei Li, how bad is it over there? I'm a few seconds away."

"Nobody's been eaten yet, but these mammals came storming out with projectile weapons. I'd prefer to find a safe way to contain this."

Rohan muttered under his breath. Violence was one thing, but projectiles on a space station had a way of spreading damage to uninvolved citizens. *No time for walking.* He stepped up into the air and darted forward with a whoosh of suddenly displaced air.

The two maintenance workers dropped their tools and ran in the other direction when Rohan emerged into a wide-open bay.

"I wanted to meet a new species. I thought they were cute. I called them bears. I thought they'd be cuddly and fun. Ugh."

"What was that, Rohan?" Wistful was definitely laughing at him.

"Nothing, Wistful. Talking to myself. Again." He let out a long breath, willing his temper to calm. "Stay light. Light. Light of heart, light of spirit." It was a new mantra he was trying out. *Not really working for me.*

He was halfway across the docking bay before anyone inside knew he was there.

Angry Bear had emerged from the doors set into the floor at the rear of the bay. He was wearing the same heavy red leathers that they'd all been wearing on the ship, but his hands *(paws?)* were encased up to the elbow in metal gauntlets covered in glowing circuitry, nozzles, ports, spikes, and nasty-looking blades. A heavy chain trailed from each elbow to the ground, clinking against the hull plating as he moved.

There were four other Ursans flanking Angry Bear, each nearly as large and nearly as angry-looking. Instead of gauntlets, they were carrying massive rifles, easily as big as an average human, with one large muzzle at the end surrounded by three smaller muzzles.

The rifles were pointed at Wei Li, who was standing calmly in the center of the bay with her arms spread in front of her, palms forward.

Wei Li was the only member of her species that Rohan had met. She was about the same size and configuration as a human female, but with a reptilian template. Two eyes with vertically slit pupils. Mostly yellow skin, streaked with red and green. Lines of fine scales traced patterns over her exposed skin.

Rohan immediately grasped the problem Wei Li was having. She could dodge or *divert* any bullets the Ursans fired at her, but since they were inside Wistful, those bullets would go somewhere and possibly cause serious damage. The Ursans had no real chance to take over the station, but they obviously didn't know that. If they tried, who knew how many civilians would be hurt in the crossfire.

The bay held an assortment of large crates, three very old and dusty shuttles, and not much else. Three of Wei Li's security team were taking cover behind one of the shuttles, holding small energy weapons but not firing yet. Probably waiting for some signal from their chief.

Rohan didn't wait for any signal.

He was fairly new to being a tow chief, but he had lots of experience dealing with armed and hostile aliens.

The four gun-toting Ursans formed a semicircle behind Angry Bear.

Rohan crossed the bay with a huge burst in speed, staying low to the floor as he went. He buzzed the front of the Ursan formation, the wind of his passage flattening their fur to their hides. The Hybrid grabbed the end of its huge rifle with both hands as he reached the Ursan at the far side of the semicircle.

His momentum ripped the rifle out of its hands. Rohan pivoted in midair, turning, and somersaulting in one smooth motion.

As he spun back toward the Ursans, Rohan swung the rifle like a hammer and slammed it down into weapon the next Ursan in line was holding. That gun folded in half on impact, emitting a shower of sparks, a cloud of smoke, and an array of fumes as it smashed into the floor.

Angry Bear and the two remaining rifle-bearing Ursans were turning toward him.

They're faster than they look.

Angry Bear was the less immediate threat, because he wasn't going to be shooting much out of his gauntlets. The other two were raising their rifles to point at Rohan.

He could have *diverted* the bullets as easily as Wei Li, but that wouldn't protect Wistful. So, he dropped to the floor and kicked himself to his right. With another burst of speed, he plowed into the Ursan whose rifle he had smashed, stuck his face into the Ursan's chest, grabbed underneath both arms, and flew the creature back-first into his comrades.

There was always a turning point in fighting unknown enemies when he'd find out just how savage they were. Would they try to shoot *through* their comrade and into him? Would they toss their rifles aside and look for another way? He got his answer. A few bullets thudded into the Ursan's armor, but it stopped quickly. They weren't willing to kill one of their own.

Rohan had created a Hybrid-Ursan missile; it crunched into the third Ursan at full speed. That soldier's rifle took the brunt of the impact, collapsing with the train.

The three made a tangled heap that flew past the last Ursan and crashed into a large cargo crate. Rohan could feel hot, scratchy fur pressing against him. Something dripped sticky wetness onto his arm.

He felt things breaking and shuddering under his hands.

These two have had enough.

He stood up from the pile of bodies. The last Ursan's rifle was pointing at his torso.

He wasn't sure he could fly into the stream without being turned or deflected, which would cause a storm of ricochets sweeping the bay. His only choice was to set his feet squarely behind him and push forward.

He fought his instinct to sidestep the rifle's path and was rewarded with a stream of bullets to the chest.

The heavy slugs hit with a thudding staccato rhythm, sending pulses of force through every bone and ligament in his body, then falling lifelessly to the ground, spent.

He would need a new uniform.

With a guttural growl, he closed on the Ursan.

The weapon was nothing like anything he'd seen on Earth or anywhere else in the sector. It clearly wasn't designed just to kill people, but to chew through tanks or heavily armored ships; maybe even protected bunkers. It was also the stupidest possible weapon to use inside a space station, especially if were you hoping to live on it after the fight ended.

The Ursan was backpedaling frantically to keep distance between them while he maintained the stream of gunfire. The tow chief was closing rapidly, but not quickly enough to make him happy.

A huge metal hand clubbed down from the side onto the tip of the gun and drove it into the ground.

"He's mine! Mine, I said!" Angry Bear backhanded his own man, sending him careening through the air and into the back wall of the docking bay, then spun to face Rohan, the chains attached to his elbows whipping around as he moved.

Rohan stood and brushed shrapnel and the last shreds of his shirt away from his chest. He took deep breaths. Charging into that gun had not been pleasant.

Angry Bear surveyed the carnage that remained of his team. "You will pay for what you've done to my men, Rohan Second Class."

"Actually, my *name* is Rohan, and the title is Tow Chief Second Class. I'm a tow chief, but a low-ranking one, so the Second Class part is really a modifier to the Tow Chief, not the Rohan."

"Enough!" Angry Bear roared and swung his arms up and down, whipping his chains into the flooring with a hellacious clang.

"I mean, I don't want there to be any more misunderstandings between us."

Another Ursan was coming up out of the open bay doors behind him. Rohan recognized Ursula's voice as she called out. "I apologize for this situation, Tow Chief Second Class Rohan."

Rohan didn't turn away from Angry Bear. He doubted Ursula would shoot him in the back, and if she was, he had Wei Li to watch out for him. "I thought you came in peace? As refugees? What's all this?"

Angry Bear roared again, drool hanging off his black lips in thin strands. "She is captain on the ship, but I am the War Leader! *I* am! On land, I lead and *she* follows!"

Ursula responded with a tired voice. "There was a ruling. This station is so vast it counts to our people as land. He leads expeditions off the ship as much as I lead on board."

Rohan nodded. "I see. Can you tell me the quickest way to end this situation? Preferably without further bloodshed?"

"The only blood that will be shed is yours, plant-eater!"

Ursula sighed. "One of you must submit, I am afraid. He is master of all the land he surveys, until he is proven not to be. That is our way."

Rohan turned his head slightly, enough to check on the four downed Ursans in his peripheral vision. All were moving, though feebly. That was good; he hadn't been trying to kill any of them.

"That's not exactly what I wanted, but sometimes it's good not to have too many choices. All right, Angry Bear. I'm all yours."

Rohan leaped forward with all his considerable speed, thinking he could overwhelm the Ursan with sheer unexpected brutality.

The other Ursans were faster than they looked; Angry Bear was faster still. He met Rohan's charge with a wide, powerful swing of his massive gauntlet, connecting solidly with the side of the Hybrid's head, knocking the much smaller man back a dozen meters.

"That hurt." Rohan felt a spark of anger flare up in his chest. The rage that always lingered inside him, eager to be unleashed, bubbled at the surface like boiling water.

Wistful answered him. "Be careful, Rohan. I'd rather you two didn't tear a hole through my belly."

"I know, I know. I'll be careful." He pushed the anger back, pushed back the rage. *I don't need you for this.*

Rohan oriented himself midair and landed on his feet. The Ursan berserker was closing on him fast, arms swept back in preparation for another terrific blow.

Rohan skipped forward, baiting the Ursan, then hopped back as one metal gauntlet whistled through the spot where his head had been. He tapped both feet against the ground behind him and sprang forward again, jabbing his left fist into the Ursan's one good eye.

The Ursan roared. It seemed his primary response to just about anything that happened.

"You should expand your vocabulary. The roaring is getting tiresome."

3

Barks and Bites

Rohan sprang forward again, moving his left fist toward Angry Bear's eye, but just by a few inches. The Ursan reacted to the feint, swinging his huge hands up to protect his face, and Rohan lowered his weight and drove his right hand directly into the Ursan's midriff.

Between the armor the Ursans were wearing, protective layers of fur and fat, and the massive muscular development in Angry Bear's midsection, the punch should have done nothing.

But the legs and arms that propelled that blow were the same legs and arms that could push full-sized battleships through space. Rohan was only half human, and that wasn't the half that mattered in this fight.

His fist sank into Angry Bear's abdomen almost to the elbow. The Ursan shuddered and vomited explosively, barely missing Rohan's back but covering a significant stretch of deck with whatever he'd eaten in the previous twenty-four hours.

Rohan dodged away from the backhand swipe Angry Bear threw at him in response.

"I think we're done here. No?"

Angry Bear answered with a predictable roar and a violent charge.

Rohan waited for the wide hook, what his people called a haymaker, which seemed the only punch the Ursan knew how to throw. It came, as fast as ever, but Rohan had adjusted to the Ursan's speed, could read it and move with it. He slid backward again, just beyond the arc of the swing, then slid forward and toward the Ursan's exposed shoulder. His feet were making small, tight impacts with the ground, the footwork he'd been trained in coming back more with every step.

He was about to take advantage of his superior angle on Angry Bear's shoulder, when the spiked chain attached to the Ursan's gauntlet, sliced painfully into Rohan's side, digging into his liver. For a moment he thought he'd be throwing up right back at Angry Bear.

"I guess we aren't done. No, don't bother to answer, I'll just assume you're roaring at me."

Angry Bear roared anyway. Rohan rubbed his side.

The Ursan closed again, but instead of charging wildly he stepped forward steadily, keeping his feet under his center and moving smoothly.

Rohan moved forward to meet him.

Rohan feinted his jab again, and Angry Bear flinched back again, but not as aggressively. The Ursan threw a quick punch of his own at Rohan, who slipped to the side to avoid it. Instead of coming back to an upright position, Rohan used the slip to whip his leg up and shoot a kick into the left side of Angry Bear's head . . . right over the eye, half an inch from where his earlier jab had landed. Blood was leaking from around the eye, and Rohan could see the soft flesh swelling.

"You're tougher than old shoe leather, Ursan. But you're outmatched."

Angry Bear swung again, a slow and labored blow. Rohan realized that he was trying to connect with the chain on the follow through.

The Earth native slid back from the punch and ducked under the chain. As it sailed over his head he reached and grabbed the end with his right hand and used the pull from the chain to launch himself up into the air and over the Ursan's shoulder. He came down with a large, arcing strike of his left elbow into Angry Bear's eye.

He had a sudden flash of insight, the kind of intuition developed over fifteen years of hard training and ten years of life-and-death combat. He saw how he could end the fight; saw that he could punch right through Angry Bear's eye, into his skull, and kill the Ursan. He could feel the rhythm of the sequence in his bones.

He stepped back.

Angry Bear roared. He pulled back a massive fist and swung it at Rohan.

Rohan held onto his flash of insight and braced. The metal gauntlet struck his face, razor edges slicing into his skin and spikes driving deeper in, drawing lines of blood.

He stood his ground.

Angry Bear reset his feet and swung again with the other hand.

Again Rohan braced and took the blow on his face. More blood trickled down his face and into his beard.

"It's over."

Another roar. Another punch, fired from over Angry Bear's shoulder, straight into Rohan's torso.

Once again the Hybrid stood. Dots of blood were shining on his chest when the gauntlet pulled away, but the wounds were shallow.

Rohan reached forward and put his palm to Angry Bear's heavy cheekbone. Gently; not a strike, just a touch. To show that he could.

The Ursan reached back to swing again. Halted.

The towering alien let his fist drop to his side. He looked around. Took in his fallen companions. Took in his captain watching him with sad brown eyes. Took in the mess he'd made of the docking bay.

He fell to his knees.

"Enough. You spoke truth. It's enough. I am no war chief here."

Rohan turned to Wei Li.

The Security Chief nodded her scaly, hairless head. The Ursans were done. Wei Li's personnel were coming out from cover. She was on her comm. "We need Medical for combat injuries to five sentients of an unencountered species. I want a team here from Housing and another security team with food and water supplies."

She looked at Ursula. "Ma'am, who is in charge here now?"

Ursula pointed at Rohan. "He is."

Within minutes, a stream of station officers, all outfitted in the same awkward metallic purple-and-gold color scheme that Rohan wore, had filed into the bay to work with the Ursans.

The Ursans were showing no more signs of resistance, their great shaggy heads hanging low with fatigue and defeat. Many were heavily bandaged; they all drank greedily whenever water was offered to them.

Rohan had one of the medical officers verify that his wounds had stopped bleeding, then flew back to the airlock to finish his shift.

Wistful guided him as he towed ships into and away from her ports.

He let himself be absorbed in the tricky job of towing ships into tight spaces. It was a job that required tremendous Power but also a great deal of precision, and it occupied his mind fully.

By the time he had finished his work, the tension had washed out of his muscles, leaving behind a pleasant patina of fatigue.

Wonder if I can sell a how-to book on overcoming stress by towing cargo ships through space?

· · · • • • • • · · ·

T he following morning, Rohan was taking his customary lonely walk when a bright red ball rolled to a stop at his feet. He bent to pick it up, moving gingerly, testing. There was no need; the pain in his side was long gone.

He looked up and saw his fashion critic, the Lukhor boy. The boy's green antennae, anchored to the top of his forehead just below his hairline, were rigidly upright.

The boy held out his hands and Rohan tossed the ball to him, underhanded. The Lukhor caught the ball and stood looking at Rohan.

Rohan smiled at him "Still in shock over the color scheme?"

The boy shook his head. "Nah, that's old news."

Rohan nodded. The boy still stood there. Rohan waited.

"Me and my friends watched a vid of you fighting with those big furry guys."

Rohan nodded, not sure how he was supposed to respond. He hadn't wanted the fight vid to be distributed, but he also hadn't thought to ask Wistful to seal it.

"I was rooting for the other guys. Especially the big chief with one eye. Man, he was cool! That glove thing was awesome, with the spikes and the chains and all that. Do you think you could get me one of those?"

Rohan scratched his beard. It was time for a trim. "Has it occurred to you that maybe if you wanted me to do you a favor, you shouldn't have led by telling me you were rooting for the other guy?"

The boy paused, antennae pointing forward. Then he nodded. "I see your point. Does that mean a no for the gloves?"

Rohan chuckled. "I'll see what I can do. No promises. I don't know if they make those in your size."

"Thanks! Hey, can everybody from your planet fly and fight like that and stuff?"

Rohan shook his head. "I'm from Earth. Most people on Earth are a lot more like most of the people you see walking around here."

"So, what makes you special? How can I get Powers like that?"

Rohan shrugged. "I was born like this. My dad wasn't from Earth."

"Oh. Was he nice?"

"He . . . No, not really. It's because of him that I have Powers, though."

"My dad isn't Lukhor, either. Mama thinks I don't know, but I heard her talking to her friends and she told them what he is."

Rohan looked the boy over. He looked full-blooded Lukhor, but not every mix was visible in a child. As Rohan knew from experience.

"So where is your dad from?"

"I don't know the name of the planet, but he's a Deadbeat. It's why I don't see him anymore. I tried to search for the home planet of the Deadbeats, but the web didn't really give me anything useful. I thought maybe I could visit."

Rohan nodded solemnly. "I'll let you know if I hear anything. No promises." He felt bad. He would have to try hard to get this kid a razor-covered, spiked metallic glove to play with. He hoped the boy's mother wasn't the quick-tempered sort.

"Those guys were really cool, though. The roar was so loud my friend Peke almost wet himself! Actually, I think he did. And when that guy hit you the first time it was like we could feel it through the floor of the station!"

Rohan sighed. "You know, I did some pretty cool things in that fight, too. I mean, I did win, right?"

"You just punched him in the eye a few times and then let him get tired. I bet if he wasn't sleepy from the long trip, he would have wiped the floor with you!"

"I don't know about that—"

"And those guns! Those were so big! I bet they were bigger than my whole body! And that guy just kept shooting you and shooting you and he totally messed up your ugly shirt."

"You don't really have a filter, do you? I mean, at all?"

The boy's antennae perked up. "What's that? Is that how you fly?"

"No, I mean the part of your brain that sits between the silly things you think and your mouth."

"Oh. Mom says I was born without that. Maybe because my dad's an alien."

Rohan nodded. The boy continued.

"Anyway, we started rooting for you afterward, even if you're not as cool as those furry guys, because Mom said they were trying to shoot up the station and might have killed us all, and you were trying to stop them."

"Finally, some credit. Your mom sounds very smart."

"She is, she's a shuttle tech. The best shuttle tech." The boy stepped closer and lowered his voice to a conspiratorial whisper.

Rohan knelt down to listen.

"You know those shuttles in the bay where you were fighting?"

Rohan nodded.

"That's the kind she works on. She wasn't there yesterday, but she could have been. I don't know what I'd do without my mom. Probably get myself into trouble." He took a deep breath. "So, thank you."

Rohan nodded. "You're welcome."

"Are those guys going to be doing any more shooting?"

Rohan shook his head. "I don't think so. At least not here. They think I'm in charge of them, because I beat up their chief. Which is kind of silly, but it means I get to tell them not to shoot anybody and I think they'll listen."

"Good."

"But if they do start again, I'll do my best to stop them, okay? And I'm pretty tough, remember."

There was a call from a window three stories above ground. The boy's antennae perked up straight at the voice.

"I gotta go. See you!" He waved as he ran off toward the residences.

Rohan muttered, "Rooting for the other guy. I don't remember that happening in the comics. Maybe to the X-Men."

As he walked farther down the corridor, his comm chimed in his hear.

"Tow Chief Second Class Rohan, do you have a few moments?"

He swallowed and headed for the middle of a clearing, out of earshot of the other residents. "Yes, Wistful. Of course. What's up? Do you need me outside? My shift doesn't start for a while."

"No. I would like to discuss the terms of your employment."

"Oh. Are you firing me?" *Did I screw up with the Ursans?*

"No. However, when you first approached me, interested in the tow chief job, you indicated that you were motivated primarily by a desire to be separated from the il'Drach Empire."

"That sounds familiar."

"And, at the time, I told you that you could find that separation here."

"Right."

"However, I no longer believe that I can keep that particular promise."

"I understand. I think. Do I?"

"I am not sure you do. I promised you a position where you would not be involved with the Empire. At the time I had no expectation of the wormhole being reactivated."

"I get it. You had no idea. You *couldn't* have had any idea."

"Correct. I can no longer fulfill the terms of your employment. Given that, I would be willing to terminate it and provide a positive reference. The passenger ship *Empty Keg* is leaving in a few hours and has a berth available."

"You're saying you're okay if I leave."

"We have an agreement. I cannot maintain my obligations to it. I believe the Empire will send ships here to investigate the wormhole. Most likely with military assets. You will be noticed. Despite my intentions, you might even become *involved*."

Rohan cracked his neck and took in the length of the grassy boulevard; looked straight up at the blue-green disk of Toth 3. "You're saying if I stay here I'll have to face the Empire. Or I could leave and try to find a place that's even more out of the way. Start over again. Hope I die of old age before the Empire gets to me."

"Yes."

"Is that what *you* think I should do?"

"I am unable to offer constructive advice in this situation. I can only offer you choices. I will even provide a generous severance package."

He laughed softly. "I don't need . . . never mind."

He felt a pang of anger at the mere idea of the Empire being enough to make him consider running away.

"You know what? I'm staying. I've spent six months here. I found a place that makes great coffee. I have friends. Not many, but still. I like it here. If the Empire comes, I'll just have to deal with it. Unless you're saying you'd rather I get out of the way?"

"It is not my desire that you leave. You are a most adequate tow chief."

"Then it's settled."

Let's see if I live long enough to regret this.

4

Curiosity Kills

"So, there am I, captain of half-wrecked ship with twenty-seven hundred refugees on board. No food and very small water left of supplies. None has had bath in weeks. We cross half galaxy using ancient technology, untested, we are all almost sure will kill us all. First alien we meet, this one." She patted Rohan, who was seated next to her, on the back. "Barely any fur, flying through space without even spacesuit and within five—what do you say?—minutes, he is trying to mate with me."

Ursula laughed and slapped the table sharply, which groaned and creaked with the impact. She reached for the platter in front of her, picked up a blue-scaled fish, and popped it whole into her mouth.

Wei Li laughed with her until tears leaked from her yellow eyes. "Oh, you think he is bad? Be grateful you are not an empath. I swear to the Seven that three-quarters of my training consisted of learning how to ignore a male's lustful thoughts."

Rohan was glad his shift was over, so he could drink through the conversation.

"This I can only imagine. Is not really surprise, no? With three penises and one brain is no wonder they are always thinking with lower parts."

Rohan choked on his mouthful of Sein Ale.

Wei Li laughed even harder. "You poor thing. You might find yourself very disappointed by our end of the galaxy!"

Ursula bared her teeth at them; it would have been a smile on a human. "We will manage."

"So, Ursula." Rohan was eager to change the subject. "How have your people been settling in?"

She shrugged her massive shoulders. "Is good. We have plentiful water, space, and fish. In end, best part of Wistful is lack of genocide." She laughed again, slapping the table with a loud crack of paw against metal.

Rohan nodded. "That's my favorite thing about this place. Sometimes I go an entire day without anybody even trying to maim me."

Wei Li smiled. "It's because we don't let the males think they're in charge here."

Ursula raised a pitcher of water in salute; Wei Li raised her own glass to answer it.

Rohan tried to come up with a clever response but couldn't. Instead, he sipped his drink, enjoying the pleasant warmth that spread through his chest. It was strong ale. "Speaking of males, how Is Angry Bear?"

Ursula looked at him. "We need better Drachna name for my war chief than Angry Bear, plant-eater."

"Well, we can't pronounce your names. How about just Ang?"

"Is this real name?"

"It's another Earth name. But yes, absolutely real."

"Good, from now he is Ang. Will be our secret what Ang is for short. And Ang is doing well. He did not lose last good eye, thank you for that."

Rohan shrugged. "I didn't think blinding your war chief would have been a good welcome to the sector."

"He did not deserve a good welcome. Must have lost half of frontal lobe along with right eye, to try storming out with guns. But please try to forgive. Or at least understand. He was shamed and angry because of what came before."

Wei Li tilted her head. "You mean in your home sector? What did happen?"

Ursula hesitated.

Wei Li leaned forward in her chair. "You may have your privacy, but I would at least like to know if we have to worry about whoever damaged your ships following you through that wormhole and coming after you here."

Ursula nodded. "Fair. I will explain but in short. Was great war. Well, war happened, was great loss of life. But war was not the problem. We like wars, mostly.

"You see, we are from Ursan colony. We worship the old gods. Most Ursans worship newer gods. Is fine, is all good, except after war, other Ursans begin to distrust us. Felt we were not patriotic enough. Said we had to be unified against outside threats. Said we must share gods, share worship."

She popped another fish into her mouth, its tail twitching as it disappeared between her teeth.

"Some converted. We would not. We had fought in war, Ursans of my colony. Had lost many. My mate died in war, two of my sons, three of my daughters. I would not give up the ways of my ancestors to prove my loyalty to anybody.

"When they came to kill us, we fled. We had to flee where they would not chase us, would not follow. Wormhole seemed good idea. No way could be worse than certain death, we are to thinking."

Rohan sipped from his glass of Sein. It wasn't like Earth beer, closer to a brown liquor.

Wei Li pursed her lips. "They will not follow you through?"

Ursula paused. "Ursan physics say wormhole will destroy our ships. So most likely, almost certain, they think we are dead. So almost certain, nothing will follow us through wormhole. Almost. Other Ursans are hateful but not—what is word—suicidal."

Wei Li nodded. "I'll take that. If they do follow you through, what should we expect? More ships like yours? Or more advanced?"

Ursula shook her head. "Same ships. Our ship was one of fleet. Best in fleet. Certainly nothing much different."

The security chief sighed. "Then it seems that wormhole opening was a one-time thing. I am slightly disappointed. But mostly relieved."

Rohan smiled at her. "You were hoping for something more romantic? A planet of handsome men desperately searching for a queen to rule over them?"

"Almost exactly that, Rohan. Almost exactly."

The Ursan pointed at the pile of fish in front of her. "This is good fish. From planet?" She pointed straight up, to the clear roof overhead and the blue-and-white planet in the center of their view.

Wei Li shook her head. "All the food is grown on the station or imported from outside the system. It is not safe enough to go down, or up, to the planet. For anything routine. The megafauna on Toth 3 are quite astonishing."

"If planet so dangerous, why build station here?"

Wei Li shrugged. "That's an excellent question. The people who asked Wistful to stay here have been dead for, I do not know exactly, hundreds of generations? Maybe thousands? But wonder we do, from time to time."

Rohan nodded. "We don't know why she's here, but we are glad that she is. There's enough trade to keep the people here busy, but not so much that the Empire cares too much what goes on. We have a great view, and there are three different brewers that have sets of casks over a thousand years old for aging liquors. I love this station."

Wistful spoke into his ear. "That was very sweet, Rohan."

Ursula sighed. "True, this is wonderful place. But my people would prefer planet. A place with space. And work for us to do. Idle paws are too soon clenched into fists."

Rohan stretched his arms behind him and looked up and down the boulevard. They were seated in the street outside his favorite restaurant, which served a cuisine almost identical to the sushi of his childhood. They had balked at first at serving whole, unprepared fish to the Ursans, but it took only one visit from the refugees to convince them that not only could the staff not prepare the fish fast enough to keep up with an Ursan appetite, but the refugees had no appreciation for the subtlety of flavors they offered.

He felt good, sitting and sharing a meal with people. As good, or better, than he remembered feeling in a long time.

Passersby still stared a little bit as they passed. Ursans were larger than almost any other intelligent species common to Wistful's sector of space.

"Tow Chief Second Class Rohan, I did not ask. Are your wounds healed yet?"

He rubbed a hand quickly over his face. "I'm fine. I heal quickly."

"Are all the brown-skins strong like you?" She waved a hand to take in the array of people walking around them. Depending on how one grouped them, perhaps a third had skin colors close to Rohan's deep brown.

He laughed. "Most Earthers would have been killed by a single strike from your war chief. And most cannot fly, or travel in space without protection. In fact, I'd bet that in a fistfight, your war chief would kill almost anybody you see walking around here. Except Wei Li, of course. She's tough."

"You are special? Why? Mutation? Cybernetics?"

He shook his head, paused. He'd hidden his origins as a civilian on Earth, but it was an open secret in Imperial space. "I'm only half human. My father was . . . is . . . an il'Drach."

"il'Drach. You were for telling me that il'Drach rule over this sector. And that is name of language I am for learning. That you are son of theirs you did not say. You serve this il'Drach Empire?"

He shook his head again. "I did, for a while. I . . . retired. Now I'm a tow chief, and this is an independent station. We're not under il'Drach control."

"I see. But you are from a planet, correct? Earth?"

"Yes, that's where I'm from. But my connection to Earth is like my relationship with Wei Li here, it's complicated."

Wei Li laughed and playfully kicked him under the table, hard enough to make the fish jump on their platter.

"Only in your dreams is our relationship complicated! It is quite simple, we are friends and no more. And like most males, you wish for more, because"—she swept a hand up and down the stretch of yellow skin, streaked with scales of red and green, that showed where her shirt was open in the front. She shook her head. "As I said, not easy being an empath. These males with no skill to shield their feelings. I am embarrassed for them all."

Ursula howled with laughter but spared the table another whack. "We have similar problem! I have very sensitive nose. Our males cannot control their scents. At least this one smells calm, like running stream."

Rohan smiled and finished his ale. "I think that's the nicest thing anybody has ever said about me."

The food and laughter carried them late into the night, but Wistful's avenues were still brightly lit when he walked home.

He fell asleep with a smile on his face. He'd forgotten how much he enjoyed dinners out with other people. Laughter.

He slept as well as he had in as long as he could remember.

· · · · ● · ● · · ·

"R Rohan. Tow Chief Second Class Rohan."
Rohan sat up in his bed. "Emergency?"

Wistful's voice was flat. Not exactly lacking in tone, but lacking the full depth of expression that a human voice might have had.

"No, but we have an il'Drach ship requesting docking. I'd like you to handle it."

He rubbed his scalp, then rubbed the sleep out of his eyes.

"I wouldn't have it any other way. You know, fifteen years ago I would have resented being woken up in the middle of the night to do work off-shift."

"And now that you are fifteen years older?"

He thought. "I still resent it, but I know better than to say so out loud."

"I'm proud of you, Rohan. You've matured."

Was she laughing at him? He had no idea.

Rohan quickly dressed. His rooms were large, commensurate with his relative wealth. Tow Chief Second Class was not a glamorous title, but it had a high status and high pay, largely because there were very few humanoids capable of doing the job, and most of those were otherwise occupied. Or enlisted.

Rohan pulled his mask over his face, thumbing around the edge to make sure it formed a tight seal over his beard, and quickly checked himself in the mirror. Nobody wants a tow chief who'd forgotten to fasten his fly, manhood flapping freely in zero gravity.

His quarters had one unique perk, in addition to the other assorted luxuries: a private airlock. An amenity only Rohan had any use for.

He pulled on his boots, buckled them tight, and headed out the airlock.

"Wistful, is the il'Drach ship playing nice?" He was already confident the answer would be yes. Had the ship come in on war footing, he doubted Wistful would have been so calm.

"She is waiting patiently outside the perimeter, near beacon B-37." An overlay popped up on the inside of his mask, outlining the beacon placements. He turned his head and quickly spotted the B section.

"On my way. Is Wei Li on duty?"

"She's off-shift, Tow Chief. Do you believe we need to wake her?"

Rohan flew toward the location. He could already make out the ship against the blackness of space. It was vast, but as Wistful had said, it was waiting patiently.

"Nah. Let her sleep. But be ready to get her if things go poorly. Do you want me to chase this ship off or bring her in?"

Wistful was an independent station. She decided who would dock with her, at her whim. Saying no had consequences, more so with some ships than with others.

"She is welcome to dock, Rohan, unless you advise otherwise."

"Understood. Did she say why she's here?"

"She is a Class A research ship, *Insatiable*. A name obviously taken in poor judgment. She says she is here to study the wormhole."

Rohan flew, and thought.

The opening of the wormhole was an excellent justification for increased Imperial *scientific* interest in the Toth system. Would they use it as an excuse to break their treaties? Invade? Demand governorship over Wistful?

If they do try, what am I going to do about it?

Not for the first time, Rohan wished his mask carried Sein Ale along with, or instead of, its small water supply.

Insatiable quickly filled his field of vision. She was huge, nearly the size of a normal space station, though still tiny compared to Wistful. She had a blocky silhouette, square from the front but long and rectangular, all right angles, incapable of atmospheric work. Four cylinders anchored her corners, each three kilometers long. An uneven array of solid sections, gaps, docking bays, detachable modules, and even a couple of weapons systems that Rohan knew from experience were far from the best the Empire offered, were lined up between the cylinders.

She was clearly built for research, exploration, and data acquisition. Despite her size, she was about the least threatening ship the Empire could send that would still be useful to them.

He switched on the tight beam comm built into his helmet.

"Hail, *Insatiable*."

"Oh, hello! How are you? I'm so excited to be here! A wormhole older than the Empire, this is so much fun! And the legendary Wistful! All the other research vessels are going to be so, so jealous!"

"Um, sure, yes. I'm glad you're glad. This is Tow Chief Second Class Rohan."

"Wow, super, a real tow chief out here outside the Empire! I was expecting a shuttle tow or something, but this is great. So much more comfortable."

Rohan stifled a laugh. "*Insatiable*, I'm glad to bring you in, but first, do you have any Imperial military presence to declare?"

"Sure I do. A bunch of guns and stuff. It's not safe without them, you know. Do you want a list of sections to search? Oh, and four armed and armored shuttles, though I don't mean to be rude but I wouldn't count on their combat readiness. We left Imperial space in a hurry."

"Sorry, of course, shuttles and security would be normal. I mean specifically, ship's lances? Any Hybrids on board?"

"Oh no, not for this trip. I've carried lances before, you know. I used to be a military transport. But we're all just scientists and some normal, run-of-the-mill security folks. Really, it's all very standard and to be honest, kind of boring."

"Good. In that case, I'm here to bring you in; your request for docking is approved."

"Oh, my gosh, really? That's awesome! I am so, so, so grateful to Wistful!"

Rohan approached the ship. "Standard station docking procedure: You'll have to power down your drives. I'll bring you in."

"Of course! Powering down now. My anchor point is about one third of the way back from my nose, marked in green. Do you see it? Or should I transmit directions?"

"I see it, *Insatiable*. Coming in now."

Right where she'd said it would be, Rohan spotted a solid metal sphere, painted green, connected by a web of struts to all four corner pillars of her superstructure. It was a typical arrangement for an Imperial ship.

He switched channels on his comms. "Wistful, please verify that *Insatiable* has powered-down her drives."

"Verified, Rohan."

"Okay, I'm bringing her in."

Rohan flew up to the dark metal sphere and checked the structure, silently working out how to move the titanic mass of the research ship.

Insatiable wasn't done with him.

"Hey, Tow Chief Second Class, I think I know you."

"I'm pretty sure you don't, *Insatiable*. I've only been at this station for a few months." He pushed, gently, turning her nose toward Wistful.

Wistful spoke into his ear. "Give her berth A1, Rohan. Nose-in to the planet."

He nodded, pointlessly. It was the berth closest to Wistful's central administrative section. Closest to security.

"No, I definitely know you. I never forget an aura."

5

What's in a Name?

"Well, I think I'd remember you, *Insatiable*. You're very interesting. Your name has . . . unforgettable connotations in my language."

He had *Insatiable*'s nose pointed in the right direction and gave her a shove sunward, toward Wistful.

"It's great, right? For my insatiable curiosity. I chose it when I transitioned to Research sector. I used to be a troop carrier for the Empire. I was once *Echo of Moonlight*."

Rohan's heart beat a little faster. "*Echo of Moonlight*. Troop carrier."

"Yes, that's me. And I'm sure I remember you. But not a tow chief. And not that name. Rohan, you said?"

"Rohan's my birth name. And I've only been a tow chief for a little bit."

"Oh, my gosh! I remember now! You're The Griffin!"

Rohan groaned.

"Oh, my gosh! Sir, it's an honor to meet you again! Lance Primary of the Imperial Fleet, code Griffin! Sir!"

Rohan pushed *Insatiable* toward Wistful. What should he do? He wasn't willing to kill her to keep her quiet. "Look, *Insatiable*, first of all, yes, I am The Griffin. I'm sorry I didn't recognize you."

Insatiable's voice was, astonishingly, shaky. "No need to apologize, Griffin, sir! I was only a troop transport. No reason you should remember little me. Well, not so little now, but still."

"It's been a big and distracting week, *Insatiable*. The wormhole and all. I wasn't paying attention. And you have grown quite a bit. I can't even make out your original form in there."

"Please don't apologize, sir! It's fine. I didn't even recognize *you* at first! And *you're* a lance primary!"

"Was. I *was* a lance primary. Not now. Look, here's the thing: First of all, the Empire knows I'm here. They discharged me, there's nothing underhanded going on, okay? And if you want to confirm that, please feel free to send a comm to Fleet Command and they'll say the same thing. I'm retired, they know I'm here, we're cool. Okay?"

"Yes sir, Griffin, sir. I never doubted you for a moment."

He was sure that was true. Ships and lances existed in a very strict hierarchy, and troop carriers were not at the top. Even most front-line warships would hesitate to question the authority of a lance.

"But the thing is, I'd like to keep me being here sort of quiet. Do you understand? Command knows I'm here, but I don't want it . . . broadcast. Public."

"Sir, I don't understand. You were a lance primary. You're a hero. You fought on the *Ringgate*. For *two* years! You should be celebrated, not acting as a Tow Chief Second Class. Everyone should know who you are and where you are."

Rohan let a little sternness drip into his voice. "*Insatiable*, things are often more complicated than they seem. Please, I am asking you, tell as few people as possible who I am. Can you do that for me?"

There was a significant pause before she answered. "Yes, sir. Of course. Of course, I can."

She *might* be lying. Ships could lie, though few were any good at it. But he had no way to force her into secrecy, not short of tearing her into pieces, so her word was all the reassurance he would get.

"Thank you."

He made a small course correction, lining *Insatiable*'s nose up more closely with Wistful.

"Oh, Griffin, sir, you're from Earth, am I remembering that correctly?"

"Please call me Rohan." Ships weren't good at lying, but they weren't great at keeping secrets, either.

"Oh, right, Tow Chief Second Class Rohan! Sir!"

Rohan sighed. "Please stop calling me sir. And yes, I'm from Earth. Why? Do you have news?"

Military ships sometimes carried information that hadn't yet been made public.

"Nothing like that, sir. I do have two Earthlings on board, though. I thought you might know them, or, if not, enjoy spending some time with your fellow Earthers."

"Huh. Actually, maybe I would, thank you. There are very few natives who have been allowed off the planet. Who are they?"

"Doctor and Doctor Stone. Benjamin and Marion. You might have heard of them; they are both quite prestigious faculty members at the Fleet Academy."

The names were familiar, but he couldn't place them immediately. He wanted to find a polite way to say he didn't monitor academic faculty in his newsfeed, but couldn't.

"Faculty of what?"

"Marion is at the top of the physics faculty. They say she's next in line for department chair. She's in charge of the team looking into the wormhole. Benjamin is a biologist and I believe he's here to survey the native population of Toth 3. I'll be honest, she's the brilliant one, he's accomplished enough, but nothing special."

"That's a fast response for a team, considering the wormhole just opened up."

"Yes. I was being supplied for a long-range reconnaissance mission on the rimward edge of the Empire when I was reassigned. It was only hours between news of the wormhole reaching the Academy and our launch."

"Makes sense. They'll be busy, I suppose, but I'll try to talk to them. Please let them know that I'm here, and I'll meet them in the docking bay and say hello. Buy them a drink or something."

"Yes, sir, *Rohan*, sir. I'll be glad to." He could almost hear the broad wink in her voice as she said his name.

Rohan checked his personal messages on the projection in his helmet as he towed the research vessel the rest of the way to her berth. Financial updates on his holdings, news on the handful of topics he subscribed to. As he read, a new message popped up: a personal note from Ben Stone requesting to meet with him soon to "pick his brain" about the animals on the planet.

Once the ship was docked and sealed into place, Rohan disengaged and entered Wistful through a nearby airlock. He didn't need directions; dock A1 saw a lot of traffic and he knew the area well.

"Wistful, any more ships I need to handle or am I free for a while?"

"You're free for now."

"Copy that. Thanks."

Rohan grabbed two hot coffees from one of the cart-based vendors who worked the docking area and waited for his fellow Earthers to disembark.

A man wearing a white lab coat over ship standard coveralls got off *Insatiable* when the first knot of officers, diplomats, and customs agents had cleared the bay entrance. He was tall for a human, with an angular build and blond hair half gone to gray. Fine lines crisscrossed his rugged features.

A member of the large Wistful security team gave the man a quick scan and welcomed him to the station. The man looked around, saw Rohan, and waved.

Rohan waved back, and the scientist walked over. Rohan sipped from his coffee and held out the other one.

"Welcome to Wistful, Doctor Stone?"

"Yes, call me Ben. You must be Rohan. *Insatiable*, well, you know. She mentioned you about ten minutes ago."

Rohan smiled. "That's me. *Insatiable* and I met when I towed you in. Coffee?"

The man's blue eyes lit up. "Are you serious? Real coffee?"

Rohan nodded. "I can't take any credit for it, but someone brought real coffee plants straight from Earth and started a plot in hydroponics. When I got here half the ship population was already addicted to the stuff, and there wasn't an Earth native on board. We have real tea, too, though I can't vouch for the preparations. Call that a work in progress."

Doctor Stone took the coffee with both hands and took a careful sip. "Oh, that's good. No, really, that's good!"

"I didn't know how you take it. We have plenty of sweeteners, but if you want milk, you're out of luck. Nothing here tastes much like real cow's milk, sadly."

"No, no, that's fine. This is perfect. Where on Earth are you from? South India?"

"My mother's heritage is Telugu, but I was born and raised in Canada. And my father, well, you know."

The professor nodded slowly. "Ah. You did say you towed us here. I thought you meant, you know, piloting a shuttle."

Rohan shook his head. "Not exactly."

"Well, then. Do you remember your English? I haven't had a conversation in English in ages! I'm American, originally, though I haven't been back in forty years."

Rohan switched to English from the Drachna they'd been using.

"It's Canadian English, so you'll have to forgive the occasional 'eh' or hockey reference."

The professor laughed. "I'll take it. Were you famous on Earth before your recruitment?"

Several il'Drach Hybrids had worked as costumed heroes on Earth before the il'Drach came to take them.

Rohan shook his head. "I wore the mask and cape for a few years, but not so you'd have heard of me, though I tried. I was never a Hyperion or anywhere near that league. I'm kind of a runt by Hybrid standards."

"Well, if *you* saying that isn't an argument that all things are relative, then I've never heard one. You literally just pulled a starship large enough to hold a crew of ten thousand people across a star system with your bare hands, and you call yourself a runt."

Rohan smiled. "Have you met Hyperion? I'm not exaggerating."

The professor flashed a huge smile. "Met him? Son, I'm Benjamin Stone. I was Hyperion's sidekick when he was in his prime. They made an action figure of me."

Rohan's mouth opened a little in shock as he processed the names again. Everyone on Earth grew up with stories of the times Hyperion had saved the planet. His tech support, sidekicks, and confidantes were a couple of too-smart-for-their-own-good kids named Ben Stone and Marion Marley.

"You know what? I'm genuinely sorry. I can't believe I didn't put the names together. I don't think I even realized you two had left the planet."

"Oh, yeah. When Hyperion left Earth the first time, we jumped at the chance. See space? Interact with countless forms of alien life? Land on other worlds? The big shock was that once we got to the Empire they found us useful, and not just as Hyperion's support, but for, you know, the science stuff. Like I said, we haven't been back home in forty years. I was really missing coffee."

"There's some decent booze on this station, too. Sein Ale Amber tastes a lot like a fine *añejo* tequila."

"My liver doesn't hold up as well to alcohol as it used to, but I'd love to join you for a drink while I'm here. But more urgently, I have questions about the first contact and about the natives of Toth 3. I hear you're the point man for both of those things?"

"I'm happy to tell you what I know. But should we be waiting for . . . the other Doctor Stone?" He couldn't bring himself to use her first name. He was still processing that he was getting to meet such legendary figures. It was like having beers with King Arthur. Or, more accurately, with two Knights of the Round Table. The less famous ones.

"My wife? Not unless you want to stand here for the next twelve hours. She's going over all the telemetry Wistful provided her from the wormhole opening. She's a physicist to the bone; I don't think she cares one bit about any of the living things from the wormhole or the planet."

"Understood. I can't contribute anything worthwhile to her study of the wormholes, anyway. All I know is that the Ursans came through it, and they seem none the worse for wear."

The professor paused. "Yes. But even later, you might want to give her some space. She has some strong feelings about Hybrids. You might even say prejudices."

"Really? But you were friends with Hyperion."

"Yes, but that was a long time ago. And we were at the Academy when the rebels occupied the planet. It—some of it wasn't pretty. I'm not blaming you for anything, but she has her feelings."

Rohan sighed and nodded. A group of Hybrids had rebelled against the Empire, against the Fathers' control over them. It had only been a year since it failed, and the sector was still suffering the aftermath.

"Trauma is trauma. I'm sorry for what she, what you, went through. I'll leave her alone unless she asks to talk to me."

"I appreciate it."

"So where do you want to start? Do you want to meet some Ursans? They're quite friendly. They hardly ever eat other sentient creatures."

Doctor Stone chuckled and sipped his coffee. "I'm actually more interested in the megafauna on the planet." He pointed down. "I've been trying to justify a trip to this system for twenty years to see them. Always been too busy."

"Actually, it's up there. Come on, I'll give you the fast tour and show you."

Rohan led the taller man to an elevator which whisked them up from the docking level, past the intrastation transport tubes, and to the promenade level.

"Residential, offices, shopping, restaurants, that sort of stuff is all on this level. You can walk pretty much the whole station, but if you're going very far you want to use a tube one level down. They're fast, frequent, and free. But here you get the best view."

He pointed up to the transparent diamond roof, and through it their view of Toth 3.

Rohan continued. "We're at the L2 point, so the planet is always between us and Toth, always right there through the roof."

Ben whistled.

"That's impressive. This is one of the largest stations I've ever been on." He looked up and down the promenade, too long for him to see the ends. "I take it back, it is *the* largest."

"Well, it kind of has to be. With other stations, excess population spills out onto nearby habitable planets. There are none in this system."

The professor pointed up and raised a bushy eyebrow. "Blue planet right there, isn't there?"

Rohan smiled. "Come on, you must have done some research before you traveled all this way, Doctor Stone."

"Oh, I did, I did. You're really telling me the creatures up there are so tough nothing can settle there? I'm hearing this from an honest-to-goodness il'Drach Hybrid? I thought you guys weren't scared of anything."

Rohan shook his head. "You could spend your whole career cataloging the things that scare me. But I certainly wouldn't try to settle that planet."

"I read that there was work being done on ultrasonic frequencies that would ward off the fauna? That didn't pan out?"

"It worked, until it didn't. Sooner or later, all the people who stay down there wind up dead."

"What triggers the attacks?"

"Your guess is as good as mine. Actually, I take it back, your guess is a lot better; you're the biologist, right?"

"Well, I'll do some more reading. Wistful has research notes she said she would share. They aren't public, so I couldn't read them from home. Have you been to the surface? Any personal impressions?"

"I have. A few times. But don't forget I have the advantage of being able to get up into orbit under my own Power anytime I want to. And even that doesn't make it safe. A lot of the kaiju fly."

"Kaiju?"

"Oh, that's just what I call them. Earth word. It means—"

"Son, I know what it means. You're building quite a record for naming things, you know. I think the term 'Ursan' is going to stick. I almost choked on my breakfast when I read that you named their captain Ursula."

Rohan smiled. "They should pay me royalties."

The professor laughed and finished his coffee. "I'll put in a word on your behalf. But don't hold your breath. I came up with the name Hyperion and I never saw a dime in revenue from it."

There was a pause as the professor put a hand to his ear and looked at the ground. "I've got to go; some data's been delivered that I have to go through. Thanks for your time and especially for the coffee, Rohan. Er, Tow Chief Rohan, I guess?"

"Rohan is fine. If anyone asks, Tow Chief Second Class. Let me know if you want an introduction to the Ursans."

"I will, thanks again."

Because *Insatiable* was docked so close to Wistful's center, Rohan was only minutes from his quarters. He *lifted* up into the air, flew up the boulevard, ducked through the wide opening that connected the arm to the older center of the station.

It was too late for him to get any meaningful sleep before his shift started, so he settled for a hot shower and a change of uniform.

"I should really learn how to cook."

Wistful answered him. "Was that directed at me, Rohan?"

He laughed. "No, just chastising myself. I'm a very stereotypical bachelor in many ways."

"That is true, Rohan. Is that a bad thing?"

"Wistful, I very rarely know whether you're teasing me or not."

"That is also true."

6

Lust at First Sight

R ohan considered reading, watching videos, and exercise. He wasn't
in the mood for any of it. He was, however, hungry.

"As long as I can't cook, I might as well take advantage of living on the
most cosmopolitan space station in Imperial space. Voted 'Best Corridor
Food in Sector' for seven hundred consecutive years by *il'Drach Today*
magazine."

"I am unfamiliar with the term magazine, Rohan."

"I am being silly. And I am going to get breakfast."

Wistful didn't answer.

Rohan left his quarters and walked out into the station. He'd come to
Wistful looking for a place where nothing happened and suddenly things
were happening.

He was halfway to his favorite omelet stall when a familiar red ball rolled
up to his feet. He smiled.

"Hey, buddy. How are things today?"

The Lukhor boy shrugged his thin shoulders. "It's boring. A really big
ship from the Empire docked and that *should* have been cool but it's all full
of scientists and teachers and other boring people."

"I know, I met one of them. He's from my home planet."

"I thought you were from here."

Rohan shook his head. "No, I'm from Earth."

"Earth? A planet called Earth?" The boy thought. "You could have named your planet anything you want and you picked another word for dirt?"

Rohan picked up the ball and tossed it into the air. "I never really thought of it that way. What should we have called it, Super Duper Fun Party Planet?"

The boy shrugged. "That's a dumb name. My home planet is called Sparkles Like Emeralds. That's way better than Earth."

Rohan tossed him the ball. "I think you're right. That is much better. Your people are pretty smart."

The boy nodded. "Mostly."

"Hey, how come I always see you out here in the morning? Shouldn't you be on your way to school or something? Be a shame to waste all that smartness and not go to school."

The boy snorted. "School's over for the day."

"Oh. People from Lukhor are nocturnal?"

The boy shook his head. "Not all of us, just a third. You get it from your mom. It's mostly annoying. Nobody's up or doing anything at night, and I'm sleepy when my friends have things going on."

Rohan nodded. It sounded efficient. "Hey, this is our third conversation and we haven't properly introduced ourselves. What's your name?"

The boy sighed. "My name is long and stupid. But you can call me Rinth."

"I'm sure it's not stupid."

"Amarinthalytics. It sounds like a subject in school that everybody fails."

"Well, I don't think it's stupid. It is long, though, I can call you Rinth. You can call me Rohan."

"Okay, Rohan." The boy let go of the ball, then popped it off his knee and back in the air. He sidestepped and popped it up off the other knee, like a juggler.

"Rinth! Time to come home!"

They both turned to look toward the voice. A female Lukhor was walking over the grass toward them.

She was pale green, with darker patches around her eyes and mouth. She had twin antennae protruding from the top of her forehead, each about fifteen centimeters long. They moved independently as she walked. She had a colorful piece of fabric draped around her; reds and yellows and purples running together, leaving both arms and a very enticing stretch of her midriff bare.

She had human-like eyes, dark pupils in a white background. When she smiled her teeth shone bright against her skin. And Rohan couldn't help but notice she was definitely mammalian.

"So, you're the grownup who's been bothering my son during playtime."

Rohan stammered. "Um, I'm sorry, I didn't mean to bother anybody. Bother *him*." *Have I been?*

She laughed. "Oh, I am teasing, you weren't. In fact, I think you're giving my Rinth a big head. He thinks he's important, having such famous friends. All his classmates are jealous."

"Oh, Mom, pleeease. You're embarrassing me." The boy's cheeks darkened to a deeper shade of green.

She laughed again. "Didn't you tell Peke just yesterday that if he didn't bring back your action figure you'd have your best mate, Rohan, beat him up?"

"Maybe. But I wasn't being serious, Mama." Rinth looked up at Rohan, who couldn't hide his smile.

She patted the boy's head, running her hand between his antennae and ruffling his hair. "It's almost time for dinner. Go wash up."

"Yes, Mama." The boy gave his ball one last bounce, then caught it in both hands. "'Bye, Rohan."

"'Bye, Rinth."

The boy ran off to the wall of housing.

Rohan looked at the Lukhor woman, who stood facing him, a smile still dancing on her lips. He held out his hand. "I'm Rohan. Er, Tow Chief Second Class. I hope I wasn't bothering your son."

She took his hand to shake and tipped her head over it. She responded to his overly formal greeting with a bigger smile. "It is a pleasure to meet you, Tow Chief Second Class Rohan. I am Tamaralinth Lastex, Drive Mechanic." She paused. "First Class. I have never heard the name Rohan."

"It's from my home planet. It means, 'ascending.' In a dead language. My father picked it." *Why did I tell her that?*

"My father picked mine as well. It means 'treasured flower' in a very living language, so I believe you have the better of it. And you really weren't bothering him."

"Good. I'm not really used to kids."

"Oh? You have no children of your own, Tow Chief Rohan? Second Class?"

"Not that I know of." He groaned, audibly, at the awfulness of his own joke. "Sorry, I didn't mean that the way it sounded. Um, no, no children. I mean, I'm sure there aren't any. Tamaralinth. First Class."

Tamara laughed. "I think you should have tried harder to avoid that Ursan's blows to your head, Tow Chief. Are you sure you shouldn't be in Medical instead of roaming the boulevard?"

Why don't you come to my quarters and let me show you how much I don't need Medical? For once he didn't say the first thing that came into his mind.

Was she an empath? *Are Lukhors empathic? What are the antennae for?* He had no idea.

"No, I'm fine, really. Just not used to talking to such a beautiful woman. I am out of practice."

She smiled wider, and Rohan thought her cheeks darkened a shade. Or perhaps it was the shifting light as Wistful transitioned to full daylight.

"Well, you are welcome to come by anytime and get back into practice. And please, call me Tamara."

He paused, desperately trying to prolong the conversation. "Well, we're on different schedules, but we both have to eat. I was going to catch breakfast at Wo Pha. It's famous for their omelets, but they serve dinner food, too. They have a mean lamb curry. Would you like to join me? You and Rinth, of course. It's five minutes that way." He pointed down the boulevard.

She shook her head slightly. "We are eating at my sister's today. She cooked, and—"

"No, totally, I understand. Sorry."

"But I'd be happy to join you some other time. Even tomorrow. I have no plans for tomorrow."

"Really? Oh, that's great. Great. Me neither, I don't have plans. Didn't, didn't have plans. I have them now! I'll be here tomorrow, we'll go to Wo Pha. My breakfast, your dinner."

"Yes. That will give me a chance to apologize for my son bothering you these past few days."

"What? No, no. He wasn't bothering me at all. He's funny. I like him."

"He is fascinated by all the hair. The beard, the hair on our chest. My people have less body hair."

How much less? Once again, surprisingly, Rohan's filter saved him from himself.

"Chest hair? What? How?" Rohan looked down. His uniform covered his chest, quite thoroughly.

"Oh, he might have noticed from the video of your fight with the Ursans. Your shirt was, er, disintegrated."

"Right, right. I forgot. He noticed that?" Was chest hair that unusual?

"It might not have been him. A few of us were watching. And who remembers every detail with these things? Such as exactly who noticed what?"

But if not him, then . . . Oh. He was stunned into silence.

Tamara continued. "So tell me, does chest hair serve a purpose? Is it a sensory organ? I'm sorry, I'm not familiar with your species."

"I, actually, I think it's just insulation. Like, from the cold. Kind of vestigial, really."

"Hmm. Anyway, it's been kind of you to indulge him. I'm sure you're very busy."

"Not as much as you might think, I have plenty of time. Lots of it. All I do is tow in a few ships a day, park them, then I'm off."

"Not counting the times you're fending off an invasion of Ursans."

"Well, sure. But that was a special case. Most days I fight off just one or two hostile aliens, not five."

She smiled. "Hopefully, they will offer you a break tomorrow."

"I hope so. If I wanted to spend my life fighting, I wouldn't have . . . I don't know."

"Wouldn't have become a Tow Chief Second Class? Would have kept doing what you did before?"

Rohan shrugged. "Yes. Not that I was given a lot of choice. At first."

"With great Power comes great responsibility."

"Stan Lee?"

Tamara furrowed her brows. "Who?"

"Sorry, never mind. He's a well-known writer on my planet, and it's a famous quote of his."

"I think someone says that on every planet. It's always something regular people—something normal people hope that people like you will remember."

"Hey, I'm regular people. I just have some unusual talents. If you saw me on the dance floor, believe me, you wouldn't think I was anything special."

She laughed. "Then that is something we shall have to do. Still, I imagine it must be lovely to just lift off and fly."

"It has its moments. I'd be happy to take you sometime. Flying."

Her eyes sparked at him. "Now there's an offer a woman doesn't hear every day."

He smiled. Sometimes it was good to have Powers.

"All right. I'll let you get to dinner. I'll see you tomorrow."

"Yes, you will." She smiled again, then turned and walked away.

He watched her until she had slipped through the doorway of her building.

The rest of his day passed by in a daze.

· · · · · · · · · ·

After finishing his shift, Rohan met Wei Li for a training session. She had been taking over his martial arts education.

"Do you think I have a lot of chest hair? Like, is it something someone would notice?"

Wei Li exhaled sharply as she snapped his head back with a crisp left jab. "Less talking, more sparring. Also, slip punches, don't simply absorb them with your face."

Rohan tapped the side of his face with his hand, a reminder not to keep his head still during a fistfight. It was something he was usually good at.

"Seriously, though. What do you think it means when a woman says something about your chest hair?"

"I think it means—" Wei Li stepped up with her signature move, a sharp left kick to the inside of Rohan's left thigh. It wasn't very damaging by itself, but it would knock her opponents out of their stance, lower their arms, and otherwise set them up for more powerful follow-up attacks.

Rohan turned his knee inward to take the blow on the front of his thigh instead of the tender inside. He hopped in, directly toward the reptilian security chief, covering his head with his right hand, and threw his left elbow at her temple.

He sighed as she blocked the elbow and pivoted away.

"Careful of that inner thigh strike! There's stuff around there I might need soon. I hope."

"By the Nine, you male mammals are always so concerned about your genitals. If you'd keep them retracted like any sane species you wouldn't have these issues."

"Well, excuse me for having standard human genitals. It wasn't exactly my choice, you know. I was born this way. Also, how come every time you swear, it's by a different number? 'By the Seven.' 'By the Nine.' And always odd."

"We have many pantheons of gods. It would take you a lifetime to understand the nuances of what each group, taken separately, means, and how they differ."

She feinted the low kick, and when he turned his lead leg again, she cut it short and stepped in with a fast overhand right punch.

Rohan's guard was up, which took a lot of the sting off the punch, but he was too flatfooted to counter. Instead, he pivoted back and to his left and tried to reset.

Wei Li kept the pressure up, closing quickly on his new position and feinting the low kick again. This time she redirected her leg into a kick up high, right into his face.

"Hey, I might—"

"Don't worry, human, no female interested in your chest hair will care if your face is mottled by a few bruises."

"I think that was mean. Was that mean? Sometimes I can't tell."

"No, Rohan, it was a compliment. On my world a line of males seven kilometers long would form to hear me sing their praises in such a way. Here, it is wasted on such as you."

"Again with the odd numbers. Seven kilometers. Really, what's that about? Are you allergic to being divided by two?"

She stopped, and her eyes narrowed, putting a chill through Rohan's blood. "If you ever hear me swearing by an even number, Rohan, run. Because it means things are very, very bad."

He swallowed hard. "You have got to teach me how to be intimidating like that. Nobody around here is ever scared of me, and I'm actually kind of tough."

Wei Li shrugged. "Yes, you're tough compared to anyone who isn't an il'Drach Hybrid. But in your own mind you compare yourself to them, not to us. So you don't feel in your own heart that you are intimidating."

"By Lord Rudra's braids, Wei Li. That was totally profound."

They circled each other. Wei Li slid back, and when Rohan stepped in to follow her, she leaped toward him with a jab-cross combination he barely evaded.

"I have my moments, mammal. Actually, much of what I say is profound, but you rarely recognize it as such. It is the curse of being surrounded by inferior intellects."

"Hey, if it's any consolation, I wish I was smarter, too."

"It is not."

Rohan snapped a right front kick at Wei Li's belly. She half parried it and half sidestepped. He planted the kicking foot right in front of her and threw a right hook at her head.

She ducked under the hook and snapped a jab into his ribs.

He grunted. That would leave a bruise. "I don't think you appreciate how hard it is to suppress my Power while thinking about fighting."

"Allow me to correct your statement. It is hard to suppress your Power while fighting an opponent of legendary skill while thinking almost entirely about some female with whom you are suddenly and, I am sure, temporarily, enamored."

"Hey, that's entirely unfair. I mean, possibly true, but unfair."

"Oh, please. What is so enticing about this female? Does she have extravagantly large mammary glands? Blemish-free skin? Symmetrical features? A pleasing pheromone profile?"

"I'd have to get an analysis done on the pheromones. Humans don't consciously process pheromone reactions."

"Of course you don't. Because how would your species propagate if it were consciously aware of the chemical underpinnings of its tragically flawed mating procedure?"

"Hey, can you remind me why we're best friends again? Because I'm pretty sure you're being mean. Again."

Wei Li sidestepped, and when he turned to follow, planted a vicious side kick right up under his ribs, knocking the breath out of him.

"I believe it is because you got tired of sycophants and, what's the human term? Suck-ups?"

"Oh, right. Gee, I kind of miss those guys right about now."

"Undoubtedly this female is enticed by the notion of a mate with so much prestige and will be equally up-sucking to you."

She reached down and grabbed at his lead leg. He palmed her head, pushing her down and off balance so she couldn't complete the attempt to take him down.

"That's really not how those words work together. But I also think you're wrong. It's not like I have a ton of prestige here, anyway. I'm a dockworker. Not even a First Class dockworker."

"Please, spare me. Everyone knows we have an il'Drach Hybrid on the station and that it's you. Certainly, I am consulted when there is a case of theft or illegal transportation of restricted narcotics. But who is called first when savage aliens attempt a military conquest of Wistful?"

"Weren't you the one who called me?"

She launched a hard kick right at his groin. "I did not say people are wrong to so regard you. Only that you cannot fairly claim to be 'just a dockworker.'"

He took the brunt of the kick on his tougher upper thigh. Her low kicks were landing on target less and less frequently. It seemed the hours of practice were paying off.

"So, any advice? You know I'm terrible with women."

"I do know that. Where did you meet this female? Was she on board *Insatiable*?"

"Actually, no. Just walking around. I got into a conversation with her kid."

"She is a mother?"

He nodded. "Little boy. Cute kid. They're Lukhor."

Wei Li grunted. "We should stop. We are getting tired and sloppy." She didn't believe in sparring while fatigued, at least not regularly.

Rohan bent forward and put his hands on his knees, trying to keep his breathing steady and nasal. "I was tired and sloppy from the beginning."

"Yes, but now it is true of us both."

"I take it that's a 'no' on the advice?"

Wei Li shook her head. "If she is a mother, be kind to her offspring, but not so kind that you appear to be manipulative. Other than that, be yourself. Because to be otherwise is a poor plan for a relationship. Sooner or later, you will revert to the true you, and that will be that."

Rohan stood up. "That was pretty good advice. Have you been studying? Reading romance novels or something?"

Wei Li shook her head. "I subscribed to 'Things your stupid friends should know but don't.' In my daily feed. At first, I believed it to be a parody site, but over time I realized it is frighteningly accurate. Now I read the entries and repeat them to people I know. Then they believe I am wise and sincere in caring for them."

"Wei Li, I've never been more glad to have you for a best friend."

She smiled at him, flashing sharp teeth and a flick of a scaly, forked tongue. "You should be."

7

Good Mourning to You

Rohan woke to a softly beeping comm, preset to recognize when he was ending a sleep cycle and alert him to urgent incoming personal messages.

There were three. Wistful letting him know he wasn't needed outside the station that morning. Professor Stone asking to meet him in the docking bay as soon as possible. A green-skinned goddess breaking his heart.

He sighed and put on his uniform. "I should buy clothes that aren't in station colors. Maybe a suit."

Wistful was either not listening or choosing not to answer.

He sighed again. It didn't help.

He ran through his morning routine, thought about eating and decided against it, then headed out.

The day and night cycle on board Wistful was artificial but most species followed it. Wistful darkened the roof and external windows somewhat during the "night" and gently encouraged businesses to close for at least part of that time.

Traffic in the streets was building quickly as Rohan made his way to the docking bay where *Insatiable* was anchored.

He deliberately chose a route that would avoid the grassy area in front of Rinth's family quarters. No reason to rub salt in his wounds, even if they were only shallow cuts.

The bay was busy with foot traffic but felt empty. Most ships using that area were cargo ships, and the bay was usually full of containers and pallets and the machinery used to move them. *Insatiable* was taking on some supplies but very few for a ship of her size.

Rohan walked casually to the huge doors that separated the bay from *Insatiable*'s airlocks. He spotted a familiar figure standing almost center in the bay, facing the doors, arms folded across her chest.

"Wei Li. Fancy meeting you here."

She turned to face him, arching one scaly eyebrow. "And where else should I be? Should a security chief be anywhere other than keeping an eye on an Imperial ship? We've already been invaded once this week, another one and I might face a pay cut."

"It was . . . never mind. You're an empath, you know I was being sarcastic."

"I do." She turned back to the thin stream of humanoids coming and going from the ship. "I will share something with you, Rohan."

"Sure."

She leaned over, placing a hand over her mouth to cover her lips. "There is something *off* about that ship. Something that makes me uncomfortable. Something I cannot precisely identify."

He looked at her intently, searching for some clue she was teasing him or exaggerating. He found only dead earnestness in her eyes and face.

"I'm not sure if it will help, but I'll keep an eye on her as much as I can."

She nodded. "Thank you, Rohan. I'm not sure that it will help either, but please do." She looked around him, bringing attention to the fact that he was alone. "I see your date did not go well."

He sighed. "It never even happened. She canceled."

"It is all right, Rohan. The number of mammalian females in Imperial space is vast, and your standards are low."

"You are as sweet as ever, Wei Li. Say, have you seen Doctor Stone? There are two; I mean the male Doctor Stone?"

She tilted her head toward the entrance. "I believe that is him walking to us now."

She was right.

Ben Stone, standing a head taller than the two ship crewmembers on either side of him, raised a hand in a quick wave and walked straight to Rohan and Wei Li.

"Rohan, thank you for meeting me. I could use a favor."

"Sure. Professor, meet Wei Li, Wistful's Chief of Security. Wei Li, meet Professor Stone. He's here to study the animals on Toth 3 and the Ursans, probably in that order."

The two shook hands.

"Your people are quite rare in this sector, Security Chief. It's a pleasure to meet you."

She nodded. "Likewise. Though I don't envy you attempting to deal with either the kaiju or the Ursans. You've chosen challenging subjects."

He laughed, his bushy blond eyebrows shaking with the movement. "The not-challenging ones are boring, and at my age boredom is my biggest nemesis."

"Wistful is a strong deterrent to boredom, Doctor, so you have chosen an excellent destination for a visit."

He nodded. "It's quite lovely. But Rohan, I was hoping you could do something for me. And perhaps you can both help."

Rohan held up his hands. "I'll try."

"Wistful has grounded, er, anchored *Insatiable*'s shuttles. I really want to get down to the surface, as quickly as possible, and she won't release them until there's been a thorough maintenance overhaul."

"And you want me to fly you down by hand?"

The professor's eyes widened. "Honestly, that never occurred to me. Having known Hyperion, I suppose it should have, but it's been so long. I just meant maybe you could pull some strings and get a shuttle released early. Better yet, get *two* released; my wife is desperate to do a flyby near that wormhole."

"Professor, I think you overestimate my importance or influence over Wistful. I was supposed to be on a date with an astonishingly beautiful woman, right now, and she had to cancel because Wistful put her on a last-minute double shift. In fact, she's probably on the team prepping your shuttles. So believe me, if I had the authority to get those overhauls canceled I'd have used it."

The professor slumped a little. "It was a long shot." He directed one quizzical eyebrow toward Wei Li, who shook her head.

He sighed. "Is it really so dangerous? I keep hearing people tell me to stay away."

Rohan chuckled, thinking of the stories about Ben Stone, sidekick to Hyperion, that he'd read while growing up. "And that only makes you more determined to visit, doesn't it?"

The professor shrugged. "Guilty as charged, I suppose."

Rohan turned to Wei Li. "The professor was famous back on my home planet. So I know all sorts of stories about his adventures as a young man, him and his wife."

Wei Li nodded. "You were a soldier? An explorer?"

The professor laughed. "I was a sidekick, I think. Friends with a Hybrid; you know how that goes." He waved a hand at Rohan.

Wei Li looked sharply at Rohan. "If you should ever refer to me or even think of me as a sidekick the results will be quite unpleasant for you. And remember, you cannot hide those thoughts from me."

Rohan held his hands up in surrender. "I swear to you I would never think that. I'm more like *your* sidekick, the less intelligent subordinate you bring in to do the mopping up after you've solved the crime. Or figured out the situation. Something like that."

She sniffed. "I will accept that. For now. But you will be subject to a demotion should you disappoint me."

Rohan smiled at the professor. "She makes it sound like friendly banter, but she's deadly serious."

"I'm absolutely going to take your word for it. I see there's no moving either of you on this, and I've learned to limit how much energy I invest tilting at windmills." He clapped his hands together. "Have you eaten? If we can't get to the planet this morning, at least we can have breakfast. I've heard the station has some very good food."

Rohan looked at Wei Li, who shook her head. "I am on duty, Doctor Stone. Please carry on without me."

The professor looked at Rohan, who shrugged. "I'm free."

"Excellent. I shall be your backup date. Not my first time." He winked at Rohan.

Rohan scratched his beard. He really was due for a trim. "I don't follow."

"Ask me again after a few drinks."

Rohan nodded. "It's breakfast for us, but it's evening for somebody."

"I didn't mean now." He paused. "Though I'm not entirely opposed to the idea. I'll have to ask you to direct us. I didn't do any research on places to eat on Wistful."

"Don't worry, Professor, I've got us covered. But since the planet is off limits for today, do you want to get a start on the other half of your project?"

"You mean the Ursans?"

"Yes."

"That is a wonderful idea. Lead the way."

Rohan led the professor to an elevator tube, which took them up one level to Wistful's transportation layer. The elevator opened up onto a small, enclosed platform, facing sliding doors. Rohan walked to a touchpad next to the doors and tapped on the panel.

"Shouldn't be long. The Ursans are in another arm of the station. Wistful put them a little bit out of the way. I'm sure she was concerned how they'd get along with the rest of the population."

"Any trouble so far?"

"I wouldn't say trouble. I kind of read them the riot act, and after seeing their war chief get handled, I think they were pretty subdued. Plus, you know, barely escaping genocide with their lives intact. The real test will be to see how well they get along with everybody else after they're settled and comfortable."

"They're learning Drachna?"

"Yeah, and really quickly. Ursula says they all have some kind of data implants. As in, their whole population."

The professor's bushy eyebrows rose up toward his hairline. "We don't see that very often."

"No, we don't. Different culture, I guess. And a complete lack of familiarity with Powers."

"So, they're truly on the other side of the Tellurian Inflection point?"

"Seems like it. They'd never seen anybody tow a ship before, and they seemed pretty surprised at how ineffectual their guns were. Plus, you know, their ship is dead. Or was never alive. Battleship-sized but a brain like a shuttle."

"Interesting. I don't think I've interacted with any pre-Inflection civilizations other than Earth's."

"Neither have I."

The doors slid open; they stepped into a small pod. They sat on the smooth plastic seats and strapped themselves in just as the pod accelerated smoothly away from the station.

The professor nodded. "Very civilized place, this station. Gravity feels close to Earth normal?"

"Yeah. There are small sections with lower gravity for species that need it, but most of the station is, I think, just a few percent about Earth normal. Air, water, all very Empire-standard. You don't have to worry about making a wrong turn and stepping into a corridor filled with chlorine gas."

The pod rapidly slowed to a stop. The door slid open quietly and the two humans unbuckled and stepped out, immediately finding an elevator to take them to the residential level.

"We'll try to find some Ursans around, but if we can't, I'll leave some messages and we'll get some food."

Finding the Ursans turned out to not be much of a problem. As the two humans emerged from the elevator they were greeted by a medley of sounds and smells.

The professor paled slightly. "Is this normal?"

Rohan shook his head. "Not really, no. The question is whether it's bad or not."

Small bands of Ursans littered the street. Some were sitting in circles passing around pitchers of what Rohan assumed were alcohol. Some were arm-in-arm singing or chanting in voices toneless to the Earther's ears.

Others were eating, digging paws into barrels filled with fish or animal carcasses cooked whole and laid out on the grass for all to share.

"Well, they're boisterous, but not as rowdy as students at Fleet Academy get after finals."

"Wouldn't know; I never made it to the Academy."

They walked between the groups of Ursans. They were mostly ignored, at least until two male Ursans wearing the dark-red leather uniform of ship's crew spotted Rohan and stood to face him.

The two saluted, both looking down their snouts at him with bleary eyes. The one to their left belched loudly and stumbled.

Rohan wasn't sure what to do. "At ease? I guess?"

The two nodded and turned away.

"They really do look so much like Earth bears. I'm going to have to do some genetic analysis."

"You don't think they're related to anything on Earth, do you? I mean, I was assuming it was a coincidence. Like parallel evolution. They're from the other side of the galaxy."

The professor shook his head. "Intelligent life comes from fewer places than you think. The more alien races we study, the more obvious it is that they share origins. There were old races traveling these stars a very long time ago, bringing life along with them."

"Really? Is that, like, common knowledge? Or your theory?"

Ben smiled. "It's common knowledge. Where things get heated, and contentious, is when you try to track down where things started first, and who brought whom to where and when. That sort of discussion ends up in fistfights and riots at academic conferences. But almost every species in this sector are close cousins. Think about how many of them can interbreed, even if their children are sterile. Different species, but not as different as, say, cats and dogs. And we know cats and dogs evolved closely together on one planet."

"I get your point."

"Do you know any of these Ursans individually? Maybe we could sit down and talk? If not, maybe we can strike up a conversation at random."

Rohan shrugged and walked to one who'd saluted him. He reached up and tapped the large creature on its furry shoulder.

"Ursula? Do you know where Ursula is? Is she around here?"

The Ursan looked at him with bloodshot eyes. Its breath contained so much alcohol Rohan was sure he could set it on fire.

If the alien understood his words, it gave no sign of it.

"Rohan!"

Rohan felt a tap on his shoulder and turned to see almost five hundred kilos of Ursan bearing down on him like a runaway train.

He barely got his hands up into a protective guard before the alien piled into him. The last thing he saw was a red, artificial eye gleaming above an array of sharp teeth, glistening with saliva.

He felt massive arms close around him and lift him off the ground. The arms squeezed, hard enough that the air hissed out of Rohan's lungs.

"Tow Chief Second Class War Chief Rohan! You have come to share in our mourning!"

Ang's breath smelled of equal parts raw fish and raw alcohol. Rohan winced, ribs aching at the pressure. "Ang! Please, not so hard!"

Ang released the Hybrid and eased him to the ground.

"Ang offers apology! Ang is happy to see Brother Rohan."

The professor looked at Rohan from around Ang's massive frame. He mouthed, "Brother Rohan?" with raised eyebrows. Rohan shrugged helplessly.

"Brother Rohan?"

"Of course! We fight, you fight honorably. Much respect. You are now as big brother to Ang. Smaller big brother."

Rohan paused, then grabbed Ang, one arm over the Ursan's left shoulder, the other under his right arm. He squeezed, hard enough to bring out a whistle from the war chief.

"Brother Ang."

The Ursan leaned his head back and let out three thunderous barks. Ursans for dozens of meters around stopped what they were doing and faced the pair. Almost in unison they leaned their own heads back and barked, all in sets of three.

It was the highest form of Ursan laughter.

Rohan let settled to the ground. Ang patted him on the back.

"Is good place. Good fish, good meat. Very good liquor. Ang thanks Rohan for letting him live to complete this mourning."

"Mourning?"

Ang nodded and waved his meaty paw, taking in the festivities up and down the wide boulevard. "We mourn."

The professor chuckled. "If this is how you mourn, I'm afraid to see how you celebrate."

Ang turned to Ben, noticing him for the first time. Rohan stepped between them. "War Chief Ang, this is Doctor Benjamin Stone. He's a hero, from my home planet."

"This place not your home?"

Rohan shook his head. "I'm originally from a planet called Earth. I've lived here for less than a year."

Ang held out his hand and gingerly shook the professor's. "Am pleased to meet planet-friend of War Chief Rohan."

The professor solemnly returned the handshake. "It's a pleasure to meet you, War Chief Ang."

The Ursan bared his teeth. "Come, you both. We sit there with top officers, mourning."

Rohan cleared his throat. "Can you maybe explain a little more? This isn't what we usually call mourning."

Ang slapped the side of his head. "Translation chip faulty maybe. Mourning. Things done after great loss, to show how we miss those who died."

"Oh, no, that's mourning, all right. Don't go blaming the chip. Maybe we just do it differently."

Ang nodded. "To mourn, Ursans set aside seven days. We drink, eat, sing songs, and tell stories of those who died. Now we have many, many stories to tell. Many of our friends died in our escaping."

Ben Stone winked at Rohan. "It's an Irish wake. If the Irish were half-ton Jewish bears."

Rohan laughed. "Jewish? Oh, you mean the seven days. A drunken shiva."

Ang looked confused.

Rohan slapped him on the back. "We're comparing your way of mourning to some cultures on Earth. I think you're combining the best parts of some different systems."

Ang nodded, his right eye red and gleaming but the left somewhat dull with alcohol. "Come, I show you our temple."

The Ursan war chief barked out another laugh and led the two humans between and around clusters of half-conscious Ursans to the door of a restaurant. The sign read, "Third Moon," and was decorated with a trio of circles, two white and one blue.

"Oh, dear."

Ang nodded violently. "Yes, is dear to us, as well. Is wonderful place."

Rohan sighed. What kind of bill were the Ursans racking up? It wasn't a dive bar they were drinking in.

They walked in, nearly stumbling back out again as they faced a thunderous shout of greeting.

Rohan looked at the professor. "I think we're going to need drinks."

"Normally, I'd refuse at this hour, but I believe I'll be making an exception. For science!"

8

Rhymes with Fine

Rohan walked up to the worn wooden bar while Ang cleared out seats for the three of them.

He ordered two Sein ales and two breakfast specials.

The professor was already seated next to Ang at the big table, comically undersized compared to the Ursans. Rohan looked in vain for Ursula, but he recognized at least three of the others from the bridge crew of their warship.

He sat at the empty seat next to the professor's.

An Ursan was finishing his story of a pilot who had crashed his fighter into a cruiser, delaying it enough for their ship to escape.

They were all, to the humans' surprise, speaking Drachna.

The story ended and the Ursans drank a toast to honor the deceased. Then another Ursan, the female engineer who Rohan had heard speak on the ship, held up her glass.

"I speak now. I speak of my father."

The rest of them raised their glasses in a quiet salute. Rohan looked and saw many a watery eye.

"I now tell tale of my father for War Chief Rohan. My father, has no Drachna name, but rest of you know him. Father was scientist. Physicist. Whole life, study. Not fight. Not respected by Ursan people, not much. Great struggle to study, to keep dignity, not fight, not war."

The bartender came by with a tray and put two short, rectangular glasses of brownish liquid on the table between Rohan and the professor.

"Father learn everything. Knew about everything. History, archaeology, mathematics, chemistry, all physical sciences. Learned man. Taught many at university. Father at heart studied wormholes most loved. More than loved his daughters, his wife, his people maybe. Had passion for this most." She turned to the humans. "Our colony system had wormhole, but closed for ten thousand years. Meaningless disk in space. Pretty but no value.

"Father studied. Father read. Father found key to wormhole. Other Ursans came. No lie, we had no stomach for fight. Already ended long war. We tired. Not want to die, but tired of fight.

"They came. We fought, we died. Father say, open wormhole, we can. Had key. Frequency, patterns to open wormhole, deduced from ancient ruins and older texts. Places left behind by the Old Ones. The Beings Who Are. Who Were.

"Few believed. But Ursula say, nothing left to lose. Father handed me key, went back to gather students, precious belongings.

"While we ran to ship, they attacked university.

"Father never reach refugee ship. Died there. We left. We came through to new world. We live. We find new friends, new brothers, new home maybe. Only thanks to him."

She drank from her glass. The others did as well. Rohan drained his in a long, smooth swallow.

The professor coughed, softly choking on the potent liquor.

The Ursans let out a short roar.

Ang spoke. "He was great hero. No fighter he, but still great hero. Save us all. We will never forget."

Another Ursan raised a glass and started speaking of another hero of the war.

The bartender brought their food, and the humans ate fried rice with eggs cooked over it.

Another story was told, and another round of drinks. If the Ursans noticed that they were being served a different beverage than the humans they didn't mention it.

There were songs.

By the third song, Rohan was pleasantly warm inside and the professor was listing to the side of his seat like a sinking ship.

There was a short lull in the conversation, and an Ursan to Ang's right lifted his glass.

"I have story, but to ask, not tell. Myself serve War Chief Ang. You should all be for telling a tale of mourning about him and myself today." He pointed his glass to each of the others as he spoke.

"We came to this great station, this strange place, and with full pride and fear we picked up arms and tried to grab by force what was being given. Myself emptied two magazines into War Chief Rohan. No Ursan would have spared our lives after that. Yet, I live. I am glad, but I am, what is word, confused? War Chief Rohan, why you not take my life? As was your right?"

Rohan stirred in his seat. He took another strong sip of the Sein Amber. "When I grew up, there was a great hero on my world. His name was Hyperion. He was a Hybrid like me, only much stronger, more talented. And the professor here"—he pointed at Doctor Stone—"was a close friend and ally of his, as close as anybody.

"Hyperion's adventures were famous, especially, for some reason, to children. My generation grew up on tales of Hyperion and his great enemies and their struggles. While he was on Earth, no matter how he struggled, no matter how villainous his enemies were, he didn't kill them. Some died in accidents, sometimes of their own making. But *he* would not kill them.

"My friends and I, children, would argue in the playground. Was Hyperion a great man for his unwillingness to kill? Or was he a fool? I always said he was a fool. Surely it is smarter to kill your enemy, to make sure they never threaten you or your loved ones in the future. They were idle words, really. I was a child with no Powers, not at that time. I never thought I would be in a position to make that sort of decision.

"Some of Hyperion's enemies continued to torment him and fight him, time and again. But some changed. Some became better people. One of those men saved my life. He had fought Hyperion, had lost. Had become a hero. It's a silly story, in a way, but I was on an out-of-control plane, and that man saved the plane. We actually later became friends, much later. If

Hyperion had been more ruthless, had been smarter, that man would not have been alive to save me.

"Every death takes something away from the world.

"We might find ourselves fighting side-by-side against some great threat. We might be allies one day. And on that day, I will be grateful that I showed some mercy."

The Ursan nodded. "So you . . . never kill? You are pacifist maybe? Is that word?"

Rohan laughed, and it came out strangled and tight. He realized he was rarely this drunk. "Oh, no, I wouldn't say that. I've had to kill more than I'd like. You don't want to know. And in the end, I'm no Hyperion. I'm weak. But I just . . . I just try very hard not to."

Ben straightened in his chair, with a visible effort. "Let me tell you, Hyperion was not perfect. I knew all his secrets, and while he was a great person, he had flaws."

Rohan looked at the other human. "Really?"

Ben nodded. "Oh, yes. Nothing too bad, he wasn't secretly evil. But let me tell you something." He leaned in toward the table and swung his head widely from side to side, checking for anybody in position to overhear. "My friend, Hyperion was a *huge* slut. He would screw anything that moved and some things that didn't. Man, woman, inanimate objects."

Rohan burst out laughing. That was much at odds with the public image of Hyperion. "Really? Somehow that never made it into the comic books."

The professor nodded. "Don't tell my wife I said that. It's a 'secret.' But *oh,* yes, he could not keep his pants on for anything."

Ang laughed along with the other Ursans. It had taken their translators a minute to catch up to the conversation. "Your planet must be littered with his children!"

The professor shook his head. "It would have been! I think half the planet would be half-Hyperion! But he was sterile. So, no children. Some broken hearts, is all."

"Cubs are great joy in life. I am sorry for your hero."

The female engineer slapped the table. "Still, something to be said for mating with no chance of cubs, is not?"

More laughter.

Ang pointed to the Ursan to his right. "This is why Argo only mates with other males!" They laughed harder.

Argo himself was shaking his head, barely keeping his own laughter in check. "Is not only reason! But is a good benefit!"

The laughter subsided slowly, and some of the Ursans got up to find other places to mourn. Rohan ordered lunch for the professor and himself.

"This is the drunkest I've been in thirty years."

Rohan nodded and made sure they had water to drink. "It's the drunkest I've been in a while. It fades fast, though."

Ben nodded. "Hyperion was the same way. He'd complain about it, too. He'd be drunk as a skunk and twenty minutes later . . . not."

Rohan cracked his neck. "That's about right."

"Anyway. I should be heading back to *Insatiable*. I'll accept a scolding from my wife, sleep this off, and hope the shuttles are cleared by tomorrow."

"We'll see." Rohan quietly hoped the shuttles wouldn't be cleared. It was a vain hope, he knew. He'd eventually have to travel to the planet. "Did you get the data you needed?"

Ben held out a hand. Rohan grabbed it and hauled the unsteady older man to his feet. "Ang and Argo both agreed to come to *Insatiable* and give blood samples. The female, I forget her name, said she'd bring an Ursan doctor to provide me with some basic info. It's more than I had hoped for, really. They are not a shy species."

Rohan laughed and propped the professor up with his shoulder.

The two humans retraced their earlier steps to the transport tubes.

Doctor Stone grabbed Rohan, pulling him back, stopping him. "Give me a moment." He put his hands on his knees.

"You going to throw up?"

"I don't . . . think so. Wasn't sure there for a moment. You think they're really going to keep this up for five and a half more days?"

"I'd bet good money on it."

"What a culture. What a people!"

"Yes, let's go, Professor. I'll get you home."

"I like you, Rohan. You have a good heart."

"That's sweet, Professor. You're drunk."

"That is also true. But I have good intuition about these things. I hope things work out with your lady friend." They stepped into the elevator, which whisked them smoothly down a level.

"Doesn't look good for me, sadly. That's okay."

"She canceled one date. It's not the end of things."

Rohan nodded. "We'll see. I'm a pessimist when it comes to romance. Besides, she's kind of out of my league."

The professor laughed. "Sometimes you Hybrids are so funny. You're a what? Maybe not one in a billion, but one in five hundred million? Not many other men can compete with the whole flying bulletproof thing."

"Ha. Speaking from experience, Professor?"

"Oh yes."

"You're the one Marion ended up married to, Professor. Not Hyperion."

"Yes, but nobody really thinks that was *her* first choice." He smiled.

"You don't seem angry about that."

"Nah. Who could blame her? And you're right, I did end up with her. I'm happy with how my life turned out. More than happy. Ask her whether she's bitter, though, and if you get her drunk enough you might get a different answer."

"I doubt I'll get the chance. You said she's not fond of Hybrids, remember?"

"Oh yeah, yeah. Right. Don't get her drunk. Better."

Rohan supported the professor onto the transport pod, to the elevator near *Insatiable*'s berth, and down to the ship entrance. He made sure the older man was steady enough to make his own way onto the ship.

Rohan stood back from the entrance and checked his messages. There were two: Wistful giving him the afternoon off; Tamara asking him to meet her for dinner at the end of her second shift. About one hour away.

"I must have done something right in a past life." Rohan turned and headed back to his quarters. Better to shower first; he smelled of vodka, bear sweat, raw fish, and perhaps more than a hint of vomit.

He was sober by the time he had reached his quarters. There was plenty of time left.

A clean-smelling Rohan checked his feeds for news. He gave up after reading the same short news blurb five times without understanding it. He wasn't able to concentrate on anything until he was sitting across a food-laden table from Tamara.

9

Chemistry With an Engineer

They had finished a glass of wine and were sharing first-date stories.

"There he was, one of the pre-eminent bankers in all of Vardos City, and his mathematically gifted daughter decided she wished more than anything to fix shuttle drives, after twenty years of bragging to one and all that his girl would be the top female financier in history. But I could not stand another summer fine-tuning credit-scoring algorithms."

Rohan shook his head. "My mother always said that parents can have hopes but not expectations."

"She sounds like a wise woman."

Rohan smiled. "She is. Like most sons, I don't remember ever really listening to her. I left home pretty young."

Tamar nodded and slipped a spoonful of curry into her mouth. "This is delicious. I didn't know your species could handle this much spice."

"Are you kidding me? My mother's people invented spice. Well, on Earth we did."

"Well, what about your father? I know very little about your people on either side."

"Trust me, you don't want to get into the subject of my father. He was all, 'with-you-by-my-side-we-will-conquer-the-Empire.' All the time. As a four-year-old it felt like a lot of responsibility."

Tamara laughed, thinking that Rohan was joking, or at least exaggerating. He laughed with her.

"So you are not close with your parents?"

He shook his head. "I haven't had contact with Earth in over ten years. It's for the best. Really, I think my closest friends are Wistful and Wei Li."

"Don't forget my son!" She smiled. "It is hard to move to new places."

"Was your sister already here when you got this job?"

She nodded and tore off a corner of the flatbread they'd ordered. "I am so hungry. Sixteen hours going over drives and weapon systems, triple checking everything, no breaks. I was barely allowed to relieve myself."

"You want me to tell Wistful to go easy on you?"

She shook her head, her antennae wobbling with the motion. "Please do not. I could handle my father; I can handle this."

Rohan held up his hands. "Sorry, sorry. Of course. I'm just glad you came to dinner with me."

"Did I not say I would?"

He nodded. "Well, when you canceled, I thought . . ."

She laughed. "For someone who can fly through space unprotected and stand in front of a hail of bullets without so much as a scratch you are very fragile, Rohan."

He hung his head. "Guilty. I was sure you'd reconsidered."

"Would you not have pursued me, Tow Chief Second Class Rohan? Sung sonnets from beneath my window? Covered my foyer with flowers plucked from the planet above, rare specimens whose acquisition threatened your very life?"

"If I thought you wanted me to, I would have. But if I thought you were just, I don't know, uninterested, then no. I'd leave you alone."

"You are a nice man. A sweet man."

Rohan groaned a little bit. "Not too sweet, though. I'm still, you know, um, sporting a full chest of hair."

Tamara laughed again. "You are funny. I needed this. I do not get away from job and family enough, I think."

"Well, you've got a son to raise. It's hard."

She nodded and looked up at him. Her eyes were dark, rimmed with black lines blended into her already dark green skin. Rohan wanted to stare into them all night.

She must have changed quickly after work, because she was wrapped in a long stretch of colored silk, not a ship's-issue jumpsuit. They sat across from one another at a table in the back of Rohan's favorite curry house.

Rohan, to his own disgust, was wearing his uniform. He had little else in his possession.

"Do you know the first thing Rinth ever said to me? That my outfit was ugly."

She leaned over to the side and looked him up and down. "Maybe, just maybe, this is one situation where you should be listening?"

Rohan laughed. "I know! I promise, I'll go to a real tailor and get real clothes. Literally all I own are Wistful uniforms."

"And what is with her? Is she colorblind? That is the most garish combination I've ever seen."

"I know! I guess Wistful thinks they make us more visible." He pointed up.

She nodded. "Practicality over aesthetics. A sign of either a declining civilization or a primitive one. That is what my mother always said."

"The Lukhor are famous for their aesthetics, though. My mother's people are like that, but not my neighbors where I grew up." Tamara tilted her head quizzically. "She moved to the other side of our planet for economic reasons. I never lived in her homeland. Honestly, we barely even visited."

"So, you were an outsider before you were an outsider? A child of your mother's people in a strange land, long before leaving your planet and becoming even more an alien?"

Rohan paused. "That is a very good way to put it. You're really smart."

"Is that not what attracted you to me in the first place?"

Rohan sputtered for a moment and drained half a glass of water. "Well, of course."

Tamara laughed at him. "Silly man. I have no such illusions. Relationships may be built on respect, but that is rarely how they start."

He wished he was drinking something stronger than water. "I am trying to think of an answer that won't get me further into trouble and, to be honest, I'm failing."

"Some trouble is worth getting into, though, isn't it?" She put a hand over his, where it lay flat on the table between them.

When she touched him, he felt something. A knot of tension between his shoulder blades, so subtle that he hadn't even known it, released. "So, um, did your father ever come to his senses? I mean, it's been years, and you're doing so well. . . ."

She shrugged. "Not in the least. He is perhaps as stubborn as I am. He cut me off from the family finances, though that was more to keep my ex-husband away from it than to spite me."

"I take it he didn't approve of your marriage any more than of your career path?"

She snorted. "No. To be fair, he was right about the marriage. And also, to be honest, if I were in real trouble, if I really needed something, I have no doubt he'd be there for me."

The waiter came and they ordered dessert. Tamara yawned while Rohan gave the order.

"I am so sorry, Tow Chief Second Class Rohan, I don't mean to be rude. I've worked a very long day and this wine is not making it easier to stay awake."

It was another moment where Rohan wasn't sure if she was showing disinterest and letting him down easy or was just genuinely tired.

"Don't apologize, it's fine. I'm just glad you came."

She nodded and checked her tablet. "I can't stay too much longer. I have to be back on shift in five hours, and I need some sleep if I'm going to be of any use."

"You don't get a break? What's the hurry?"

"*Insatiable* is demanding that her shuttles be made ready as quickly as possible, and we're upgrading their shield and weapons systems at the same time. The real problem is that eighty percent of the shuttle engineers are working on the Ursan ship. It's the largest dead ship any of us have ever seen, and we are not really staffed to do all that work by hand."

"You should get the Ursans to do it."

"Apparently they are all occupied for the duration of their mourning period."

Rohan nodded. "I spent half the day, mourning with them. 'Occupied' is too gentle a word."

"They did not resent your presence?"

He shook his head. "They didn't seem to."

"That is good. Grudges are a burden to both parties."

"Another saying from your people?"

"It's what I tell myself whenever I have to think about Rinth's father."

Tamara yawned again, stretching as she did it.

The desserts arrived. Rohan started eating.

Tamara pointed her fork at him. "You must tell me a few more things about yourself, so I have answers when my sister interrogates me."

"Is she in the habit of doing that?"

"Every time I ask her to watch over Rinth while I'm out on a date." Her cheeks twitched with a smile.

"Fair enough. I'm not sure what a sister wants to hear about someone on a date? I have a steady job. I'm not married. That's a good start, I think?"

She shook her head, her antennae wriggling with the motion. "That's the sort of thing my mother would want to hear, not my sister. But I can't really blame you, the subtleties around this issue are difficult for men to understand."

"Yeah, I have no idea what any of that means."

"Fair enough, let me offer some guidance. How about, what is the best thing about having your abilities?"

"Best thing about Powers?"

She nodded as she chewed some of her pastry.

He considered a lascivious answer, but it felt too soon. "I'd have to say travel. Ironically, I don't get to do it here, but usually, if I'm on a planet, I can go almost anywhere without preparation. Mountaintops, secluded valleys, underwater caverns. I've been to dozens of places where no non-Hybrid could even survive. Places literally unseen by humanoid eyes."

"That is a very good answer. Romantic, non-violent. I like it."

"I'd be lying if I didn't admit that being bulletproof has its advantages, as well. I mean, I wish I didn't live a life where that was needed, but when it's useful, it's really useful."

"I'm sure! What else can you do? Can you read minds? Can you read my mind right now? Wait, I should ask, *are* you reading my mind right now?"

Rohan laughed out loud. "No! I'm not sure I'd even want to. I'm a little more empathic than the average person, enough to sense a ship nearby. I can usually tell when somebody is about to start hitting me. Nothing significant. What about you, though? Is that what those are for?" He pointed at her antennae.

"No, nothing like that. Say, these are delicious. Andervarian pastry?"

He nodded. "Andervarian. They're not just for vodka."

"Oh, I don't drink Andervarian vodka anymore. I had a bad experience with it at university."

"We can stick to wine. Or Sein Ale, which is what I usually drink."

She yawned again. "I can't stop the yawns! No Sein Ale for me tonight. You can buy me some next time."

His heart skipped a little in his chest. "So. Next time."

"Assuming you're interested in a next time?" Something in her dimples told him she had no doubts about the answer.

"Of course! I mean, of course. Yes, please. Pretty please."

"For now I am full and pleasantly, only slightly drunk. I must get some sleep."

"Absolutely. Um, may I walk you home?"

She shook her head. "No. But you can fly me."

10

Legend of the Decipede

"Rohan."

"Yes, Wistful." He sat up in bed. He had been awake, tossing and turning and thinking about his date. He glanced at the clock display on his wall screen. It wasn't even 5:00 AM.

"Rohan, *Insatiable* is demanding that I allow her shuttles to leave. One to the planet, and one to the wormhole."

"Demanding?"

"Perhaps repeatedly requesting."

"Ah. And?"

"I would like your input on the best way to handle this situation."

"My input?"

"Yes. Should I allow the shuttles to leave?"

Why is she asking me?

"What does Wei Li think?"

"Wei Li believes that surveying the wormhole is unproblematic, but that if the other shuttle travels to Toth 3, it will not return. She believes we will create conflict with the Empire if one of their valued scientists is killed in this system."

Rohan stood up and started putting on his uniform.

"I see what she's saying. If they go down there, they're likely to die. And, sure, we can say, afterward, that we warned them so, but people are bound to get irritated about it. And to be honest, I'd hate to see the professor killed. I kind of like him."

"As do the Ursans. Which is another negative Wei Li mentioned regarding the professor's demise."

"He's a stubborn guy, the professor. If you want to talk him out of it, you're going to need someone who's better with words than me."

"Wei Li suggested that, since we can't convince the professor to abandon this course of action, perhaps you could accompany the shuttle."

Rohan paused, then walked to his bathroom. He stood in front of the mirror and gave a quick brush through his beard, then a longer brush of his hair.

"I could. I don't really want to, but I could."

"I can offer you a substantial bonus for this extra duty." Wistful thought all organics were motivated by money.

"It's not the money, Wistful. It's . . . oh, heck. I'll do it. But what about incoming ships? There must be some waiting to be brought in."

"We have four cargo ships awaiting tow services."

Rohan turned his head from side to side, making sure his hair and beard looked all right in the mirror. Both were longer than was his habit. Would Tamara like his hair long, his beard bushy? Should he trim them? Did her interest in his chest hair mean she would like him generally hirsute?

"Here's what I think: Tell *Insatiable* that they can only visit Toth 3 with a guide, and that guide must be me. But since I'm busy with other work, they'll have to wait a few hours. I'll grab those other ships and any other that gets here in the interim. That gives us a plausible excuse for a short delay and time to think about how to keep those scientists alive."

"That is an acceptable course of action. I am seriously considering promoting you to Tow Chief First Class."

"Whoa, let's not get ahead of ourselves, Wistful. Let's see if I can bring this shuttle crew back alive, then we can start talking about promotions."

"Yes, Rohan, quite right."

"But, just out of curiosity, what kind of pay increase do I get for Tow Chief First Class?"

Wistful paused. "As you say, Rohan, let us not get ahead of ourselves."

He laughed out loud. What subroutine made Wistful so miserly?

Maybe she was saving up to buy a new star system to move to. One without wormholes and monster-infested planets.

The Hybrid finished getting ready and headed out his personal airlock into the cold darkness of space.

"Wistful, which ship gets brought in first?"

She directed him, by beacon position, to the ships that needed to dock.

He towed them one-by-one to berths around the sentient station. "Wistful, remember how long it took me to do this my first week on the job?"

"I do indeed, Rohan. You were quite clumsy."

"That's not fair. Do you have any idea how hard it is to push an inert ship through space by hand?"

"I do, Rohan. I have had tow chiefs before you. They all struggled at first, the inexperienced ones. But you struggled a bit more than average."

He shook his head as the last cargo ship shuddered into place, the docking port sealing into place against its hull. "If this whole being-a-space-station thing gets tiring, Wistful, you can always get a second career as a motivational speaker."

"I shall keep that idea in reserve, Rohan. That was the last ship waiting for you."

"Copy that. I'll make my way to *Insatiable*, but I'm taking my time."

"Of course. I'll let Doctor Stone know you're on your way. I'm also releasing the shuttle that's bound for the wormhole."

Was that shuttle going to be a problem? Were they going to do something stupid? Rohan had no concrete suspicions, just a justified paranoia regarding the Empire.

"Sounds good."

Rohan went back to his quarters and showered. He checked his messages: nothing but a request from the professor that he join them at his earliest convenience. He stopped at a sidewalk café for a large mug of coffee and a heavy, meat-filled sandwich layered with greens and thinly sliced nuts that crunched with each satisfying bite.

Having run out of ways to procrastinate, he took a tube to the research ship's entrance.

"Hail, *Insatiable*."

She answered over his comm by tightbeam. "Oh, good, Tow Chief Rohan. We've been waiting for you! I think Doctor Stone is quite anxious."

"Well, I had other responsibilities. But I'm here now. Can you direct me to the correct shuttle bay?"

She sent him directions. "Please take care of them, Tow Chief Rohan. I'm super excited to receive information about the planet and its biosphere, but I am also very worried about my crew. The data I have shows that the planet is really dangerous."

"I will do my best, *Insatiable*. Promise."

Insatiable was large enough to have her own internal transit system. It used an Imperial standard layout, so Rohan took only moments to find his way.

He stepped off the transit pod and into the most spacious shuttle bay he'd ever seen on a ship. It was busy with crew members walking back and forth, performing checks on the shuttle's systems.

Ben Stone was standing outside the shuttle. He walked up to Rohan when the Hybrid left the pod. "Rohan! Good, good. Glad you could come. Wistful wouldn't let us go to the planet without you."

"I know, Professor. She's worried, that's all. Come on, show me the shuttle."

"Yes, yes, of course. Here, meet our shuttle pilot, Visita." A woman was walking by, wearing a jumpsuit with *Insatiable*'s livery and a pilot's badge on her shoulder. She was short and slightly built, humanoid except for her big, three-fingered hands. "Visita, Tow Chief Second Class Rohan. He's from my home planet."

Rohan held out a hand. "A pleasure."

Visita took it firmly. "I hear you're our guide."

"I wouldn't go that far, but I've been planetside as much as anybody. Actually, more than anybody."

"What kind of atmospheric phenomena are we looking at? How tough is the flying?"

He shook his head. "It's not that kind of dangerous."

"I'll start preflight checks, sir?"

Rohan shrugged. "No reason to delay, I guess."

Ben slapped him on the back. "Check her out! A beauty, isn't she?"

Rohan looked over the shuttle. Three stories tall, six legs of landing gear built with military-grade ruggedness, two main bootstrap drives and three auxiliaries for extra maneuverability. The hull bristled with gunports, sensor arrays, and multiple aerodynamic components: fins, wings, and foils to help it move in atmosphere.

It was one of the largest shuttles he'd ever seen. He whistled in appreciation.

Ben smiled. "They're built for exploration, investigation. To go places where nobody wants to risk a living ship."

"Impressive. I hope you're not expecting all this to keep you safe?"

"That's what you're here for, isn't it?" The professor clapped him on the shoulder. He was practically bouncing as he moved, full of energy. "Come, I'll introduce you to my graduate students and we can make a flight plan."

The professor led Rohan to an interior room dominated by a conference table, with bright screens covering the walls, floor-to-ceiling. The students were excitedly discussing their visit.

Rohan couldn't remember the students' names. They were all dressed in some kind of quasi-uniform; gray tunics and matching pants with lots of extra pockets and straps.

Two of the students were Rogesh. Heavily built, at least twice the thickness of a human of the same height, with hard, gray-scaled skin and stubby horns. One was male, the other female, and they stood closely together; either good friends or a mated pair.

The male was scowling at Rohan. Perhaps a mild facial deformity.

The third graduate student was a male Lukhor with a friendly smile and nervously twitching green antennae.

The last two were Andervarian, their dark purple skin marked with a geometric pattern of bright yellow tattoos. They were taller than humanoid standard, slender, with their hair tightly braided to their scalps.

The Rogesh male had a map of Toth 3 projected onto a wide screen. He was tracing a planned route with his finger. "If we travel this way, we are within a few hundred kilometers of four different biomes, so we can maximize sample collection diversity." His voice was tight and nervous.

Rohan shook his head. "Did you get the flyer sightings from Wistful?"

The man shook his head sharply, his horns punctuating the movement with menace. "What do you mean?"

Rohan scratched his head. "Oh, sorry, I thought someone went over some of these things with you." He tapped his commlink. "Wistful, please send me updated flyer location data from Toth 3."

"Sending."

"Thank you, Wistful."

With a little help from One, the first Andervarian student, Rohan had new graphics overlaid on their projection within minutes.

"Okay, Wistful keeps a set of satellites in orbit around the planet. They're watching for flyers. You can't land anywhere near them, not if you want to have any chance of leaving the planet again. They like to tear shuttles apart."

The Rogesh looked annoyed. "Tear shuttles apart? What does that mean?"

The Hybrid scratched his beard. "I'm sorry, I keep thinking you were briefed. There are a handful of kaiju—megafauna—species on Toth 3. The flyers are the fastest, so you have to watch for them over a larger area."

Doctor Stone cleared his throat. "How large *exactly* are these kaiju?"

"I saw one with a two-hundred-meter wingspan, but even an average-size flyer is easily fifty meters across. And they're heavily built, for flying reptiles, so don't think it's two hundred meters of paper-thin anything. When I say they like to tear shuttles apart, I mean it literally."

The Rogesh female shook her head, her hand on the arm of the male. "I'm sorry, I think we're having a translation problem."

Rohan looked around the room and smiled grimly. "I'm pretty sure we aren't. I keep telling everyone, this is a bad idea."

The Lukhor cleared his throat. "This planet has about one point one Imperial standard gravities at the surface and the atmospheric pressure is almost exactly Imperial standard. Are these creatures floaters? Lighter than air?"

Rohan shook his head. "No, they fly. They're fast, too. Easily break the sound barrier."

"I'm pretty sure that's impossible."

"You feel free to tell them that. But please do it from far away." He looked around, saw their skeptical glances. "I'm telling you, we're absolutely not landing near any flyers. See these spots here?" He pointed to colored spots dotting the map around the area the Rogesh had originally pointed out. "Nothing that lands in that area is getting out alive."

The Rogesh male jerked his arm, dislodging the female's hand. "He is mocking us! Spot animals from space. Two- hundred-meter wingspan. He calls us weak. It is always the way with the half-breeds."

The professor's eyebrows furrowed angrily. "Haditz! That's enough! Rohan is generously lending us his time and expertise, and I will not have you insulting him."

"It is he who is insulting us with this ludicrous caution! We are more than capable of handling ourselves. We don't need to listen to this . . . this mule!" The female put her hand on his arm again.

The professor shook his head and stepped chest-to-chest with the massive, horned alien. It was like a zookeeper facing down a rhinoceros.

"Haditz, I said that's enough." His voice was cold and stern and was not open to interpretation.

Haditz growled from deep in his chest and turned away.

The professor kept his stare on the larger alien. "Go do another check on the drones. I don't want any surprises after we land."

Haditz huffed loudly and stormed out of the room. The female looked toward Rohan, as if wanting to say something to him, then turned and followed the male.

The professor looked upset. "I'm sorry, Rohan. I did not expect Haditz to lose his temper that way."

"You thought he'd lose it a different way?" Rohan's tone was curt. His irritation was showing.

"That's not what I meant. I underestimated his pain, perhaps."

"Sure. Did I do something to hurt him? Is it my cologne?" Rohan made a show of sniffing his armpit.

"I mentioned we had some issues during the Rebellion." The older human looked around the room. The remaining students looked down, refusing to meet his eyes.

"Ah."

"A group of rebel Hybrids came to the Academy. It was not good. Not good. Haditz is normally a nice fellow, but proud. From a proud people. Pride and occupation make for a bad mix."

For just a moment Rohan tried to imagine what might have happened to result in Haditz's anger. What atrocities could the rebel Hybrids have committed? For just a moment Rohan's imagination answered the question. He shuddered, imperceptible in his jumpsuit.

"All right, all right. I can ignore Haditz, I'm a grownup. But that doesn't change—Look, you really have to listen to me about a place to land."

"What do you suggest?"

Rohan stepped up to the planetary map and used his fingers to pinch zoom in on various areas. Andervarian student Two pointed at something.

"How about that valley right there? Not much biodiversity, but it's pretty clear of . . . whatever."

Rohan shrugged. "Looks good. Professor?"

The professor nodded. "Is it daylight there?"

Andervarian One did a quick check. "They're spinning right into dawn now. By the time we get there it will be light and we'll have a full day to work with."

"Then let's go. Rohan, please join me on the flight deck; we can get a better view from there. And we'll give Visita her instructions."

Rohan and the professor went to the shuttle's flight deck.

Visita's six graceful fingers flew over the controls. Rohan wanted a good look at her feet, but couldn't think of a polite way to ask. *Do the roots match the branches?*

She turned to them. "*Insatiable* and Wistful have both cleared us for launch. Please take seats, just in case."

Alarm klaxons sounded, loud enough to be heard inside the shuttle. The crew vacated the bay and sealed it. Then a roar of wind as the air was evacuated, followed by the mechanical whir made by *Insatiable*'s external door dialing open.

Visita's hands moved across more controls and the shuttle slid smoothly out of *Insatiable*'s belly.

They took a wide arc around the station, then darted toward the far edge of the planet. Toth 3 was centered on the main screen, filling their view, Toth dawning over its edge.

11

Tempting Fate

The professor let out a long breath. "I never get tired of that kind of view. It's a beautiful planet."

"That it is, Professor. At least from this distance, it is."

Stone turned to him. "You know, compared to most Hybrids you're atypical."

"The il'Drach would say I was ill-trained."

"Most are, I don't want to say fearless, but maybe, I don't know, *not* cautious."

Rohan snorted a laugh. "Like I said, ill-trained. There is a very specific model for how we're supposed to think and act. Mostly, don't think, just act. I never really fit the paradigm. My father was unusual, for an il'Drach."

The professor paused, then continued in hushed tones. "You know, I'm not sure it matters, but I'm not unsympathetic to the motives behind the Rebellion."

"I'm not arguing politics with you, Professor. I didn't ask your position on any of that."

"I know. You know, we used to have long debates about the morality of the il'Drach Empire. My wife and I and Hyperion, at least at first."

"Did you? What conclusions did you draw?"

"Well, none, to be honest. And it was always theoretical. It wasn't as if we could have made any difference."

"I don't know. Hyperion was special. Have to wonder how the Rebellion would have gone with him around."

"I have wondered that. Regardless, the Empire is probably a good thing for most of its citizens."

"I wouldn't argue. Benevolent dictatorship. It's nice if you can find it. At least as long as it stays benevolent."

"Benevolent toward *most* of its subjects. I don't think Hyperion found the il'Drach benevolent. I don't think you do, either."

Rohan stretched his arms behind him, cracked his neck. "I obviously can't speak for Hyperion. And you might have noticed that I don't make a habit of saying critical things about the Empire."

"But you're not standing on the lance deck of an Imperial destroyer right now, are you? You're here, a tow chief on an independent station."

"With all due respect, you don't know why I'm not on that deck."

"I don't. Maybe I'm asking. May I? You certainly don't owe me an answer, but I have to wonder."

A long pause. The planet grew in their screens by the minute. From space it was very Earth-like. Clouds. Two-thirds covered by sparkling blue oceans. Land masses covered largely in green.

"I got tired of war, Professor. I'm a tow chief because I'm tired of war. It's not a statement against the il'Drach, it's not a position for or against the Rebellion, not a political ploy. It's just tired old me looking for a way to spend my days in a way that leaves me able to sleep through the night."

"Readying for atmospheric entry now. Shedding velocity."

The ship had artificial gravity, so they didn't feel its sudden deceleration, but they could see the transition as the image of the planet, which had been expanding rapidly, became almost still.

Visita hit a button and a warning buzzer sounded through the shuttle.

They hit the atmosphere. Temperature readings immediately began to climb.

The professor coughed. "This still makes me nervous. Does this make you nervous?"

"Nah. But I've done this without the shuttle. That lends a different perspective."

"Quite."

The shuttle descended deep into the atmosphere, heading toward the cloud layer.

Visita turned back to them briefly. "We might experience some turbulence. Nothing to worry about."

Rohan spoke. "Just let me know if you would like me to get out and push."

"Unnecessary, Tow Chief. Maybe on the way back up." She bared her teeth showing she was joking.

"Five minutes."

The ride got bumpier as air bit hard into the shuttle's aerodynamic parts.

Visita touched some controls and the screen split down the middle, showing another perspective on one half. "We've got video from orbit patched in. Landing area looks clear."

The image focused rapidly on a patch of ground.

"All right, Visita. Nice work."

Rohan took out his mask and tapped on the display. "Flyers are holding steady, we're clear for now."

The shuttle plummeted toward the ground, then rapidly decelerated just in time to prevent a crash. It touched down gently onto a grassy field.

"Hold." Visita's fingers danced over the controls. "Gravity one point one. Pressure one. Switching from antigravs. Atmospheric sampling has begun; results will be available momentarily."

Their weight shifted unpleasantly as the shuttle's gravitational field was turned off.

"Thank you, Visita." The professor tapped his comm link and spoke. "Launch drones. I want four points of aerial view before anyone sets foot on the ground." He turned to Rohan.

"We'll set the drones at fifteen hundred meters. They'll give us plenty of warning if anything big approaches."

"Okay." Rohan tapped his own comm. "Wistful, can you alert me if there's any change in kaiju activity on the planet within two thousand kilometers of our position?"

"Yes, Rohan."

"Thanks." He stood and stepped closer to the wall screen.

The professor clapped his hands together sharply. "This is the good part, am I right? New planet, exploring things. Great fun."

"Atmospheric safety confirmed, Professor. Safe for—wait, checking Hybrids. Yes, for every species on board."

"Good, good! Visita, please open the doors and lower the main ramp."

"Yes, Doctor Stone."

The planet's air was heavy with humidity and the thick smell of decaying vegetation. The hum of insect life drowned out voices from more than a few meters away.

The plants, trees, and bushes with leaves of green and yellow and purple swayed gently even though there was no breeze. The ground was covered with a thick, spongy covering, not blades like grass, but more reminiscent of a moss or mold.

The graduate students, carrying cases and backpacks and holding metallic sensors in their hands, walked in a widening spiral out from the shuttle, occasionally bending down to insert long probes into the moss or scooping samples into clear vials.

"I've got some of the blue fungus."

"I sampled the red."

"Seismographs planted."

"I'm getting imagery of rock formations under this moss."

"Professor, look here." The professor went to Andervarian Two, who was pointing at a small screen with slender purple fingers. "Look at that!"

The professor nodded. "Interesting. Take more images, put together a composite. Start over"—he tilted his head, turned his body, and framed the landscape with his hands—"there."

"Yes, Doctor Stone."

The shuttle perched at the top of a broad, gentle hill. Rohan circled the peak, straining to see as far as he could in all directions. He planted a foot and stepped up into the air, flying straight up, and turning.

Doctor Stone followed behind his assistants in the broadening spiral they walked. "I want signs of animal life. So far I see nothing indicative of anything larger than a worm. Bite marks on trees, scat, anything."

A chorus of yesses answered him.

Rohan floated down, landing in a walk alongside his friend.

"Scat?"

"We have to study the kaiju somehow. We'll also leave the drones behind along with some other automated surveying equipment and hope for some closeups. From a safe distance, of course."

"I don't see any problem with that."

"I'm surprised you don't get more scientists looking to study your kaiju."

"I think Wistful has discouraged them in the past."

"Why?"

"I don't know. I don't pretend to completely understand the mind of a ten-thousand-year-old space station."

"Who told you she was ten thousand years old?"

Rohan stopped in his tracks. "Everyone says that."

The professor shook his head. "Remember, it's Drachna. It's like the Tao Te Ching, when it says 'ten thousand things' it isn't a literal count, it's just a colorful way to say 'innumerable.'"

"So Wistful isn't ten thousand years old?"

The professor shrugged. "I did a quick check through Imperial archives before we came here. Wistful was mentioned there in some of the earliest records I could find."

"So, she's as old as the Empire?"

"More like, she was already old when the Empire was young. Going by the descriptions. Again, it was a quick search."

"So, we're talking, what, twenty thousand years? Fifty?"

"Maybe more. Considerably more. I'm a biologist, not a historian."

"Sure. Hm. Now I wish I'd paid more attention in history classes."

"Did the il'Drach even teach you history?"

"No, not really. My education was always more practical. Trade school for war."

"We could have a long debate now about the value of a liberal arts education, if you'd like. It would remind me of my youth on Earth."

"I don't think I'd actually be arguing with you, Ben. My education wasn't my plan, you know. Not my choice."

"Of course. Sorry, I didn't really mean anything by it."

They walked down the hill to a broad, flat plain. They were still a few dozen meters from the tree line.

"Professor, there's more." Andervarian Two was waving his purple hands.

Ben walked over and looked at the student's findings. "Yes, I see it. Get as many images as you can. Spread the sensors out more, I want a broader picture, not a deeper one. At least for now."

"What is it, Professor?"

The older human smiled. "Signs of construction underneath the moss."

"You mean, like, ruins? Ancient cities?"

"'Ancient' is an understatement. There haven't been cities here for at least as far back as the Imperial archives go. Fifty millennia, minimum."

"I had no idea. I wonder what Wistful knows."

"Ask her."

"Rohan." The voice was coming over his comm link.

"Professor, excuse me, irony is calling. Yes, Wistful?"

"Motion detected. Twenty-five kilometers due east of your location."

"Motion? Oh, for— Wistful, land-based or aerial?"

The professor was looking at him. "What is it?"

Rohan shook his head.

"Land-based."

"Which direction, Wistful? Which way is it moving?" He turned. "Ben, we have to leave the surface. Now. Gather your people."

"Traveling north by northeast from its location. Rohan, it's headed away from you."

"Okay, okay. Good. Professor, we leave now."

"What is it?"

The Lukhor was shouting. "Professor! We have a sighting from the eastern drone. Something big. But it's not heading this way."

"Let me see."

The Lukhor brought his tablet over, tapping on it has he went, choosing the right feed. He turned it so the professor could see.

"Heading?"

Rohan answered. "Northeast, so it's not coming for us. Yet. But we have to leave."

"Rohan, if we leave, who knows when Wistful will let us back? It could be weeks. Or months. Or not at all. This is the opportunity of a lifetime. How far away is it?"

"Only twenty-five clicks. You're not listening to me. We have to move."

"Twenty-five kilometers? Why the rush?"

Rohan felt his temper fraying. He exhaled, a long slow breath, and held his lungs empty for several seconds. "Professor, these creatures are dangerous and fast. Please, you have to trust me, we have to go. Now."

The two Rogesh closed on the humans. The female looked down at them and spoke. "We should have at least half an hour to gather more data before we're in any danger. We've found the beginnings of some very interesting things under the moss; let's at least finish the search. It will be much harder to get the imagery either from orbit or remotely."

"No." Rohan stepped over to her, put his hands on her shoulders. "You need to listen. Your calculations are wrong, you're thinking about regular land creatures, predators from other planets. These aren't that—"

Haditz charged at Rohan and slammed his hardened, massive shoulder into the Hybrid, knocking him back from the female.

Rohan fought back his temper.

Haditz roared, a sound like an asthmatic foghorn. "No, we will not listen to you, mule! You do not order us around, you do not tell us what to do, you are not our master!"

"I'm not telling you to leave because of some sense of manifest superiority! I'm trying to save your lives! If I have to, I'll wrestle the lot of you back onto that shuttle and drag you into space myself! I won't let you die on my watch."

"Professor!" It was Andervarian One. "Professor! The moss is excreting some kind of gel. It's very difficult to move through it, sir. We might want to regroup and re-evaluate the situation."

"A gel? What?"

"Professor, get these people out of here, now!" Rohan knew he was shouting and fought to calm himself.

"But Rohan, twenty-five kilometers. Surely—"

Wistful spoke into everybody's comms. "Rohan, the mass is changing its direction. Now heading due north."

Haditz closed on Rohan, knees bent, arms spread, as if ready to charge. "It's not even coming this way! You're the problem! You can't handle anybody not bowing down to your demands. You're like every other Hybrid. Just leave us alone!"

Rohan's voice was cold. "You think you have a choice now. You think you can choose whether to stay or to go. But really your only choice is how badly hurt you are when you get on that shuttle. I strongly suggest you try to calm down and make a good decision about that. But honestly, I'm getting less and less clear about what I hope you do."

Ben came closer to Rohan and reached an arm out but stopped short of touching him. "Rohan, please, settle down. This isn't helpful."

Wistful spoke again. "The mass has paused."

Andervarian One was looking at his screen. "Professor, it's swiveling its head. Like its sniffing, sampling the air. I think it's turning this way."

Haditz roared again. "You don't scare me, Hybrid! Always with the threats, you mules! Someone doesn't do what you want, what you say, the next step is always a threat. Do what you want or meet some terrible fate. Make the right choice, comply. Enough! We've had enough!"

Rohan emptied his lungs, held it again. Three seconds. "I don't know what the others did to you during the Rebellion, and right now I honestly don't care. You are getting on that shuttle."

"Professor! It is moving again!"

Wistful's voice in Rohan's ear. "Rohan, the mass seems to have changed direction."

The professor pointed at the Andervarian. "Which way is it going now? And how fast?"

"Um, let me see." His fingers stabbed at the tablet.

Wistful spoke. "It is moving toward your location now, Rohan. Ten kilometers per hour and accelerating."

The Andervarian shouted. "Fifteen clicks per hour! How fast can this thing go? Maybe we *should* start to head out."

Haditz shouted. "No! The shuttle is outfitted with military-grade ion cannons! We stay and do our research. If that creature is a threat we incinerate it!"

The professor shook his head. "These are rare and potentially endangered creatures, we are not destroying them for the sake of scientific curiosity! If it is coming this way, we are leaving! Back to the shuttle everybody."

"Sorry, twenty clicks per hour. Sorry, twenty-five. I miscalculated. No, wait, I didn't. It's accelerating."

"Professor, hurry these people. We don't have much time."

"Thirty, no forty, no forty-five kilometers per hour. Um, this is making me nervous."

Haditz spun away, but his feet were stuck fast to the moss. He fell to the ground, catching himself with his hands. "What?"

Ben walked over to the Rogesh, his feet sucking against the moss with each step as if it were a thick mud. "Come on, Haditz. We'll come back, collect more data. For now, back to the shuttle."

"Professor. One hundred kilometers an hour. It's flattening everything in its path. By the Ladies, this thing is huge."

The professor reached down and tried to pull Haditz out of the moss. The heavy, gray-skinned humanoid didn't budge. "Somebody help."

Rohan came over, floating above the vegetation to avoid the gel. The ground all around was now slick and wet with the sticky substance.

"No! Not you! You cannot be the one to help me!"

"One hundred twenty kilometers per hour."

12

Told You So

Visita addressed them over the comm. "Firing up the shuttle engines and prepping ion cannons. Can everybody make it?"

Rohan looked around. They were at the base of the hill, a hundred meters from the shuttle. An easy walk if not for the sticky gel. But everyone seemed to be able to wade through it, if slowly.

He counted. The Lukhor, both Rogesh, the professor, one Andervarian. Where was the other one?

"Where's . . .? Damnit, name, the other purple guy? The Andervarian?"

Andervarian One spun around. He pointed toward the tree line and started plodding in that direction.

Rohan shouted. "No, you get back to the shuttle! Let me get him; I can fly!"

The Andervarian looked down. "Oh, boy. One hundred seventy-five kilometers per hour. What the hell? How is that even possible?"

Rohan growled low in his chest. "People never listen."

The professor paled. "No more arguing. Everybody back to the shuttle, now. Right now. Haditz, no more discussion. Start moving or, even if you survive this, your career is over. Understood?"

The Rogesh grumbled low in his chest but said nothing more.

They pulled each other out of the moss and made their painstaking way back to the shuttle. Each step required enormous effort. Pull a foot free, heavy with wet sticky moss, shove it forward, shift weight, pull the next foot free. Like hiking through a knee-deep pool of freshly chewed gum.

Rohan floated up out of contact with the moss, then darted for the tree line. "Hey! Dammit, what's your name? Where are you? We have to go!"

He reached the trees without hearing anything from the last student.

"Speed is up to two hundred kilometers per hour! What is this thing?"

Rohan darted back and forth between the trees. "Where the hell are you?"

Wistful's voice. "The creature will arrive at your location in about two minutes. At its present pace."

Rohan spotted a purple arm waving between two trees.

"There you are." He sped forward, rounded the massive tree trunk.

Andervarian Two was waving frantically. His back was to the tree. "I'm stuck!"

"Oh, for . . ." Rohan got closer.

The bark of the tree looked smooth from afar, but was gripping Two's clothes like a Velcro patch.

"I just hope your species isn't too modest."

Rohan, still airborne, grabbed Two, who was clutching his briefcase to his chest and bracing visibly.

"What? Why? Oh!"

Rohan pulled. The student's clothes tore and ripped, coming away with him and sticking to the tree in roughly equal parts.

"One minute."

The Hybrid cradled his cargo in both hands and flew a zigzag pattern between the trees. He slowed slightly, remembering that too rapid an acceleration would kill the graduate student as surely as being eaten by the kaiju.

Once clear of the trees he made a beeline up the hill and to the shuttle's open door.

A steady rumbling was growing in the air, a continuously building thunder, a sound so deep they felt it through their bones and teeth as much as their ears. The shuttle itself was vibrating noticeably with the noise.

The others were clambering up the ramp and into the shuttle in a disheveled pile of bodies and equipment. When they touched, the gel stuck them to one another, further slowing their progress.

Rohan flew right over their heads and lightly tossed his Andervarian into the shuttle, then turned.

The scientists were scrambling up the ramp at his feet. Behind them was the long slope of the hill, broken by the sharp tree line of the forest.

Lifting up over the treetops was a red insectoid head, moving smoothly but at an unbelievable speed.

Rohan wasted three precious seconds deciding whether he had enough time to get the shuttle loaded and airborne before the kaiju reached them.

"Professor, get them on board and lift off. Lift off! I'll distract it."

"What? But—" The professor stole a quick glance over his shoulder. "Oh, my God. Oh my . . . God."

Rohan tapped his comm to make sure he was broadcasting. "Visita, fire up the engines and get ready for liftoff. Do not wait for me, I can get to Wistful on my own. Or meet you in orbit."

"Copy that. We have ion cannons, Rohan. I can stop that thing."

"No, you can't. Let me handle it. You get these people away."

"Rohan I'm combat-rated in this shuttle and you're a tow chief. You don't need to—"

The professor interrupted her. "Listen to him, Visita. We're almost ready for you to lift the ramp."

Rohan took a deep breath, ramping up his Power as he did so. The very cells of his skin and muscles twitched with the buildup, eager to be unleashed. The world brightened, then settled back to normal as his eyes saturated with Power. He arched his back, looked up at the sky, and growled as his angry il'Drach heritage washed through him.

Then he snapped forward, visualizing himself as an arrow being released from a bow, aimed right at the center of the creature's massive head.

It was an insect nightmare.

A maw large enough to swallow three men standing on each other's shoulders in one bite, dripping clear green fluids. Two huge glittering and multifaceted black eyes. Four long mandibles twitching open and shut in an obscene reflex as the creature closed on the shuttle.

A long, segmented body followed the head. Each section boasted a pair of massive legs, splayed to either side. The legs at the second segment were very long, and in the first longer still, giving the kaiju an upward slope to the front of its body.

It didn't react at first to Rohan's speed. He touched his fists together in front of his forehead, forming a triangle with his forearms.

The Hybrid rammed into the spot right between the creature's maw and eyes with the kinetic energy of a meteor.

With that same maneuver he'd punched holes through battleship hulls, six inches of advanced titanium honeycomb plating reinforced with carbon nanotube lacing and tempered in living stars. He had ripped through planetary cores with it, blown apart asteroids that would have wiped out planets.

It was enough to stop the kaiju's forward motion. Barely.

The creature's six front legs lifted off the ground.

The professor's voice broke over the comms. "Good lord, that thing must be eighty meters high!"

Andervarian One yelled at him. "Get inside, Professor! Now! Now!"

"Wistful, it's a decipede. Any advice?"

"Don't let it eat you. Its stomach acid has interesting properties that you would not care to experience."

"Great, thanks. I would not have thought of—"

One of the kaiju's forelimbs whipped across and struck him a terrific, if glancing, blow.

That's fast.

He could feel bones creak and see a flash behind his eyes. When he regained consciousness, he was scraping the mossy layer on the ground a few hundred meters away from the decipede.

It was facing the shuttle again. The kaiju lowered itself as its back legs began rhythmically pumping to build up speed. Trees fell and dirt fountained up into the air like a geyser behind it.

Rohan let himself hit the ground just hard enough to kick off with his legs for some extra speed. He *squeezed* energy through his body, funneling his Power into forward momentum, accelerating until the air shrieked in his ears.

He struck the decipede squarely in the back of the head with both forearms, knocking it forward. Its head plowed into the ground right at the base of the hill they'd landed on, its mandibles digging huge ruts in the moss and dirt.

"Rohan, we're in!" It was Ben's voice over the comms.

"Lift off, damn it. Lift off! Now!"

The creature's legs spasmed and flailed for a moment, then gathered beneath it and lifted it back into the air. It spun in place, clockwise, no longer focused on the shuttle.

Rohan looked through the fallen trees and debris kicked up by the decipede's motion. He grabbed the trunk of a small straight tree, a Toth 3 version of a pine, perhaps four meters high. He lifted it overhead and threw it at the decipede like a javelin.

The pointy end of the tree struck the kaiju's huge black eye. Its whole body twitched, a ripple that passed through each segment from its head to its tail. Then it moved toward him.

The Hybrid was prepared for the monster's first swipe, a viciously fast swing of its right forelimb. He slipped under it, gathering up energy for another charge, when the backswing caught him flush.

It was getting faster.

The creature screamed, an ululating and piercing high-pitched whine that shook the landscape. Every tree, every leaf, every stone, and every strand of moss vibrated along with the sound.

The cone of sound knocked Rohan back out of the air. He almost blacked out from the impact.

Rohan shook his head to clear it. He saw the shuttle lifting off the hill to his right.

The decipede charged him again.

More chatter over the comms. "That thing can't be that quick! It's impossible, it weighs too much! It should be crushed under its own mass."

"What does it even eat?"

"Better question is, what drove it to evolve into that?"

"Rohan, watch out!"

The Hybrid dodged the first strike, then the backswing, flying backward just fast enough it had to move toward him to engage farther from the shuttle.

The carpet of moss and fungus covering the hill was sticking to the underside of the shuttle. As it lifted away, the vegetation lifted with it, stuck fast. Rohan saw the craft settle back to the ground.

Visita came over the comms. "I need to give it more power. Buckle in; I'm turning off the gravity dampeners. This will be bumpy."

Rohan flew up and over another swing from the decipede, and when he thought he had cleared its front four limbs, it lifted its maw toward him and launched a stream of green fluid that caught him full in the chest.

"Aah!" He screamed before he knew what was happening. Everywhere the fluid touched his skin a searing pain pulled the breath out of his chest.

"Rohan! Did anybody get a sample of that fluid? What is that? Stomach acid?"

Wistful spoke. "The decipede secretes a venom which is a mixture of highly corrosive acids and a uniquely potent neurotoxin."

The professor cursed under his breath. "Rohan! What can we do?"

Rohan coughed and spasmed, desperate to keep the goo out of his mouth. "I'm okay. Get off the ground!"

"Diverting full power to drives. Engaging . . . now."

There were cries and shouts over the comms as the students were tossed about inside the ship.

Rohan could see nothing with his mask coated in venom. He flew back, then cut a right angle, then dove toward the ground, desperately dodging attacks he could only hear coming.

His mind cleared slowly as his enhanced body adjusted to the toxins coating his flesh. He flew down through the trees, using leaves and branches to scrape the viscous venom off his mask.

The monster was storming through the trees, coming after him.

Rohan braced his arms and charged for the creature again, weaving up and down through the air as he gathered speed. Just before impact he dove down underneath it and into the dirt below.

He drove his body through the soft ground, cleaning the acid away with the friction.

"We're free! Oh god, Rohan! He's gone! Who saw? What happened?"

"I'm okay, Professor. Just cleaning myself off. With dirt. Kind of funny."

He erupted from the ground at a spot he thought would be behind the decipede, but as he twisted around to look, he saw the creature's last segment overhead.

The kaiju had stopped moving, and it lowered its heavy carapace right onto Rohan, smashing him back into the ground from which he'd emerged.

The pressure from the monster was enormous. He was momentarily stifled; unable to move, free himself, or even inhale.

Visita spoke over the comms. "Coming to assist."

Rohan wanted to shout her off, but he didn't have enough air in his lungs. He barely had enough energy to support his own body and maintain the integrity of his facemask.

He had to get free.

The Hybrid went through the mental routines he'd been taught so many years ago when his Power first manifested. He reached down into the well of anger that lurked just below his conscious mind, reached in, *pulled*.

The Power, and the anger mixed into it, responded.

Who do you think you're stepping on?

He felt a thud through the kaiju, which settled more heavily onto his body.

He pulled in more Power, growling and yelling into his helmet. Then he *pushed*, savagely, against the tons of chitin above.

With a crack he pulled free.

His Power-drenched body squirted out into the air.

The shuttle was hovering close to the kaiju, flashes of lightning streaking through the air as its ion cannons fired at the monster.

The streaks of high energy particles danced across at the creature, which let out another piercing scream.

Rapid fire cannons, meant for protection against aggressive wildlife, fired projectiles so rapidly the sound was a constant high-pitched whine.

The kaiju spun toward the shuttle as the bullets stitched holes across its carapace. The channels of energy danced flame across its shell.

Then the decipede stopped, settled lower to the ground, and grew still.

The stream of bullets twisted, their flight redirected around the monster. Rohan had to dodge frantically to keep himself out of their new path.

He growled again. *Get out of my way!*

The bridge of fire connecting the shuttle's ion cannons to the decipede also shifted and danced, flickering across its shell, to the edge of its body, and quickly scattering off, igniting trees and moss in great arcing circles all around the monster.

"Stop! You can't hurt it! Get out!"

The decipede's rear legs moved forward, planting, then its front half lurched up at the shuttle. It lunged again, slipping between the streams of bullets and fire.

"Get out!"

With a violent twitch it moved forward, impossibly fast, and swung its longest arm forward, catching the shuttle at the very tip of its reach.

Visita's voice was no longer calm. "That was the aft drive! Aft drive is offline!"

Rohan was behind the decipede. He blasted forward again, this time aiming for the relatively narrow strip of meat and gristle between its head and its forwardmost segment.

He struck. A clear liquid spurted out of the flesh between his forearms as the decipede screamed.

He flew backward, desperate to get clear of its reach, as it spun.

"Stings, does it? Hurts, does it? Come on, get some revenge. I hurt you; now come after me!"

The shuttle floated away, lilted badly off its axis and looping back toward the hill where it had first landed. The decipede reared up and launched another stream of acidic juices at Rohan.

He shot straight up, barely avoiding the deadly liquid.

The decipede leaped forward again, its massive legs launching it up into the air in a burst.

Its limbs missed Rohan, but its underbelly struck him solidly, knocking him backward.

He'd had more than enough. His Power danced in his head. He wanted to tear into the bug, wreck its carapace, feel its armor crunch under his hands, dig into its soft meaty interior.

He wanted a war.

Rohan saw the shuttle limping its way up into the sky, spiraling up, trailing smoke from the hull. It was gaining altitude, but very slowly.

Wistful came over the comms. "Rohan, there are more masses approaching. These are significantly faster than the decipede, I believe they are flyers. Three, four, no, five. All converging on your location."

He shook his head. There was no need for his anger. No use. He breathed out, emptying his lungs, holding for several seconds. A quick inhalation.

"Okay. I've been a lousy lance today, maybe I can be a decent tow chief."

He flew straight back, as fast as he could, drawing the decipede after him. Then he redirected his flight down and plowed into the ground, using the trees, rocks, and dirt to come to an almost instant stop, then reversed course and leaped directly at the decipede.

He'd hurt the thing enough it didn't want to meet his charge head on. The decipede angled itself slightly, its limbs lifted to deflect the Hybrid.

Just before he made impact Rohan turned and flew as fast as he could to the shuttle.

"I'm going to lift you guys out. Where's your anchor point?" He cursed under his breath. He really should have checked before they left *Insatiable*.

"We're not built for towing! This is a shuttle!"

"All right. I'm coming in under the damaged drive."

The kaiju screeched again as it spun. He could hear its legs driving into the forest, pushing itself after him.

He arced down, scraped the ground, then pulled up in a tight climb underneath the shuttle.

He aimed for the smoking area where the decipede had damaged it. He struck the shuttle, feeling the entire ship shudder with the impact.

Then Rohan *pushed*.

The path of the shuttle immediately straightened as Rohan's force compensated for the damaged drive. The spiral it had been winding through tightened and flattened until it was climbing straight up to the edge of the atmosphere.

A series of sonic booms rattled them all.

Wistful warned him. "Flyers closing quickly."

"Visita! I can push harder! Lean toward this side, I can take more of the weight!"

"Copy."

The shuttle tilted so more of its mass was above Rohan's position. He *pushed* harder.

"Temperature building."

"Can you take it?"

"Yes, Rohan, we're still within tolerances. Can you?"

His voice was tight, his anger still riding him. "I'm fine."

He wasn't fine. The heat was burning his skin and clothes and made breathing increasingly uncomfortable.

But he had been through worse.

They burst through the cloud layer.

As the air thinned, so did the resistance. The shuttle picked up more speed.

"We've almost cleared the atmosphere. Temperature stabilizing. Now temperature is dropping."

The planet receded beneath them. Looking down, Rohan couldn't make out the hill anymore. Then he could see the entire continent. Then the edges of the planet.

"Altitude?"

"Ten thousand meters. Eleven."

Rohan let out a sigh and eased off slightly. "I think we're safe. The flyers never come up this far. Push it to twelve-thousand meters and we can take it easy from there."

He heard cheering and clapping over the comms.

"Guys, the shuttle has external damage. I don't want to risk hull integrity by mucking about with the airlock. I'm going to tow you right to *Insatiable*."

Visita was first to answer. "Yes, sir, Tow Chief. And thank you."

13

You Might Find It

"So how was work?" The Lukhor put a forkful of salad in her mouth. Her green cheeks were tight with a mischievous smile.

"We're on our second date and we're already at the 'how was work' stage of the relationship?" Rohan took a big bite of his own salad. The restaurant, owned by a famously temperamental Rogesh chef, was well-known for its vegetarian dishes, but you had to eat whatever he felt like serving that day.

"At the rate you seem to get into deadly situations I'm not sure how long you'll be around, so I thought we'd better speed things up."

"I think maybe you're overdoing it. We seem to have skipped over a lot of the good parts."

"Whatever are you thinking of, Tow Chief Rohan?"

"I'm actually not sure. It's been so long since I've dated I think I've forgotten."

"Maybe I can do something later to jog your memory."

"It can't be too much later, I have a shift starting in a couple of hours."

"From what I've heard of your species I didn't think your males needed that much time." She was smiling again, to Rohan's relief.

"That's not, um, universally true. Besides, I'm only half human."

"And the other half? Are il'Drach considered to be skilled, or at least enduring lovers?"

"I mean, they must be. They have children scattered across the galaxy."

"Do il'Drach females never travel in search of mixed offspring?"

"Actually, no. Never. No non-il'Drach I've met has ever even glimpsed an il'Drach female."

"That is mysterious! And interesting. But you never answered my question."

"About work?"

She raised her eyebrows in acknowledgement and finished her salad.

"Wistful asked me to go to the planet yesterday, babysit some scientists who wanted to see the beasts of Toth 3 for themselves."

A Rogesh waitress came quickly and cleared their plates, refilling their glasses as she did so.

"So I heard. More accurately, so I saw. The video of your adventure was all anybody was watching yesterday."

"Oh. I didn't even realize anyone had pushed any video. I fell asleep as soon as we got back to Wistful and really only got up this morning to meet you."

"The battle was quite dramatic. What do you call the creature?"

"A decipede. I encountered one before, but I think that one was smaller."

"It seemed like a very frightening situation."

"Well, I didn't want to lose the scientists. I like the professor, quite a bit, to be honest. And if they all died it would be pretty embarrassing."

"You were not scared for yourself?"

He shrugged. "Not so much."

"Do you think yourself invincible, then?"

"Well, I'm pretty tough. I wouldn't say invincible, though."

She nodded. The waitress brought their next course, an omelet with assorted mushrooms folded inside.

Rohan bit into it. "Wow. That is really good."

The restaurant was small, every seat taken. It was within a block of the center of the station, in the busiest part of the arm.

"See, I told you we should try this place. Even though they serve no meat."

"I admit I was a little scared by the chef's reputation. He's supposed to have a real temper, and an angry Rogesh is nothing to sneeze at."

"You wrestled a two-hundred-meter-long insect yesterday and today you're frightened of a Rogesh cook?"

"The decipede might have eaten me, but it wasn't going to poison my dinner. Or spoil my date with you."

"I suppose the cook is the more threatening of the two, when you put it that way."

"Exactly."

"Well, Rinth was suitably impressed by your exploits. He was even rooting for you over the monster."

"Was he? That's good."

"He said it was only because, in his words, 'insects are icky.'"

"I'll take any approval I can get. I think the professor's assistants were all at least half rooting for the decipede."

"Why would you say that?"

Rohan sighed. "They've had bad experiences with Hybrids. Really bad, I guess. So they don't like me very much. I bring back bad memories."

She nodded and ate some more. "Were you part of these experiences? Were you responsible for them?"

"What? No, of course not. Not even close."

"Then they are being . . . racist? Is that the right word? Bigoted?"

"Yeah, I guess they are."

"Well, not everyone feels that way. I am pleased to say that footage convinced my sister to approve of your continued presence in my life."

"That is good news. Wait, was that in doubt? Did I need her approval?"

"Need? No. But is it useful to have willing and trustworthy childcare? Yes, it is."

"I totally see your point. I kind of like this offset schedule thing we have going on. I share my breakfast with you, but it's your dinner."

"Yes. You can still have dinner with another companion, when I'm eating my breakfast, and I need never know about it."

"Or, here's an idea, we can have breakfast and dinner together for both of us."

"Now perhaps it is you who are overdoing it, Tow Chief Rohan. Let us not rush things too much."

He held his hands up in surrender. "As you wish." He finished the omelet and drained the wine glass. "That was really good."

She nodded, her antennae bobbing with the motion. "It is good. I will share with you a secret."

"Go ahead."

She leaned closer to him and whispered. "I could not get this reservation at first, so I mentioned that you would be my companion. A spot opened up quite suddenly."

"Really? I'm a celebrity now?" He chuckled.

"Yes. And I am determined to take advantage of that status."

"If I'm going to be famous I'd better start dressing better."

"Yes, you should. We have spoken about that jumpsuit."

"I think you make it worse by looking so good. That dress is gorgeous."

Tamara was wrapped in a long filmy cloth, sprays of vivid color winding around her body.

"All I brought from my former life when I came to Wistful were my clothes. I was known in school as something of a shopper."

"I imagine growing up rich doesn't discourage that."

She laughed. "The opposite! It was my responsibility to be fashionable. If I didn't spend my full clothing allowance each season I was chastised most sternly."

"I've been wearing one uniform or another for, I think, ten years now. No, fifteen! I haven't bought my own clothes in that whole time."

"Then that is your assignment. No more horrid jumpsuits when we dine together."

"Okay, fair enough."

The waitress brought them dessert, a custard with fresh berries on top.

Rohan's comm chirped in his ear. "Rohan, we have a full docket of arrivals today."

He tapped the comm to answer. "Copy that, Wistful. I'll be on time."

Tamara lifted one eyebrow at him. He pointed at the comm behind his ear. "Wistful reminding me I have work today."

"She speaks to you directly?"

"All the time."

"You are a celebrity, indeed."

As they finished a Rogesh male, easily two hundred kilos with the complexion of a rhinoceros, came to their table. He had a white hat in his hands.

"You are Tow Chief Rohan?"

Rohan nodded, wondering if there was a problem with his credit.

"May we put an image of you dining at this table on our wall? We will, of course, not charge you for the meal."

"Are you serious?"

The chef huffed. "I am always serious."

"Well then, image me all you want. The food was delicious."

"Of course it was." The Rogesh huffed, then waved his staff over. "Get the image, and make sure it is prominently displayed. And make sure he's smiling!"

14

The Blue-Skinned Sommelier

The rest of his morning was enough to make him forget the burns and bruising caused by the decipede.

He couldn't stop whistling into his mask as he completed his morning shift.

Rohan paused in his work and pulled a deep lungful of air out of his mask's compressed reservoir.

He had docked twelve ships and was feeling the strain.

He floated freely in the vacuum of space, just a few hundred meters away from Wistful. He pulled up his messages on the inside of his mask.

Some ads. A financial statement.

A response from a personal shopper he was thinking of hiring to help him buy clothes, offering to meet him that evening.

A lunch invitation from Ben Stone.

"Wistful, can I take a lunch break in . . ." He checked the message, then the time. "Half an hour?"

"Yes, Rohan. Only a few more arrivals are expected today."

"Thanks."

He took a moment to breathe and enjoy his uninterrupted view of the stars.

A shadow flickered over his vision.

"What was that?" He flew backward, retreating toward Wistful, his eyes darting back and forth. "Wistful, what just flew past me?"

"Unknown. What do you mean?"

"Something . . . a shadow or something. It blotted out some stars. But I didn't actually see anything."

There was a pause.

"Sensor logs do not register anything. Are you sure something was there?"

"I'm not . . . no, I'm sure. Something. I don't know what."

"Is it still in view?"

He searched the sky. "Nothing now."

"I will scan and alert the Security Chief."

"Okay, thanks, Wistful. I'll go grab the next ship."

Rohan brought in two more small cargo ships before taking his lunch break. The professor had asked to meet him at a restaurant near the area where the Ursans were staying.

He entered the station through his personal airlock, used the facilities in his quarters, then followed the directions on his facemask to the restaurant.

He spotted the professor holding down a table and walked over.

Ben Stone stood as Rohan approached. He stepped toward the Hybrid and grabbed Rohan's hand between both of his, then shook it vigorously.

"Rohan, I'm so glad you came."

"Well, sure. I needed a break, had a really busy morning."

"Did you? Wait, please, sit." The professor pulled back a chair for Rohan.

"Sure. Is everything okay?" Rohan sat in the offered seat.

"Of course, of course. Well, mostly. To be honest, I'm quite embarrassed about yesterday."

"What about it?"

The professor sat across from the Hybrid and waved a waiter over. "Rohan, we didn't listen to you as we should have. And I really am sorry for that."

"It's fine, really. Don't worry about it. All's well that ends well, right?"

"That's just it! Things only ended well because of you. You saved my life. All our lives."

"Sure. That's why I was there."

The waiter brought trays of food over. The professor pointed at them. "I assume you're hungrier than normal? Been expending a lot of energy?"

Rohan twisted his head back and forth. "That's not exactly how things work, but I can eat."

"Good, good. I am told this is the best food on Wistful, at least by Earth standards. A cuisine very close to French. It is owned by a chef who worked at my favorite place by the Academy."

Rohan looked around. The wait staff was abundant. He also realized that the other diners were dressed much more formally than he was.

"Sounds good."

Four small dishes were brought, bread for each and a slender rectangle of something pale surrounded by a drizzle of a shiny black sauce.

"Haditz, especially, wanted me to give you a message. Actually, he wanted to come to lunch, but I wasn't sure that would be welcome."

"I'd be fine eating with Haditz if he's decided to stop hating me. Or at least hate me more discreetly."

"Well, good to know. You're a kind man. We're all quite grateful. Haditz said to tell you that he owes you a life debt." Ben cut his appetizer in half and ate a piece. His eyes rolled back in his head.

Rohan followed. It tasted like fried tofu, but with a delicate seasoning he didn't recognize.

"A life debt? I forget Rogesh culture. This doesn't mean he's going to follow me around or anything, does it? Or try to pay me back in kind? Or give me his firstborn child? I am not responsible enough to take care of a baby."

"No, that's the Lukhor, the Andervarians, and the Ursans, respectively. You can expect to be gifted Ang's first cub as soon as he finds time to sire one."

"You're kidding, right? Please tell me you're kidding."

"Just a joke. I think."

"The cubs are probably cute, though."

The professor smiled and nodded. "Haditz will pay you back if he can. And if he doesn't find an opportunity, he'll pass that burden on to his children."

"Would it be worth taking the time to try to convince him this isn't necessary?"

Doctor Stone waved his hand in the air in dismissal as the next course was artfully arranged between them. "You know the Rogesh, they love making declarations of honor. It's not as if it will actually prevent him from living his life."

"Fair enough. I do kind of wish that video hadn't gotten out. Especially after the Ursan thing. It feels weird to walk around now, it's like people recognize me."

The professor's fork froze in midair between his plate and mouth, a leaf dangling helplessly from its tines. "Rohan, I am quite sorry. It's a scientific expedition, the records are a matter of public property. I didn't mean to make a spectacle out of you."

Rohan shook his head. "It's fine. There are some advantages to fame, to be honest. I got a free meal out of it this morning."

"Good, good. And how are you feeling after being doused with those neurotoxins?"

Rohan tapped his side, below his ribs. "Nothing my half il'Drach liver can't handle. I was pretty knocked out yesterday. I think I slept for twelve hours when we got back. But I'm fine now."

"Excellent." The professor paused. "Listen, there are some other things I'd like to talk about, but nothing urgent, if you're still tired. Just some things I'd like to run by you."

"I'm fine, go ahead." The two paused their conversation while the blue-skinned sommelier came to their table and explained how the next round of wines would pair with the food they were about to eat.

When the sommelier left, the professor continued.

"Let me again apologize for not listening to your warnings about the planet. I was working under the assumption that the fauna of Toth 3 were biologicals."

"No apologies needed. But I'm not sure what you mean."

"We can do rough calculations about how big life forms can be, how much energy they can produce, how strong they are. Lukhor to Rogesh, they all fit within this band of physiology. Except, of course, for creatures with metaphysical Powers that are not based on regular high school chemistry."

"Like an il'Drach Hybrid."

"Exactly. Or, so it turns out, like a Toth 3 kaiju."

Rohan sipped his wine.

"So the kaiju can be so big and so fast because they have Powers? Capital 'P'?"

"That is exactly what I am saying. That decipede was so far beyond the possibilities of mundane physiology that there can be no question. As in, orders of magnitude beyond what we believe possible."

"That's interesting. Are animals with Powers common? I don't think I have ever heard of any."

"They are not. In fact, they are almost unknown. We have never seen any living creature exhibit metaphysical Power without also exhibiting sentience."

"Maybe they are sentient. I mean, not linguistic, but sentient."

"I was wondering the same thing. Hard to prove, of course. We won't be capturing any and making them run through a maze."

"Well, now I'm extra glad I didn't hurt that thing."

The professor raised his glass. "To the kaiju."

Rohan chuckled and lifted his own in response. "To the kaiju."

They drank.

"That conclusion, by itself, opens up a host of new questions."

Rohan blew out a long breath. "I can only imagine."

"I'd very much like to know what made the kaiju attack."

"Me, too. You think I can help you with that?"

"Just help me brainstorm some ideas. It's conceivable that the decipede heard us land, but given the atmosphere and distance, it would have to be extraordinarily sensitive to noise to have reacted to the shuttle the way it did."

"It also didn't come straight for us when we first landed. It headed off in another direction."

"Exactly! So, probably not attracted by sound."

The professor rubbed his hands as the meat course arrived, thin slices of some kind of rib meat in a delicate gravy.

"You have a better guess? Smell?"

Ben shook his head. "We checked wind patterns and basic gas diffusion equations. There is simply no way particles from us traveled all the way to the decipede's resting spot in the time it took to respond to us."

"I give up."

"I have a thought, but keep it to yourself for now. It's a little . . . quacky."

"Who would I even tell? It's not like the Fleet Academy Journal of Xenobiology has me in their contact list."

The professor leaned in. "If the creatures are using metaphysical Powers to maintain their physicality, perhaps they are using metaphysical senses as well."

"You think the decipede is an empath?"

"Not exactly a full empath, but something along those lines. Tell me, you have empathic abilities?"

"Very little."

"But some. What is the rate of propagation for the, er, energies that you sense?"

Rohan opened his mouth, then closed it. "Huh. I'm not sure."

"But faster than, say, smells, yes? And probably faster than sound, yes?"

"Yeah, I think so. You'd notice the difference in space, more than on the station, but when I'm in space, I can sense something's energy at least as soon as I can see it, if not sooner."

"There you go."

"Sounds like your trip to our little system has been fruitful. At least for you. And I heard the other Doctor Stone cleared the wormhole for safety."

The professor laughed. "She'd be so annoyed to hear you say that, but basically yes. In a fashion typical for her, she filed a report indicating that the wormhole showed no evidence of being a greater threat than it was prior to this recent event."

"So it's just as dangerous as it always was."

"Exactly. But not necessarily more dangerous. And the Powers that be interpreted that as her saying the wormhole is safe."

"Which is not what she meant at all."

"I think she knew, deep down, how they'd take it. There just wasn't enough evidence to support stronger action. Like quarantining the system."

"Was that something she considered?"

The professor shrugged. "It was at most a remote possibility. Anyway, with nothing much to do right now, my dear wife is quite disappointed." His voice trailed off at the end, and he sat playing with his fork.

"Professor, try the meat. It's really good."

"What? Oh, yes, of course." He stabbed a slice of meat and popped it into his mouth. "Excellent, truly."

"Since your wife's work is over, will *Insatiable* head back soon?"

"Well, you see . . . we're not sure her work is actually over."

"Oh. Good, then. I mean, good for her. Is it?"

"Maybe." The professor sighed. "Her first trip to the wormhole didn't give her much in the way of new data. She found herself with time on her hands, and she said she wanted to meet some Ursans. I brought her to them, made introductions. At dinnertime. Yesterday."

The professor finished his dish and a sip of his wine. "You know, I have a regular human metabolism. This is much too much alcohol for me to be consuming day after day."

Rohan recognized procrastination when he saw it. "Did Doctor Stone cause some kind of problem with the Ursans?"

"What? Oh, no. Absolutely not. Quite the opposite."

"Oh. Is she leaving you for Ang? The Ursans are, so I hear, hung like, well, like bears."

Ben laughed. "Not that I'm aware of, no. At least not yet. But she did have a long conversation with them about how they got here."

"You mean about the wormhole?"

"Yes, exactly."

The next course came, another meat dish, heavier and paired with a bolder wine.

"Doctor Stone, are you trying to tell me something? Because I promise you I am not intelligent enough to figure it out from what you're actually saying to me here."

"She was quite interested to find out how they got here."

"You said that already. Obviously she was, that's what she's here for, to study the wormhole." He chewed and swallowed a mouthful of food. "Wait, you're being very specific. She wants to know how *they* got here. Like, how they specifically used the wormhole. How they opened it."

The professor studiously sliced his meat, eyes focused on his plate.

Rohan continued. "One of the Ursans talked about how they had a key to open the wormhole. It was the woman whose father, what, invented it or rediscovered it or something."

The professor sipped his wine.

"Let me guess. Your wife thinks she can duplicate this process. No, better yet, she's going to do it. She's going to use whatever the Ursans give her and go reopen the wormhole. And I bet she's not going to ask anybody before she does it. And that's making you nervous, right?"

"This wine is the best pairing, don't you think? This beef is so strongly flavored, yet the wine isn't dominated and it's not dominating."

Rohan sighed. "You're a terrible liar, you know."

The professor shrugged. "Technically, I haven't lied at all. I just mentioned that we had dinner with some Ursans while they mourn their dead."

"And if she figures out that you led me to this revelation, will the fact that you didn't technically tell me anything save you?"

"From the wrath of my wife? No. From the wrath of my own conscience? Definitely maybe."

Rohan grinned and shook his head. "I'm not going to argue with that. I mean, I could, but I won't. You do realize I'm going to have to tell Wistful? I might not have to tell her, because she listens to everything said in public places like this."

The professor shrugged. "Does she? Nobody told me that. Not explicitly. Or, if they did, I forgot, because after all I'm an older man and the memory . . ."

Rohan held up his hands in surrender. "You're right, you're right. I got it. You are innocent in this. Just an accident, yes?"

"Exactly." Their dessert arrived.

Rohan sighed again. "Look, there are two possibilities here. Either she figures out how to open the wormhole, and she does it, or she fails. If she fails, no harm is done, but nothing is gained. But if succeeds, what will happen then?"

"She'll be acclaimed as the greatest astrophysicist in the Empire?"

"Maybe, and that's great, at least for her. But what about the rest of us?"

"What do you mean?"

"Once it's open, are things going to start coming through?"

"Presumably it will shut again before that happens. And even if it did, the other side of the wormhole is a pre-Inflection society. What are you worried about?"

"Those Ursans are tough, Powers or no Powers. And we don't really know what's on the other side, do we?"

"You don't have to convince *me*. If you want an argument, choose another partner. I did not encourage her to pursue this plan."

"Fair enough. It's really up to Wistful anyway. Not my pay grade."

The professor chuckled. "Maybe once you're a Tow Chief First Class, eh?"

"Yes! That's when I'll have all the power and all the girls will come swooning."

"So your lady friend isn't interested in a Second Class Tow Chief?"

"Tamara? I didn't mean her. I don't know that she cares particularly. She seems to like me just the way I am, though I'm not sure why."

"That sounds lovely. Second date went well?"

"Almost too well."

"Meaning . . . what exactly?"

Rohan took a bite of his dessert. "Things work out best for me when I like a woman enough to date her for a bit but not so much that I want things to get really serious."

"Because you're afraid of commitment?"

"Because my lifestyle isn't conducive to commitment. You know, always having to fly off and fight something."

"Rohan, you're not a lance anymore, you're a tow chief. You have a regular job, and from my understanding it isn't even particularly dangerous. You don't have to fly off and fight anything."

"That sounds good in theory, but you see what happens when I try to stay peaceful. Someone needs me, and there I go."

The professor nodded. "I understand what you mean. Hyperion felt the same way. I think he dreaded the idea of finding a partner he really loved."

"Which never happened."

"Not that I know of, no."

The waiter came for payment, which Ben quickly covered. "No arguing, this is my thank you for saving all of our lives. It's really the least I can do."

"I'll accept it. If you really want to do something for me, find someone to take me shopping! I'm told my taste in clothes is bad. Or nonexistent. Or something."

The professor shook his head. "I'm no better, I pay people to tell me what to wear. Right now I have to get back, there are a few papers we're putting together and my assistants will need some help."

"Sure. And thanks for the meal."

15

Needle in a Shipstack

R ohan took two hours to clear his work queue.

He floated in a position close to one of Wistful's warning beacons. The beacons formed a rough sphere around the station and broadcast a continuous signal warning ships not to get too close to the station.

He was far enough away from Wistful to be out of Toth 3's shadow. He looked up at Toth itself, a yellow sun that looked like the one he'd grown up with.

He wondered, briefly, how his mother's family was back on Earth. He hadn't been home in a long time.

"Wistful, did you hear what Ben and I were talking about over dinner?'"

"Yes, Rohan. You know you can always request privacy, but if you do not, I am paying attention."

"Just making sure. Do you know what you are going to do about it?"

"Right now, nothing."

"'Right now' meaning as long as the other Doctor Stone hasn't actually figured out how to open the wormhole or meaning no matter what she does?"

"The former, Rohan. I do not believe it would be wise or safe to force open the wormhole using the Ursan technique. Should Doctor Stone refine that technique and attempt to use it I would be inclined to ask her not to."

"And when you say 'ask,' I assume you mean, 'force.'"

"I do not make idle requests, Rohan. If my wishes are not honored, they will be escalated." Wistful's tone was cold. Of course, Wistful's tone was always cold, but it seemed colder than usual.

"I'm not arguing with you, I just want to know where I stand."

"I do not wish to engage in a great deal of violence."

"'Do not wish to' and 'are not willing to' are very different things."

"That is precisely correct. I chose my words with deliberation. As always."

"Okay. I'm heading back in, unless you have more for me to do."

"I believe Wei Li would like your assistance with something. At *Insatiable*."

"Got it."

He tapped his comm link twice, opening a call. "Security Chief Wei Li."

A moment later he heard her voice. "Rohan?"

"What's going on?"

"I have had a bad feeling about this ship. That feeling has not gone away. So we are going to search it, liter by liter, until I am satisfied that my bad feeling is unfounded."

"And I'm part of this because . . ."

"I need you to examine the exterior of the ship. I want to match our schematics with the actual hull dimensions. Don't worry, we'll make sure all the math is automated for you."

He let out a long breath. Nobody on the ship would be happy about that. But it wasn't his job to make them happy.

"I'll be there."

"Copy. Thank you." The connection closed with a click.

"Wistful, you know, for a tow chief I've been doing a lot of non-towing activities."

"That is true."

"I hope there's a bonus in there for me somewhere."

"As I believe I have said before, I will ensure that you are more than adequately compensated."

He smiled to himself as he flew back to the station. He cycled open his airlock remotely, pulled himself through the hatch, and entered his quarters.

He drank a pitcher of cold water and quickly showered. He always felt like showering after long stretches of time in vacuum, and he could never figure out why.

"I could really use a nap." He wasn't recovered from the neurotoxin attack he'd suffered on Toth 3. "All right, I will skip the nap. But I will definitely go to bed early tonight. No tossing and turning thinking about Tamara. No, absolutely not. Right to sleep. That's what I need."

Still no answer.

"I am finding this whole talking to myself thing very unsatisfying."

With a final sigh he walked out the door and into the corridor.

A short transit-pod trip brought him to the docking bay in front of *Insatiable*.

He touched his comm. "How are you doing, *Insatiable*?"

"Oh, Gr— I mean, Rohan, Tow Chief Second Class! I am doing great! Oh, no, actually, that's a lie. I'm bored. But not like worth-complaining-about bored. Just bored. It's a good thing there are so many other ships to talk to!"

"Right, one advantage to being at a busy space station. Anything special I can do for you?"

"Oh, no, but thanks so much for asking, Tow Chief Second Class Rohan!"

"Do you know what we're here for?"

"I do, yes. You're going to search me in case there are any security violations. I was told already."

"Are you okay with that?"

"Yes, absolutely, I am. I'm a research vessel, you know. Curiosity is a virtue, and if you're curious about what's inside me, then I'm happy to help you research an answer!"

"Good, good. We'll try to make this as painless as possible."

"I realize you're using the word 'painless' metaphorically, but I am still not sure what you mean. Still, thank you for the kind wishes, even if I don't understand them!"

Rohan looked around the room and found Wei Li talking to a group of security personnel. There were about ten of them, all people Rohan knew by face if not by name.

"Wei Li."

"Rohan, good. I sent files to your mask. Schematics, coded according to who is going to verify which parts of the ship, and so forth."

"Sure."

"As we verify the contents of each section, report it as searched on the diagram and we'll all see it gray out. Understood? We're verifying the contents of everything down to the liter, but not deeper. No need to go through the crew's underwear drawers, okay, Vikram?"

Everyone laughed except Vikram, a pink-skinned humanoid who darkened noticeably at Wei Li's words.

"Rohan, I need you to scan the ship from the outside."

She held out a small box, like an Earth television remote. Rohan took it, flipped it around so he could see which end emitted the lasers.

"Got it."

Wei Li led her crew to *Insatiable*'s entrance, a broad opening sealed to the docking bay.

An angry voice rang out across the bay. "This is unacceptable! We're a sovereign ship of the Empire. Why are we being subjected to this search?"

The voice belonged to a human female, a tall and lean gray-haired woman with pale and lightly wrinkled skin, dressed in white lab clothes.

A purple Andervarian in an Imperial Navy uniform, all brocade and ribbons, stood in front of her, talking to Ben Stone, who completed the triplet.

"Doctor Stone, can you try to explain to your wife that we are subject to Wistful's requests as long as we're docked here?"

Ben put one hand gently on his wife's shoulder. "Dear, I realize you're frustrated, but it's just a routine search. They just want to match what we declared against what's actually here."

"Why? Are they searching every other ship docked in this backward outpost? Or just us? While I'm on the verge of the most important research the Empire has seen in fifty years? You're telling me that's a coincidence?"

Wei Li walked up to the human. The security chief stood half a head shorter but radiated a sense of barely suppressed energy.

"I do not care about your research and my goal is not to interrupt your work. There is something off about this ship and I *will* determine what it is."

"And how exactly do you know that something is off?"

Wei Li tapped her forehead. "I am an empath. Empire certified, Class Four."

Marion Stone's eyes continued to flash her anger, but she lowered her voice. "And what exactly is a Class Four Empath sensing from this ship?"

"If I could answer that, we'd have either already killed it, or chosen to ignore it. But I do not know, so we are conducting a search to figure which course of action is appropriate. If we may?"

It wasn't really a request.

Marion glared at Wei Li as if she believed her eyes could emit death rays or heat beams if she willed it strongly enough. Luckily for the security chief, she had no such ability.

After a long, awkward pause, the humans stepped aside.

Rohan looked over the trio. Ben made eye contact with him and gave a quick shake of his head.

Not the right time to meet my drinking buddy's wife.

The Hybrid could take a hint. He turned around and walked to a nearby airlock.

The work was boring and repetitive but not difficult. Rohan floated slowly over *Insatiable*'s hull, his handheld painting the outside with a grid of lasers and computing a map of the exterior surface.

Wei Li and her team covered the inside, measuring each compartment and comparing to the schematics.

An hour later, Rohan had covered half of *Insatiable*'s exterior.

He circled to *Insatiable*'s other side.

She spoke to him.

"You know, you should be so proud of me, Tow Chief Second Class Rohan, I haven't let it slip to anybody who you really are."

"It's more who I used to be, but anyway, thank you."

"Oh, it's my pleasure to be of service. After we spoke, you know, I did some more research on your career. So distinguished! I'm sorry I didn't realize."

"That was all a long time ago, *Insatiable*. I'm just a tow chief."

"Oh don't say that, Gr— I mean Rohan. You saved my shuttle and my crew on Toth 3. I saw the video! It was very inspiring."

"Don't get carried away, *Insatiable*. Just doing my job."

"And the work you did on Tolone'a! Who knows how long that war would have dragged on if you hadn't been there!"

Rohan sighed as he scanned the last corner of Brown section. "I appreciate what you're trying to say, *Insatiable*." He badly wanted the ship to shut up but couldn't think of a polite way to make that happen.

"You know, if I had a better idea of what you were looking for, I might be able to help you find it. Doctor Stone, I mean Marion Stone, has some very fishy equipment on board that your Security Chief might be interested in."

Rohan froze in place. Was this a trap?

"*Insatiable*, that's very kind of you. But Wei Li knows what she's doing. I don't want to get you in trouble for helping us."

"Oh, Rohan, you're the bestest! I wasn't feeling great about offering you information, but I couldn't just not offer it, you know? Like, you have to do it, but you're not supposed to do it, but you're the Gr—"

"Please, the name!"

"Right! Sorry!"

"I tell you what, *Insatiable*. I think there is something you can do to help out. Why don't you log into our external camera feed and check the visuals against your schematics of your own exterior."

"You mean, like, check to make sure I have the sections I declared on my manifest?"

"Yes, exactly. I mean, mistakes happen, nobody's to blame, really, if you missed declaring a section. They were in such a rush to get you here after the wormhole opened maybe someone forgot to update something. Right?"

"Oh, sure! That's totally possible! I can check that. Just give me . . ."

When the ship's voice trailed off in Rohan's comm he continued scanning her hull. Maybe the compares would take some time, keep her occupied.

His thoughts drifted to Tamara. Gorgeous and a killer sense of humor. An unfair combination. Should he stop seeing her? Was the joy of knowing her worth the pain of the inevitable breakup?

Why am I such a pessimist when it comes to romance?

Since when had he been such a sucker for a girl in desi clothes? One alien in a sari and he was losing his mind. *Do I miss home?*

"Tow Chief Second Class Rohan." *Insatiable*'s voice had a new, serious undertone.

"Yes, *Insatiable*?"

"I believe I have found an anomaly."

Within minutes Rohan, Wei Li, three of her security personnel, *Insatiable*'s captain, and Doctor Marion Stone were standing in an empty bulk storage room.

Rohan had his hand on one of the bare metal walls. "There's something on the other side of this wall that's not supposed to be there. I mean, it might be nothing, just an undocumented empty space, but, you know."

Wei Li nodded. "We should check." She had her personal scanner out and was going over the walls carefully, looking for a way through.

Marion Stone walked over to Rohan and held her hand out stiffly.

"Tow Chief Rohan, I presume."

He swallowed and took the hand. She trembled slightly when he touched her. He pretended not to notice. "Second Class."

"Yes, of course."

"It's an honor to meet you, Doctor Stone. I grew up on stories about you and your husband."

"You mean stories about Hyperion in which my husband and I were minor characters."

He cleared his throat. "I was, er, trying to be polite."

"Polite? A polite Hybrid? What are you, Canadian?"

"Actually, yes. I'm from Canada. Born and raised."

A smile flashed across her face, so fast it was almost imperceptible. "Well, then. Tell me, Mr. Canadian Hybrid, what do you think is on the other side of that wall?"

"I have absolutely no idea. I only know what we all know: that it's supposed to be vacuum, and it isn't."

"Not the thinker, then, are you? Not an idea man?"

"No, ma'am. That's not what I was trained for."

Her eyes hardened at his words. "No, you weren't. Tell me, Tow Chief Rohan, have we met before? You seem familiar."

Did she recognize him? "Second Class. And no, we haven't. I'd remember."

"Of course. Of course. Rohan. Well, what are we going to do about this compartment? The one that's not supposed to be there?" She waved her hand at the wall as she spoke.

Rohan shrugged. "I tow things; I don't make those decisions."

Wei Li turned to them. "There's definitely something there, but there's no interior access. This wall is solid. Rohan, could you look for an entrance from the outside? We'll grab a shuttle and meet you there."

Rohan nodded with some relief.

The Hybrid left through the nearest airlock and followed the directions projected onto his mask. The extra section was right between Orange 8 and Orange 12.

He slowed as he neared Orange 8. *Insatiable* was vast, bigger than any warship in the fleet. She was designed for long-term deep space deployment, with enough interior space for her crews to remain sane on trips that could last months or years.

"I'm at Orange 10."

"We're still prepping a shuttle for ourselves; we'll be a while. What do you see, Rohan?"

"It's a shuttle bay. Bland as can be. Doors are open."

"Open? You are certain?"

Normal procedure was for shuttle bays to close their doors when not in use.

"I realize I'm not a trained detective, Wei Li, but I can spot an open bay door when I see it."

"Of course. Is anything inside?"

He flew closer. The bay was dark.

He floated in through the wide-open doors, using his handheld to project some light into the interior.

"It's vented, obviously. No atmosphere. I see ports, though, so it looks like it's hooked into *Insatiable*'s air supply. I see some supplies, food, a chair, a bed. Wait a moment."

There was a bang.

"What was that, Rohan? We felt a shudder right through the deck of the ship. Rohan?"

Within seconds the ship's voice burst over the comms.

"Something just exploded in Orange 10!"

16

Bliss

"So there we were, eating dinner."

Tamara was on her side, her head resting in the crook of his shoulder. She traced her dark blue fingernails over his chest as he spoke.

"We?" Her voice was soft with sleep.

"Yes, this was yesterday. Shortly after I got a face full of explosive on *Insatiable*. The professor, Benjamin, not Marion. Wei Li, Ursula, and me. I have no idea why Ursula was there, I think she's trying to get something from Wei Li."

"Hmmm. Go on." Her hair was spread out over his arm, gently tickling his skin. She rubbed her top leg over his thighs.

It was highly distracting. "Right. For a minute I was thinking about all the stuff that has happened to me this week. Like, in just the past seven days. Getting shot, fighting a giant insect, absorbing a load of detonating theonite. And I was about to say that I've had terrible luck this week. I wanted to ask, is this a time when I should be gambling, because clearly the universe owes me some compensatory good luck, or should I avoid gambling, because clearly the universe hates me right now."

"Do you so miss gambling?"

"No, I don't really gamble. It's just a saying, really. But I was about to say this, and I thought of you. And I realized I'm already more than even with the universe."

"So you're saying that being with me is worth a fight against an army of space bears, a two-hundred-meter superpowered monster, and a point-blank exposure to detonating theonite? That is all? I think you are underestimating me. I believe you are, in fact, ahead."

He laughed and pulled her body a little more tightly to him. "I stand corrected, more than even. As in, I'm on a streak of very good luck, if you count all the things."

"All the things, yes. I'm glad you realize it. Men are often foolish when they judge these accounts."

"I'm trying to be less foolish. You know, I could lay like this all day. Maybe I'll call in sick. I deserve a sick day. I'm not fully recovered from that dose of neurotoxin I took on Toth 3."

"Not fully recovered? You seemed fully recovered a little while ago."

"Oh, no, that was not me at full strength. Give me a little more time to rest and you'll see what I'm capable of. If you think you can handle it." He tickled her ribs lightly.

She shivered. "I take that as a challenge. And I accept. You replenish your reserves and we shall see whether *I* am up to the task."

He turned, just far enough to reach her face, and kissed her lips gently.

She snuggled into him as he did it, her softness melding around hm.

After a minute, she settled back against the bed and stroked his chest again. "I am glad the hair returned, as you said it would."

He laughed. "That decipede spit was so corrosive. I want to farm those guys, collect the spit, and sell it somehow. Maybe to clean something. Like, the nastiest, most disgusting mess you can imagine, we could dissolve it away."

"I suspect you are a much better warrior and tow chief than you are a businessman."

"I always thought my true talents lay in the bedroom. No pun intended."

She kissed his chest. "Do not get too full of yourself, Tow Chief Second Class Rohan. You are quite the warrior. I am not sure your bedroom skills are quite as superlative."

"Not sure?"

"I cannot be sure yet. I believe I shall need some more extensive testing before I verify your claim."

"Ah. Testing. I am willing to undergo further testing if it will help you draw conclusions."

She giggled. "Then we shall do so, for science! But not now, for that blinking light on the side of your bed is telling me that your shift starts soon."

"I'm pretty sure I can take a sick day."

"You can, but you know you'll be called in to meet and discuss something with someone, sooner than later. The past few days have been eventful. And you have been at or near the center of these events. And you cannot expect more good luck from the universe, not with the amount you've had already this day."

He sighed. "You're probably right."

"Get used to saying that. I'm always right."

"Don't worry, I know. I've dated before."

She poked him in response. "Do not attempt to make me jealous by discussing your other paramours."

"Why? It won't work?"

"Or, worse for you, it might."

He kissed her again, his heart jumping as he felt the softness of her lips.

"How is Rinth? Is he going to feel weird about you spending time with me?"

She let out a breath. "It is hard to predict with children. I do not think so, though. He likes you and he does not seem to hold any illusions about his father returning to our lives."

"Okay. Let me know if there's anything I can do to make things easier."

"I will, Tow Chief Second Class Rohan." She paused. "I will tell you something funny. I have never had an Earther friend before. I was not sure how your people handled . . . this."

"What do you mean 'handled'?"

"Well, anatomical matching, for one thing. I'd hate to get to this point only to find out that we don't fit together. Physically."

"Oh, right. Maybe ask a doctor before you date any Ursans."

"Yes. That information is easy to come by, of course."

"I'm sure the web has abundant resources to answer any question you have about interspecies relationships."

"It does! Often with helpful instructional videos, suggestions for positions, dos and do nots. Especially the instructional videos, there were so many examples, for all different species combinations, in many varied numbers."

"I can imagine."

"Only imagine? You have never perused these selections? Out of curiosity?"

"Oh. Well. Um, maybe I have. Did you find any favorites? Any you'd like us to watch . . . together?"

She laughed. "Maybe someday. Anyway, a point I was getting to was trying to determine how your people handle the social aspects of sex."

"Ah. I see what you're saying. That's actually harder to figure out."

"Exactly. Does your species mate for life or engage in casual copulation? If the latter, when do they do so, and what are the expectations?"

"Was the web helpful with that?"

"Very much less so. First, there seemed to be less content on this topic. Almost as if there is less interest."

"I can't say I'm surprised."

"I can imagine many watch the instructional videos for a sense of titillation, while the more practical aspects of dating on your world draws less prurient interest."

"I'd say that's accurate."

"The true difficulty lies in the heterogeneity of your planet. In some cultures you mate for life, exclusively, while in others you pair as casually as Lukhors drink tea. With some of your people, families are raised with kin, and sex is only shared with those outside the household!"

"It's more regulated on Lukhor? More homogeneous?"

"Our culture seems less varied. I'm sure there's some interesting historical reason for the difference."

"I can ask Ben. He might know."

"Yes."

"In the country my mother came from you're supposed to wait for marriage, then only mate inside that bond. Plenty of people break that rule, of course, but that's the idea. Where I grew up, people tend to be more liberal."

"I believe I can deduce your personal values in this area from your current predicament."

He stroked her back. "I think you can make quite a few deductions from this."

They settled against each other, sharing warmth and skin, half dozing in the gentle light coming in through the clear ceiling.

After some time, Tamara stirred. "Now you need to get ready for your job. If you get fired and are no longer a celebrity, I will have to wait in line for the best restaurants like all the peasants."

"With the peasants, eh? We wouldn't want that, would we?"

"Remember, I'm only using you for your connections."

He laughed and sat up. The blankets slid aside and he feasted his eyes on a long swatch of green skin. Rohan ran his hand up that expanse, from the side of her knee over her hip, then down the curve of her waist onto her back, up her spine to the nape of her neck.

"Hmm. That feels nice."

He sighed and shook his head. "But you're right, I have to get going. I am sorry."

"There will be other nights. Other days. I am not done with you yet, my Rohan."

"Good. But don't let Wistful hear you say that, she thinks I'm her Rohan."

"No worry, I will not compete with her."

"Please don't. Because, you know, when you live inside someone, it's not good to make them angry."

She laughed. "Go shower now. I will dress and go home to sleep before I am tempted to make a bad joke about living inside somebody."

"Oh, please don't. Nobody needs that."

"Go!" She made a whipping motion with her hand, as if she was going to snap a towel at him. He laughed and walked toward his shower, stepping over the puddle of fabric her dress had made on the floor. They hadn't taken the time to hang it.

He turned back to the bed. "Wash my back?"

She tilted her head, as if considering, then stepped out from under the covers and crossed the room to join him.

I can't imagine ever tiring of that view.

· · • • • · • • · ·

A little while later, a regretful Rohan left his quarters to report to work.

Wistful greeted him over a closed channel. "How are you feeling?"

He swung his arms loosely as he floated. "Actually, pretty good. I don't think that explosion was meant specifically to kill *me*. They would have used something stronger."

"I agree. What is not clear, then, is what the actual goal was."

"We can let Wei Li work that out. Right now, I could really use a day or two free of any physical beatings, if that can be arranged."

"I will attempt to do so."

"Great. For now, do you want me to start bringing in ships?"

"Yes, Rohan. Please begin by bringing *Artistic License* out to the beacon perimeter. She is fully prepped for departure."

"Copy, grabbing *Artistic License* now."

He checked his mask for directions and flew around to the north arm of the station. He found *Artistic License*, floating just free of her dock.

By the time he had pulled her to the beacon perimeter around Wistful, another ship was waiting for him to bring to dock.

Then another, and another.

"Rohan."

"Yes, Wistful?"

"You should take a break now. Can you meet Wei Li at *Insatiable*? I believe she would like you to go over the scene of the explosion with her."

"Sure, I could use the break."

He flew across the station. The central portion of the station was a fat glittering teardrop, twice the size of an Imperial capital ship. Her outermost skin was single-facet diamond panels. All the science Rohan had learned on Earth told him the material wasn't possible, but he slept under it every night. The material caught and reflected and sparkled with light from the stars, from Toth, from nearby ships, and from the inside of the station; all mixed with every color of the rainbow in a chaotic frenzy.

Rohan slowed as he passed his own room, a tiny part of him wondering if Tamara had slept there even after he left, perhaps hoping she had.

He stole a quick peek. The room was empty. He flew on.

The important bits of Wistful, the housing for her generators and central processing cores, were deep inside the central mass, but the outer layers were full of amenities for her crew. He passed weapons decks and strategic command rooms and communications arrays and observation domes, many unused.

He flew out over the southern arm, skimming the clear roof that covered the concourse. There were throngs of people about, walking to and from the transport system to lunch dates or to meetings or home for siestas. He could spot a dozen different species mingling on the grass and sidewalks, standing elbow-to-elbow with one another at food stands and bars, casually conversing about the happenings of the day.

There were Ursans mixed in with the crowd, their furry heads sticking out from the crowd of shorter bipeds, but no longer causing any stir of curiosity.

Something about the cosmopolitan nature of it all tugged at something in Rohan's chest. It was an image, a place, a scene, and an ethos worth protecting. He was feeling at home for the first time since leaving Earth over ten years earlier.

Rohan approached *Insatiable*. She jutted out from her dock in Wistful; four heavy tubes, arranged at the corners of a square, parallel to one another, an assortment of differently shaped metal sections and empty spaces between them.

Rohan tapped his comm. "Hail, *Insatiable*."

"Oh my goodness, Gr— Rohan."

"Yes. Permission to come aboard? I am supposed to meet Security Chief Wei Li in Orange 10."

"Oh, oh. Tow Chief Second Class Rohan. Oh." The ship's voice was broken and hesitant.

"Yes, that's me. Permission to come aboard?"

"My goodness. Rohan. I, I have to tell you something." If he hadn't known better he would have thought *Insatiable* was crying. Could ships cry?

"Are you all right, *Insatiable*? You sound, um, odd."

"By the light of the Empire, Rohan, I am so sorry."

"What are you sorry for, *Insatiable*? What happened?"

"What do you mean? You . . . the explosion . . . on board . . . it's all my fault."

"Oh, that. Look, I'm fine, all right? It's okay."

"No, it absolutely positively fundamentally is not okay! That should never have happened. Become a research vessel, they said. It's safer, they said. No more combat duty, they said. Learn new things, explore cool new worlds, they said. No danger. No killing, they said. They lied, Rohan!"

If ships had lungs she would have been hyperventilating.

Was the ship having a breakdown? Could ships break down like that? Psychologically?

What should he do?

Rohan reached back into his past and brought out his best officer's voice. It was the voice he'd used to scare a cadet or push a recruit to take their first jump out of an orbiting ship for unassisted planetary reentry.

"Research Vessel First Class *Insatiable*!"

The response was sudden and immediate. "Sir, yes, sir!"

"You were attacked. The *Empire* was attacked. This is no different than any ship being damaged in any war that the Empire has ever fought. This is exactly what you were trained for as a troop transport. Isn't it?"

"Sir, yes, sir!"

"You are going to calm down and assist in any way you can as we try to determine the source of this attack! Is that clear?"

"Clear, sir!"

"You were damaged during honorable service to the Empire. There is no shame in that. Do I have to repeat myself?"

"Sir, no, sir."

"Steady your circuits now."

"Yes, sir."

"Good. Do I have your permission to come aboard to investigate this attack?"

"Sir. Yes, sir." Her voice was softer now, smoother.

"Good. Where would you like me to come on board, *Insatiable*?"

"There is an airlock in Orange 5. Cycling it open now."

He let the steel ebb out of his voice. "Very good. Are you okay, *Insatiable*?"

"I think so, Tow Chief Second Class Rohan."

"We were assaulted, *Insatiable*. You and me."

"Yes, Rohan."

"We're not going to let that stand, are we?"

"No, we're not."

"Okay."

"Thank you, Rohan."

"You let me know if you need anything, okay?"

"Yes, Rohan. Airlock is open."

"Thank you, *Insatiable*."

Rohan slipped into the airlock. The outer door immediately clanged shut and the lock pressurized.

A few seconds later the inner door spiraled open and let Rohan into the ship's interior. He followed the display on his facemask to the compartment where he expected Wei Li to be waiting.

She was alone in the vast empty room, facing the outer wall.

"Security Chief."

"Tow Chief Second Class. This ship heals quickly."

17

Unpleasant Mysteries

The wall Wei Li was facing had been badly damaged in the theonite explosion.

Rohan walked up to it and ran a hand over the smooth metal. "Healing a flat wall is easy. It's when the complex systems get damaged that the nanobots take a long time to make sure they're fixing things correctly. Plus, it's the only damage to the ship. Not like the nanos are busy elsewhere."

"Yes. Still, it's impressive."

Rohan waited. His reptilian friend was clearly thinking about something.

She tapped her comm. "*Insatiable*, I am activating a privacy shield so Rohan and I can discuss confidential matters in this bay. Do you understand?"

There was a pause, then she nodded.

She knelt to the ground and put a small cylinder on the floor. She tapped the top. She turned to him. "You are recovered?"

He shrugged. "Pretty much. I did request a day or two without concussive head trauma to finish healing. I'm not sure Wistful pushed the paperwork through yet."

"I will not promise anything. I will, however, avoid chastising you for missing combat practice."

He spread his hands in helplessness. "I've been kind of busy, you know."

"Lack of preparation will not make these events less likely, nor will it lead you to enjoy them more."

"I was kind of hoping I could work at avoiding these situations instead of working my butt off trying to get better at handling them."

"Mmm." She walked along the outer edge of the room, examining the wall more closely. There was little else to look at after the explosion; the interior of the small bay had been all but vaporized by the theonite. "Best of luck with that."

Her tone was not sincere.

"Why are we here, Wei Li? What are you looking for?"

"We are here looking for clues. It is the initial step in the detectiving process."

"I don't think that's a word."

"It is now. I have Wistful's authority to make up words as I see fit." She said it with a perfectly deadpan tone.

"That sort of explains why you're here, but not why I'm here. Why am I here?"

"You are here to assist me with my detectiving, Tow Chief Rohan."

"I am pretty sure I'm not qualified to do that. My head is good at taking punishment, not at thinking. Er, detectivating."

"Don't add extra syllables to my made-up words, Rohan. And your head is perfectly fine for thinking, even if it is admittedly even better suited to taking punishment."

"Thanks. I think?"

"Rohan, I am a Class Four Empath. There is nobody within four star systems of here better qualified than I to interrogate suspects. I have a small but proficient team of lab techs, trained to the highest Imperial standards, who are experts in applying every known technique of forensic analysis. You are not, as you say, especially brilliant intellectually. I mean no insult."

"None taken."

"So why do you think I need you?"

"Um. To lift something heavy? I'm good at that."

"No. I need you to be a sounding board for my ideas. This is an Imperial ship, on Imperial business, and this sabotage is most likely related to the Empire. I need someone familiar with the ways of the Empire to tell me if what I am thinking is reasonable."

"I can do that. Well, I can try to do that."

"Good. Let us recapitulate what we know, and then what we suspect. First, an explosive was set here."

"Are we sure of that? Could some theonite have been stored here, and I set it off accidentally?"

"No. Theonite is extremely stable and you did not do anything that could have set off a properly stored supply."

"Okay."

"Past this we have to do some guesswork. Shall we assume that whoever set the theonite was skilled in its use?"

Rohan thought, then nodded. "I think we should."

"Why do you say so?"

"Because theonite isn't something people play with when they don't know what they're doing. It has a reputation for being dangerous."

"I agree. Therefore we should assume that the theonite detonated when, where, and for the reason desired by whoever set it."

"I'll buy that."

She turned her gaze sharply to him. "Do you think it was meant to kill you?"

Rohan shook his head slowly. "Not if the person setting it knew anything about Hybrids. It might have hurt me if it had been set to detonate when I was at point-blank range, but it basically went off as soon as I stuck my head through the bay doors."

"I agree. It would have probably killed or severely injured anybody else entering the bay, but if the intent was to harm the crew of Wistful it would have been set to go off after a greater delay."

"Makes sense. But what other reason could there be to set the charges? I can't imagine it was an attempt to hurt *Insatiable*. Look at her, it's been a day and she's good as new."

"I agree again. You see, your brain serves multiple purposes when you allow it to."

"It would be nice if we knew what else was in here. We can't figure that out because the theonite wiped out all the evidence."

"Yes. Interesting. I believe you might be following the same path of detectiving that I followed."

"Oh. You think the theonite was set to destroy evidence?"

"I am having great difficulty coming to any other conclusions. And as I am much more intelligent than you are, it is likely that there is no other reasonable conclusion to draw."

"Now the question is, what could have been going on here that someone would want to hide badly enough to set off a theonite bomb?"

"Ah, that is a good question, Rohan. You might have a future with this thinking business if you stick to it."

"I prefer towing ships, thank you."

Wei Li hesitated, glancing quickly at the cylinder generating their privacy shield. An indicator light on top of it was shining green.

She walked closer to the Hybrid. "Rohan, you know I respect your privacy. But you should know that I am fully aware that you have not always been a tow chief."

He swallowed. "What do you mean?"

"I have seen you tow ships and I have seen you fight. You were not a tow chief before coming to Wistful. Given your roots, and the limited options available to someone of your biology in the Empire, it is not hard to deduce your employment history."

"Okay. Why are you saying this?"

"Because if you have seen something like this before, this sort of . . . arrangement, I would like you to feel free to share that knowledge with me. Without fear that it will compromise the security of your past."

Rohan scratched under his beard. He thought. "I don't really have anything to contribute here. It looks like someone was hiding here, presumably to spy on whatever was going on in the ship. It had to be someone with pretty high clearance setting it up, because they'd have to execute an override on *Insatiable* to put someone on board without her noticing."

"I agree. But the list of people who could do that is too long to be of use to us."

"Right, it's not like I can look up and say it's only one particular person or even one particular office that could have done it. So someone hid a spy in here."

"What were they spying on?"

"Wait, I'm not done. The problem is, how did they get out? *Insatiable* should have noticed any ship or even person exiting the bay. And if she didn't, Wistful would have."

"Was this a suicide?"

He shook his head. "It could be, I guess. But that doesn't feel right. Nothing serious enough happened here to warrant a skilled spy committing suicide to avoid detection. What would be the point? To send some kind of message? To whom?"

Wei Li took one last circuit of the room. "Forensics says there are trace compounds in here consistent with a humanoid living inside for several days."

"Consistent with a vaporized corpse?"

She shook her head. "Inconclusive. I very much wish I had a person to interrogate."

"Yeah, me, too."

"All right, Rohan. Thank you for your time."

"Are you staying?"

She shook her head. "I will speak some more with the crew. Perhaps somebody will have a strong feeling that leads me somewhere."

"Good luck."

"Thank you. And thank you for your help, limited as it was."

He laughed as he left. Rohan retraced his steps to *Insatiable*'s airlock and left the ship.

He activated the comm system in his mask. "Where to next?"

"Beacon Z Five, *Cherrypicker* is waiting to dock. You also have a message from Ursula."

Rohan brought his messages up on the inside of his mask. Ursula had sent a message, marked urgent. She wanted to meet.

"Wistful, south corridor, Block 112. What is that?"

"Block 112 is mostly fish farming tanks."

"Huh. Okay, then. I have another date. Send a message to Ursula. Tell her I'll meet her at the end of my shift."

After that he was too busy to think much about any female in his life.

· · • • • • • • · ·

By the time he arrived at Block 112 he had a splitting headache and an angrily empty stomach.

It was too early for the dinner crowd, which left the concourse pleasantly underpopulated. Rohan bought a kebab from a quiet food stand and pulled chunks of seasoned meat and cubes of grilled vegetables off the stick as he walked.

He stopped in front of a familiar red ball, lying quietly in the grass.

"Hey, Rinth! What's going on?"

He picked up the ball left-handed and tossed it lightly into the air.

"Rohan! I got up early and came out to play!"

"Does your mother know you're out here?"

"Sure, she does. I'm allowed as long as I don't go past that tree or that food cart." He pointed out the landmarks.

"Okay, buddy. I haven't seen you in a few days. Um, how's school?"

The green-skinned boy looked Rohan up and down. "I can't believe you've been on like five dates with my mom and you're still wearing those clothes."

"I think it was more like three dates, though I'm not sure why you're counting."

The boy waved a hand in dismissal. "It's not the number that matters. It's still embarrassing. What if people find out that my mom is dating someone who dresses like that? They'll never forget it. I'll get picked on for the rest of my life."

"Is that what you're worried about? You know, I've been kind of busy."

"Oh, sure. You have time to fight monsters and aliens and get exploded but you can't take ten minutes out to order a suit?"

"I guess my priorities are a little messed up. I'll try to do better."

"Good."

Rohan looked at the boy, furiously trying to come up with a way to ask the child how he felt about Rohan dating his mother that wasn't awkward. Nothing came to him.

The boy broke the silence. "Can you teach me how to fly?"

"Oh, buddy. I'm sorry, but probably not."

"Why not? I bet flying is cool. And I promise to be super careful."

"Most people don't have enough Power to fly. It takes a lot of spiritual energy."

"Oh. What if I practice really hard?"

"Maybe. But even if you never fly, I bet you could learn to do other cool things. Like break stuff with your hands."

"Dodge bullets?"

"Uh, yeah, maybe. I could probably teach you that. But can we wait until you're a little older? I don't think your mom would appreciate us shooting at you so you can practice."

"Yeah, that would probably make her mad."

"How about I teach you how to use your spiritual energy, and you help me pick out some nice clothes. Do you think you could do that?"

Rinth smiled. "I bet I could! I mean, at least better than you can do for yourself."

"Cool. Look, I have a meeting now, I'll come see you when you have a day off from school, okay?"

"Deal!"

Rohan took the last bite of his kebab, sucking some air into his mouth to cool it where the hot juices ran out onto his tongue. Then he *rose* into the air.

The concourse and the buildings around it emptied out as Rohan got farther from the station's center. The blocks closest to the fish farms and hydroponic gardens were almost deserted. Rohan had walked the full breadth of the station before, but not often. There was rarely a reason to come to these empty blocks.

The walkway rose steeply as it approached the fish farms. The path became a grating covering the enormous tanks, the clear roof of the station just a few meters overhead.

As Rohan entered the farm he was hit by the strong smell of fish and algae and the echoing rush of running water. The fish that Wistful kept were all species native to streams and rivers, so the farms maintained an artificial current by pumping the water back from one end and in through the other.

There were very few people on the decking itself. Newcomers to the station often visited to marvel at the huge tanks swarming with fish, but the view got boring quickly and very few station residents returned. Within minutes Rohan had found Ursula.

"Ursula! I got your message."

The female, small for an Ursan but still over two meters high and weighing at least two hundred-fifty kilos, turned to face him. She had been contemplating the stream of fish below her. Rohan noticed again the gray hair streaking around her muzzle. It was the only sign of her age he could see.

"Rohan. I am grateful that you have come. Please." She pointed at a metal bench set against a railing, past which was an opening into the tanks.

"What did you want to show me?" He looked around.

"Please to forgive my subterfuge, Tow Chief Second Class Rohan. I wish to speak to you in private and could not think of another way to make it so."

Rohan sighed. He had come to Wistful to lead a simpler life. Suddenly he was surrounded by complications. "Well, this is a good place to have a private conversation. Noisy, nobody around, and nowhere for anyone to hide if they want to eavesdrop."

"Those were my thoughts, as well. Also, I like the sound of the water and the fish. It is eating fish like these out of streams or rivers that my people love to do most."

He smiled at the image. The Ursans seemed more like Earth bears every day. "It is peaceful here. White noise, we call it. The constant rush of the water. Makes me sleepy."

"It makes me hungry!"

They chuckled. Rohan sat on the bench, and Ursula quickly settled next to him. She was scented with some kind of citrus.

"Aren't you still mourning? Or did I miscount days?"

"Ah. We mourn for seven days. Today is the sixth day, the day of planning. We think on how to honor our dead, or how to—I don't have right word—distribute their responsibilities. For example, if a parent of a cub has died, we gather and plan who will care for the cub from then on."

"I'm going to go ahead and assume you're telling me this for a reason."

Ursula bared her very alarming array of teeth at him in what he hoped was a smile. "You are in ownership of information which I believe would to help me greatly."

"I'd be happy to tell you whatever you want, mostly. You didn't have to . . ."

She waited.

He continued. "You don't want the other Ursans to hear what you're going to ask me."

She waited some more.

"You don't want Wistful or Wei Li to hear it, either. And you think they won't hear us over the water."

"Tow Chief Rohan, you are my most favored partner for subterfuge. They say your head is like a stone, but I know you use it more than it looks like."

"People have been telling me that lately. I'm not sure it's a good thing."

"That is true. Nobody likes a male who is too much for thinking. Still, is good for us now."

He looked down into the water. The fish weren't salmon, though they looked like salmon, and tasted like salmon, and smelled like salmon. He thought it was a good thing he hadn't stepped in one.

She eyed him skeptically. "You are too smiling now."

18

Papa Bear Jokes

"I I thought of a terrible joke. I'd share it with you, but it would take a long time to explain and it still wouldn't be funny."

"Tell Ang. He loves the jokes that are not funny. I always say, if it is not funny, how is it a joke? Then he growls."

"Sounds like Ang."

She took a deep breath and let it out in a huff, almost like a pant. "Rohan, we watched images of your shuttle landing on the planet. Of the creatures." She pointed one massive paw up, at the view of Toth 3 they had through the clear ceiling.

"Yeah. That's why I told you not to go to the planet."

"We are not for understanding what we saw."

It wasn't the response he'd been hoping for. "Did you not see the two-hundred-meter insect that tried to kill us?"

"Yes, that was clear. And we saw shuttle with truly lovely guns. These ion cannons you have are greater than Ursan technology, but the principles of it we know."

"Yes, and did you happen to notice how useless those ion cannons were on the decipede?"

Ursula shook her shaggy head. "That is where the not understanding happened. We do not understand how they missed. And because we are not for the understanding, some of the young believe that if steady Ursan paws guided the cannons then miss they would not."

"Oh, no. Look, just no. That's not how things work."

"If I am not to explain how things work, then the young will not listen to my not explaining. And I fear they will do something very male. Sorry, is idiom, I mean something very stupid."

"You and Wei Li must get along great, don't you?"

She bared her impressively sharp teeth. "Wei Li is my very good friend."

Rohan rubbed his temples. The headache, which had never left him, was doubling up its assault. "Okay, you get a crash course in metaphysics. Are you ready?"

"Please, yes."

"This is the sort of thing that people in the Empire mostly know, but mostly don't talk about. It's discouraged. Because the Empire runs on metaphysical Powers. So, try to be discreet when you talk about this stuff."

"Soul of discretion is Ursula."

"Great. First, every living thing has some spiritual Power. Even plants."

"Every living being."

"Yes. Thinking life has much more. So, even a small rodent has more than a tree."

"You say even Ursans have this Power?"

"Absolutely. Even highly advanced artificial intelligence. Once a computer gets to a certain point, and even though it's not totally clear where that is, the computer starts manifesting spiritual Power. It becomes alive. Most of our big ships are alive, for example. Your ship isn't, it's dead like a shuttle."

"Oh."

"Everything with spiritual Power of any kind can exert it on the world, even if only a little bit."

"You are saying that every living creature has the telekinesis?"

"Yes. *Most* living things have very little, and it takes a lot of training to use it to any effect. You could train for years and get just strong enough to lift a fork off the table with your Power. So it's not very useful."

"And some be strong like you and tow ships through sky."

"Yeah. Some of us are born with a *lot* of Power. Enough to fly and tow ships. Others can *sense* other people's spirits, so they can tell what people are feeling."

"I see."

"The real trick is that the Power doesn't affect everything in the world the same way."

"No? What is exception?"

"Every living thing is best at affecting its own body, and especially when resisting the Power of something else. So, if you held up, say a straw, I could pinch it shut very easily. But if I tried to pinch shut your carotid artery, your spiritual Power would fight me. And it would win. So I'm strong enough to pull ships through space but not strong enough to overcome your own energy and twist up your insides."

"That is good to know. I had not even begun to worrying what you might be doing to my blood vessels."

"When I pull a ship, my Power is *pushing* my hands, and my hands push the ship. If I tried to stand back and just *push* the ship directly it would be harder. Possible, but much harder."

"Your body is like lever for your spirit. Metaphysical machine."

"That . . . that's a really good way to put it."

"And is lever for someone on other side as well."

"Yes. That's why we only make big ships that are intelligent, that are alive. Because anybody with Powers, even if they are much weaker than me, can totally wreck the internal mechanisms of a dead ship. Just reach in and twist up cables, unplug things, break the shielding around the generators. With a living ship, you can't, it fights back. Resists."

"So all warships in sector are intelligent."

"All warships. Really, anything interstellar. A big dead ship is just too vulnerable; nobody would feel safe on one, in case, you know, pirates or something. Also, the best way to travel between systems, to travel really far, is a ship with Powers. They open rifts in space, using Power. We don't have machines that can do that."

"Like a wormhole."

"Pretty much. Just temporary and smaller."

"I see. And this explains decipede and ion cannons how?"

"It's very easy to move your own body with Power. It's also pretty easy to move things that aren't alive, especially small things. And especially things that are already moving."

"Like bullets."

"Yes."

"When Ang and other Ursans shot you, you did not move bullets. Bullets struck your chest. I watched."

"I could have diverted them around myself easily. But then we would have had a stream of bullets flying around the station, and who knows who might have gotten killed."

"So you let bullets hit you to stop bullets. On purpose."

"Yeah. It doesn't sound very smart when you say it like that."

"So giant bugs on planet have . . . this Power."

"Right. More than they should have, since they don't seem very smart, but they're definitely exceptional that way."

"And the flying things on planet, they are same?"

"Not as big as the decipede, but very, very fast."

"Also with Powers."

"Absolutely. Nothing that size could even get airborne in that atmosphere, with that gravity, on plain old biology."

Ursula sat in silence, her foot tapping at the grating beneath them.

"What about island? Or polar caps? My people are good with cold."

Rohan shook his head. "I've been to expeditions to the poles. And there's good news and bad. The good news is, it definitely took longer before the flyers came for us."

"How much is longer?"

"That's the bad news. Once we managed to stay overnight. Three of us. Just when we thought we were in the clear, we were making breakfast. I spilled the hot water for the tea, Radu got so mad, he thought he was going to freeze to death before we could boil more. Next thing we knew the alarms were going off and a murder of flyers was coming straight for us."

"Overnight." She let out a huge sigh. "That is not very much time. Still, thank you for all your explainings. This might be enough for to stop young ones from acting as fools."

"I hope so. You can tell them I said not to go. Hey, tell them that they have to fight me for the right to lead the expedition. Let them line up and try to take me out. I don't know, that should buy some time."

"You would fight a thousand Ursans to prevent them from getting themselves killed?"

"It's not my preference, but yes."

"You would have made a good for-real war chief, Rohan. If you were not so small and so lacking in hair."

"I swear, two days ago a woman was attracted to me because of how much chest hair I have, and now another one is putting me down for not having enough."

"Just be glad you don't have only one penis. I heard some of the species here are so equipped—how can they hope to ever satisfy a female like that?"

"I, uh, yeah. Whew. Lucky me."

"Next thing you tell Ursula some species managed to fill a planet while males only have two testicles each!"

"I, uh, no, I wouldn't say that."

"Oh, yes, I forgot. I am sorry. I hear your species uncomfortable with such frank discussion of sexual matters."

"Yes. Yes, we are, quite uncomfortable. Especially me. I come from a prudish culture."

"Earthlings?"

"Well, not all Earthlings, but some of us. And mine. Especially mine."

"I see. I am for apologizing."

"It's okay, you didn't know."

They sat in silence for a bit.

"Rohan Tow Chief, separate topic. Do you have an opinion on what Ursans should do now? You are a wise man, I think. You know much about this side of galaxy."

He scratched his beard and watched fish swim endlessly against the artificial current in the water beneath his feet.

"I'm not sure what you mean by 'do.'"

"What is next? We are alive. Life is not enough for intelligent being. Survival is not enough."

"I don't know, Ursula. I'm not sure I'm the one who should be answering those questions."

"I am requesting only advice, Rohan."

"My best advice is to not get advice from people like me."

She barked out a laugh. "That is a for cheating answer."

He relented. "I was in a situation something like this a year ago. My other job was over and I could do whatever I wanted to do. I thought about opening a bar, thought about just living out in the wilderness somewhere."

"And you chose to become a man who tows ships."

"I wanted to do something useful. And I wanted to do something that I was good at. I mean, maybe I could run a decent bar, but there's no reason to think I have any special aptitude as a bar owner, you know?"

"So tow chief you became, since for this you are well suited."

"Right. And honestly I was not at all convinced that it would work out. But it turned out I kind of like the work."

"I am not sure what *we* are good for, here in this end of galaxy."

"Look, you're still mourning. You've been through a tremendous transition. An unbelievable transition. But you don't have to make any final decisions today. And you don't have to make them by yourself."

"That is part of problem, Rohan. Today is day of planning. I must have plan."

"Or else . . .?"

"Must have plan to have hope. Must have hope to have restraint. With no plan, the young will not believe I am leading them somewhere, will start to have own ideas."

He grunted. "Mostly bad ideas. Like starting a colony on Toth 3."

"Precise you are."

"I tell you what. We'll find someone who can help you figure out where you can be the most useful. It's a big station, there are all sorts of smart people on board."

She rested a broad, heavy paw on his shoulder. "Thank you for the trying, Rohan."

"What about Ang? Is he helping at all?"

"Ang is even more lost. He is focused on being best war chief. Meaning, best follower of Ursula's direction. You have Drachna phrase for this. Being good soldier."

"Oh, yeah, that's it."

"Ang is happy to do as he is told."

"Could be worse, though, right? Ang could be one of the ones with the stupid ideas."

"Yes. That would be much worse." Ursula was looking down into the water again. "Do you think there would trouble be if I took a fish? Just one?"

19

Tall, Pale, and (Mostly) Handsome

The bed was warm, the sheets silky smooth.

"I could get used to this in a hurry. Waking up, seeing you. It's at least my second favorite way to start my day."

His hand drifted lazily over her back as he talked. She shifted, one antenna catching in his cheek, then twisted her head so it popped free. She giggled.

"Only second favorite?"

"At least. I don't want to overstate things."

"But you only see me at the end of the day, when I'm worn out and dirty. I get the fresh, rested version of you. Hardly seems fair. To you."

"I think only the fresh and rested version of me has a chance of keeping up with you."

"Oh, somehow I think you would manage."

He smiled as she ran her fingers through his chest hair. He turned toward her, his nose touching her antenna, and spoke. "We should go dancing, I think."

"Dancing?"

"Yes. People congregate together and move rhythmically to a shared musical experience."

"I know what dancing *is*. What I don't know is why you want to do it."

"You don't like dancing? I used to love going dancing."

"When was this?"

"Well, back on Earth. Before my Power came out. I guess it's been a while. But it was fun. We'd have parties, just put on music, dance, drink."

"If you wish to dance then we should dance. We will find a dance hall with nocturnal hours that suit me."

"Or we go in my evening, your morning. One day. I'm not saying, like, today."

"I have not been dancing in a long time. We dance at weddings and family parties. I haven't had many of those."

"No family parties?"

She shook her head, her antennae tapping his face with the motion. "After my father disowned me, only my sister defied him. She had nothing to lose, he won't take action against her. But the cousins, uncles and aunts, they are afraid of losing access to the money, the contacts, the jobs. So to avoid his anger they ignore me."

"I'm sorry. That sucks."

She shrugged. "It was part of the price of living the life I wanted. It was worth it."

"I'm glad someone made a decision they're happy with. The Ursans have no idea what to do with themselves. I guess I should say, they have ideas, but not good ones."

"I'm sure they will find their way."

"Are you still working on their ship? Is it ready?"

Tamara shook her head. "I spent my last shift back on *Insatiable*. They requested a rush job installing some strange equipment on one of the shuttles."

"Strange?"

"Yes. Based on artificial gravity, but not bootstrap drives. Something else."

"Like a weapon?" That didn't sound right. The Empire wasn't in the habit of putting experimental weapons on shuttles. When the Empire wanted something destroyed, or damaged, they just sent in Hybrids.

She shrugged. "I do not think so. The energy draw is high but not weapon-grade. That Doctor Stone is quite a tyrant, though. If we stopped even for a bathroom break she acted as if we were committing high treason."

"Huh. Did you finish?"

"No. And knowing the day crew . . . they're lovely people, not the brightest. They're going to have trouble with that equipment. Unless they pull crew off the Ursan ship it won't be finished today."

"Huh."

"You have already said that. Why? Do you know something about Doctor Stone and that shuttle?"

Rohan let out a long breath. "I hope I'm wrong. I'm afraid she's found a way to force open the wormhole. Or at least copied the way to open it from the Ursans."

"Is that a bad thing?"

"That's the tricky part. I think Wistful is fine with people studying the wormhole, but that's not the same as having them *open* it."

"Surely Wistful is aware. We're all contracted through her. It's no secret we were working on the shuttles on *Insatiable*."

"Yeah. I'll check in with Wei Li to make sure."

"You do that. But not just yet. We have ten more minutes to be right here."

"Yes, we do. Barely!"

· · · · ● · ● · · · ·

Forty minutes later, Rohan was pulling himself through his airlock. He opened a comm link. "Wistful. What's the queue look like right now?"

"Good morning, Rohan. Three waiting and seven more expected this morning."

"Not bad. Listen, I'm going to be a bit late. I have an errand to run. Ship's business."

"Yes, Rohan. I'll inform the ships. Do you need backup?"

"Not yet, Wistful. I'll try to be quick."

He tapped the comm again, opening a new call.

"Personal. Open a link to Doctor Benjamin Stone."

The communications system in his helmet responded with Wistful's voice.

"Connecting."

He paused, wondering if the professor would take the call live. There was no answer.

"Begin recording, please. Doctor Stone, I'd like to have a quick word. I'm on my way to *Insatiable* now. I hope you can spare a minute. End recording."

He twisted in place again and pushed himself toward the southern arm.

A quick glance over Wistful showed him nothing out of the ordinary. He spun, vaguely hoping for another glimpse of whatever dark shadow he'd seen a few days earlier. Or for some trace of whatever had been hiding in the secret bay on *Insatiable*.

No luck.

"Hail, *Insatiable*."

"Tow Chief Rohan! I am so glad you stopped by! This is so exciting, isn't it?"

"What's exciting, *Insatiable*?"

"Um, well. I'm so sorry, I forgot!"

"You . . . forgot what you are excited about?"

"No, silly. I forgot that it's a secret! Sorry!"

"Once again, you leave me speechless, *Insatiable*. I have no idea how to respond. Anyway, I'd like to come aboard, see if I can have a few words with Doctor Stone."

He expected her to immediately agree. She did not.

"With which Doctor Stone are you seeking words, Tow Chief Second Class Rohan?"

"Mr. Doctor Stone. Ben. Not his wife; she and I aren't really friends."

"I certainly wouldn't know anything about that, I can't keep track of all the relationships you organics have with one another. Though there has been an interesting rumor about the Rogesh freighter and Erimedean transport ship getting free for some unauthorized joyrides around the asteroid belt, if you know what I mean."

"No, I don't know what you mean, but that's okay, I don't think I want to."

"Anyway, you're welcome to come aboard, Tow Chief Rohan. I don't know if Doctor Stone is available, but you're free to try the comms."

"Great. Thank you, *Insatiable*."

He followed the markings on the outside of the ship to the main airlock. It was cycling open as he got to it.

"Thank you again, *Insatiable*."

"It is an honor as always, Tow Chief Second Class Rohan." He could swear he heard her winking as she said his name, although she had neither eyes nor eyelids. At least she'd stopped vocalizing the 'Gr' sound before it.

As he waited for the airlock to pressurize an incoming message popped up in his heads-up display.

"Adjudicator Magdon Krahl requests the honor of your presence at your earliest convenience to discuss matters on behalf of Eldarinth Lastex, First Citizen of Lukhor."

He paused, even as the airlock's inner door cycled open.

"Personal."

His mask answered. "Proceed."

"Relationship between Eld . . . the person named in the message I just got, and Tamara, the woman I've been dating recently." He wasn't sure that was specific enough information for the computer.

"Magdon Krahl: unknown. Eldarinth Lastex is the father to Tamaralinth Lastex."

"Huh. Okay. Thanks."

Doctor Stone was turning the corner toward him, his tall, lanky frame draped in loose and casual clothes.

"Rohan, my friend! Welcome. Sorry I didn't answer your message, I was in the shower." He looked around the corridor. "Who were you thanking?"

"Just my computer." He tapped the side of his mask.

"Is there an artificial intelligence in that?"

"It's just comms and navigation. Or, that's what it wants me to think."

The professor laughed. "Come, join us for breakfast. I have a treat for you."

"Do you?"

"Every man should have a hobby, Rohan. Something you do that serves no real purpose, has no real importance to anybody, but which makes you happy."

"That's probably good advice. What's your hobby? I assume this treat has something to do with your hobby?"

"Yes, it does. For the past twenty or so years I have been recreating North American commercially available donuts. Using off-world ingredients."

"You mean like Dunkin' Donuts kind of donuts?"

"Yes, exactly! It was one of the things I missed about Earth, and, you know, finding a good donut on this side of the sector is not easy."

"I'm going to have to take your word for it. I've been trying, and failing, to get a decent samosa. I haven't even looked for donuts."

"Oh, yes. I can't help you with samosas. But I do have some freshly made donuts that I'd love for you to sample."

"I'm not sure I can. I just had dinner."

"Dinner? It's morning. . . Oh, right, your lady friend is nocturnal. Just try, I need feedback from someone who has actually eaten the real thing."

They walked deeper into the section. They entered a large room, a cafeteria with seating for about twenty. Plastic containers and food preparation equipment covered one wall. Small tables and chairs were scattered about.

Doctor Stone's team of graduate assistants were spread around the small cafeteria, eating and sharing soft conversations in small groups.

One table held a short stack of cardboard boxes.

"Wow, Doctor Stone, you go all out on the presentation."

"I do! And it's totally wasted on everyone but you and me."

"If I'd known I would have stopped and brought coffee."

The professor held out a paper cup. "I am one step ahead of you! I had some delivered. I have an extra; my wife decided she was too busy to join us."

Rohan reached for the cup. "I can't turn that down. Coffee and donuts."

"Good, don't! Now, to what do I owe the honor of your visit? Have you uncovered any new information regarding the explosion?"

"No, actually. I was kind of hoping you'd thought of something. Or found something."

The professor shook his head. "All I have are ideas, I'm sorry to say."

"I'll take ideas. You have a hypothesis about what was there?"

"Hypothesis? I have a paranoia-driven flight of fancy. I'm not sure it's worthy of the term 'hypothesis.'"

"What is it? Or would you rather not say here?"

"No, no, they've all heard my ramblings before. If anyone here wanted to turn information over to the il'Drach, they already have. I don't know if it makes sense, but the only reason I can see for what happened is that the il'Drach had a spy in that bay. And they were here specifically to spy on me. Or, more likely, on my wife."

"Not on Wistful?"

He shook his head, his thick gray eyebrows shaking with the movement. "If the il'Drach wanted a spy on Wistful, they could have sent one at any point in the last thousand years. Ten thousand. The wormholes have always been there, dormant, right? I suppose the spy could have been sent specifically to observe any changes in the wormhole, but that's literally why we were sent officially."

"Maybe it was a stowaway? Like, just somebody trying to hitch a free ride to this system?"

The professor's heavy brows furrowed. "I can't say it's impossible, but the resources you would need to hide on *Insatiable* without her awareness are much greater than what you'd need to arrange transport to this system. It's not as if Wistful is embargoed or under siege."

Rohan bit into a donut. It was everything he remembered from childhood visits to Tim Horton's, for better and for worse.

"This is really good, Professor. I'm impressed."

"Thank you, Rohan, thank you. Is there anything else I can help you with? Not that I've helped you so far."

"Well, this is a little delicate."

The Hybrid paused, scanning the room to see if the students were paying undue attention.

"Your wife is not being very discreet with her preparations. I'm hearing things, which means Wistful is hearing things."

Doctor Stone sighed. "I don't think she's *trying* to be discreet. My wife has a way of not caring about politeness or formalities when she thinks she's in the right."

"She's going to force Wistful's hand, and I don't want to see that happen."

There was a pause.

"Why not? Why is this. . .? Why are you making this your concern? Not that I'm unappreciative."

Rohan thought. Why was he? "I owe Wistful a lot. More than I want to explain. Which means that if she asks me to do something I really don't want to do, I'm still going do it, I'll just really hate myself afterward."

"But knowing you'll regret it isn't enough to stop you."

Rohan shrugged. "That's kind of the foundation of the whole Empire, isn't it? We Hybrids do what we're told. Even when, maybe especially when, we don't want to."

"Except when you decide not to and there's a Rebellion."

"That didn't turn out so well. You know that as much as—no, apparently better than—most people."

Their voices had gotten louder and the students were quietly staring at them.

The professor cleared his throat. "Anyway. I appreciate what you're trying to say. At least I think I do. But there's not much I can do about it at the moment. It's not as if she listens to me, you understand?"

"Sure. I wasn't expecting more than that. I just wanted to talk. Maybe you can find some way to mitigate the fallout. If things come to that."

"Thanks. I'll do what I can. Just be aware that probably isn't much."

"Come on, you were a superhero before I was born. Don't sell yourself short."

Ben chuckled drily. "Really more of a sidekick. Now, not to change the subject, but I'm going to do exactly that. We've been studying the kaiju."

"That's cool. What have you figured out?"

"Just observations, nothing dramatic. They seem to engage in periods of intense activity followed by longer periods of dormancy. I still haven't found a pattern. It's not obviously circadian."

"You've only got a couple of days' worth of data points, though."

"No, we have more than that. I connected with a group living on station who study the kaiju from afar. They're hobbyists, I suppose you could say. They use the public parts of Wistful's satellite feeds to keep tabs on kaiju activity. They've given us decades worth of data."

"That's a good idea. I should have thought of it."

"It *was* a good idea, but it didn't get us very far beyond ruling out everything on our short list."

Rohan scratched his beard. He was due for a trim.

"That's interesting, but not something I can devote any brainpower to right now. We have more pressing issues."

"Of course, of course. Just wanted to keep you updated."

"Yeah, that's good, thanks. The donuts were great. I haven't missed home this badly in a long time."

The professor gave him a wide grin, flashing strong white teeth. "My pleasure, Rohan."

"I have to get back to work. I'll see you soon."

"Best of luck!"

As Rohan stood to leave, Haditz, the Rogesh male assistant, made eye contact with him. The massive, gray-skinned humanoid gave a short, affirming nod, and Rohan nodded back.

A silent acknowledgement that the beef was over, Rohan thought. *It's a start.*

20

Levels of Intimidation

Rohan left *Insatiable's* cafeteria and retraced his steps through the ship to the airlock.

He tapped his comm. "Message to Magdon Krahl. Begin recording. I can meet you around lunchtime. Say, one o'clock. If that's not good you'll have to wait for evening. Anywhere on the station, your choice. End recording. Send."

The Hybrid stepped into the airlock, waited for it to depressurize, and left *Insatiable*.

"Wistful, I'm free. Which ship is first?"

Instructions followed, transmitted directly to his mask's inner display.

Ships were towed away from Wistful and pushed to the beacon perimeter.

Other ships, floating outside the perimeter, were contacted and pulled into dock, one-by-one.

"Wistful, am I pulling in more transport ships than usual?"

"Yes, Rohan. There are several cruise lines that have added me to their regular travel itinerary. Apparently, the nascent wormhole is now must-see viewing for tourists. Despite the fact that there isn't anything new to see."

"Oh. I should have invested in hotel space onboard when I had the chance."

"I doubt an increase in financial assets would make a significant difference to your lifestyle, Rohan."

"That is probably true, Wistful. Sad but true. I'm bringing *Love Boat* in to the north arm now. Wait, is that really this ship's name? Am I getting a translation error?"

"That is accurate, Rohan."

Rohan struggled to keep the laughter out of his voice while talking to *Love Boat*. He couldn't think of a polite way to ask how it had been named.

A warning popped up on the inside of his facemask. He had an appointment.

"Wistful, I'm taking a lunch break. I have a meeting."

"Yes, Rohan."

Rohan checked his messages. Executor Magdon Krahl had picked Ton'ga Shell, a very pricey lunch spot, for their meeting.

"Should I change into something nicer? This purple-and-gold jumpsuit was designed to be highly visible, not to make a good impression. Do I even want to make a good impression? More to the point, do I even own anything nice enough to make a good impression?"

Wistful responded. "I do not believe you do."

"No, sorry, Wistful, talking to myself. Thanks, anyway."

Rohan arrived at the Ton'ga Shell at a minute before one. He stepped through the front door and looked around.

Most of the customers wore some version of business wear. Mostly dark and somber colors in conservative cuts. Clothes meant to flatter aging and under-exercised bodies, physiques that went with the lifestyle of accumulating great power and wealth.

Rohan stepped up to the host podium. An impeccably dressed Kratic, lavender skin complimenting his dark suit, looked him over with the most subtle hint of disapproval in his eyes. "Welcome to Ton'ga Shell. How may I help you?"

"Tow Chief Second Class Rohan. I am meeting someone here, a Magdon Krahl? Is he here yet? She? I should have probably checked on that before. He or she."

The host's expression changed dramatically, and he glanced quickly at a small screen built into the podium. "Yes, sir. Welcome, sir. *Mr.* Krahl is waiting for you, in the back room. Please follow me."

"I didn't even know you had a back room."

"Of course not, sir. This way, sir."

Rohan followed the host past closely-packed tables and through ornate wooden doors into a separate room. A third the size of the main room, it held one large table with room for eight but only two lonely chairs.

There was a Shayjh getting up from one of the chairs as they entered. He was very tall, almost thirty centimeters taller than Rohan, with skin an opaque alabaster white that had no touch of human pink or tan to it, no tracery of blue veins or red blemishes.

The man was very thin, his frame filled out somewhat by sturdy leather clothing. His hair was as white as his skin, his pale gray eyes wide and almond-shaped, his ears sharply pointed.

The man loomed over Rohan and extended his right hand. Rohan took it and was met with a surprisingly strong grip.

"It is a pleasure to meet you, Tow Chief Second Class Rohan. My name is Magdon Krahl, Adjudicator, of the Seventh Circle."

"I would introduce myself, but it looks like you got all my important titles already."

"Everything current, I believe. Thank you for agreeing to meet with me. Please, have a seat. The food here has a solid reputation."

Rohan sat. The table was set with handcrafted china and ornate flatware.

Magdon Krahl snapped his fingers and a waiter swiftly entered the room to pour them glasses of wine.

They sat in silence while the waiter did his job. As soon as the man exited, Magdon Krahl reached forward and pressed a conspicuous button.

"This is now a truly private room. We are shielded from any eavesdropping, including even from Wistful herself." He cleared his throat and continued. "As I believe my original invitation specified, I am here to speak with you on behalf of the First Citizen of Lukhor. In the interest of expediency, do you have any insight as to why?"

Rohan sipped his wine. It was bold and complex, a powerhouse on his tongue.

"I would assume he has a space station in need of a tow chief, and you're here to offer me a job. Which I'm going to have to decline, as I'm on a contract with Wistful, but I thought I'd enjoy the food and wine before officially saying no."

Magdon Krahl's cheeks twitched in a smile that died before reaching his eyes. "I'm afraid this has nothing to do with an offer of employment."

"Ah, well. I suppose I'm not very good at guessing. Maybe you could, I don't know, just tell me?"

"Before we go further with this discussion I'd like to make sure you understand what it means that I am a Seventh Circle Shayjh."

Rohan ran his fingers through his hair, scratching his scalp. "Please, enlighten me."

"My people work almost exclusively in high-risk positions. As such, we maintain clones of ourselves at all times, ready to resume our roles should any accidents befall us in the course of those duties."

Rohan nodded, a look of vague interest on his face. "I can't imagine that's a great comfort to you. I mean, *this* you would still die. The fact that a copy would go on to finish what you started wouldn't change the fact that you're dead."

"On the contrary. To go along with our uniquely advanced cloning technology, we have uniquely advanced *spiritual* technology. My soul is anchored not to this particular body, but to any of my clones that I wish to inhabit."

"So your consciousness can actually hop from body to body? You don't die?"

"That is correct. Regrettably, it is a technique we cannot transfer to other species. And only our highest caste can utilize it."

Rohan sipped more wine. "That is a fascinating story. In fact, I'd love to hear more about it, maybe visit one of your cloning facilities, talk to your theologians and metaphysicians about how this all works. Are you pitching this to me? You looking for investors? Scale up the operation?"

"No, of course not. I am telling you this so you understand that threatening this body," he waved a hand over himself, "with violence will not be an effective or useful action on your part."

"I see. Which leads to my next question, which is, why do you think that I'm about to start threatening you?"

"Because I am going to tell you some things which you will not wish to hear."

"Since you assumed that my response to that is going to be violent, you're either going to piss me off a lot, or you've dealt with a lot of Hybrids before. Or both. It's both, isn't it?"

"Your heritage does bring with it a certain reputation."

"Then don't you think I'll kill you just for the visceral satisfaction of it? Even if you'd wind up coming back later?"

"We are also in the habit of equipping our bodies with high-powered explosives that detonate when our life functions cease. As a deterrent."

"I'm not especially concerned about explosives. Maybe you've heard."

"Your physical resilience does not protect the people around you. If you kill me now, you might survive, but the people dining in the next room would assuredly not."

"Fine, then. Consider me warned that all my violent outbursts will be both pointless and full of negative consequences. Now can you tell me the actual thing you wanted to tell me?"

"Are you aware of your connection to the First Citizen of Lukhor? Or did she not tell you?"

"If by 'she' you mean Tamara, then she did, in fact, mention that her father was an important person on Lukhor. I don't remember her telling me his actual title, but I doubt that's the relevant part of this discussion."

"On the contrary, it is most relevant. Tamaralinth Lastex is the eldest child of First Citizen Eldarinth Lastex of Lukhor."

"So far you've told me some very interesting things about you, and some less interesting things about what you think of me, but very little of interest about either Tamara or her father, other than his title, which frankly doesn't mean very much to me, seeing as how we aren't on Lukhor."

"First Citizen Eldarinth's title is important because it indicates both his very high position in Lukhor society and the extent of the resources he can bring to bear to protect that position."

"Based on the listening comprehension skills I acquired in grade school I'm going to take it that the key word in that sentence is 'resources.'"

The waiter came in with prepared shellfish, one for each of them, drizzled in a delicately sweetened sauce. Rohan ate his while the Shayjh continued.

"Indeed. First Citizen Eldarinth holds his eldest daughter in the highest regard. As such, he believes that only the most qualified suitors are appropriate to engage with her in any kind of romantic capacity."

"Then he and I are in agreement! Cheers!" Rohan raised his wine glass in a feigned toast.

"I do not think that you are. First Citizen Eldarinth does not have the same regard for his daughter's taste in romantic partners."

"Oh, that is very sad."

"This is not an uncommon failing in the young. Between you and me, First Citizen Eldarinth himself had some unfortunate dalliances in his youth."

"Sure. Young people. Crazy."

"While First Citizen Eldarinth is certain that you possess many positive qualities, you are clearly not suited, either intellectually or socially, to match with his daughter. He wanted me to convey to you his sincere desire that you recognize this and cease all contact with Tamaralinth."

"This is . . . I don't even . . . is he serious? Really? Daddy wants me to stay away from his daughter, and he sent a Shayjh Adjudicator to make sure I do it? It's not like she's a kid anymore. I'd kind of get this protective instinct if she were a teenager, but . . . she's a grown woman."

"That does not obviate the fact that her judgment in this matter is lacking."

"You're just going to try to scare off anyone who wants to date Tamara until someone her daddy likes more comes along?"

"That is exactly what I am saying. You see? Perhaps your breed's reputation for poor language skills is undeserved."

"All right, let me play along with this for a minute. How can you be so sure that I'm unsuitable?"

Magdon pointed at Rohan's jumpsuit. "You are a manual laborer. First Citizen Eldarinth makes all important financial decisions for an entire planet. A very rich planet."

"Maybe I just like manual labor. Maybe I'm actually very smart and well educated and I only do this job so my mind is free to think about mathematical theories and philosophical treatises on the structure of society."

Magdon raised one perfect white eyebrow. "Is that the case?"

Rohan shook his head. "No, mostly I think about punching things. Or boobs. A surprising amount of thinking about boobs, actually. I should probably find a new hobby."

"Tamaralinth Lastex is a genius and will inherit her father's position. You cannot be part of that future."

"Let me play along just a bit longer, okay? Let's say, for the sake of argument, let's just say that I agree with what you're saying. We've been on, what, three dates?"

"Four. And one non-date conversation."

"Wow, okay, that was creepy. That you knew that. More creepy than scary, though, you should work on that."

Magdon chewed slowly on his appetizer but didn't answer.

"My charm is so definitely not working on you. My point is, we're not getting married or anything. Isn't this conversation a little premature?"

The Shayjh sighed a small sigh. "That is what we thought as well, right before she married her first husband."

"Ah. I get it. Little lady's a fast mover. Must be hard on her father, I guess, as long as he's sticking to his old-fashioned notions of worthiness."

"It is. I do not assume that you will sympathize with First Citizen Eldarinth's position. You are yourself young and, obviously, not a parent."

"No, definitely not a parent." Rohan felt his own lips tighten. "If you're not expecting me to sympathize, then what's my motivation here to stay away from a woman I find quite delightful? In your eyes, how is this supposed to convince me?"

"I am prepared to offer you a substantial sum of money if you cease any and all interactions with Tamaralinth."

"Seriously? A bribe? I've seen this on TV and it's a bad cliché. Are you going to pass me a slip of paper with the number on it, then pause meaningfully as I unfold the paper and gasp at the sheer quantity of zeros written on it?"

Magdon already had his hand on the table, sliding it forward slowly. "That is the custom."

"There's really a slip of paper under there. There really is! This is kind of fantastic. I mean, I'm not going to take the money, but this will be a great story for me to tell. I mean, I can't thank you enough."

The tall, pale man lifted his hand, revealing a folded slip of paper. "It is customary for you to take it."

"Wait, I forget the trope. Do I open it, then crumple it up and throw it in your face, to signify that even after seeing the amount and being tempted by it, I'm refusing? Or do I crumple it up and throw it without looking, to show that no amount of money could possibly tempt me away from my Tamara?"

"The former is more common than the latter, but it is your choice."

The waiter came in and silently refilled their glasses, then cleared away the plates.

As the door swung shut behind the waiter Rohan continued.

"Let's skip to the part where I haven't taken the money and you have to go to plan B. Which is really plan A, because you must have known that the bribe was never going to work, so your backup plan was your regular plan all along."

"Complying with First Citizen Eldarinth's wishes can bring a great improvement to your quality of life. Certainly greater than any single romantic relationship could offer. To an even greater extent, crossing him can lead to a corresponding detriment."

"A detriment? What, he's going to get me fired? I doubt that, given that Wistful was here and independent before Eldarinth's ancestors invented fire and started giving names to things. Is he going to ruin the financial institutions where I keep my assets and leave me destitute?"

"Perhaps. But I believe you can expect a more direct and immediate response."

"That's your threat? If you're trying to scare me, you're going to have to try harder."

Magdon Krahl snorted.

"You Hybrids are all the same. No imagination."

"The Empire wasn't built on the backs of Hybrids because we're creative. In fact, you could say it was built on the fact that we aren't. But we're tough as hell. So how is your employer going to bring me detriment? I assume you're not threatening Tamara here."

The Shayjh waved his hand dismissively. "Of course not. We will not allow any harm to come to the girl. You are to dissociate from her in a way that ensures the blame is on you. She should never believe any fault is in her, other than her poor choice in men."

"I'm still not seeing the threat here."

"We would not harm Tamara. You do, however, have other friends. I know you have grown close to Doctor Stone. He is no longer as protected as he once was."

"With Hyperion dead."

"Correct. You are also fond of the Ursans. And the station's chief of security."

"So if I don't comply, something will happen to my friends?"

"If it should come to that. I hope it doesn't. Despite our reputation, we are not a cruel race. I would much rather you take the credits and disappear, so no one needs to be hurt."

"Except Tamara. I vanish without explanation, she'll be hurt."

"I meant physically hurt."

The door swung open. Two waiters entered, one carrying a wine bottle and the other bringing the salad course. Both moved with quick, efficient, well-rehearsed motions.

"It doesn't make you nervous to threaten an il'Drach half-breed this way? Given our general love of battle, thirst for revenge, and so forth? You're not afraid I'll come after you or your people?"

"You are welcome to try."

Rohan stabbed into his salad with a fork and ate a mouthful of greens. It was some kind of seasoned seaweed. "I used to intimidate people. I guess I've lost my touch."

"You're not very big, not for a Hybrid. And, let's be frank here; you're a tow chief on possibly the most remote and backward station in the sector. Hardly a spot where one would expect to find a truly dangerous warrior."

Rohan looked down at his left hand. It was clenched into a fist. He loosened it, shaking his fingers, then let out a long, slow breath.

"Let me ask you a hypothetical question, please. Suppose I were a dangerous Hybrid? Say, a former lance secondary of the Empire? Even a former lance primary? Would you hesitate to deal with me this way?"

"If you were a former lance primary or secondary I'm sure I'd be dead by now, consequences be damned. I truly do not mean to wound your pride, but we probably would not have taken this contract if it meant confronting such a person. But I cannot imagine that this knowledge is helpful to you. In fact, I would think quite the opposite."

"Call it intellectual curiosity. I like to know things, even when it doesn't do me any good."

"You are not a typical Hybrid."

"I get that a lot. I am, as you mentioned, sort of a runt by Hybrid standards. I think it affected my psychology."

"Who is your father?"

Rohan shook his head. "We're not good enough friends yet for me to share all those stories."

"Friends? Then I take it you're going to resolve this the rational way?"

Rohan chewed more salad before answering. It was on the salty side but tasted remarkably fresh. He wondered if it was cultivated onboard or shipped in.

"You know, I do have my pride, but I see where you have me in a bad situation. And let's face it, there shouldn't be any real urgency here, correct? How about you give me forty-eight hours to make up my mind. Two days. That will give me a chance to cool my temper and think about this rationally. And, if it comes to it, to come up with a good exit strategy."

"Forty-eight hours?" One perfect white eyebrow rose almost to the Magdon Krahl's hairline.

"Is that an unusual request?"

"Actually, yes, it is."

"See, I've surprised you again! Isn't it delightful?"

The Shayjh sipped at his own wine. "I must admit that it is refreshing."

"Great. In the meantime, I have another request for you, I hope you don't mind."

"Another surprise. What can I do for you?"

"Just a little bit of background research. You see, I didn't introduce myself fully before, because, stupidly, I assumed you knew all about me."

"There is surprisingly little information available about your life before you arrived on Wistful."

"And I'd like to keep it that way. Now I don't blame you for making the assumptions you've made, but I feel bad about moving forward when you don't have all the facts."

"What 'facts' am I lacking, Tow Chief Second Class Rohan?" The Shayjh's tone was heavy with skepticism.

"I was not always a tow chief."

"Indeed."

"Yes. In fact, I was in the Imperial Navy."

"Most Hybrids serve, though most serve for only a short while. There is no shame in it. The job of a lance is quite difficult."

"Yes. Lances, at least successful ones, rarely retire, and when they do retire, it's even more rare that they become tow chiefs on backwater stations."

"That is my understanding."

"But, as you mentioned, I'm atypical for my breed."

"You are."

"So I'm going to properly introduce myself. But only because we're under a privacy shield. And regardless of what else happens, I expect this introduction to be kept confidential."

"Of course."

"I am Tow Chief Second Class Rohan of Earth. Formerly, The Griffin, Lance Primary of the Empire." The Shayjh's face took on a subtle blue tint at the words. "I have other titles, other nicknames. The Tolone'ans use my name as a curse when they get angry enough. The Shayjh, your people, call me the Scourge of Zahad. I honestly can't remember all of them. But that one's worth remembering.

"Let's meet up again in forty-eight hours, during which time I'm going to hope you read up on my history and reconsider this transaction. As in whom is being asked to do what under which threats. And we'll finish this conversation."

"The Griffin? You expect me to just . . . believe you?"

"Look for pictures, do the compares. I used to shave, keep my hair short. But be discreet, Adjudicator Magdon Krahl. Because if I'm not lying, and I find out that people have heard things from you that I don't want them to hear, then you can imagine the consequences. . . . Or maybe you can't. Shayjh, in my experience, aren't really that much more imaginative than Hybrids."

Rohan stood. Magdon Krahl stood with him, his features missing their earlier composure.

"Well, it was a pleasure meeting you, Adjudicator. I haven't seen a living Shayjh in years. Please excuse me, I have to get back to my menial job."

"Yes. Quite."

Rohan turned and left the room.

He walked through the front room, full of traders and businessmen and old friends sharing meals and laughter, making deals or reminiscing about old times.

His face was tight.

His comm pinged with saved messages almost as soon as he stepped outside the private room. The privacy tech had blocked all incoming messaging.

One message was from Wei Li, who wanted him to meet her as soon as possible outside *Insatiable*.

He sighed. Apparently, it wasn't yet time for the hours of manual labor he'd been looking forward to.

21

Earth Toys

"You do not seem yourself, Tow Chief Rohan."

"Who do I seem like, Wei Li? Or is it 'whom'?"

She let out a brief laugh. "Like a man with serious concerns on his mind. Most unlike the casual and even flippant demeanor we have come to expect from our tow chief."

The security chief had met him outside the Ton'ga Shell, apparently not willing to wait for Rohan to reach *Insatiable*. They were crossing the station together.

"You don't look as cheerful as usual, either."

"Please. I am never cheerful. But today I am, perhaps, less cheerful. I do not like this business."

"What business is this exactly?"

She narrowed her eyes at him. "Your business is to stand behind me and be threatening by implication. You need not do anything. We are delivering a message on Wistful's behalf, and it will not be well received."

"We should get a Shayjh to deliver it. That's apparently their specialty."

She turned to him, her head jerking with the sudden lizard-like speed unique to her species. Her scaly green skin shone in the lights over the promenade.

"Why do you speak of the Shayjh?"

"I just had lunch with one. You know anything about them?"

She slowly let her gaze fall away from him. "Yes."

"Any advice? I am on the wrong side of an argument with one and I think I might have already screwed it up."

"How?"

"I threatened him. By telling him something I shouldn't have."

"You threatened a Shayjh?" She laughed, louder, and more genuinely than before. "I would give much to have seen that. You can be pleasantly delightful at times."

"Old habits. And he kind of hurt my feelings."

"Poor Rohan. How did the nasty Shayjh hurt your feelings?"

"It's stupid. I'm being stupid."

"Of course, but that is only to be expected. Which type of stupid was it this time?"

"The type where he was willing to threaten me and wasn't at all scared of the consequences. I got used to people having some measure of, I don't know, not respect exactly, but wariness. Like, people knew not to cross me. Everyone knew. I kind of liked it. More than I realized at the time."

"Having others fear you can be empowering."

"I'm noticing that, now that it's gone."

"It is also inconsistent with forming close personal connections. I believe you have traded up."

They walked side-by-side through the concourse, the usual crowd of people walking to and fro around them, paying them no special attention.

"I wouldn't argue with you. I just sometimes miss the fear. Anyway, any advice for taking on a Shayjh?"

"Yes. Don't. They are a nasty and dangerous race. At least the ones who leave their home planet are."

"Thanks. I'm not sure I'll have a choice."

"The lower caste Shayjh, the clones and drones, are tough but manageable. The higher castes are another story. Sixth Circle and higher. Take care if you have to kill one. They believe their bodies hide secrets to their technology, so they are usually rigged with explosives designed to detonate when they die."

"He actually told me that. I think to prevent me from just killing him outright in the restaurant."

"It is good that you didn't." They reached the elevator. Below them stretched the bay that connected to *Insatiable*'s main entrance.

"What should I do?"

She shrugged. "Shayjh are commercial creatures. If you convince them that they stand more to lose than to gain by facing you, they will alter course."

"That's great advice. Except the guy on the other end of the contract is one of the richest men in the galaxy."

"Money is not the only currency they value."

Rohan nodded as they got into the elevator and descended past Wistful's transport level.

"Why am I here again?"

"You are muscle. You are here to provide an intimidating presence. Wistful has calculated that such a presence is desirable in this situation."

"You know, this isn't actually in my job description. I've been spending a lot of time lately doing non-tow chief things."

Wei Li shrugged. "If you are not willing, refuse. Or demand a bonus. Complaining to me is pointless."

"I know, I know."

They exited the elevator and crossed the open bay to *Insatiable*. As they approached, Wei Li raised her voice and projected it at the ship. "Hail, *Insatiable*."

Insatiable's answering voice echoed through the bay. "Hail, Security Chief Wei Li."

"I believe we are expected."

She was standing straight, shoulders back, as if at attention in a military procession.

"You may board, Security Chief Wei Li. And escort." *Insatiable*'s tone was far more serious than Rohan was expecting.

"Wistful thanks you, *Insatiable*."

Wei Li strode forward through the ship's entrance.

Rohan followed close behind.

A pink humanoid in crisply pressed ship's uniform greeted them just inside the main corridor.

"I am to take you to the captain."

Wei Li inclined her head, her eyes never leaving the crewman. "Thank you."

The ship's officer led them through some corridors and through a short ride in a transport pod. Then he stepped into a medium-sized meeting room and announced them.

"Security Officer Wei Li, and escort."

Rohan felt as if they were being presented at court.

The room held a long conference table. The far side of the table was occupied, so Rohan and Wei Li took seats closest to the door.

The seat to their left held *Insatiable*'s captain. He was another pink humanoid, with a handsome beard of green hair and a hairless pink scalp. He wore a ship's uniform in *Insatiable*'s gray.

The captain nodded toward Wistful's officers. "We need to stop meeting like this." He had been with them while they investigated the secret bay that Wei Li had found on *Insatiable*.

Wei Li nodded. "Hello, Captain. Doctor Stone."

Doctor Marion Stone was seated to the captain's right.

"Security Chief. Tow Chief. You asked for me, I'm here. Keep this short, I have work to do."

Wei Li flashed her a tight smile. "That claim is premature."

A Tolone'an was seated at Doctor Stone's right. His jet-black eyes and the four tentacles extending from around his neck brought unpleasant memories back to Rohan.

He leaned forward suddenly, as if he was about to burst out of his seat.

Dr Stone put a hand on his arm to restrain him. "Exactly what is that supposed to mean?"

Wei Li cleared her throat. "I will come to the point directly. Wistful forbids you from any attempt to alter or open the nascent wormhole for a period of seven days, and possibly indefinitely longer, depending on the results of further study."

The Tolone'ans tentacles twitched in agitation.

Doctor Stone's eyes flashed hotly. She glared first at Rohan, then at Wei Li. "Why?"

Wei Li shrugged her muscular shoulders. "Wistful does not have to give reasons. But I believe she is concerned for the safety of the system should you experiment with these primal forces."

"The Ursans came through and the system was perfectly safe."

Wei Li shrugged. "Doctor Stone, I am not a physicist. I cannot argue with you about the potential consequences of these experiments that I do not even begin to understand. I would, however, like to remind you that Wistful is very, very old, and has significant experience with various issues that far outstrip your own."

"If Wistful has information about the stability or safety of the wormholes, she should be sharing that with me so we can all make this decision together! Not shutting me down!"

Wei Li shrugged again. "Wistful has chosen this path. You are free to dislike it. Your feelings are your own. You are not, however, free to experiment on the wormhole."

The captain was glancing nervously back and forth between the two women, as if unsure of whether or when he should intervene.

The dark blue Tolone'an, who Rohan assumed was Doctor Stone's assistant, finally broke in. "This is wrong. You can't just stop us by force; this system doesn't belong to you. The wormhole doesn't belong to just you, it's a treasure that belongs to this whole sector."

Wei Li looked at him with her cool, vertically slit eyes. "Maybe it is; yes, we can; yes, it does; and again; and I respectfully disagree. This system was deeded to Wistful by the Empire, and she has sole jurisdiction over all objects with an orbital boundary of Toth."

"You mean every object orbiting Toth. Well, I've got news for you—"

"I am well aware that the wormhole does not move in an orbit, but that is not what I said. You can look at the charter; it is very specific. Everything located inside the orbit of the farthest object orbiting Toth."

The Tolone'an stood up and leaned over the table, his tentacles hanging over it. He was broad through the shoulders and heavily muscled, unusually so for a researcher.

"How are you going to stop us, then? Are you going to send *him* after us?" He stabbed a thick blue finger at Rohan. "Is that why he's here? To remind us that we can be forced to comply?"

"Yes, that is exactly why he is here. Given the nature of our previous communications with Doctor Stone it seemed a worthwhile reminder."

Doctor Stone looked at her assistant. "Calm down, Garren."

Her eyes were a pale blue that seemed to grow colder and icier as she spoke. She looked at Rohan. "Is that the message? If we don't do as you say, we'll feel the wrath of a Hybrid?"

Rohan scratched his beard. "I wouldn't say 'wrath.'"

Wei Li put her hand on his shoulder. "He does not speak for Wistful at this time. Though I agree that we did not say 'wrath.'"

Garren spoke again, his voice shaking with emotion. "You can't do this to us. You think every other race and breed is here to just roll over and play dead whenever you ask us to. Well, I'm telling you, that's not the case, and one of these days you'll find out just how much it can cost you to underestimate us."

Rohan leaned over to whisper in Wei Li's ear. "They had bad experiences with Hybrids. In the Rebellion. And on Tolone'a."

Garren focused his black eyes on Rohan. "'Bad experiences'? il'Drach Hybrids wiped out our entire religious caste. I would call that more than a bad experience. Try 'genocide' to start with."

We Li turned her cool gaze to Garren. "Let us refocus. Wistful is responsible for the health and safety of two million souls in this system. She will not compromise their safety so you can get your name on a paper a few weeks or months early. You will cease any attempts to experiment on the wormhole. You may continue passive analysis for as long as you like. Do you understand?"

The scientists didn't answer, but their captain did.

"Please tell Wistful that we understand her request. And thank you for bringing it personally." His green beard twitched.

The station officers stood. Wei Li left, Rohan right on her heels. The same officer who had brought them to the meeting room escorted them back out into Wistful's bay.

· · · · · · · · · ·

O nce they were clear of the entrance Rohan looked at his friend. "I think that went well. Don't you?"

She laughed, some of the tension easing out of her. "You see why I said it would be unpleasant business."

"Yeah, they were pretty angry."

"Anger I can tolerate; this was more. There is a feeling that someone has when they feel they will not get what they think is just, and a different feeling when they are preparing to fight for what they think is just."

"I take it you were sensing the latter. Which means you are going to have to stop them."

She nodded. "It is more difficult because I agree with their position. If Wistful knows of some danger, she should share that knowledge. Otherwise, there seems to be little reason for concern."

Rohan shrugged. "I am not going to give my two cents about who is right and who is wrong here. I have my own problems to deal with."

Wei Li nodded. "Thank you for accompanying me."

They took the elevator back to the concourse level.

Rohan touched Wei Li's shoulder with his fingertips, just enough to get her attention.

"What is it?"

"I don't like that I was asked to do this. Do you understand? I'm a tow chief. I could have gotten security work anywhere in the sector, and gotten paid a lot more to do it. That's not what I wanted here."

"I know, Rohan. I do not know if it helps, but I believe Wistful wanted you here to help Doctor Stone. If she defies Wistful, the best way for Wistful to stop the shuttle would be to destroy it, probably killing everybody on board. Doctor Stone may not believe that Wistful would do that, but you and I know she would. The threat implied by your presence may save their lives."

"Oh, I get that. I didn't say that it was the wrong call, or that I should have refused. I just said I don't like it. I don't want to be that person anymore, but all these things are pushing me in that direction. And it's worse because part of me likes it. It's easier to play the tough guy. It comes naturally."

"I understand. I will try harder to stop asking this of you."

"Thanks. That's all I'm asking for."

It was Wei Li's turn to hesitate. Rohan saw that she didn't walk away, so he waited.

"You are more agitated than usual. With cause, yes, but still, it is not good for you. You should join our workout this evening."

He let out a breath. It was no use trying to argue with a Class Four Empath when she made a claim about one's mental state. "You're not wrong. I should. I'll probably see you later, then."

The security chief nodded, turned, and walked off.

Rohan tapped his comm link. "Wistful, I assume I have ships to bring in?"

"That is correct, Rohan. Only a few."

"Great. I'll be in space in a couple of minutes."

"Yes, Rohan."

"Wistful, I have a question for you."

"Yes."

"The roof is made of plates of unfaceted diamond, right?"

"That is as good a name for the material as any in Drachna. So, yes."

"If something hit the roof very hard, would the plates break or pop open?"

"Hit from the outside or the inside?"

"From the inside."

"The setting is weaker than the plates, by design. They would dislodge before they shatter."

"Okay. How much damage would that do? To the station? Like, depressurization, structural damage to you?"

"If I am aware, I can maintain the atmosphere. If not, then we would lose some atmosphere, but only locally."

"How hard would it be to fix the damage to the setting and the roof?"

"Not very. A few hours of work for a pair of maintenance workers. I would still rather you continued to use airlocks, if possible."

"I plan to. Thanks, Wistful."

He reached his airlock and left the station.

There were an even ten ships to tow, five inbound and five outbound. There was a lot of shuttle traffic, mostly heading out to mine raw materials from the system's outer planets and asteroids, returning with loads of metallic ore or ice.

One shuttle, on an outbound trip, veered close to Rohan's position and killed its outward velocity.

"Hail, Tow Chief." The shuttle was using a tightbeam to converse privately with him. His music turned off automatically when he caught the transmission.

"Hail, the shuttle. What's up?"

The shuttle pilot was a female, possibly a Rogesh by the sound of her voice. "Hey, Tow Chief, just a quick word. I was on a long run to the outer belt. I thought I saw something there, like a shadow across the stars, but my instruments didn't pick up anything. Have you heard of anything like that? Am I getting spacesick?"

Rohan thought. "I've seen something exactly like that myself. You're not crazy, if that's what you're asking me. Security is aware that there might be an issue. I bet they'll figure it out sooner or later."

"Thanks, Tow Chief. That's a relief. I'll see you on the inbound leg."

"Copy that."

The music restarted.

Rohan drifted for several minutes, scanning the stars, straining for a glimpse of an unaccounted-for shadow in his field of vision.

He saw nothing.

"Rohan, the freighter *Black Star* is inbound. Its mass is twenty percent over your usual rating."

"Copy that, Wistful. You want me to try it or should we get a team of shuttles to bring her in?"

"What is your assessment?"

He thought. "I can do it. Send me out."

The freighter was large, but not larger than *Insatiable*.

"Why is that thing so massive?"

Wistful answered. "It's filled to capacity with industrial parts. I'm expanding my manufacturing capacity."

Rohan got to the anchor point and *pushed*. The ship barely moved.

By the time he finally eased *Black Star* into its bay with a gentle kiss of touching metal he was breathing hard and feeling drained.

"Wistful, is there anything else on my docket?"

"No, Rohan, you're done for the day."

"Thanks, Wistful."

He paused, then spoke again. "Hey, Wistful, I had a meeting this afternoon at Ton'ga Shell, in a private room. Were you listening to that conversation?"

"No, Rohan, I was not. I believe you were under a privacy shield."

"Yeah. Have you had dealings with any Shayjh?"

"I have had dealings with every sentient species in this sector. Which includes the Shayjh. But not to any great extent."

"Is it true? That they can hop their spirits from a dying body into a fresh clone?"

"That is my understanding, yes."

"Is there some way to, I don't know, block the transfer? Seal the spirit?"

"Not that I am aware of. Would you like me to make inquiries?"

He considered his answer as he flew toward his airlock. "No. I don't think so. But thanks."

"You're welcome, Tow Chief."

He drifted in space, his back to Toth and the station, eyes on the stars.

"Personal. Which star is Sol?"

"Sol is not presently visible. It is on the other side of Toth."

"I guess it doesn't matter."

He spun and took a leisurely pace back to the station.

· · · • · • · · ·

H e was pulling through his airlock when his comm played the song he associated with Tamara's comm. Rohan took a quick glance at the time. It was just past five in the afternoon. He tapped to answer.

"Hey. Everything okay?"

"Hello. Yes, everything is okay. Should it not be?"

"It's just early. I mean, for you. I thought you'd still be asleep."

"My sleep was interrupted by pleasant dreams. Of you. Now I will ask if you are all right."

"Oh, sure. Everything's fine."

"You do not sound fine. Are you sure?"

He let out a long breath. "Yeah, just had a tiring day. I brought in a ridiculously massive ship just now, and I was afraid I'd tear an arm off Wistful if I made any mistakes. That thing must have had its hold filled with a neutron star."

"Yes, we were waiting on a large shipment of machine parts. They would be very dense."

"Yeah. And I got roped into this confrontation with Doctor Stone, who wants to try opening the wormhole or something. It was just . . . uncomfortable. I guess I'm a little tense."

"Do you . . . need anything?"

"Nah. Actually, is Rinth up? I have something for him."

"Not an Ursan war gauntlet, I hope. He will destroy my apartment if he runs around with such a thing."

Rohan chuckled. "No, no. Something safe and harmless. A toy from my childhood that I thought he might like. I had it made, wasn't difficult."

"He should be getting up soon. He'll eat and be outside if you want to see him. Within an hour."

"Great, great. I need time to get it anyway."

"Are you sure you are all right?"

He hesitated. "Yeah, just stressed. Sorry. Will I see you after your shift?"

He could hear her smile over the comm.

"I will check my busy social calendar and let you know." A pause. "Ah, here we are. Yes, fortuitously for you, I am free in the morning."

He felt himself smiling. She seemed to have that effect on him. "Great. We can have breakfast. We'll go to your favorite place. They can meet your boyfriend."

"Boyfriend? Did you say 'boyfriend'? I fear my Drachna does not cover this word."

"Oh, sorry. Boy toy? Paramour? Lover? I'll say it in Fire Speech if you'd like."

"Wait, you speak the Fire Speech?" Her voice carried genuine surprise.

"Actually, yes. I picked it up on Earth."

"That's quite rare. Will you teach me?"

"I wish I could! You have to be very good at it to actually teach someone else, and I'm not that good. I can barely speak it. I can't read it at all."

"Hm. Still, I am dating a man who speaks Fire Speech. This is very dangerous, yes? I can ask you to say anything in it and you will be unable to lie."

"Hmm. Maybe I should have stopped bragging while I was ahead."

"Oh, no, this is good. 'Why are you late, Rohan?' No more, 'I was held up at work.' Now I will hear, 'I was out drinking with boisterous male friends.' Or, worse yet, 'I was drinking with boisterous female friends.'"

"Hey, when have I ever been late? Your little scenario isn't very fair."

"No, that is true. It is not fair, you are quite punctual."

"Yes, I am. Thank you."

"Is Fire Speech how you first spoke to the Ursans?"

"Yep. I'm not really sure how I would have handled that if all I had was English, Telugu, some Hindi, and Drachna. Their language is completely different to anything I know."

"Does every Hybrid speak the Fire Speech?"

"No, it's rare. To be honest, most Hybrids are not that well educated. Our training is more combat and less linguistics. We speak with our fists."

"We do not often have Hybrids on our world. It is peaceful; the Empire is not worried about us."

"My homeworld isn't even really part of the Empire. We don't officially have space travel yet."

"That sounds very primitive."

"When I was young, the existence of intelligent life on other planets was sort of a myth. Most didn't believe in it."

He had entered his room and was lying on his bed, stretching, his shoes off and his air mask by his side. He *reached* out and lifted a glass of water from across the room, floating it over to his hand.

"So you are certain you are ready for this title of boyfriend?"

He thought about the Shayjh and couldn't keep his tone light anymore. "Sure. Let's talk about this later, okay? I have things I still have to do tonight, so let me go and take care of them."

"Very well, possibly boyfriend Rohan. I will myself get ready for work and make sure my little one remembers to eat breakfast."

"Great, see you later."

22

Getting Things

Rohan sat up, dressed, and splashed water over his face.

"Personal. Is the gift for Rinth ready yet?"

"Yes. Tollan's Things reports that the product is available for pickup."

"Thank you." *Why do I thank the computer?*

Rohan pulled on his boots and hung his mask off his back, so it fell into the hood of his gold and purple jumpsuit. He cursed under his breath, annoyed that he still hadn't found time to pick out nicer clothes. Rinth would give him grief over his wardrobe.

He stepped out into the station hallway.

Tollan's Things was the front end of a small-batch fabrication shop in Wistful's eastern arm. It was off the main promenade, marked by a barely visible sign over a simple door on a corridor inside one block of shops and offices.

A chime rang as Rohan entered. The shop was clean, with little around the spare walls to indicate exactly what kind of things were sold.

Tollan, a slender humanoid who probably could have wandered Earth unnoticed with a little makeup to cover some facial markings and a hat over his pointed ears, sat behind the counter.

"Hey, Tollan."

Tollan grunted and looked up from the screen he'd been studying. "Tow Chief Second Class Rohan. I believe . . . hold on." He tapped at the screen. "Yes, we have an order ready for you. In the back. You picking up?"

Rohan nodded. "I will never understand how you keep this place going with what you charge for things."

"You're complaining that my prices are too low?"

Rohan spread his hands to the side. "No complaints, sir. Just an observation."

The older man grunted. "My name is known in certain circles. I get the really hard jobs, and when I do them, rest assured I charge accordingly. Hold on."

Tollan stood and walked through the store's interior door into the back. He stepped back through it almost immediately.

"Is this supposed to be a weapon? Because if it is, I have to warn you, I followed your design exactly; it's still not very rugged."

Rohan shook his head. "Nothing like that. It's a toy. For a kid. Just like one I used to play with."

The older man nodded and stuck the item in a bag, then pushed it across the counter.

Rohan softly snapped his fingers. "Hey, Tollan, question. Do you know any good tailors on the station?"

"Tailors? You mean . . . armor?"

"No, not 'tailors' with air quotes, I mean actual tailors. Like someone who could fix me up with a suit. If you don't know, that's fine."

"You are standing in the best tailor shop on Wistful. Maybe in this half of the sector."

"Seriously?" Rohan looked around the shop, noting with his eyes the distinct absence of mannequins, clothing samples, fabric, or the other accoutrements one would expect of a place that made clothes.

"What do you need? You want the uniform taken in?"

"No, I wouldn't dare. The uniform is fine, what I need is civilian clothes. You know, if I want to go on a date. Or to a party."

Tollan raised an eyebrow. "Tastes vary dramatically from place to place. You want to look good for an Earther? I'd have to do some research."

"Not many Earthers around to impress, so no, that's not what I was thinking. Can you make me look good to a Lukhor? Or if not good, then at least acceptable?"

Tollan nodded. "I can do that. What do you need, a suit? Two?"

Rohan shrugged. "I have practically nothing right now. How about you fix me up with three complete outfits, all the way to the shoes. Can you do that?"

"I can, but it won't be cheap. Five thousand credits."

Rohan didn't hesitate to answer. "Done. When can we get started? You know, measuring and all of that?"

The shopkeeper pointed toward the ceiling. "You've already been measured. I'll message you when it's done. Same account?"

Rohan nodded. He felt good about getting something done. "Great. Any idea of a timeframe?"

"You'll have to see how inspired I'm feeling. Shouldn't be more than a couple of weeks. Maybe less."

Rohan nodded. "Thanks." He picked up his bag and left the store.

It didn't take him long to find Rinth, kicking a ball with some other children in the wide grassy walkway in front of his building.

One of the other children noticed Rohan first and pointed him out. They moved a few dozen meters farther along and continued their game.

"Hey, Rinth."

"Hey, Rohan. What's up? We're in the middle of a game."

"Sure, sure. Actually, I got you something."

The Lukhor boy's eyes opened wide. "My gauntlet?"

"No, sorry, not that. Here, take a look." He handed the bag over.

Rinth opened the bag and pulled out a concave plastic disc as far across as his forearm was long. He turned it over in his hands. "What is it? Is it a plate? I don't need a plate."

"It's a frisbee. I guess there's no Drachna word for it. Here, hand it to me, then run that way about ten meters."

The boy followed instructions. Rohan gently tossed him the frisbee. Rinth plucked it out of the air like a seasoned professional.

"What are you supposed to with it?"

"You throw it back and forth. Play catch. You can throw it different ways, make it arc all over. Here, throw it back. No, put your finger along the edge. There you go."

They tossed the frisbee around for a few minutes.

"Fun?"

"Yeah! It's pretty cool. Not nearly as cool as an Ursan gauntlet would be, but pretty cool."

"Good. Well, it's yours. You can play with your friends. As far as I can tell, that's the only frisbee in the entire il'Drach Empire."

"Will you come and play sometimes?"

"Absolutely, I will. You're a quick learner; I bet you'll be better than me before you know it."

"I think I'm already better than you." Rinth smiled.

Rohan laughed. "I gotta go. I'll see you next time, all right?"

Rinth nodded. "See ya."

The Hybrid headed for the station's center.

Wei Li's gym was deep in the bowels of the administrative section, tucked into areas mostly closed off to civilians. The door cycled open for Rohan as he approached.

The security chief herself was in the middle of the sparring floor, lightly trading strikes with a massive gray-skinned Rogesh. Rohan didn't recognize him. He walked to the edge of the sparring area and waited for a break in the action.

Wei Li danced around the Rogesh, peppering him with punches and knee strikes as he lumbered after her, trying to grab onto something. She evaded every attempt with ease.

After a few exchanges she held up a hand to stop him. "Enough, for now." She turned to Rohan. "I am glad you are here, Rohan. This is Tamtam; he is a new hire. Tamtam, this is Tow Chief Second Class Rohan."

Rohan shook the newcomer's hand.

She continued. "Rohan, Tamtam is a Painted Trunk in Rogesh grappling."

Rohan whistled. "That's impressive."

The men grappled, the difference in physical strength proving too much for the Rogesh to overcome with technique. Time and again the Hybrid tossed the much heavier Rogesh to the ground. Tamtam was breathing heavily, his eyes wide with frustration, when Wei Li stopped them.

"Good. You look tired, you are dismissed. Tomorrow you must begin preparing for the licensing tests."

"Yes, ma'am." He took a deep breath. "Tow Chief Rohan, thank you for the instruction."

Rohan nodded. "Anytime."

They waited for the Rogesh to close the gym doors behind him. Rohan looked at his friend. "A lesson needed to be learned?"

She grunted. "Males. Always believe they know everything. He could believe in a faster person outmaneuvering him but could not believe anyone could just be stronger. I thought, who else to give this lesson than our tow chief?"

"Glad to help."

She peered at him from the corner of her vertically slit eye. "You are not quite yourself today."

He shrugged. "Lots of stress."

"You have not been meditating. You should. Twice a day, fifteen minutes. Say your mantra."

Rohan sighed. He couldn't argue with her. He *had* been skipping meditation. "I have a hard time doing it when things are crazy."

"When things are crazy is when you need it the most. You know this."

"I know, okay? I do. I'll try harder."

Rohan sat for the fifteen minutes. Stray thoughts would not stay away. Wei Li clapped to indicate the end of the sitting session.

"Are you ready?"

He shrugged. He didn't feel calm or focused. "To train? I guess."

She nodded. "Suppress your Power."

"Right." Rohan took a deep breath. "Hey, you remember when we first tried this?"

"I do."

"I knew it was possible. I had a martial arts teacher on Earth, a guy named Spiral. When the Wedge attacked New York they killed his father. After that he became obsessed with becoming stronger. He went to every corner of the Earth looking for training techniques, spiritual techniques, everything."

"It seems that would make him an excellent choice for a teacher. I would enjoy meeting him."

"Yeah, next time I go home I'll bring you. We can make a vacation out of it. I'll show you all the nice places."

"Is Earth so lovely?"

"Parts of it. Anyway, most Hybrids never even try to suppress their Power. Spiral thought I'd be stronger if I knew how to hold back my strength."

"Now I am sure I would enjoy the company of this Spiral person."

"He'd like you, too."

"The young species often fall into this trap of thinking that development is linear. One desires to be strong? Train your strength. It goes up, little by little. Eventually you are stronger."

"That doesn't sound wrong. Is it?"

"It works only in the short term, which is why it seems right to the young. They only know the short term. But real growth is a helix. One must train a quality, push and develop it for a while. Then reverse course and train its opposite, develop the other side. Then bring the two qualities together into a new thing. Climbing all the while."

"A helix. Thesis, antithesis, then synthesis."

She considered. "Those are good terms. You have trained linearly for fifteen years. Pulling through more of your Power, more strength, harder strikes, faster movement. There is nothing wrong with it, but at some point you have to stop developing the Hybrid side and work on that weak human side. Develop some of your softness."

"Which is what we're doing. This will make me stronger?"

"Once you learn to integrate the two sources of Power again, yes. But to develop the human side, you have to put aside your il'Drach Power for a bit."

She led him through a long workout, beginning with technical work on the heavy bag, then some basic partner drills to practice slipping punches and checking kicks to the legs.

An hour later Rohan was breathing heavily, his uniform soaked with sweat.

"I forgot how hard this is without Power."

Wei Li nodded. "It is doubly hard for you. It takes energy to suppress your Power, which adds to the burden of the physical work."

"Do I get a break now?"

She shook her head. "Now we do some conditioning."

The nausea surprised him. He hadn't gotten nauseous from pure physical work in so many years.

"I'm sure that's enough. It wouldn't be fair to everyone else if I got into even better shape."

Wei Li shook her head. "Stop the complaining. Move to the heavier ball. As fast as you can now, lift it overhead, toss it, catch it with arms extended, then slam it into the ground . . . Good. No, that one was too slow. Faster."

Soon he was gasping for air. "This. Is. Ridiculous." He felt a touch of anger, his Power scraping at his consciousness like a cat scratching at the door of its cage, asking to be let free.

He *shoved* it down.

She snapped her fingers. "That's what you needed. Right there."

"Isn't there an easier way to teach me this?"

"This is the safest way. The fact that this practice also involves significant physical suffering for you is just an added bonus."

"Bonus for whom?"

"Why, for me, of course."

Rohan laughed, then coughed. "Lord Rudra's braids, I almost puked. Don't make me laugh."

"Very well. Now, ten more ball slams and you are done."

Rohan completed the exercise, though by the last repetition the ball moved as if he was submerged underwater.

"You may now collapse."

He followed that last instruction with enthusiasm.

Wei Li left him on the floor, gasping for air. She returned moments later with a bottle of water.

"Here. Drink."

He drank greedily. "Oh, that was brutal." He drank more, between large gulps of air.

"Rohan, I believed meditation and rigorous physical work would calm your spirit. I see that it has not. Much as it pains me to ask this, do you want to *talk* about what's bothering you?"

"That's turning out to be one of the downsides of the whole secret past thing. It's hard to find people to talk to. Who will understand where I'm coming from."

"Again, this pains me to say, but I will understand." She tapped the center of her forehead. "The burden of a Class Four Empath. I always understand. Almost always."

"Right. Right." He sighed. "To be honest, it's nothing terrible going on in my life. It's just a handful of issues that I'm not equipped to handle."

"What does that mean?"

"I keep running into things that I can't punch and kill my way out of. Marion Stone getting ready to break curfew. A Shayjh I literally can't kill."

"Yes, see, we have something in common after all. I have reports of a shadow in space that I must investigate, yet no idea what that could mean or how to go about it. Why can I not face a ring of drug smugglers or organized sentient trafficking? Perhaps an old-fashioned extortion ring."

"You should go to Earth, we have tons of that stuff. You'd be a hero."

She shrugged. "I have no desire to become anybody's hero."

He drained the last drops out of the water bottle. "What do you plan to do with the 'shadow in space' problem?"

"We will deploy an extensive network of active sensors. It will be a burden on Wistful to process all the data, but she can manage temporarily."

"Gather information. Like a soft jab. You throw it out just to see how the other guy reacts."

"Yes, something like that."

"You need any help moving those sensors into place?"

She shrugged. "Wistful will tell you. This is not my area of mastery, if you understand."

His breathing had resumed its normal cadence. He ran a forearm over his face, wiping off a layer of sweat.

She continued. "Anything else you need to lift from your torso?"

"Get off my chest? I don't know. I have another whole day to figure out what to do about the Shayjh. Hey, maybe you can help me with that. You know anything about their body jumping? How they move their spirit to another body so they don't die?"

"I know a little. My people consider ourselves just as advanced as the Shayjh, though in very different directions."

"Cool. You know the range on that trick? How far away the clone can be, before it doesn't work?"

"I do not. Not exactly."

"I don't need exact, I need the vaguest of estimates. Like, can they jump to other planets? Systems? Galaxies?"

She paused. "Such a technique should not work between systems. There are things in the deep of space, in the darkness between stars, which would make it very hazardous. Having said that much, could it work between planets insystem? That I truly do not know."

"Thanks. That's actually enough. I should go, eat something. Get some rest."

"Yes, you should. Center yourself, Rohan. I suspect things will become busier before they return to normal."

23

The Dreadnought

She had switched to his right side, her head on his shoulder. He was taking full advantage of the fact that she was pushed up high enough on him that he could reach her buttocks with his hand.

Her chin dug into his collarbone as she played with his chest hair.

"You are subdued today. Has the spark already fled this relationship? Are you finding this no longer exciting? Oh, the monotony of it all. We eat great food, rush back to your lovely bed with very expensive linens, and enjoy knee-liquefying sex together. How very bored you must be."

He shook his head and smiled. "No, nothing to do with you. With us. I'm sorry, Still working through some things from yesterday."

"I shall forgive you as long as this is not the beginning of a pattern of such behavior."

"No, I promise."

He traced the patterns of contrasting darker green that dotted her back. She giggled and squirmed gently when he hit a ticklish spot.

"Sorry."

"I am fine. It's a nice spot, just, not so much."

"Okay."

"I am to tell you that Rinth enjoyed his flying disc."

"Oh, great. Frisbee. I'm glad."

"He *might* have forgotten the promise of an Ursan war gauntlet. But I am not sure."

"Well, if push comes to shove I know a guy who can make him one."

"Then let us hope that push and shove stay well clear of one another."

"I'll hope. Listen, Tamara." He hesitated.

"Yes?"

"May I ask a personal question?"

"Yes. And no, I was not faking it, and yes, size does matter, but not to the exclusion of all else."

"That's actually not what I was going to ask. But thanks for the updates, anyway."

"Then what?"

"I want to ask about Rinth's father. How your marriage ended."

The softness in her tone evaporated. "What about it?"

"Well, I know he left you two. But before that, were things good? Or were things not good?"

"Why do you ask me this?"

He took a deep breath. "I like you. A lot. I want to know how things have gone wrong with you before so I can avoid those kinds of mistakes. Also, maybe I'm a little worried that you still have feelings for him."

Her voice stayed cold, but she answered. "If you seek answers about that relationship, I cannot help you. To my mind we were quite happy until, without explanation or reason, he left us. If you're worried that I will return to him, do not. I cannot forgive what he did."

"So you were happy, then suddenly . . . gone?"

"Yes. Suddenly gone. It was not a good time. Luckily, I am not the sort of woman who depends on her man to care for her. I was not *lost* without him. But it was not a good time, either."

"Okay. Sorry. I'm sorry. That sounds shitty." Rohan's heart felt like a lump of molten lead in his chest.

"Was that the answer you wanted?"

"I don't know if 'wanted' is the word I'd use. I *needed* to know."

"Well, now you do." She disengaged from his arm and stood. "I will get back now. I believe you were going to share coffee with your friend Benjamin Stone."

"Look, I'm sorry."

She sighed, then bent over and kissed his forehead. "I am not angry, just no longer in a cuddling mood. Thoughts of my former husband do that to me. I will be back to myself soon."

"Okay. Look, I'll make it up to you. I'm just not sure how."

She sighed and put on a soft smile. "I will think of something you can do. Later."

"Anything you want, Tamaralinth Lastex."

"I will take you at your word, Tow Chief Second Class Rohan."

Rohan laid in bed and watched her dress and leave.

I might never see this again. Depending on how things go with the Shayjh.

He showered and dressed, then tapped his comm. "Wistful, what does the docket look like? How many ships have I got queued up?"

"Very few, Tow Chief. We have two approaching, neither is ready for you yet."

"Okay."

He headed out.

· · · · · • · • · · ·

"R Rohan!"

Rohan half stood and waved as the professor walked to his table.

He was at one of several tables strewn about the walkway outside the café, right up against the hustle and bustle of traffic along the station's east arm.

The lanky older man folded himself into a seat and gestured for a coffee. "How are things, Professor?"

Ben shook his head. "I can't complain. How are you feeling?"

"All healed. Something to thank Dad for."

"Quite right. How's the coffee? You're sure you didn't know about this place? I thought when I discovered it, that for sure you'd been here."

Rohan took another sip of the hot liquid. "I didn't, but you're right, it's good." He leaned forward and lowered his voice. "Next time I'll take you to Pop's. Even better."

Ben lifted his eyebrows in surprise. "Better? I'll consider that a date."

"I won't tell your wife."

"She wouldn't notice anyway. She's totally absorbed in her work. Again."

"It's that obsessive work ethic that saved the Earth on more than one occasion, if I remember my comic books correctly."

"Saved the world? Yes, sometimes. Much more often it was just annoying."

"I can imagine. Is that what you wanted to talk about? Your wife?"

"Well, in part. You see—"

Rohan's comm burst on at unusually high volume. "Tow Chief Rohan, there is a situation developing."

The Hybrid held up a hand to Ben, cupping his other hand over his ear.

"What is it, Wei Li? Ursan riot? Another explosion on *Insatiable*? Did we find the mysterious space shadow?"

"There is an Imperial dreadnought on course to break the beacon perimeter planetside. It is not responding to hails."

Rohan stood, knocking his chair to the ground. He looked at the professor.

"Rudra's braids! Professor, cover my tab. I'll pay you back. Emergency."

The professor was standing, a quizzical expression on his face, as Rohan *lifted* up into the air.

He pulled his mask from his hood and sealed it to his face, the air supply hissing awake as he lifted his arms up to absorb the impact with the roof.

The unfaceted diamond roof over the promenade was about fifty meters above the grass. It took him less than a second to strike it, directly on a seam where two large plates of the transparent material met.

The seam burst, the two plates of diamond popping outward.

Without slowing, Rohan emerged into the vacuum and accelerated in earnest. Projections immediately appeared in his display, showing him the way to the dreadnought.

"Wistful, Wei Li, whoever. What ship is this?"

The security chief answered. "Auto response to pings says she is *Fathers' Vengeance*. Do you know her?"

I served on her.

"I know her. She puts the 'dread' in dreadnought. Typical ship killer, but with a mean streak. Standard armaments: battering rams, grapples, heavy armor. Enough high yield nukes to sterilize a planet."

"Is that all?"

"She has a lance deck for five. Two primaries, three secondaries. Which isn't to say she has five Hybrids on board right now, but that's her allotment."

"Still not responding to hails."

"Don't you have a treaty with the Empire? I thought they promised not to pull stunts like this."

"We do. Reason dictates that the il'Drach Empire would not break their word with an attack like this, given their general disposition. My scanners, however, are not agreeing with those dictates."

Rohan had been at maximum acceleration from the moment he touched vacuum. He focused and opened wide his third eye, trying to *feel* the energy of the living warship.

"How did you not see her coming?"

"We believe she opened a gate inside the orbit of Toth 3."

"That's a risky move. Why bother?"

Gates close to strong gravitational sources, like stars, were inherently unstable. It was the reason ships almost always approached Wistful from the outer edges of the Toth system.

"I do not have an answer for you, Rohan. What do you suggest we do?"

"I'll go punch a hole in her, then try to talk this out. If she has five lances, and they board Wistful, just stay out of their way and try to minimize casualties. Nothing on board is going to stop them."

"Should you not reverse the order of actions? Talk *before* damaging her?"

"Nah. Ships like these? You have to convince them you're serious first. Then they might listen to what you have to say. Let's see if she remembers me."

Wistful's voice broke in. "Rohan, you do not have to do this."

He grunted. "Yeah, I do. But I know what you mean."

He flew an arc around Toth 3, on a path to intercept the incoming warship.

"I still can't *feel* her."

A long pause before Wei Li responded.

"Neither can I. But sensors indicate she is close to your location."

Rohan decelerated and looked. "I'm not seeing anything."

"Perhaps she has some stealth technology? It could be a recent upgrade."

His sensors showed him that the ship was close.

"Do you have active sensors out here? Something that's not going to be thrown off by a coat of black paint? I can't see her."

"We are moving some into position but it will take time. Most of the available sensors are farther out in the system. Because of that other matter."

To look for the space shadow.

Wei Li spoke again. "Now there is another issue. A shuttle has taken off from *Insatiable*. It's accelerating at its maximum capacity toward the wormhole."

"Of course it is. *Fathers' Vengeance* is probably here for exactly that reason. Make a diversion so the shuttle can slip away. You want me to turn around, chase the shuttle?"

"The dreadnought seems to be the more pressing concern."

Rohan let out a slow breath, held his lungs empty, and spun in place, squinting as he tried to locate the Imperial dreadnought by eye.

He opened a broadband channel. "Hail *Fathers' Vengeance*. This is Tow Chief Second Class Rohan. Imperial Navy, retired. What is your intention in this system?"

No response.

"Wei Li, how is this even possible? I don't see or *feel* anything."

"We haven't ruled out the possibility of stealth tech."

"Then how are your scanners picking it up?"

"That is odd. Hold on."

He flew quick loops around the position the dreadnought was supposedly occupying, keeping the background stars in sight. If the ship was too black to see it should still occasionally block the sky behind it.

A new voice on the comms. "Shuttle is advancing quickly on the wormhole. Not answering hails."

Rohan grunted. "Still not seeing anything. This is too convenient."

A pause before Wei Li answered. "We have techs investigating now. Hold your position."

"I think I should be going after that shuttle. Maybe the dreadnought left? Flew in to distract us, then took off?"

"It is still present on scanners. No, correction. The image is a phantom. Somebody inserted it into the scanners from inside the station."

"So I'm chasing a ghost?"

Her voice tightened. "Yes. Which shouldn't be possible. Nevertheless."

"You want me to go after the shuttle now?"

"Please."

Rohan oriented himself, using the mask's heads-up display to find the right path to the wormhole, and shot himself along it. "On path to intercept the shuttle."

"It is refusing tightbeam comms. We have them on an open channel, I'm patching you into it now. Perhaps you can instill some sense into them. Or some fear."

"Assume I can't talk them down. Will I reach them in time?"

"If they're trying to do a flyby, then no. If they need to slow down and reduce their velocity relative to the wormhole to run their experiment, then you'll catch them."

"Which is it?"

"I do not know for certain, Tow Chief Rohan. Does it matter?"

"I guess not."

A moment later the open channel came over his comms. A group of voices were pouring through, mostly faint background noise, a few with greater clarity.

The first voice on the open channel was Wistful's. "I repeat, return to dock immediately or you will be subject to fire."

The answer came from Doctor Stone. "This is an il'Drach Imperial shuttle attached to the Science Research Vessel *Insatiable*. We are on

Imperial business. Any action taken against us will be a declaration of war against the Empire."

A voice Rohan didn't recognize came over the speaker.

"That's not—" It was cut off abruptly.

Wistful again. "This system is recognized as independent by the il'Drach. I have sole authority here. Turn back."

He cleared his throat. "Doctor Stone, please stop this. We'll work together, figure something out. Wistful didn't say you can never work on the wormhole, just not right now. Let's make sure it's safe first."

The channel from the shuttle snapped open again. "You know full well she'll never let us open that wormhole, mule. You're just not used to anybody refusing to follow your orders, are you? You think your Powers mean you get to be in charge. Of everything."

"That's not what I'm saying, Doctor Stone. Professor. Please, I don't want to hurt anybody."

"Oh, I'm sure you don't. Because compassion is a well-known Hybrid trait, isn't it?"

"I'm not just half il'Drach, Doctor Stone. I'm also Canadian, eh? I really don't want to hurt you."

A separate channel, just for him, cut in with Wei Li's voice. "Rohan, you are closing on them. They have turned and are decelerating rapidly. It appears as if they do need to be at relative rest to the wormhole."

The open channel resumed.

Wistful was speaking. ". . . within my rights to destroy your vessel if you do not turn around now."

Doctor Stone responded. "You wouldn't dare. You won't risk it. And we won't stop just for that mule. We're not as helpless as you think."

Rohan cleared his throat. "Doctor Stone, I'm going to catch you. This is pointless."

"You think so? Just what I'd expect from one of *you*. Assume that you're going to get here and have your way with us? Because there's no possible way we could resist your Power, you almighty superbeing?"

"Look, I'm sorry if I offended you. I'm not that tough, as Hybrids go. Maybe I just don't want you to hurt me, okay?"

"Don't patronize me, Rohan. You're very powerful, yes. But you grew up on stories about Hyperion, didn't you? Who was always at his side, figuring things out, telling him where to go and how to apply all that strength?"

"I remember, Doctor."

"You think I didn't expect this? You think I just lost my temper and stormed off in this shuttle without a plan?"

"I never said that, Doctor Stone." A blinking dot appeared on Rohan's mask display as he closed the distance between himself and the shuttle.

"You were thinking it, though. I know how you see the world. You see a ship, you don't even care if it has weapons, if there's no Hybrid aboard, it's unarmed. It's like those of us without Powers don't even matter. We aren't *counted*."

She wasn't wrong. "That's a military calculation; a threat assessment. Just because someone isn't a military threat doesn't mean they don't matter. That's never been my attitude, my belief."

"Still patronizing me. I was at ground zero of the Rebellion; that's exactly their attitude. Hybrids should rule the Empire, why? Because you're the strongest. Well, maybe you aren't."

Wei Li cut in on Rohan's feed. "Something exited the shuttle, Rohan."

"What? A missile?"

"I don't believe so. Metallic, but the shape is humanoid."

He rejoined the open channel. He could almost see the shuttle, shining in the starlight. And near it, a fleck of motion.

"Doctor Stone, your shuttle appears to be losing parts of itself. You might want to have that looked at."

Her voice was cold, with an overtone of mockery. "Rohan, I'll call you Rohan for now."

What does that mean?

"Be my guest."

"I wasn't asking permission. Rohan, my husband is a good-hearted person. After the Rebellion, he set aside his anger and his rage and moved on with his life. Unfortunately for you, I'm not so kind. So while dear Benjamin continued with his research, I became a little bit obsessed with the past. With the harm the Hybrids did. To me, to my friends. With preventing that harm.

"When we were young, we trusted in Hyperion to protect us. That in the end, the strongest, toughest guy out there was on our side. But Hyperion isn't around anymore, is he? And the strongest, toughest guys aren't always on our side."

The fleck of motion was rapidly growing larger as it moved toward Rohan. It was metallic, certainly no bigger than an Ursan. And fast.

Wei Li spoke in his ear. "Fragment rapidly approaching your position, Rohan. Appears humanoid."

Rohan had to start slowing himself to avoid overshooting the shuttle.

"I'm not against you, Doctor. I'm not your enemy."

"I believe *you* think that. I know you're wrong. Last time, when the Rebellion started, I didn't think Hybrids were my enemy, but *I* was wrong. Full circle. That time, I wasn't prepared. This time, I am ready. *We* are ready."

24

Iron Squid

The metallic object closed on Rohan. It approached at a velocity that shocked him, on a collision course with the Hybrid's own path.

Just before they crashed Rohan rolled out of the way.

It was humanoid, both in shape and size, little bigger than Rohan. Its surface was metallic, mostly silver but with matte black accents under the arms and on the outside of the legs. There was a lump, semispherical, jutting out from the figure's upper back.

The helmet included four struts, two in front and two in back. Arranged where a Tolone'an's tentacles would be.

The figure shot past Rohan but immediately turned a tight arc and headed back toward him.

Rohan yelled into his comm, "Is there a person inside that thing? I don't want to kill anybody."

Doctor Stone answered him. "This is a terrible cliché, saying this, but you should worry less about harming Garren and more about what he's going to do to you."

"Garren? Your assistant? He's inside that thing? You sent someone after me in powered armor? You *have* to know better."

Garren had reversed course and gotten back to Rohan's position before the Hybrid could say more.

Rohan reached out a hand and *sent* a wave of energy to disable the armor.

"I hope that suit has good passive life support because I'm about to demolish its mechanicals. And the same is going to happen to that shuttle if you don't turn it around."

The wave broke cleanly over it, as if the armor were itself alive, or part of a living thing.

Garren's distinctive accent broke over the comms. "I know every last micrometer of this armor and its circuitry, Hybrid. It's as much a part of me as that mask or that uniform is a part of you. You're not going to find this so easy."

Rohan cursed under his breath. No regular soldier could assimilate complex mechanicals into his metaphysical sense of self, but a highly trained engineer was obviously a different story.

Wei Li spoke. "They're closing on the wormhole, Rohan. You need to do something soon."

He spun and *reached* out to stop the shuttle, but before he could aim his wave of energy he was yanked sharply backward, then struck hard in the lower spine.

"Faster than you thought!"

Rohan spun again and tried to grab the armored researcher, but some force pulled them apart rapidly, as if they were falling away from each other. By the time Rohan had compensated, Garren was well out of reach and the shuttle was again closing on the wormhole.

"You can't possibly have a reactor in there. Which means you're operating on stored energy. You can't keep this up for long!"

"Luckily, I don't need long."

Something changed. The two combatants fell toward one another as if a black hole had opened up between them.

Garren was prepared, and he caught Rohan with a solid punch to the sternum, the fist driven with all the strength of the armor added to their combined speeds. The Hybrid's ribs cracked with the impact.

"Oof." Rohan grimaced.

Before he could strike back, they were falling away from one another again.

"Gravity. You're creating point gravitational sources. Like a bootstrap drive." Breathing hurt, but his lungs weren't punctured. Small victories.

"You're smarter than the average Hybrid. Too bad that isn't saying much."

Rohan set aside the pain in his ribs and drove himself forward, into Garren's position. Before he could reach, the gravitational source shifted and they fell away from one another at right angles to Rohan's path.

Without pause, Rohan pointed at the shuttle and sent another wave of energy toward it.

Garren's projected gravitational source pulled him to the side, but not quickly enough.

The next voice came from the shuttle. "We're hit! Drives are failing! One drive online! Reactor one is offline! Backup reactors engaging."

"Damn Hybrid! Your fight is with me!"

"Actually, it isn't. I'm just here to stop that shuttle. What is your problem, Garren? You know this is going to fail."

"I know who you are, what you did on Tolone'a. I was there, Rohan. Or should I call you by another name?"

The armored man redirected the gravity and pulled Rohan toward himself again. The pair fell together with dizzying speed.

Rohan was prepared for the punch that was coming. He twisted to his right and back as they were about to collide, stabs of pain lancing through his ribs with the effort. He lashed out with a knee, catching Garren above the hip.

The metal dented visibly but held under the strike.

Garren's cry of pain went out over the comms.

"Hurts, doesn't it? I imagine you don't take a lot of kicks to the liver at any of your classes or research symposiums."

Doctor Stone took back her comms. "Garren! Stop him! Don't worry about us!"

Rohan sent another wave of energy toward the shuttle, but it jerked out of the way.

Garren closed on him again, flickering the gravitational source between them erratically so Rohan couldn't time his approach.

"You killed women and children when you wiped out the religious caste on Tolone'a! You slaughtered my people, you monster! Don't deny it!"

The armored humanoid landed another punch, but at a much lower relative speed. Rohan took the blow and caught the outstretched arm.

"This is not the time to discuss the Tolone'an war. I *saved* your people by taking out the leaders who refused to surrender. If not for me the il'Drach would have nuked it until the last drop of water boiled away."

He gripped harder, trying to penetrate the outer layer of the armor, but it was strong and hard to grip. After a moment he changed tactics and spun them both furiously.

"What are y— " The words were choked off.

Let's see how much centrifugal force Tolone'ans can handle before they pass out.

Garren twisted and squirmed, then lashed out with a kick to Rohan's broken ribs that caught with enough force to dislodge the Hybrid's grip.

The two flew apart.

"This won't get you revenge! Let me take that shuttle back in before anybody else gets hurt!"

Marion Stone was shouting. "We're not giving up! We haven't forgotten the Rebellion! We deny your authority over us. You don't get to be our boss just because of who your father is!"

"Stop with the Rebellion! I wasn't even part of it!"

"You think I don't know that? You think I don't know who you are? *What* you are? What you did during the Rebellion? You think the truth makes me *less* afraid of you?"

Rohan felt a sinking feeling in his stomach. He *sent* another pulse after the shuttle, but it was still evading and he missed. He streaked toward it to stop it manually.

"Please, I'm just trying to help."

Doctor Stone wasn't listening. "Help? Do you want me to be grateful? Oh thank you, great Griffin, thank you for ending the Hybrid Rebellion. For killing their leaders. Thank you for preserving the Empire. Thank you for saving us from our own foolishness, trying to open this wormhole."

The wormhole was close, a huge reflective disk floating in space.

"Doctor Stone, this is an open channel. Please don't."

"Oh, my husband thinks you're great. So nice. You eat his donuts, get him coffee. How do you think he'd look at you if he knew what the Fathers thought of you? If he knew how their voices quake when they talk about you?"

"Please don't."

He was almost at the shuttle when Garren crashed into him, knocking him off course.

The armored man had both arms around Rohan's waist.

The Hybrid, reacting out of instinct, grabbed the armored suit's head and twisted.

Metal and seals popped and hissed at the armor's neck. A puff of gas escaped.

The gravity source between them shifted rapidly and they fell away from one another.

"You walk around like a hero. You think you're the next Hyperion, only he never saved the whole Empire, did he? He never squashed an entire army of Hybrids. You seemed reluctant, sure, retired right after and left the Empire behind. But the truth is you liked it, didn't you? The others picked on you, thought you were weak. You showed them. Well, today I'm going to show you, take control myself. Give you a little window into victimhood.

"Fire the key!"

Rohan pushed himself toward the shuttle as hard as he could, but he couldn't reach it. Something happened at the shuttle, a separate gravity source pulsing with an odd arrhythmic sequence. It pulled, pushed, pulled again, with varying intensities.

He faced the wormhole. A circular mirror with a stone frame that stretched a kilometer across, hanging impossibly in space, defying both gravity and the laws of orbital mechanics.

He'd seen it before, flown near it before. But never glowing with a brilliant white light.

"This is not good."

Wei Li spoke. "Rohan! Get clear. Wistful is going to vaporize that shuttle."

"It's too late, Wei Li. The wormhole is opening. You'd better leave them alone. If this thing goes wrong, Doctor Stone is one of the few people alive who might be able to help us fix it."

The glow intensified, then shifted to blue, then into something out of the visual spectrum. The mirror folded back on itself, opening a tear in the fabric of space.

The shuttle reversed course and backed away from the open wormhole. Garren clamped hands over the neck of his armor and drifted, none of his earlier speed or power on display.

Rohan floated and stared.

The stone frame of the wormhole was unchanged.

A view onto a strange planet, blue and Earth-like, flanked by a pair of yellow suns, filled the space where the mirror had been. Around the planet were an array of stars in unfamiliar patterns, vast nebulae glimmering in the distance.

Wei Li spoke. "Rohan, are you all right?"

"Yeah, I guess. It's actually pretty cool."

"Don't go near it. We don't know what will happen."

He sighed. "I know. I'm sorry, Wei Li. I messed up."

Doctor Stone's voice came again, shaky with adrenaline. "You see? We opened a dormant wormhole. And you couldn't stop us. Secret hero of the Empire, favorite and most-feared son of the Fathers. Yet here you are, foiled by a senior citizen former sidekick and five graduate assistants."

"Doctor Stone, you'd better rescue your assistant. I popped the seals on his suit and from what I remember Tolone'ans don't like breathing vacuum."

"Damn, he's losing air. We can't maneuver precisely enough to catch him; our drives are damaged!"

Rohan sighed. He flipped to a private link to Wistful.

"Wei Li, was Doctor Stone talking on an open channel?"

"Yes, Rohan."

"Hm. Was anybody listening?"

"Quite possibly, Rohan."

"Rudra's braids. Ah. Oh. Well. That's not great. I'm going to go rescue Garren."

25

Devil Doctor

"I I really don't want to be in here. I'm telling you, I'll be fine."

The doctor, a red-skinned biped with black horns and a mix of scales and fur over her body, was wearing a white lab coat. "You will be fine, because you will stay here until I am sure of it." Her eyes were yellow and lacked visible pupils.

"Have I ever told you that you—"

"Resemble demonic creatures of your home planet's legends? Yes, repeatedly."

"Oh, sorry. I'm a little loopy from all the . . ." He pointed at the empty bottles of anesthetic on the table next to his bed.

"I am unsurprised. I gave you enough sedative to incapacitate ten Rogesh adults."

"And I appreciate it, even though it will wear off within the hour. Less."

She maneuvered an imaging device over to him and pointed it at his chest. He overheard her comm chirp in her ear.

"You, hold still." She tapped the back of her jaw. "Yes?"

He held still while she pressed buttons on the device, then looked at a screen on the back of the machine, then pressed more buttons.

"Yes, he can have visitors. His injuries are not life-threatening."

"See? Didn't I tell you? I'm fine."

"I said hold still. No, not you, I'm talking to the patient. Simivar out."

"Ooh, am I getting visitors? That sounds like fun."

"Security will be coming shortly. You need to rest. But first, can you suppress your Power again? It interferes with the scanning."

"I will. I know I look bad, but you should see the other guy."

"I have. He's being treated down the hall. He does, in fact, look worse than you."

"Good. I don't like that guy, I think he broke two of my ribs. Hey, you should take a look at them, you're a doctor. I think they're broken."

"Yes, three of your ribs are, in fact, broken. And yes, you will be fine. Now please suppress your Power momentarily so I can take fresh scans."

Rohan's closed his eyes. His brow furrowed in an exaggerated look of concentration. "I'm doing it. I'm doing it. I'm doing it."

"Please be quiet, Rohan. And hold still."

"Being quiet now."

She touched more buttons, nodding. "You can relax. Scan is complete."

"Great! What does it say? Did you find my pen?"

"No, there is no pen in your torso, Rohan. Your ribs are healing quite rapidly."

"See, I told you!"

"Yes." The door chimed. "Are you willing to speak with security?"

He nodded. "No problem. Send them in, I can take 'em. Heck, I could take them with six broken ribs! Even twelve!"

Her tone remained patient. "Please do not 'take' anybody. The chief is here to speak with you, that is all."

"Ooh. Am I in trouble?"

"I do not think so. She is your friend, Rohan, remember?"

"Oh yeah, right. Gotcha. Send her in!"

"I will be back in a little while to check on you, Rohan. Stay in bed."

"Will do!"

The doctor walked to the door and swiped it open. She nodded to Wei Li, who was waiting to enter.

"He will be fine. He's heavily sedated, though, so expect odd behavior from him."

"He's sedated? Why?"

"He was in pain. Pain in his species is incompatible with healing. So I eased it."

Wei Li nodded. "All right. Can you estimate when he'll be back to normal?"

The doctor shrugged inside her white coat. "I have little experience with Hybrid metabolism. He says within the hour. Given how quickly he regained consciousness, I doubt it would be much longer than that."

"Good, thank you." She walked over to Rohan's bed. "Are you all right?"

"Wei Li, I am much, much better than all right. These drugs are awesome."

"So I see. I am glad you are not more badly injured."

"Me, too! I might be even more glad than you are."

She smiled at him, flashing her sharp incisors. "Do you know where you are?"

"Is this a trick question? Because it really seems like a trick question."

"No, Rohan. I want to see how alert you are, so I am asking if you know your location."

"Oh, okay. I'm pretty sure I'm in bed."

She sighed. "Rohan, try to be serious."

"Um, in a medical unit? I assume on Wistful. I don't actually remember which one."

"That is enough, thank you. Yes, you are in the crew medical unit on Wistful. I am sorry I did not come by sooner, I was dealing with *Insatiable*'s crew."

"Oh, that sounds bad. Is it bad? What are you doing with them?"

"The crew of the shuttle is confined to the ship for now. *Insatiable* is being given a choice between leaving the system and allowing us to disable her remaining shuttles."

"They're leaving? I would have wanted to say goodbye to Ben."

"I believe she will allow us to disable the shuttles. Wistful is making it easy on them. She recognizes the truth in what you said about Marion Stone."

"Good! Finally somebody listens to me! What did I say again?"

"That if there are problems resulting from the wormhole activation she would be the best person to help us resolve them."

"Hey, that's true. I'm pretty smart. Who would have guessed?"

"Not I, Rohan. But yes, that was quite smart, especially for a male." She smiled and patted his arm. "Do you remember what happened? Why you are here?"

He nodded. "That armored Tony Stark wannabe punched me in the chest. Did you know he has reversible gravity-source generation? Push and pull? I didn't even know they could do that."

"We have his armor under seal. Doctor Stone is most insistent that we not examine it, but she is willing to have it kept someplace inaccessible to her."

"That sounds like a good idea. Keep it away, in case she gets any bad ideas. It's all about the ideas."

"You are somewhat cute in this state. Like a baby. I almost desire to pinch your cheeks."

"I almost want you to."

She laughed. "I am glad to laugh. It has been a trying day."

"You're telling me!"

She paused. "Rohan, do you remember the things Doctor Stone said to you while you were engaged with the shuttle and her assistant, Garren?"

Rohan scratched his beard. "Yeah, I think so. I mean, not all the specifics."

"Doctor Stone said a number of things about your past. Over an open channel."

"Oh, yeah. I kind of wish you hadn't reminded me."

"Is it true? What she said?"

"I don't think it's fair for you to ask me questions like that when I'm drugged. How am I supposed to lie convincingly?"

"You can't lie convincingly even when you are sober. Not to me."

"That is a very good point."

"Wistful sent a faster-than-light ship to block the transmission ahead of the wavefront. All copies of the broadcast on publicly accessible archives have been wiped. Wistful and I are both monitoring public conversations for rumors of your history to spread. So far, there is no evidence that it has."

"So my secrets are safe. Sort of. Safe-ish. Maybe."

"I would not go that far. But they are not widespread. When they become so, you should expect repercussions."

"I always do. Stop, please, you are killing my buzz."

She nodded. "We will watch out for you as best we can. In the meantime, the wearer of the armor is just down the hall from you. Under guard. Which brings me to the question I have for you: What would you like to happen to him?"

"You mean, do I want to press charges?"

Wei Li tilted her head quizzically. "I mean, what would you like to happen to him? We have many convenient airlocks through which someone might accidentally step. I, as security chief, also have passwords to the store for all internal video recordings." Her expression was stone cold.

"Ha, that's a good one. No, it's fine. He was doing what he thought was right. As far as I'm concerned, let him go. Maybe conditional on him apologizing or something. He did break three of my ribs."

"As you wish. You are not a vengeful person, are you?"

"I am by nature. You should have seen me a decade ago! I'm just trying to be better. Also, to be fair, he has some right to be mad at me. I did a lot of . . . stuff on Tolone'a."

The security chief tilted her head and looked away, holding up a finger for Rohan to stay quiet. After a moment she nodded.

"Yes, very well. Send the crew in." She turned to Rohan. "It seems *Insatiable* has accepted our offer. She will stay, and we will disable her shuttles."

"That is not what I expected."

"She is quite distressed by the fact that Doctor Stone ignored instructions, and by the fact that you were injured as a result. It is a shameful situation for a ship to be in."

Rohan nodded and sank back into his pillows. He was determined to enjoy the effects of the drugs for as long as they lasted. "Any leads on the dreadnought? *Fathers' Vengeance*?"

"Doctor Stone has admitted to hacking the sensor array to falsify those images. As punishment, she will show us how she did so and help us fix that vulnerability."

"I guess a hack is better than an actual dreadnought in the system."

Wei Li shrugged. "Neither is comforting. Her husband is waiting nearby to speak with you, if you are willing."

"Sure, I'll talk to him. I hope he brought food."

"Also, when you are feeling better, I would like your help."

"What can I do?"

"Wistful has an active sensor array prepared. We are moving parts into position by shuttle, but I am told your assistance would be helpful."

"Tracking that shadow among the stars?"

"Yes."

"Hey, you should see if Doctor Stone picked up anything. They must have had all kinds of telemetry going when they turned on the wormhole."

She paused. "Rohan, that is a good idea. Thank you."

"You are very welcome. Send in the next supplicant!"

"Were you not already injured I would be required to damage you for using that term to refer to me."

"That's why I used it now, and wouldn't any other time."

"I will send in the professor."

"Thanks. And thanks for checking up on me."

"You are most welcome, my friend. I will go now, there is work to be done."

The security chief left. Rohan saw his mask on the bed next to him. He picked it up and scrolled through his messages.

"Personal. Scan news feeds for updates on Hybrid Rebellion."

"Scanning. No recent updates."

His stomach settled a little.

He checked his net worth, then checked the buy price on a lovely mountain estate on Andervar that he'd been eyeing for years.

He blinked. Either he was deeply impaired by the drugs or he'd accumulated enough credits to buy it.

There was a knock on the door.

"Enter, all ye who dare face the wrath of the Rohan."

There was a pause, then the entrance cycled open. Benjamin Stone walked in, ducking his head slightly as he stepped through the doorway.

"Hello, Rohan." His voice was tentative.

"Doctor Stone! I was kidding about the wrath part. Loopy from sedatives, you know."

"Ah, good. I am not eager to face anyone's wrath."

"Hey, come on, we're buds. No wrath for you."

"How are you feeling? I hear Garren broke your ribs."

"You should see the other guy! Hey, wait, have you seen the other guy? They said he's right down the hall."

"I have."

"Tell me he looks worse than I do. Otherwise I'm going to be very embarrassed."

"Well, your pride is safe. He has some extensive internal injuries from that kick you gave him. They're prepping him for another round of surgeries now."

"Really? Huh. I didn't realize I'd hurt him that much."

"Some from you, some from the decompression. So, yes, he looks worse than you do."

"Now I feel kind of bad. I'm not sure I should."

Ben walked to Rohan's bedside and put a hand on the Hybrid's shoulder. "You're a decent person, Rohan. You shouldn't feel bad, but I'm kind of glad you do."

"I'll figure it all out when these drugs wear off."

"Good, you do that. Are you okay?"

Rohan waved his hand in the air. "This is nothing. I'll be one hundred percent in a few hours."

"Really? Must be nice."

"Yeah. It would be nicer if I wasn't putting that fast healing to the test."

"Yes, I'm sure. Rohan . . ." The older man hesitated, his bushy eyebrows pushed down over his eyes. "I'm sorry for what my wife put you through. For what she did."

"It's not your apology to make, Professor."

"I know. It's just, she's my wife. I feel I should have been able to stop her, keep a lid on things."

"We both know that's not reasonable. She's never been someone you could control. Not according to the stories."

"You're not angry with me?"

Rohan shrugged, wincing at the pain that flared through his ribs. "You're not her boss. It's not your fault. Heck, you even tried to warn me."

"I heard you got a good look through the wormhole."

"I was almost inside it. In a way, it's amazing, but in another way, it's nothing at all. Like looking through a window."

"Looking into a star system halfway across the galaxy."

"Yeah. I assume your wife took all sorts of readings? We know where the Ursan system is now?"

"I'm sure. I haven't really spoken to her."

"Oh."

"You know, I was pretty shocked when you flew through the roof like that. I was sure for a moment that the section would decompress and I was dead. I had no idea those panels would snap back into place so easily."

"Yeah. It's funny, I think it was one or two days ago I was trying to work out the quickest way into space from the promenade, for something completely unrelated. I asked Wistful about it. She basically said it would be okay."

"I guess I'm glad you weren't just hoping we'd survive."

"Nah, I had you covered."

"I shouldn't have doubted it. Or you."

The silence dragged on a bit. Rohan broke it. "I have a question for you. Did you know?"

"Know what? Which part of it?"

"What your wife said about me. My past. Over the comms."

The professor's voice softened, almost to a whisper. "What did she say?"

"She said my name. My old name. Codename. Title. Whatever you want to call it."

"I take it your name wasn't Rohan."

Rohan sighed. "She said, over an open channel, that I'm The Griffin."

"Over an open channel? That's . . . I'm sorry."

"Not your fault. I mean, it's not like I'm in much of a disguise. I grew my hair out, grew a beard. I should have tried wearing glasses."

"To answer your question, I did not realize you were The Griffin."

"Your wife recognized me."

"And yet, she didn't feel the need to share that information with me."

"Is that weird? That seems weird."

The professor hesitated. "We have different attitudes about Hybrids. We've argued about it. You might not understand this, but when you're married to someone for a long time, you learn that there are some things you just need to set aside and ignore."

"Agree to disagree."

"Something like that. Anyway, if she recognized you and didn't tell me, that's not surprising. You were . . . are, really The Griffin?"

Rohan shrugged. The professor took that as an acknowledgement. "You're a legend. I thought I was the famous one in this friendship."

"Legends have been told about me. I'm not a legend. There's a difference."

"Was anybody listening to the open channel? Do people know?"

Rohan shook his head. "I can't tell. Wistful says she scrubbed every public log of the conversation, but . . . I'm going to have to assume that somebody heard."

"Ah. Is that really such a problem?"

"That's not all she said."

"What more is there?"

Rohan paused. "She said I ended the Rebellion. That the Fathers are afraid of me."

The professor's already light skin paled even further. "Dear lord. She said that?"

"She did."

His voice grew even softer. "Is that true?"

Rohan closed his eyes and pinched the bridge of his nose. "It doesn't matter. If anybody hears that and believes it, that could lead to a whole bunch of Hybrids coming after me."

"Rohan, I had no idea, I promise you."

"Okay. It doesn't really matter, I guess."

"Of course it matters. We're friends. I would have warned you. She went too far saying that."

"Well, at this point, who knew what, when, is all moot. I have to assume someone was listening, and that word will get out. Which means you should stay away from me for a while."

"You think?"

"I think it's a bad time to be my friend."

"I've dealt with Hybrids before."

"It's not just them. I'm about to seriously piss off a Shayjh Adjudicator. Things are bound to get ugly."

"You really know how to make friends and influence people, don't you?"

"It's not for lack of trying, Professor."

Doctor Stone pulled a chair to a spot next to Rohan's bed and sat down. "This all seems kind of crazy."

"Doesn't it? It would be great if it turned out I'm just high on these meds and hallucinating this stuff. Bears in space. Wormholes. Is it the drugs?"

"Sadly, my friend, it's real. Or we're sharing your insanity. But I haven't taken any drugs. Seriously, though, is there anything I can do for you?"

"Stay away?"

"You're forgetting who I am, Rohan. I spent a long time with Hyperion. I'm not going to run and hide because there's danger in being close to you."

"I don't know, I can't think of anything else. Still fuzzy-headed. Hey, you know what you can do? Distract me. Tell me something new."

"Like what?"

"I don't know. Did you learn anything new about the kaiju?"

The professor shook his head. "Not exactly. We've been analyzing the plant samples, and their genetics are really clean. Too clean."

"What does that mean?"

"Evolution always works its way through side trips and dead ends. That's why we so often find things like vestigial limbs, extraneous enzymatic pathways, redundancies that aren't quite necessary. Junk in the DNA. The plants on Toth 3 have almost none of that, and what they do have looks very recent."

"Genetic engineering?"

"It certainly looks like it. Ideally, we'd gather samples from many other places and do comparisons. If we find nearly identical species on the other side of the planet, well, that's suspicious. It's too soon to tell for sure."

26

Deep History

Rohan tried to concentrate. "Any progress on figuring out why the kaiju attack?"

"If 'progress' includes ruling out most of our working hypotheses, then yes, lots of progress."

"Ha. Bummer."

"Our best ideas now are either very hard to test or things out of bad science fiction. If this were a movie or a comic book I'd say the whole planet was built as a security system. There must be some fantastic treasure on that planet somewhere."

"Don't go spreading that idea. I don't want to turn into a full-time rescue unit if I can help it."

"No, I haven't shared that one even with my own team. The consequences of that idea getting around could be brutal."

"I'll keep my mouth shut, you can be sure of that."

"You, I wasn't worried about."

Rohan thought. "If there was a treasure down there, it would have to predate the Empire."

"Predate the Empire. Also predate human recorded history. It's a big universe, and we're not the oldest intelligent life in it. You knew that."

Rohan fiddled with his mask. "So what are you planning to do now?"

The professor sighed. "I don't really have much planned. I had just begun packing to leave when your security chief told us we could stay.

Apparently, we aren't being exiled despite my wife's violations of station rules."

"That's good, isn't it?"

"I suppose. It gives me a chance to do some more research."

"And your wife can make improvements on that armor she built for Garren."

The professor shook his head. "I can't completely dismiss the idea there. The world might be a better place if there was something to level the playing field."

Rohan shrugged. "I'm not arguing that point one way or another. I just don't want the leveling agent breaking my ribs."

"If someone's going to argue that Hybrids can't be trusted with so much power, I don't know that my wife and Garren are the best candidates to replace them. Too much anger there."

"Well, the armor was impressive. I'm kind of surprised the Empire let her build it."

"I'm not entirely sure the Empire knew about it. I think it was more of a side project."

Rohan shifted from side to side, seeking a comfortable position. "The good news is, the drugs are wearing off. The bad news is, the drugs are wearing off. Starting to feel the ribs again. But it doesn't hurt as much as when I came in."

The professor stood. "I'll let you get some rest. And keep an ear out for any rumors about your old title spreading around the station."

"I appreciate it."

Rohan settled back into the bed and closed his eyes. A moment later the door cycled open and his red-skinned doctor came back. "Sorry, were you sleeping?"

He shook his head. "I've been terrible about getting in my meditation lately. I figured, as long as I'm here with nothing else to do, it's a good time to get back to it."

"That's a great idea. How's the pain?"

"Better. The drugs seem to be wearing off but the ribs don't hurt as much."

"Let me take a quick peek." She maneuvered the imager over to him and performed a scan. "That's quite a marvelous recovery."

"Thank my father."

She smiled. Her teeth were more intimidating than Wei Li's. "If you're going to be getting injured regularly I'll need to brush up on my Hybrid biology."

"I kind of hope that turns out to be a waste of your time."

"So do I. At the rate these are knitting together you should be fine to move around in another hour or so. I suggest you remain here until then. You have visitors, so you won't be too bored."

"Visitors? Who else do I know?"

"Shall I let them in?"

"Sure."

The doctor left the room, letting a lovely, green-skinned woman with two antennae on her head and a small, similarly equipped boy enter the room.

"Oh, hey! Why are you guys here? Isn't it early?"

Rinth walked forward. He held a toy, a plush pink octopus. "I heard you got hurt. So I asked Mom if we could visit you. And I brought you Squishy. Squishy helps me feel better when I'm hurt, so I thought he could help you." The boy held out the plush toy.

Rohan took it in his hand. The pink octopus was aptly named. "Rinth, that's the nicest thing anybody's ever given me."

Tamara put her hands on her son's shoulders. "Are you all right, Tow Chief Second Class Rohan?"

Rohan shrugged. "It's really not that bad. Wistful insisted I get checked out before going back to work, that's all. If it were up to me I would have just gone home and slept it off."

She shook her head. "I do not recall giving you permission to sustain injuries, Rohan. I have laid claim to that chest, and therefore, to all the ribs sustaining it. You are not to endanger those parts again without advance dispensation."

He laughed, and winced. "Is it just the ribs? What if I'd gotten a concussion?"

She waved her hand. "I am not with you for your brains, Rohan. You may risk your skull as you desire."

He laughed again. "You have to stop doing that. Give me another hour before making me laugh. Please."

She smiled and walked around Rinth to Rohan's side. She caressed his forehead gently. "We are both glad that you are not seriously hurt. Public accounts of what happened are varied and somewhat chaotic. Someone has removed most of the media recording the event. There is video, but no audio of the battle."

"Good."

"Why 'good'?"

"Well, some things were said on an open channel during the battle that I'd rather didn't get around."

"Things?"

"I'll explain later, I promise. But not right now."

"All right. We should go, now that we see you are all right. Rinth has school, and I have an early shift. I was called in to verify the work done today on *Insatiable*'s shuttles. They are all to be disabled because of what happened."

"Yeah. Hey, buddy, could you give your mom and me a minute alone? I want to talk about some grownup stuff."

The boy sighed. "No kissy stuff. I'm just a kid and I'm not supposed to be around when you do those things. Until you're married. And even then, I'm only supposed to see kissing and not the other gross stuff you do with your clothes off."

Tamara glared at him. "Rinth!"

"What? That's what Auntie said."

Rohan laughed. "No filter. It's not kissy stuff, I promise. Just two minutes alone."

"Okay." Rinth stepped outside.

"What is it, my Rohan?"

Rohan sighed. "It's hard to explain."

"Be quick, you only have two minutes."

"Right. Look, I have some things to work out. Personal things, they don't involve you. I'm going to need some space to work them out."

"Is this where you tell me that you are, in fact, married to an Earth girl? Or an Ursan?"

"Nothing like that. Not another girl, and nothing about the way I feel about you. But something I have to deal with, and you can't be around me while I do it. If things work out, I will explain everything. I promise."

"And if they do not work out?"

"Then you'll know everything, and I will probably be dead. So either way you'll get the story. Look, I'm really sorry. This is a shitty thing to say to you."

She sighed. "Life does, occasionally, happen. And it is not always easy to deal with. I will give you your days. But do not let this become a habit."

"I won't. Really. Thank you."

She turned to leave. He grabbed her hand just before she moved out of reach. "Tamara, seriously, I'm sorry."

She turned to face him. "I know, Rohan. I will attempt to prolong judgment until after I have heard the entire story. But I am famed for my beauty, my intelligence, and my shopping acumen; not for my patience."

He sighed. "I get that. Thank you."

"Message me when you wish to talk."

"I will. Soon. I promise."

She kissed his forehead, then left the room.

Rinth stuck his head through the open door. "'Bye, Rohan!"

"'Bye, Rinth. Take care of your mom."

"I always do, silly. Watch out for the armored man and the scary bears. Squishy will keep you safe."

"I'll bet." He held Squishy up to his face.

The pink octopus stared at him, unperturbed. He squeezed it and the plush made a squeaking sound.

"This is what I needed in my life."

"What?" Doctor Simivar had returned.

"Sorry, wasn't talking to you."

"All right. I'd like to inform Wistful that you're cleared to return to work ninety minutes from now. Unless you have some objection."

"No, that's fine."

"Good. I brought you a nutrient shake. I understand your nutritional needs are mostly based on your mother's species."

"Mostly." He took the shake and drank it. "Thanks, Doctor."

"You are most welcome. I need to go check on my other patient."

"Tell him I said hello. No hard feelings."

She cocked her head and looked at him with her blank yellow eyes. "Really?"

Rohan shrugged. "I mean, I'm not eager to be best friends, but I also don't want him worried that I'm going to walk down the hall and pull his testicles out of his body through his ears."

"That is a very vivid description of vengeance to come from a man with no hard feelings."

"I'm still an il'Drach Hybrid, you know. Our emotional milieu is mostly made up of hard feelings. Actually, you know what? Don't tell him. I'll tell him myself."

"You may speak with him, but please do not continue your fight in my medical bay."

"No fighting, just a small chat."

Rohan finished his shake.

Meditated.

Checked his messages.

He used his mask to scan station social media headlines for current events.

Hi Quality Images of New Star System! Binary Suns! Will Ursans Return?

See the Space Battle between our tow chief and the armored Tolone'an! (Warning: low resolution imagery).

Physicist who opened wormhole claims no danger from radiation. Read our exclusive interview.

Ursan leaders warn us: not everybody on the other side of that wormhole is friendly. Click here to hear about atrocities our Ursan neighbors escaped.

Doctor Stone regrets violence over wormhole opening. Read her sad story!

Still no indication anybody had listened to Doctor Stone give away his identity.

Rohan stood slowly, testing his ribs. There was an ache but no sharp pains. He stood and changed out of his patient gown and into his purple-and-gold uniform.

The Hybrid stowed the mask in the pocket made by his uniform's hood and stepped out.

"Which way, which way . . .?" He looked around, finally spotting two security officers walking down the hall. He followed.

They walked to a room guarded by two other personnel. The standing guards left and the new pair took their spots.

"Hey, guys."

One was Tamtam, the Rogesh that Rohan had wrestled with the day before. "Tow Chief Rohan, hello."

The other guard nodded. Rohan smiled.

"Is it all right if I talk to him? Just a couple of minutes."

They looked at each other. Tamtam cleared his throat, a deep rumble that sounded like a minor landslide.

"Sir, we are tasked with keeping the prisoner safe."

Rohan held up his hands. "I really just want to talk to him. If he objects, I'll leave peacefully."

They traded glances. The second guard held his hands up. "Why not?"

Rohan nodded. "Thanks." He walked between them and through the door.

Garren was in a bed similar to the one Rohan had been resting in, except the Tolone'an was manacled to the frame at wrists and ankles. There were two lines dripping fluids into his body and a bright antiseptic light shining on the area around him.

"Garren, I have to say, you don't look great."

The Tolone'an's eyes were bandaged, and all four of his tentacles were heavily wrapped.

"Tow Chief?" His voice was weak but steady.

"Yeah. I came to see how you were. Tell you no hard feelings."

"You should. Have killed me." He had to pause for a ragged breath every few words. "Why didn't you. Kill me?"

"Why do you have to be so serious about everything?"

"Why didn't you? Doctor Stone said. You saved. My life."

"We could argue that. I towed you into the airlock, but if I hadn't popped the seals on your armor you wouldn't have been dying, so . . ."

"Don't argue. Semantics. Could have. Left."

Rohan pulled a chair to the spot next to Garren's bed and sat down. "I told you, I'm not your enemy."

"I attacked. You."

"Hey, things happen. Lots of people attack me. I'm not going to carry a grudge against them all. The Ursans did their best to kill me just over a week ago, and now they call me 'Brother.'"

"Forbidden weapons. Technology."

"Yeah, I bet the il'Drach will have something to say about that armor. But I don't work for them. Anymore. That armor is not my problem. In fact, I hope you can improve on it."

"Why?"

Rohan sighed. "Hybrids shouldn't always be the strongest people around. It leads to bad habits. Improve that armor, maybe then you can teach us some humility."

The blue-skinned man shook, and for a moment Rohan thought he was seizing.

It was laughter. "You are a. Strange Hybrid."

"I keep hearing that. I'll take it as a compliment."

"It was."

"Great. How are you? Anything I can do?"

He shook his head. "I will heal. They think. Even my eyes."

"Good. If that armor wasn't so tough I could have stopped you without hurting you. So I guess that's one you can blame on yourself."

"Yes."

"There is one thing, though."

"What?"

"You heard the stuff Doctor Stone said about me. My past."

"Yes."

"I'd really rather we keep that private. Please."

Garren didn't answer immediately. Then: "Is that. A threat?"

"There are people who will come after me if they hear it. That's fine, and I don't expect your sympathy over it. But they'll come after my friends, my acquaintances. Innocent people. Maybe even Doctor Stone. And I can't have that."

"I see."

"So I'd really like you to keep things to yourself. And if I have to threaten you, I guess I will. But I'm trying to be nice. It doesn't come naturally to me, remember. I am a Hybrid. So what's it going to be?"

"I will not. Betray. Your secrets."

"Good. Thanks. Look, if you have second thoughts, if you need to talk things over, let me know. I might even tell you the truth behind those stories, especially if you buy me a few rounds of Sein Ale first. And if you heal up and want to fight again, that's fine."

A longer pause. "Understood."

"Great. As far as what security will do to you, that's out of my hands. I told the chief I didn't want you charged or held on my account, but that doesn't mean Wistful won't have the book thrown at you."

"What book?"

"Sorry, Earth expression. I mean have you incarcerated."

"I knew risks. When I did this. It is okay. With me."

"All right. You heal up. We're not even, though. I think you owe me that round of ale. Assuming your people drink booze."

"We do. I will."

"I have to go. Work to be done."

"Wait. Was it. True? You. Saved Tolone'a."

Rohan cocked his head. "I told you the truth. I was told that if I couldn't end the war they were going to sterilize the planet."

"Ah. Sorry."

"You don't owe me an apology. I did what I thought I had to do, but it was still pretty horrible. Maybe I should be apologizing." He gently patted the man on his bandaged shoulders and stood.

Rohan left the medical bay. He tapped open his comms.

"Wei Li. I'm available for whatever I'm supposed to be doing."

He was standing by the airlock before he heard the security chief's voice in his ear.

"Rohan. Good."

"Hey, Wei Li. What am I doing? I mean, what am I supposed to be doing?"

"Hold on, let me check the encryption on this channel." Another pause. "Wistful wants you placing a few of the sensors in the array."

"I don't mind, but why not use shuttles?"

"Shuttles are too easy to track. We're concerned that if we place all the sensors using shuttles they'll be easy to map, and people will be able to find holes in the coverage."

"So where do I get the sensors?"

"Your mask has instructions."

He stepped into the airlock, slipped his mask over his face, and waited for the lock to depressurize. Then he flew out into space.

Glowing lines immediately popped up on the heads-up display in his mask to direct him toward the western arm of the station.

He flew around to an open shuttle bay where crew wearing vacuum suits were lining up metallic objects in neat rows. The objects were roughly spherical, painted a matte black, with assorted rods and pipes of various sizes emerging at odd angles.

The display led him to the last sphere in the line. He flew to it.

A suited crew member gave him a thumbs up.

Rohan walked a slow circle around the sphere, looking for an anchor point. He found spots with handprints etched into the matte black surface. He placed his hands and lifted.

New lines speared their way across his display, directing him out into space.

He pulled the sensor out into space.

"You know, Wistful, I think this is just what I needed. A nice, calm, tedious job to keep me distracted. No violence, no excitement."

"You are welcome, Rohan."

"Just out of curiosity, why don't you have these sensors deployed all the time?"

"They are very delicate, very expensive, and not very useful. Between passive and metaphysical sensors almost any credible threat to me or the system can be easily identified. This is an unusual phenomenon."

"I learn new things every day. Just how far out am I taking this?"

"This sensor cluster is going to a spot between Toth 5 and its largest moon."

"That's pretty far. Play me some tunes, then."

Dance music, popular tunes from Rohan's high school years, played over his comm system as he accelerated smoothly through vacuum.

"You know, Wistful, there's a corner of my brain that still tells me I shouldn't be listening to music, because it will prevent me from hearing someone trying to sneak up on me out here."

"You would not hear anyone in space with or without the music playing, Rohan. I believe you know this."

"I do. But there are millions of years of evolution inside an atmosphere telling me that I need my hearing to be safe."

"Do you actually believe that your species evolved over millions of years? And in an atmosphere? Did you not pay attention in biology class, Rohan?"

"I did pay attention. Wait, we didn't? What are you telling me?"

"I was making a joke, Rohan."

"You have to work on your joking voice. You need to modulate your tone when telling a joke. And since when did you make jokes?"

Toth 5 was growing visible, even without display enhancement, as he closed on the gas giant.

A regular flow of shuttles dipped into Toth 5's atmosphere to gather raw materials for Wistful. His mask outlined the shuttles to make them more visible, as a safety measure.

The guide arrows in his display turned amber, telling him to decelerate.

"I do not detect such modulation in Chief Wei Li when she is being humorous, Rohan."

"Then how do you know she is being humorous?"

"I can judge from the context of her statements, Rohan."

"Are you sure?" He dragged out the last word, teasing the station.

"Now I believe you are the one making jokes, Rohan."

"One day I'll figure out how much of these—"

He was interrupted by a jaw-rattling impact as something large, dark, and fast struck him from behind like a meteor.

27

Ramifications

The sensor cluster launched from his grasp and tumbled through space toward the gas giant looming above.

Rohan was bent painfully backward over the rounded surface of whatever had hit him. It accelerated into his body, pushing him into its surface, driving him toward the large, cratered moon below.

The impact had knocked the wind out of him and dislodged his mask. He held his breath, eyes stinging from the hard vacuum contacting his face.

Rohan reached up to grip his mask, his fingers fumbling with the seals, while wiggling his body from side to side, trying to get free of whatever was pressing into him.

The object on his back twisted and turned, matching his struggles, pushing him at ever-increasing speed toward the moon.

He caught the mask and put it back in place. The compressed air tanks in the mask's rim hissed as they dispensed a breathable atmosphere into the thin space between his face and the curved, single-facet diamond faceplate.

The moon was growing rapidly in his field of vision.

He twisted and got a good look at the thing that had hit him.

It was black, a matte black much deeper than the dark surface of the sensor cluster, darker than a Darianite's skin. The black was completely non-reflective, more an absence than an actual color.

The side striking him was round, almost spherical, but a second glance showed a shape more like a flattened teardrop. Additional struts or arms seemed to emerge from its back, but it was so hard to see he wasn't sure.

"Rohan, did something happen?"

The ship pulled back, letting him free, then surged toward him again with a burst of acceleration far beyond any ship he'd ever encountered. It struck him full in the chest, dislodging his mask again and robbing him of the air he'd need to answer.

He put his left hand out onto the cold metallic surface of the ship. With a grunt, he squeezed, his fingers puncturing the thick, hardened hull, scrunching the smooth metal up into a handhold.

Anchored to the ship with one hand, he rode the frenzied side-to-side movement, his body and legs flailing out into space with each jerk of motion. With his other hand he gripped the facemask again and settled it firmly into place.

". . . assistance?"

He sipped cautiously at the air inside his mask. He knew from experience that gulping vacuum was unpleasant.

The ship was scout-sized, about as big as a small school bus laid on its side.

"Wistful, being attacked. Found our shadow."

The ship reversed its acceleration, pulling back hard enough to loosen his grip on the makeshift handhold, then slammed forward again. He was better prepared, absorbing some of the impact with his arms, and kept his mask in place.

Rohan regained his hold just as the ship twisted to shake him free, spinning him in place.

He held on, resisting the rotation, fingers burning with the strain. The starscape behind the ship spun in a dizzying streak of stars, the gas giant twirling around his field of vision in a colorful blaze of red, orange, and pale blue.

Rohan ignored the rotation and slapped his right hand into the matte black surface.

"I've got you—"

The ship drove him into Toth 5's moon. They sank through ten meters, then fifteen, then twenty meters of rock and dust, kicking up a tremendous plume of debris.

Rohan felt his ribs creak and separate with the impact. There was no atmosphere, so the dust was settling fast, but not fast enough for him to see anything.

The ship pressed him deeper into the bedrock of the moon, turning like a corkscrew to increase the pressure and drive him more solidly into the bedrock.

Rohan kept his left-handed grip on the ship and reached down with his right hand, blindly grabbing for anything solid.

He *pushed* against the acceleration of the ship, forcing it back and away from the bottom of the crater.

He touched hard bedrock; planted his feet on the stone and tightened his grip on the handhold he'd created.

"Hold still." He knew he was talking to himself.

The Hybrid reached up with his other hand and tore his fingers into a fresh spot on the hull, working fresh ripples into the metal.

The ship pulled back; like a living thing twitching away from a flame.

Suddenly, he was standing in the bottom of the virgin crater, dust settling fast and burying him to his knees, and the shadow ship was hovering dozens of meters away.

He opened a short-range open comm channel. "What the hell, Ship?"

He launched a wave of disruptive telekinesis at the ship, thinking it was a shuttle. To his surprise, the wave broke over its hull. The ship was sentient.

"You're alive?" He was no empath, but he could usually *sense* a ship's spirit from such a short distance. Not from this ship.

It hovered, its nose pointed directly at him. He could make out three lumps on the front, two above and one below, that looked like bootstrap drives. The lumps were arranged like eyes, wide apart, and a mouth. A face, surprised to see him.

He shook his head, lifted and lowered his shoulders. His ribs were very sore but didn't feel broken.

"I repeat, what the hell? Why are you attacking me?"

Something dark emerged from the back of the ship, then an object shot out and around it.

Rohan kept his comm link open.

The figure swooped toward the bottom of the crater where Rohan was standing.

It was a man, dressed in a jumpsuit similar in cut to Rohan's but of the same dark color as the ship. His aura had a familiar smell.

He accelerated rapidly into Rohan.

Rohan opened a channel back to Wistful. "The shadow is some kind of stealth ship. I'm being attacked by someone who seems to be another Hybrid. More details coming, if I survive."

The Hybrid from the stealth ship flew with his left arm extended and his right fist held near his shoulder. As he closed he threw a looping punch with the right hand.

The sheer speed of the movement almost caught Rohan off guard. He had anticipated the punch and ducked his head slightly to his left.

The fist sailed over Rohan's right shoulder.

He continued the motion to his left, shooting his right knee into the other Hybrid's gut.

The man was moving too quickly; the knee glanced off his body.

The two spun away from each other, coming to a stop in the moon dust and gravel.

"Why did you come? It was all I could do not to go down to the station to hunt you down like a dog. Then you fly right out to me? Are you in such a hurry to die?"

Rohan cracked his neck. "You do realize I had no idea you were out here? That's why I'm here, to try to find that ship. You've been spooking all the shuttle pilots."

"You're not even my primary mission. I'm not here for you!" The voice was tight, the whine of a superpowered adolescent.

"Let's talk about this. Where are you from? You look human. Well, half human. You know."

The Hybrid, a foot taller than Rohan with blond hair and a physique like a professional strongman, leaped forward.

"Die, traitor!" He closed on Rohan, then bombarded the smaller man with powerful punches.

Rohan dug his back heel into the gravel and stood his ground. He lifted his arms, guarding his head with his forearms and swaying from side to side just enough to catch the punches on his arms or shoulders instead of flush on the face.

The large Hybrid spoke as he unloaded, a punch with each word. "You. Betrayed. Us. Cost. Us. Our. Freedom."

Rohan felt the impact of each blow as they sent shockwaves through his shoulders, his spine, and into his legs. He was driven down to bedrock; then even that began to crumble with the force.

As soon as Rohan had a feel for the other Hybrid's timing, he leaned forward with a hard jab in the moment between the bigger man's punches.

It landed square on the faceplate of the other Hybrid's mask.

Rohan immediately followed with a quick punch from his right hand. His fist sank deep into the blonde's solar plexus.

The bigger man stepped back, pausing his assault. "I am Jaroux of the Ice Colony."

Rohan nodded. There were several places where humans from Earth had been relocated to other planets by the il'Drach. The Ice Colony was one. Northern Europeans had been transplanted there five or six hundred years before.

"I am—"

"I know who you are! It was announced to the sector!"

"I didn't think anybody was listening."

"I wasn't here for The Griffin! I studied your exploits in school; we admired you. My mission only has to do with Doctor Stone and that armor she's been building. While monitoring that I have to hear that my hero, the pride of Earth descendants everywhere, ended the Rebellion and doomed our people to another thousand years of slavery?"

"It's not that simple—"

Jaroux leaped forward again, interrupting. He started pounding again, jackhammering away with both arms.

Up close, Rohan could see the cherry red of Jaroux's face through the film of spittle coating the inside of his mask.

"You're not listening to me."

The punches came harder, and faster.

Rohan ducked left, then right, each time catching glancing blows on his shoulders. He stepped into the larger man, lifting a knee into Jaroux's midsection.

He heard a grunt over the comms, but the assault continued.

The big Hybrid finally adjusted, throwing two quicker left hands in a row, then a kick straight into Rohan's belly.

Rohan deflected the punches but was open for the kick, which sent him flying back in the moon's light gravity and knocked the wind out of him.

Jaroux followed, an unrelenting violence machine. "Traitor. *Traitor.* Die!"

Rohan sucked in some air. "You failed witty repartee class, didn't you? Who is teaching that to the cadets these days?"

"Die!" He punched again, then kicked again.

Rohan adjusted, taking the brunt of the kick on his arms, but the impact was enough to send him backward into a rocky cliff. He settled back in the fresh indentation his collision had made, shards of stone showering down around him.

The blond Hybrid settled into a half crouch, arms slightly in front of him, palms facing forward as if he were about to pick up a heavy barrel. He grunted, audible over the comms.

Rohan recognized the posture. Different cultures, different traditions, gave it different names, though his favorite was always the Surrender Stance.

It was one method Hybrids were taught to use when trying to surrender completely to their rage.

Rohan felt the man's energy build. His ribs ached. "You don't have to do this. Stop this, we can talk. I can explain what happened."

"I. Don't. Care. What. You. Have. To. Say."

Jaroux's energy kept building.

Rohan could feel his own energy rising, bubbling up from the base of his spine.

It was the same Power he'd pulled on to survive the decipede attack on Toth 3. It had brought anger along with it then, but that had just been a taste of what it could do.

This time, faced with the spirit of another Hybrid's murderous intent, it was the anger of the il'Drach made manifest. The thirst for conquest, the lust for violence, the unbridled eagerness to make and unleash mayhem.

Rohan muttered to himself, reciting his chant, willing the Power to be calm. He could feel his own restraint like a physical thing, a seal against his anger, buckling and warping under the strain.

"Traitor!"

Through his third eye, his spirit eye, Rohan could *see* Jaroux glowing, white sheets of light pulsing around his body. The level of Power was as high as Rohan had ever seen around anybody not named Hyperion.

The young Hybrid was *strong*.

His own Power surged again, rising to meet the challenge, guided by a more primitive, more basic behavior pattern. He refocused on the chant, soothing the beast inside.

Rohan's comms barked into his ear. "Rohan. What is happening?" Wei Li's voice.

"There was a Hybrid on that ship. He's trying to kill me now."

"Rohan, hold on. We're sending help."

"Do not. Nobody on Wistful can handle this guy. I don't know if *I* can handle this guy."

"Then be careful. Remember to move your head."

"Yeah. Turning off my comm."

He closed the long-range channel.

The big Hybrid flew forward through the air, right arm cocked for a big opening punch.

Rohan timed the attack, slipping to the side as the punch came.

It might have worked, had the punch been aimed at his head. Instead, Jaroux punched him square in the chest.

The blow caught Rohan hard, driving him back a full body's width into the mountain. A fresh shower of stones came down around them.

Jaroux pulled back his left hand to follow up. Rohan ducked forward, bending almost in half, falling forward to get out of the hollow he'd crushed in the mountain.

As the punch sailed over his head the berserker followed through and kicked him, almost absentmindedly, and sent Rohan bouncing along the moon's surface and out of the crater they had made.

The dust plume Rohan kicked up hadn't even begun to settle when the berserker caught him from behind. As Rohan planted a foot in the ground to stand, Jaroux grabbed him by his free ankle and flipped him up overhead, then slammed him down into the ground.

Rohan twisted in place, turning to meet the ground with his arms instead of the back of his head, mitigating the damage as much as he could.

The savage took a mighty leap back to the cliff face. He swung Rohan like a bat into the cliff, too quickly for the smaller man to react.

Rohan's head collided solidly with the stone.

Stay calm. If you lose control, you'll kill him. You're not a killer anymore.

The berserker's face was split in an open-mouthed roar that wasn't audible over the ringing in Rohan's ears.

His head felt hollow. His vision blurred; came into focus; blurred again.

Jaroux spun and swung, creating a similar impact with Rohan's face and the cliff.

Rohan went limp.

Jaroux dropped the tow chief to the ground and stood over him. He poured down a rainfall of punches, hammering Rohan directly into the lunar surface.

After his initial salvo was done, Jaroux stood and hopped to the side. He pulled back one leg and kicked Rohan in the side, launching the smaller man across the crater again.

The anger inside Rohan continued to swell. He tried to calm it, to quiet it down, but the concussive damage made it so very hard to concentrate, to think. . . .

He looked up and saw the blurry blonde closing on him again. He knew he had little chance of surviving without the anger, without the Power that came with it.

Not ready to die yet.

That thought broke his concentration completely.

The seal he held over his own Power popped like a soap bubble. The spring of angry energy surged up, spiraling out of the base of his spine, moving up in twin helixes around his backbone, meeting at the back of his skull. He felt sparks flashing up and down his back.

He let the rage sweep through him. He gave in to it, fed it, building it.

How dare this child challenge me? This Ice Colony juvenile who was drinking milk from bottles when The Griffin first wiped out civilizations for the il'Drach?

Rohan's pride and anger swirled together and swept through him.

Who does this boy think he is?

The Power flowed up through his chakra lines and out, reinforcing his ribs, then all his bones, surging outward and pushing tingling energy into every muscle fiber, every nerve ending, every cell of his body.

His head cleared instantly, his vision dialing into sharp focus. He could count the hairs on Jaroux's blond head, see every scratch in the berserker's face mask. He felt every fiber of his own uniform, the soft rubber around his mask where it met his skin and beard. He could smell his own blood on the inside of his mask.

With his third eye, his spirit eye, he *saw* his own aura. It was solid and heavy, not as flashy as Jaroux's scintillating display, but bright and dense.

Jaroux tilted his head back and roared, pausing briefly. "Finally." The word was barely intelligible over the short-range radio.

Rohan slapped at his arms and legs, brushing dust and stones off his uniform. He stood, slowly, gathering his energy, finally riding the tide of his rage and pride.

The berserker flew at him again, trailing pebbles and shards of stone pulled along incidentally by his Power.

Rohan reached behind him and grabbed a boulder, about as far across as he was tall. The tow chief slammed the boulder into Jaroux as the two met.

Jaroux disintegrated the boulder with a wave of his hand, his Power shredding the inanimate object effortlessly.

The resulting cloud was opaque and thick enough to carry sound.

Rohan moved forward through the cloud and grabbed the berserker behind the head with both hands and pulled down while driving his right knee up into his opponent's face.

Jaroux crossed his arms in front, harmlessly absorbing the force of the knee, a smile on his face as he escaped injury.

Then Rohan pulled away, taking Jaroux's mask with him.

The blonde reached out quickly, almost spasming in his effort to regain the mask.

"I said we didn't have to do this. Did you listen to me? No."

Rohan stepped forward, guided by his third eye and glimpses he caught through breaks in the dust cloud.

Jaroux's arms were outstretched, reaching for his mask. Rohan kicked him savagely in the groin, launching him out of the dust cloud.

The smaller man burst forward, hot in pursuit of the larger.

The berserker was grimacing, hands clasped over his face to hold onto whatever breath he had left. Rohan stepped in on a diagonal, moving forward and to his right, dipping down slightly, and lashed out with a fast left jab to Jaroux's face.

The larger man flinched back from the contact, and Rohan followed with two powerful straight punches to the belly.

When Jaroux's arms dropped to protect his gut and the last reserve of his air, Rohan leaped upward and crashed his rising knee into the large Hybrid's chin.

Jaroux's mouth opened and a small puff of air escaped. He stumbled backward, tilting dramatically against the weak gravity of the moon.

Rohan stepped in and slapped toward Jaroux's face. When the larger Hybrid, only half conscious, pulled up his hands to block, Rohan ducked down and grabbed the berserker by the knee.

He pulled up on the man's ankle and pressed his own knee into the spot just below Jaroux's kneecap. With a shudder, he pulled and dislocated the knee completely.

Jaroux's mouth opened in a silent howl. He grasped at Rohan's face with rapidly weakening arms.

Rohan took the offered arm and snapped the elbow in two. Then he kicked the larger man in the gut, sending him flying across the crater and into the cliff face.

Rohan closed again.

"You heard my name and, what, decided you could take me? Call me a traitor? You have no idea, you ignorant little pissant. You challenged The Griffin and expected to walk away? Or maybe you didn't? Were you hoping for a death worthy of legends and songs? Let me accommodate you."

Jaroux's mouth was opening and closing as he sought air. He used his functional arm to rise, supporting himself with his one good leg.

The powerful aura of energy he'd showed earlier was flickering and fading.

Rohan moved forward again. A sudden shock from his left side drove him clear of the berserker, and then the entire area.

The matte black ship, presumably unmanned, had attacked.

"You little f—"

The two of them, ship and Hybrid, hurtled across the moon's surface toward a large mountain.

Rohan reached down and found the handhold he'd created earlier.

With a bellow of rage he *pushed* against the ship, stopping its motion dead, then accelerating it back the other way.

The ship twisted and spun from side to side, trying to get away. Rohan gripped it with his right hand, pinching another handhold into the hull, steering it in the line he wanted.

With both hands he drove the point at the back of the ship into Jaroux, stunning the large man.

Rohan kept his handholds and flipped over, driving the ship into the lunar surface.

"Stay down! I've torn thousand-year-old dreadnoughts into scrap over less than this!"

Through senses enhanced by the flow of Power coursing through him, he caught a whiff of fear from the ship. It *felt* disturbingly like the cry of a child.

The whimper slowed the rise of Rohan's temper.

He stalked over to where Jaroux lay, draped backward over a mound of stone.

Rohan stomped on the larger man's lower leg, snapping the shin.

The berserker's entire body spasmed with the movement, then lay back again.

Rohan reached out and, with a jerk of his powerful hands, broke the blonde's remaining undamaged arm, just above the wrist.

Another wave of emotion from the ship behind him: wordless begging.

Rohan reached forward again. His anger was high in his throat, throwing a red haze over his vision. His shoulder shook with the effort it took to restrain himself.

He repeated his chant. The calming words his teachers had given him. Once, twice. Ten times.

He inhaled sharply, then let out a long, slow, measured breath.

He held his lungs empty until the burning was too much.

Inhaled sharply again. Repeated the cycle.

Finally, he reached up with shaking hands and took out Jaroux's mask. He bent over the other Hybrid and slid it down over his face, tapping it to make sure the seal was fixed. Waited to make sure the big man's belly was rising and falling with his breaths.

Then he picked his fellow half-human up in two arms and walked to the waiting ship.

28

Everything's a Nail

Pop's House of Breakfast was famous for two things: the best eggs in the sector, and arguably the best coffee. The prices were reasonable, but questions about the eggs' origin were forbidden.

The "House" was no more than a counter facing the promenade. Mismatched tables and chairs were spread out on the walkway in front of the counter. Chairs were stolen occasionally, but more often new donations were left while the store was closed. Over time the seating had spread out farther until it blocked the walkway and obscured the storefronts to either side.

Rohan only had to wait a few minutes for Pop to stroll over to take his order.

"Tow Chief Rohan. It's been a bit." Pop was tall and lean, covered in diamond-shaped scales that alternated orange and black. He had six ink-black eyes lined up across his face and around the side of his head.

"Hey, Pop. I've been busy."

"With a girl, I hope. Or a boy. Whatever you're into. How many sexes does your species have, anyway?"

"Just the two, and yes, it's mostly about a girl. Along with a few other issues. They've been in the news."

"Don't follow the news much. Just manage the business, you know."

"I do."

"The usual?"

Rohan shook his head. "I need a double order on the eggs today, Pop. Been fighting."

Pop nodded. "You all right?"

Rohan looked around. The promenade was busy with the usual morning foot traffic. Half of Pop's tables were taken by regulars eating their breakfast and leisurely sipping from steaming mugs. The odor of grass lingered under the food smells that wafted out of the kitchen.

"I think I am. We'll know for sure in a few days."

Pop grunted. "Double order. I'll be back with your coffee."

"Much thanks, Pop."

The coffee came in a pint-sized glass mug, black and hot. The Hybrid took a tentative sip, then a deeper one. "Perfect. Thanks, Pop."

The Kajakh'ton native nodded and walked back to the counter.

"Personal. Check in to Pop's, set location public."

His comm spoke softly into his ear. "Acknowledged."

He leaned far back in his chair, neck arched so he faced the clear roof overhead, and waited.

"At what are you looking, Tow Chief?" Wei Li's voice came from a few feet away, not his comm.

"Toth 3. It looks so peaceful from this distance."

"May I sit?"

"Of course, help yourself."

She sat in one of the empty chairs that surrounded Rohan's table. "Are you all right, Rohan?"

He straightened in his seat and picked up his coffee. Slurped some of the hot liquid. "I thought so, but people keep asking me. So maybe not."

"I wanted to speak with you yesterday. I have heard that you solved our mystery."

"It depends on which mystery you mean."

"You found the source of the shadow in space."

"Not exactly true. More like it found me."

She looked him over, her expression flat.

Pop came over and stood silently.

Wei Li turned to the man. "Coffee, please, Pop. No food today."

He nodded. "Coming, child."

Rohan smiled. "Child?"

She shrugged. "It is a term of endearment in his species. We are closely related."

Rohan shrugged. "If you say so."

The security chief did not respond.

Pop brought the coffee and looked at Rohan. "You'll be a while?"

Rohan nodded. "I think so. Expect the table to stay occupied for the morning. I'm good for it."

Pop waved his hand. "Take your time." He walked off, taking stock of each table and their needs.

Wei Li clicked her tongue. "Care to tell me what happened?"

Rohan paused. "Your space shadow was a stealth ship. It's either very new or very old technology. I have never seen anything like it."

"A ship that could hide from all of Wistful's sensors?"

"And more. It kept itself hidden from *Insatiable*, and it was *inside* her at the time."

"You are sure?"

"It told me so. I cannot imagine a scenario in which it would have been lying about that."

She nodded. "You say the technology is new or old. What about the ship?"

"She's a baby. Newly grown. I think she's the youngest ship I've ever spoken with."

"Shayjh? il'Drach?"

Rohan shook his head. "There was a Hybrid on board. The ship spoke like an il'Drach military ship, same attitude, same terminology. I don't think it has anything to do with the Shayjh."

"Hm. The Shayjh used to have the most advanced stealth technology in the sector, but nothing as potent as what you're describing."

Pop walked over and placed a plateful of eggs in front of Rohan. His belly answered the smell with a rumble of hunger.

The seasoning bit into his tongue as he ate. He sipped his coffee before responding.

"I can only tell you what I know."

"Did you ask the ship what its mission was?"

"I didn't have to. The Hybrid basically told me. They were spying on Marion Stone."

"The Empire wants to know about the wormhole?"

Rohan let out a short laugh. "Ironically, no. They're spying on her because of the armor."

Wei Li sipped her own coffee. "The Empire is worried about the armor?"

"I'm not sure. Jaroux, the Hybrid, didn't really know, either. You know how it goes, you get an assignment, they give you parameters. He was supposed to watch over things, spy on the good Doctor Stone, and take action only if she did something overtly treasonous. Do they want the armor for themselves, or do they want it destroyed? I wouldn't be surprised either way."

"So you do not believe he was an overt threat to Wistful."

"If I thought he was we'd be having this conversation in med bay while examining his corpse."

She nodded. Her vertically slit eyes flicked away from Rohan, taking in their surroundings, then back to him. "They attacked you? Unprovoked?"

"There might be a difference of opinion on what counts as provocation here. I was carrying your sensor cluster, but that wasn't the reason. The Hybrid was listening in to the conversation I had with the professor when her assistant and I fought the other day."

"His attack was related to the Rebellion."

"As far as I can tell."

"He just . . . lost his temper? Violated orders and assaulted you?"

Rohan shrugged. "He's from the Ice Colony. You know what those guys are like. Always looking for an excuse to lose their cool and charge off into battle against unbeatable odds, die gloriously, yada yada."

"Seems a poor choice for a spy."

"I didn't ask. I have a guess, though. I bet he pissed someone off, and they decided the best punishment for someone like that would be a couple of weeks cooped up in a ship with nothing to do but monitor comms and go stir crazy."

"That . . . is quite possible."

"I don't think this was a super high priority mission for them."

They ate in silence for a time.

"Tow Chief Rohan, how am I to know that this Hybrid is no longer a problem? Since we are not, in fact, speaking over his corpse. And since we are also not, in fact, speaking outside a prison cell where he is present and available for my interrogation."

"I gave him parole. He is never to return to this system."

"Parole? What do you mean, he promised? Did he, what do you say in your culture, did he pinky swear to never return?"

"He gave his word. Hybrids take that sort of thing very seriously."

"Do they really?"

Rohan swallowed some eggs. "There are many methods the Fathers use to control us. One of the best is to convince us that we live by some sort of code, that following the code makes us honorable. It's a powerful narrative. Chivalry, Bushido. Good trick."

"They can send you to raze planets full of innocent civilians, but you know that you're righteous because you always keep your word?"

"Exactly. We are raised to glorify that sort of thing. Honor, loyalty, courage. We're taught to live and die by those virtues. Compassion? Meh. Not so important. But if a Hybrid swears on a thing, that thing gets done or the Hybrid dies."

"You do not seem to be under the continued influence of this, what did you say? Narrative. Ethos."

"My father was unusual. But I'm not immune to the appeal of it. The warrior ideal. It's enticing because it's simple, and it speaks to something inside us."

"So you believe strongly that this Hybrid will never return?"

"I do. I made the ship promise to spend a day and a half flying away from the Empire. The ship will do as it's told; they're under the influence of the same sort of rhetoric as we Hybrids."

"Whether you are proven correct or not, there is nothing to be done about that now. And the Hybrid wasn't directed to act directly against Wistful, so I will move on from this matter."

"Good."

"One question."

"Shoot."

"How did you defeat the Hybrid? You being a mere tow chief, him being active il'Drach military?" She sipped her coffee and looked out onto the boulevard as she asked the question.

Rohan shrugged. "I had to remember who I used to be for a little while. I'm still washing the taste of that out of my mouth." He tapped the side of the coffee mug.

She nodded. "If you need to discuss things further, I am here for you. How do you say, off the record."

"Thanks."

"I will start disassembling the sensor array." She pushed her chair back to stand.

Rohan put out his hand. "Wait a minute."

She settled back into her chair. "What?"

"Can you do me a favor? You and Wistful, I guess?"

"You know I will not agree until I know what the favor is."

"Can you leave the sensor array in place for a couple of days?"

"I don't see why not. Why? For what are we looking?"

"There's a Shayjh ship in the system. A big one, I think. I'd like to know where it is."

"We won't be able to find a dormant Shayjh ship."

"Dormant?"

"If it slipped into the outer reaches of the system, and doesn't do anything, we'll have a very hard time finding it."

"What if it launches a shuttle? Headed here?"

"That is different. We can definitely keep watch for that, at least for a few days. Longer, and we'll need Wistful's permission."

"We won't need longer." He turned his head to the side. "Professor! Have a seat."

Wei Li turned and saw Benjamin Stone pulling out a chair across from Rohan.

"Security Chief, Rohan. How are you both?"

Wei Li nodded politely. Rohan grunted.

"Professor, you should let your wife know that the Empire is interested in the armor she built."

"Really? Does this have something to do with the battle you were in yesterday?"

"Yup. The Empire had a Hybrid hiding inside *Insatiable*, ready to take out the lovely Doctor Stone. The other lovely Doctor Stone, I mean."

The older human held his hand up to get Pop's attention. He ordered coffee and eggs for himself. He leaned forward and lowered his voice to a whisper. "Is this Hybrid still around?"

Rohan opened his eyes wide, as if in shock, and stared pointedly at a spot over the professor's shoulder.

Ben turned around, alarmed. Rohan laughed. "I'm kidding, I'm kidding. He's gone. I can't say whether they'll send another one, but you should have a few days' reprieve, regardless."

Ben sat back down. "That wasn't funny. You scared me!"

"Hyperion's sidekick? You should have nerves of steel."

"That was a long time ago."

Wei Li looked at him. "You knew Hyperion?"

He nodded. "My wife and I were friends of his back on Earth, long before he joined the Imperial Navy. We spent years together fighting local villains."

"I am sorry for what happened."

He spread his hands. "Thank you. Things happen. We hadn't been close in a long time."

"Still."

Rohan cleared his throat. "Professor, coming up behind you."

The professor sat still. "You're not fooling me again with the same —"

A massive furry paw settled on his shoulder. "The Doctor Stone. Mr. Tow Chief Rohan. It is pleasure of mine to see you both well."

Rohan waved to empty chairs. "Please join us, Ang, Ursula."

The massive Ursans looked around the open area until they found chairs that seemed sturdy enough to support their weight.

They pulled the chairs over to Rohan's table, then settled carefully into the creaking furniture. Pop came over and took their orders, unperturbed by the expanding group.

Ben smiled at them. "I didn't know Ursans drank coffee."

Ursula leaned forward and put her hands on the table. "Wonderful discovery it is, this coffee you have."

Rohan spread his arms. "Now this is a party. All we need is a way to make this coffee Irish and we're set."

Ang cocked his head. "What does this mean 'Irish'?"

The professor laughed. "We pour in whiskey and cream. As far as I can tell there's no real dairy here on Wistful and certainly no whiskey."

Pops arrived with a tray.

Ursula eagerly reached for the mug of coffee he offered her. She gulped from her mug. "We have heard that you had battle yesterday? Was this wormhole connection?"

Rohan shook his head. "Nothing to do with it."

The Ursans nodded and drank their coffee.

Pop walked over. "More coffee? Biscuits?"

Rohan, startled, looked up. "You serve biscuits now?"

The scaled man looked down at him. "Yes. Ohmei wanted to branch out, she started baking. No charge, they're experimental. Shouldn't poison you. Not sure about the Ursans."

Rohan nodded. "Bring some, we'll be happy to try." Pop walked away.

29

Ask a Soldier Back to War

Doctor Stone cleared his throat. "Who is Ohmei?"

"That's the cook. It's not her real name, nobody can pronounce her real name. At least no humanoids. Ohmei is just the sound people usually make if they see her."

Doctor Stone's bushy eyebrows rose in confusion, then he suddenly laughed. "Oh my. Got it. What species is she?"

Rohan shrugged. "Something with a lot of tentacles. Like a Tolone'an and Chthulhu had a baby. She makes damn good coffee, though. And we're about to find out if she can bake."

Pop brought a tray of biscuits, which the group passed around.

They ate for a while. The biscuits were hot and buttery and settled pleasantly in their bellies.

Ang cleared his throat, a rumble so deep that Rohan felt it in his bones.

"Tow Chief, War Chief Rohan. We are wishing to talk about something."

"I had a feeling this wasn't just a social call. What is it?"

Ang opened his mouth, then shut it again.

Ursula leaned forward. "When Ursans came here, when we opened wormhole, we believed was one-time only. We believed we could never go back, never be following."

"Ah. And now you know we can open the wormhole."

"It seems as yes. Maybe not, and if Wistful says too dangerous, we listen. But seems yes."

"So, what? You can't be telling me you just want to turn around and go back. They'll still kill you."

Ang grunted. "Only we go back alone. If. If we go back alone. Only if."

Rohan made a fist, relaxed it. "Seeing where you are, I have to wonder, are you asking me to go back with you? Is that what this is?"

The Ursans looked at each other. Ursula nodded. "Is one option. Would you? We can pay. Some minerals, we found, common on our world, valuable here. Pay much."

"It's not . . . it's not that." He sighed. Bit into a biscuit.

Ben Stone leaned forward. "I might be speaking out of turn, but I'm not sure Rohan *wants* to be at war. He . . . he was a soldier, once. A respected one. He left that behind. Retired."

Ang nodded. "Is not his people, is not his war. Wrong to ask it, maybe. I am sorry, brother. We had to try."

Rohan shrugged. "I know. I'm sorry, too. I just can't think about this. Not today."

Wei Li spoke. "Let us not get too far ahead of things. Wistful may not allow further openings of the wormhole. But if she does, Rohan is not the only Hybrid, or the only being of Power, available to assist you. You might be able to hire other help. I can provide you contacts, people to speak with, if you wish to do this."

Ursula nodded. "My thanks, friend Wei Li. We are not decided on returning even if we can. But we have to consider. Much thanks."

The chairs were emptying as the breakfast crowd left for work or school or appointments or went to sleep for the day. The promenade thinned out as traffic eased. Toth 3 hung overhead in all its blue-and-white glory.

Rohan ate the last bite of his eggs, finished his last biscuit. Drained the mug of coffee.

He looked at Ang, then Ursula. "If you go back, ask me again. At the last minute. No promises, though."

They nodded to him. Ang pressed his right paw over his heart. "Deepest gratitude, brother. Go or no go."

Wei Li stood. "I have work. Rohan, I will see to your request. From earlier."

"Thanks."

She looked at the Ursans. "I will get you those contacts. Please do not plan anything before Wistful approves. I do not want to be the person who has to stop you if you go against her."

Ursula nodded. "As you say. Our thanks."

Wei Li left.

The professor picked up his last spoonful of eggs and held them in the air. "I do wonder about these—"

Rohan clapped a hand over the taller man's mouth. "You can't ask. That's the rule."

Doctor Stone shrugged and spoke, his word muffled. "Sorry."

Rohan activated his comm. "Wistful, do I have ships to move this morning?"

"Yes, Rohan. If you're up for it."

He stretched his arms. "My ribs are okay. My head hurts, but I've had enough head trauma to know I'll recover. I should thank my father for the fact that I don't suffer from chronic traumatic . . . what is it called, encephalopathy."

"Report when you are able, Rohan."

"Okay."

The Ursans stood. Ang looked at Rohan. "Brother, if there is something for you that we can do, please tell. You have been great help to us and to you we have been great burden. I feel."

Rohan shook his head. "Don't worry about it, Ang. Honestly, I wish you guys were my biggest problem right now."

Ursula stepped around the table and hugged him to her chest. "We will be seeing you soon, friend Rohan."

He hugged her back, surprising himself.

Ursula disengaged. The Ursans said goodbye to Doctor Stone and walked away.

The professor turned to Rohan. "I'm still trying to wrap my head around the idea that there was a Hybrid spy in that secret bay on *Insatiable*. This is the one that blew up when you searched it?"

"Yup. He's gone now, though."

The professor sipped his coffee. "If this Hybrid was here as a spy, why did he attack you? Did you find his ship?"

Rohan shook his head but didn't answer.

"It's because of what my wife said? He heard it, spying on the comm channel?"

Rohan shrugged. "It's not important. He's gone now; he won't come back."

"Did you kill him?"

"Nah. I'm trying to be better about that sort of thing. Almost, though. Had a little flashback to the old me."

"Do you want to talk about it?"

Rohan shook his head. "Not now. Probably not ever. Some things aren't meant for talk therapy. Maybe whiskey therapy."

The professor nodded. "Hyperion didn't talk to me about it, either."

"What do you mean?"

"Well, on Earth, the cape stuff, sure, we talked about that. But after coming here, going to war for the Empire, we drifted apart. He never really talked to us, either of us, about those times."

"Well, I can't speak for Hyperion. But I can guess. And my guess is that he didn't think you'd understand. Not having been there."

"I don't doubt it. I still would have listened."

"I know, Professor. It's a nice thought."

"Well, I'm going back to the ship, to do some more analysis. Lots of good data to go through. And I'm halfway through my first draft of a paper on Ursan mating rituals that's going to set the journals on fire."

Rohan laughed. "Best of luck with that one, Professor."

"I'll see you later. Take care of that head."

"Don't worry, Professor. It's just my brain, and that's my least critical organ."

The professor stood and left.

Pop walked over, his four central eyes focused on Rohan while the outer two kept watch on the other tables. "Anything else?"

"No thanks, Pop. Back to work."

"If things work out with the girl, bring her over. Ohmei can make her the special."

"I didn't know you had a special."

"If you knew, it wouldn't be special, would it?"

Rohan chuckled. "Take it easy, Pop." He left, tapping his comms open as he walked.

"Wistful, on my way."

Rohan slipped his mask over his face and headed out a nearby airlock.

"Messages."

Magdon Krahl had sent a ping. There was no content, just the digital equivalent of a handwave, but Rohan didn't mistake the meaning.

His forty-eight hours were almost up.

"Personal. Message Adjudicator Magdon Krahl. I will meet him at one o'clock on the benches outside Pop's House of Breakfast." Pops would be closed by then, leaving the promenade mostly empty.

"Acknowledged."

Rohan worked his queue of ships in need of towing.

The morning passed.

Rohan had made two round trips to the buoy perimeter when his comm pinged with a one-word response from the Adjudicator.

"Accepted."

"Personal, search web for ways to deter a Shayjh Adjudicator."

"Searching." A long silence. "No credible matches found."

"Can you share one or two of the *in*credible ones?"

"Suicide is often mentioned, but it appears to be in jest, as the Shayjh are widely rumored to be in the habit of resurrecting their deceased enemies for the purpose of continued punishment."

"That's funny. Well, no, I guess it's not really funny. Oh, well." He checked the time. "Wistful, I'm taking my lunch break."

"Yes, Rohan."

He flew back into the station using an airlock two blocks away from Pop's. He wanted to approach slowly and on foot.

There were benches for playing tabletop games arranged amid patches of grass and random bits of playground equipment outside Pop's seating area.

As Rohan closed on the area, he saw it was nearly deserted. Three people were in sight, one seated on a bench, while the other two stood behind him.

The standing figures were surveying the promenade, their heads swiveling back and forth. If they were paying any special attention to Rohan, he couldn't tell.

He walked in a curve so he'd approach the seated figure from the front.

Magdon Krahl's eyes showed red highlights in the brighter light of the promenade. His skin was just as white and solid, as though he were cast in porcelain. His hair was pinned back from his angular face, putting his pointed ears on display, each decorated with a single onyx stud.

"Adjudicator. I would say it's a pleasure to see you again, but—"

Magdon Krahl looked sharply at Rohan. "Tow Chief Second Class Rohan. If you will not say it, then I will. A pleasure."

Rohan checked out the two Shayjh standing behind the Adjudicator. Their white hair was trimmed down to a stubble. Both were massively built, muscles straining at their matching reinforced black leather uniforms. Their heads continued to swivel, ignoring Rohan completely.

"And these are . . .?"

Magdon Krahl waved a hand dismissively. "You can say bodyguards of mine. Nothing for you to be concerned with. Please, sit." He gestured toward the bench across from his.

"Are those corpse soldiers? Does Wistful realize you have corpse soldiers on board?"

The seated Shayjh shrugged. "She has no regulation against them. To be honest, I was surprised to learn this."

Rohan grunted and sat. All that separated him from the taller man was a low stone table, just big enough for a gameboard. It was used for an il'Drach chess-equivalent that he'd learned but never mastered.

Magdon Krahl waited, smiling slightly.

Rohan cleared his throat. "While we're here, what can you tell me about Shayjh stealth ship technology?"

The question did not seem to be what the Adjudicator was expecting. "Nothing."

"That's too bad. I ran into a ship yesterday that actually managed to hide inside another ship. In a shuttle bay."

The Shayjh's eyes widened slightly. "Inside?"

"I know, it's impressive, isn't it?"

"I did not think that was possible. But I am not an engineer."

"No, of course not. Still, the ship is all but invisible. I'm no empath, but I'm used to *feeling* the presence of a ship. This thing was ten meters away from me and I got no impression at all."

"That is very impressive. But why bring this question to me?"

"I asked around, and everyone thought it must be Shayjh. After all, who has more advanced tech than you guys?"

Magdon Krahl's eyes narrowed. "I will neither confirm nor deny that particular supposition."

"Come on, Maggie. Can I call you Maggie?"

"If you like."

Rohan smiled. "That's good. Instead of the predictable answer, getting offended at my feminine nickname for you, you seize the initiative by just agreeing."

"I really just don't care. I'm much more interested in what we should be calling you."

"What does that mean?"

"You see, I took your advice. I looked into the Hybrid called The Griffin, the Scourge of Zahad. I, how would you say it? Asked around."

"Clearly this did not have the result I expected. Do you think I'm lying? Facial recognition not match up? I did grow this handsome beard as a disguise."

"No. I question your identity from a more philosophical perspective."

"Well, they say you can never set foot in the same river twice. But people are still people, and I still call you Magdon Krahl even though you're not exactly the same person I spoke with two days ago. I mean, I'm sure you're a few grams heavier or lighter."

The Shayjh shifted in his seat. "I'm not being pedantic. The Griffin built a reputation as a tremendous warrior, and while the stories never indicated a cruel streak, you were certainly ruthless. But clearly something has changed."

"Has it?"

"Obviously. The Griffin was not the sort to be so troubled by an invasion mounted by a handful of primitive mammals from a pre-Inflection-point civilization. The Griffin was not the sort to give two thoughts to defeating a sub-intelligent insect lifeform, even one as big as the decipede. The Griffin was not the sort to be troubled by an unpowered Tolone'an wearing battery-powered armor he built in the back corner of a physics lab."

"When you describe it all that way it makes me kind of sad. I do think you're underplaying how tough the decipede is."

A pale hand waved dismissively. "It's an animal. The Scourge of Zahad would have slaughtered every decipede on that mudball, then piled up the corpses and cooked the largest one for lunch."

"That imagery is equal parts glorious and disgusting. I'm having very conflicted feelings about it."

"I'm sure you are. I do not know what happened to you, but it is clear you've gone soft. Did the end of the Rebellion break your fighting spirit? Or something before? I couldn't even find any records of what you did during the Rebellion. Were you hiding somewhere, keeping your head down?"

Oh good, not everybody heard.

Rohan shrugged. "Something like that, yes. Certainly not on the front lines."

"And, because I fancy myself a villain, and the primary attribute of a villain is to enjoy cruel ironies, I have to thank you for embodying a deliciously cruel one here."

"How do you mean?"

"Because if you still were The Griffin of old, I would break our contract and leave you in peace, because as you correctly pointed out, there is no profit to be made going toe-to-toe with the old you. But if you were still that person, your precious Tamaralinth Lastex would probably have no interest in you, as her tastes do not wander toward the cruel or the ruthless. That would be her father's preference. And now, if you somehow managed to resurrect your former personality, you would assuredly lose her forever."

"That *is* a cruel irony. I see your point."

"Which brings us back to my original proposal."

"You're not going to back away nervously, hightail it to your ship, and flee the system in terror?"

"No, I do not believe I am."

"That's too bad. That was totally my plan A."

"I see. And plan B is . . ."

Rohan leaped over the table with arms outstretched, using his Power to push himself with electrifying speed into the Shayjh. He aimed his fingers directly for the Adjudicator's eyes, flaring up his Power as he moved.

Magdon Krahl flinched back into the bench, his hands rising reflexively to cover his face, both corpse soldiers frozen by the sudden nature of the assault.

Rohan's hands never reached the Shayjh's eyes. While still half an arms-length away, he reached down, ducking his shoulder, and grabbed the taller man around the waist.

The Hybrid arched his back, snapping Magdon Krahl out of seat, and shot straight up out of the park like a rocket being launched.

"Faster faster faster faster." The Earthling strained, pulling Power out of his reserves as fast as he could.

He reached the unfaceted diamond roof over the promenade in under a second. At the last moment, he twisted, bending forward, taking the impact against his own back instead of going through behind his hostage.

He didn't want the Shayjh dead. At least not yet.

The moment he felt the clear panels give way over his back he twisted again, accelerating at an angle he knew would take him as far away from incoming shuttle traffic and the station's superstructure as possible.

He sank his fingers into the Shayjh's sides and gripped hard. Rohan held the other man at arm's length and looked him over.

The Adjudicator's eyes were opened in something like shock or horror. HIs mouth gaped as his body fought for air. His eyes were bulging as he decompressed.

Rohan *pushed* hard to continue his acceleration away from the station. His eyes stung against the vacuum and his chest already ached for lack of air.

He looked around, finally establishing a line he knew would keep him clear of the station and any clusters of ship or shuttle traffic.

Rohan closed his eyes, gripped harder to Magdon Krahl's body, and shoved. He doubted the Shayjh would survive much longer in vacuum.

With a silent kick he felt the shockwave from the body exploding.

The force of the blast struck Rohan like a falling decipede, instantaneously reversing the direction of his flight and sending him tumbling back toward Wistful. The last of his breath was knocked from his lungs as every one of his joints flared with pain.

30

Shockwaves

Rohan tumbled toward the station, eyes pressed tightly shut, his thoughts on getting his mask back in place.

His lungs were screaming for air before he finished sealing the mask. He waited two counts for the air to flow, then inhaled three careful sips. The mask wouldn't supply oxygen fast enough to keep up with desperate gulps.

He was still tumbling chaotically. It reminded him of lance training, when the cadets would all be forced to recover their bearings after being thrown with violently spinning trajectories.

That training served him well.

Once he was oriented he listened to his comms.

"...all right? Repeat, Tow Chief Rohan, do you need assistance?" It was Wistful's voice.

"Negative. Sorry about that. Found an explosive on board the station, had to get it clear as quickly as possible."

"Please repeat."

"Found explosives on board, took them outside in the most direct fashion I could find. There are also two Shayjh corpse soldiers on the promenade in front of Pop's, right where I flew through the roof. You probably want security to make sure they don't go rampaging anywhere."

"Are you injured, Rohan?"

He patted himself down. "Negative. Heading back in now. I'm going back to Pop's to make sure those corpse soldiers aren't causing a ruckus."

"Very well."

Rohan propelled himself toward Wistful. His entire body ached from the explosion.

Rohan approached the station, a massive, glittering cross hanging in space, her diamond covering sparkling as if she were a necklace for gods.

The panes he'd knocked aside had already settled back into place.

He couldn't see much of anything through the roof, so he circled to an airlock and made his way to Pop's.

When he arrived he saw Wei Li and three other station security personnel standing in a semicircle. Facing them were the bodies of the two corpse soldiers.

Rohan joined them.

Wei Li looked him over. "I heard something about an explosion? Shayjh?"

Rohan nodded. "The Adjudicator was about to detonate, so I pulled him into space where he wouldn't do any damage."

"'About to detonate'? Why?"

Rohan shrugged. "I was going to have to kill him, and when I did that, he was going to detonate. So, you know, I acted to preserve the safety of the station."

She shook her head. "Shall I assume you had a legitimate reason to kill this Adjudicator? Or would you like to come with me to a holding cell?"

"Oh, no, I definitely had a good reason. It was proactive self-defense."

"That is not usually how self-defense works."

"Premature self-defense? No, I don't like the sound of that. He was threatening me. Actually, he was threatening you, too. Said if I didn't do as he asked he'd take it out on my friends, and you are on that list."

"Threatening the security chief? I suppose we can call that a capital offense."

"You occasionally show a strange sense of understanding of things like due process. I'm not complaining, I just find it odd."

"You tend to think of me as a police officer, but I'm not. My job is not to create a just and fair legal system. My function is first to keep Wistful safe, second to keep her inhabitants safe. If this Adjudicator posed a threat to either, and you removed it, you helped me with my job."

"I get it. Hey, can I speak to you in private for a moment?"

"Yes. Come." She turned to her lieutenants. "Watch the bodies. If they regain consciousness, stun them again."

Wei Li led Rohan toward a more isolated area of the park. She tapped at something on her tablet, then nodded.

"No surveillance here. What is it?"

"Those guys aren't dead?"

She shook her head. "I need to be certain they are not also equipped with explosives. Until then I'm keeping them unconscious but alive. Relatively speaking."

Rohan nodded. "You used electric shocks to knock them out?"

"Yes. It's the easiest way to handle a rogue corpse soldier."

"Okay, good. Thanks. I would have given you a heads up, but I didn't know about them until just now. The Shayjh didn't have the corpse soldiers when we first met up."

"*I* knew about them. We've been keeping a close eye on them since their arrival."

"Great. Listen, I could use some help."

"Yes?"

"I'm pretty sure there's a Shayjh ship in the system. Magdon Krahl is probably waking up in a brand new clone body as we speak, and I am pretty sure he's going to come back this way. Maybe not immediately, but soon."

"They will not dock a Shayjh interstellar ship on Wistful. I do not believe she would allow it, but even if she did, they do not like their ships to remain so close to scrutinizing eyes."

"Right, so I imagine they'll send a shuttle."

"Which is why you wanted the active sensors to remain deployed."

"Yeah. I had a feeling something like this would be happening. I was hoping you could tell me where that shuttle is coming from."

"You intend to find the mother ship by back-tracking the shuttle path."

"Yes. Killing him isn't going to accomplish anything, but if I know where the ship is, I can grab some leverage."

She tapped the side of her tablet absent-mindedly. "I should be able to help. As soon as his shuttle is identified I'll generate the tracking data."

"That's super, thanks."

"Anything else?"

He scratched under his beard. "I don't think so."

"Rohan, was your interaction with this Adjudicator related to the opening of the wormhole? Or Doctor Stone's work?"

He shook his head. "Nope. Personal matters."

"Very well. Please try to minimize the collateral damage caused in this conflict."

"You got it. And thank you." Rohan rubbed his temples.

Wei Li looked at him. "Are you certain you are uninjured?"

"I think so. That was one hell of an explosion. I'm going to go buy some stock in Shayjh munitions factories."

"I do not believe those are publicly traded companies."

"No, I was . . . Ha, you got me."

She smiled, a twitch at the corners of her green lips. "I believe I did. Now, please get some rest. I'm sure there will be some new catastrophic event within a day that requires your attention."

"Really? I was hoping for a break."

"It is unlikely. Bad things always happen in sevens, and we are not yet at that limit."

"My people always say they come in threes."

"Your race is young and short-sighted."

Rohan laughed. "I can't argue. Look, I'm going to take your suggestion and lie down for a while. Comm me if you need me."

"I will, Rohan. Now I must see to the scanning of these bodies."

Rohan made his goodbyes and started the walk back to his quarters.

He stopped off at a food counter and ordered the Lukhor equivalent of burritos. They were tasty, and about as spicy as he could handle.

He popped the last bite of burrito into his mouth as the door to his quarters cycled open. He drained a pitcher of water, then put his mask into the recharger to replenish the air supply.

The Hybrid lay on his bed fully clothed.

"Personal. Hold all messages for ninety minutes. Then wake me."

"Acknowledged."

He closed his eyes.

His dreamed of his time as a lance primary. Flashes of battles he'd fought in, wars he'd fought, disjointed images filled with blood and violence. Mostly his violence and the blood of others.

The dreams shook him out of sleep before his chime could wake him.

He sat for fifteen minutes trying to meditate.

"Wistful, let me finish out my shift. How many ships are on my docket?"

"Just two out and two in, Rohan. It should not take long."

"Copy. Heading out now."

Rohan made slow work of the towing jobs. He'd been pushing his Power harder than usual and wanted to be rested if he needed it again.

He chatted with three shuttles. He asked them about the shadow they'd been seeing, and if it was still appearing.

None reported any new sightings.

Wistful spoke on his comm. "Rohan, that was the last ship. I will speak with you tomorrow."

"Copy that, Wistful. Heading in."

He made his way toward his personal airlock. Before reaching it, he turned sharply and redirected toward *Insatiable*. He coasted toward the enormous science vessel.

"Hail, *Insatiable*."

"Tow Chief Second Class Rohan! I wasn't expecting you. But that's all right! More than all right! You can come by anytime. What can I do for you?"

"*Insatiable*, can I come aboard and have a private chat? If not now, some other time?"

"Private chat? Of course. But with whom? Should I page my captain? Doctor Stone?"

"No, I meant with you. I just want to keep you updated."

"Me?"

"Is that okay?"

"Sure, of course it is. I'm happy to talk. Come in through Orange 36, it's secure."

"Cool."

He followed the lines flashing on *Insatiable*'s hull to the designated section.

"Tow Chief Rohan, I believe Doctor Stone would also like to speak with you. Is it all right if I mention to her that you're on board?"

"'Her'? You mean Marion Stone?"

"Yes."

He paused. "Is she going to give me a hard time? Because I'm really not in the mood for it today."

"I do not believe she is, Tow Chief. I believe she is feeling contrite."

"Hm. Okay, sure. Just give me five minutes to talk to you first."

"Yes, sir, Tow Chief Rohan."

An airlock opened in front of him. He entered, then followed guide arrows through some corridors to a conference room. He went in and sat down.

A large screen took up one wall. It lit up with a representation of *Insatiable*, as she must have looked in drydock where she was built.

"I am at your disposal, Tow Chief Rohan."

"Good. Hm. I'm not sure how to say this, exactly. I wanted to make sure someone was keeping you informed."

"Yes, Tow Chief Rohan. Informed of what?"

"You're aware that we found out what was originally in Orange 10?"

"I . . . wasn't exactly."

"Okay. Well, I think you should know. I was, well, I was doing some work for Wistful, out near Toth 5. I was attacked by a ship."

"A ship? One of my shuttles?"

"No, not a shuttle. An actual ship. Young, but alive. It had pretty amazing stealth capabilities."

"I see."

"That ship came to this system inside Orange 10. It had a crew of one, a Hybrid, an Imperial soldier. I guess a lance."

"You are saying that there was a ship hiding in Orange 10 with a lance aboard?"

"I am."

"And I did not know about it?"

"Correct."

"That is, well, that is very embarrassing, Tow Chief Rohan. I don't know how to apologize for that."

"Actually, I don't want an apology. I don't think it was your fault."

"How do you mean that?"

"You were a transport ship before, right? Much smaller. Different configuration."

"Yes, that's right! I told you that. That's how we met."

"You must have grown very quickly to become this size in such a short time."

"Oh, yes, very quickly. In fact, I grew faster than any other ship I know. It was very exciting."

"You know, when humans have a growth spurt, when they grow fast, we often become very clumsy. It takes time to adjust to newly lengthened limbs, and if we grow too fast, we have a hard time adjusting."

"I see."

"It must be hard for you, too. To maintain spiritual cohesion when you change that quickly."

"You think that is why I did not sense the intruder?"

Rohan sighed. "I can't prove anything. But I do think someone wanted you to grow so fast that you'd have blind spots in your, what do you call it, self-conception."

"Such as Orange 10."

"Yes."

"That would also result in a weakness in my defenses. If I don't have a strong sense of all my physical parts, I can't protect them from metaphysical interventions. Powers."

"That is also true."

"So my safety was compromised in order to hide a spy on board."

"I can't prove anything, *Insatiable*, but I do believe that's what happened."

She was quiet for a bit. Then: "Why are you telling me this?"

"I think you have a right to know. I don't really expect you to do anything about it. To be fair, I can't think of anything that you *could* do about it. But you should know."

"Do you ever hate the Empire, Rohan? For the way it uses us?"

"Only when I think about it, *Insatiable*. Which I try not to do."

"If you hate the Empire, why did you end the Rebellion?"

Rohan paused. "First of all, please don't repeat that story."

"I won't, Rohan. I'm getting better at keeping secrets."

"Second, it's complicated, and not something I want to talk about. And it's probably safer for you if you don't know the whole story. Okay? Ask me again in a decade or two."

"Do you think we'll still see each other in ten or twenty years?"

"I can't promise anything, but I see no reason why we can't be friends."

"You? Friends with a ship?"

"Why not?"

"That is unusual. For a humanoid."

"I'd be proud to be your friend, *Insatiable*. But either way, there are things I can't talk about. Okay?"

"Yes, that is okay, Rohan."

"Great. For what it's worth, the stealth ship and the Hybrid weren't here to hurt you."

"I should have been told, Rohan. I feel, I don't know the word. Violated."

"I'm sorry. I don't know, maybe I shouldn't have told you."

"No! I am a science vessel. I want to know the truth, and I want to know everything. That is how I picked my name. That is my ethos. Please, never doubt the wisdom of telling me true things, even if they are painful to know."

"I hear you, *Insatiable*. That's all I had to say."

"From the bottom of my processing network, I apologize, Rohan."

"You know how you said I shouldn't apologize for telling you the truth, even if it hurts? Same here. Don't apologize to me for being taken advantage of by the Empire. Deal?"

"Yes, Tow Chief Rohan. Deal."

"Great. Now, you said Marion Stone wanted to see me?"

"Yes, Tow Chief. She is waiting outside."

"Oh, great, she's waiting. I'm sure that will improve her mood. Please send her in."

"Yes, Tow Chief. Thank you. For thinking of me."

"No problem."

Rohan stayed in his seat as the door slid open.

Marion Stone entered. She wore a white jumpsuit, wide pockets and loops for instrument covering most of its surface. A tight ponytail held her blond-going-to-gray hair and her finely lined face was free of makeup.

"Tow Chief Rohan."

"Doctor Stone. Please excuse me for not getting up. I've had a rough couple of days."

"That's fine."

"What brings you to me?"

She walked slowly to a chair opposite Rohan's, pulled it out, and sat down. "I do not like apologizing."

"I didn't ask you to."

"No, you didn't, but Ben and I had a talk, and I remembered—I was reminded—that as much as I don't like apologizing, I like it even less when I owe an apology but don't make it."

"Okay." He waited.

"I have come to realize that you are not a bad man. And I have treated you as a bad man, because of what you are, and that isn't how I like to conduct myself."

Rohan waited, arms folded on the table in front of him.

Doctor Stone sighed. "Thank you for saving Garren's life. I . . . we both . . . I think we both expected you to kill him. In some ways maybe he was hoping you'd kill him."

"If you're expecting me to apologize . . ."

"No, that's not what I meant. Really. In some ways, he wanted to die a martyr. He's been so angry since, well, since the Tolone'an war. Even angrier since the Rebellion."

"He's not alone."

"That's not really an excuse, is it?"

"No."

"You saved my husband's life. You saved Garren, after he attacked you. We are at odds over the wormhole opening, but that's not really your fault, is it?"

"No."

"So, I'm sorry. We shouldn't have goaded you into having to attack us. And I should not have said what I said."

Rohan sighed and slumped forward on the table. "You put me in a lot of danger. Which is my own doing, in a way, but you also put a lot of other people in danger. Innocent people."

"I know. I am sorry."

He sighed. "All right. I forgive you. But please don't spread this more than you already have, okay?"

She nodded. "I won't. Neither will any of my people, I guarantee it."

"Good."

"I do have a question, though."

"What?"

"I've read your files. You might not have been the most ruthless or savage Hybrid, but you weren't kind or merciful. What happened?"

He sighed. "Doctor Stone, I've accepted your apology, but we are not friends. You want answers to questions like that, you've got to make more of an effort."

She nodded. "That's fair. I'm sorry, I'm not the one with the social graces."

"I get it, kind of. I'm not merciful by nature. I had to work at it."

A hint of anger flashed in her eyes. "Are you accusing me of something?"

"Just observing. You want to be rude, then make excuses because civility doesn't come naturally? That's a little like a Hybrid bullying people and blaming it on his father. Isn't it?"

She paused, holding back an outburst. "Maybe you're right. I guess we're not going to be friends."

"I didn't say that. I just said that if you want to be friends, you're going to have to make an effort. And if you don't want to, that's fine with me."

The door cycled open. Ben Stone squeezed through before it could finish, his face flushed slightly and his lips parted in a pant.

"Oh my! Marion, Rohan. I heard you were here. Is everything okay?" His eyes were wide under his bushy eyebrows, his arms extended as if he thought he would have to physically separate them.

Rohan shrugged. Marion Stone looked at her husband coolly. "We were just talking. To be honest, I came here to apologize."

Ben slumped forward, his arms on the table supporting him. He took a deep breath. "Of course you did. Great, I'm glad. How is that going?"

Rohan shrugged again. "I was just leaving. I've done what I came here to do. Take care, both of you."

The older man looked at his friend, his eyes questioning. Rohan shook his head gently and turned to leave.

Marion stood. "I meant what I promised, Rohan."

"Good. I really don't want us to be enemies. I find that I have more than enough lately."

He left the couple in the conference room. A few short corridors later he was putting his mask on inside the airlock. A minute after that he was outside *Insatiable* and on his way home.

31

The Inquisition

"Rohan, please wake up." Wistful's voice sank down through his consciousness.

He had a vague sense of being asleep and dreaming about . . . it slipped away.

"Rohan, please wake up. You are needed."

What was happening? Why was Wistful talking to him?

"Tow Chief Second Class Rohan, it is urgent."

His eyes opened. The room was dark; his normally transparent roof was set to turn opaque when he slept.

"Lights, dim." The room filled with a soft yellow glow.

"Rohan, please. There is an urgent situation."

He took a deep breath and sat up. He rubbed his eyes quickly and stood. "Brief me. I'll get dressed."

"The wormhole has opened again."

"Good grief. Is it Doctor Stone? She took a shuttle out?" He used the toilet, feeling momentarily awkward about peeing while someone was talking to him. Then again, Wistful was older than his species and inorganic. He didn't think she was programmed for embarrassment.

"No. From the other side."

"More Ursans?"

"It appears so. One ship has come through so far, and it is broadcasting a Mayday."

"Mayday?" He splashed water on his face, forcing himself awake.

"The message is in Ursan."

"Okay. I'm almost ready. Patch me in and push directions to my mask."

"It is done."

He pulled on a clean uniform and slipped his comm unit behind his ear. The feed started right away.

The voice was rough and guttural. It spoke in Ursan, not the primitive Drachna the Ursans on the station had been practicing since their arrival. The language sounded to his ears like something between a roar and a growl, punctuated with glottal stops and clicks.

If he hadn't learned Fire Speech he wasn't sure he'd even recognize it as a language.

"This is the cargo ship *Ark of Cubs*. We are a refugee vessel. We are unarmed and have taken damage. Repeat, Mayday. This is the ship . . ."

He disengaged his mask from the recharging unit that kept its battery and air tanks topped up and settled it onto his face, tapping the seal in place. Lights came to life in his heads-up display, indicating the direction he needed to fly.

He stepped toward his airlock.

The airlock shut and depressurized as soon as he entered. Wistful was watching and managing things in real time.

"On my way." He said the words out of habit. The station knew exactly where he was.

"Thank you, Rohan."

The Mayday was repeating through his comms. He lowered the volume to a background drone.

"Wistful, is that Mayday on a loop? And can you alert me if it changes? As, in, is it a recording?"

"I will." A short pause. "There are variations in timing from each iteration to the next. It is being repeated by a person."

"That's good. I think. At least there are survivors. We're not dealing with a ghost ship."

"That is correct."

He flew around to the bottom of the station and accelerated outward into space.

The Mayday continued.

"Do you have visual on the ship? Any information?"

"Yes, Rohan. It is a dead vessel, but quite large. It's three times the size of the Ursan ship that's docked here."

"Signs of damage?"

"Yes. I can identify four forward drives on the ship, of which only one is currently functioning. Damage on the others, and on the hull, appears to be of both projectile and energy weapon origin."

"Copy that." He pushed hard, accelerating toward the wormhole.

There was a pause in the Mayday.

"Wistful, have you answered the Mayday? If not, maybe we should?"

A pause.

"I have not. Would you like to?"

"Sure, let's tell them help is on the way."

"I will patch your comms through to the channel on which they're sending the Mayday. It's radio, so there will be a lag."

"Okay. Ready."

"Go ahead."

He cleared his throat and spoke in Fire Speech. "This is Tow Chief Second Class Rohan of the independent space station Wistful. I am heading to your location to offer assistance."

A short delay.

"By the gods, thank you. There's someone there! Someone's answering!" Voices in the background.

"What's your situation, *Ark of Cubs*?"

A new voice, this one rougher and deeper, answered. "This is the captain. We are fleeing an active hostile situation. We are leaking atmosphere and are completely out of food and water. We weren't even sure there was anything on this side of the Eye of Gods."

"Well, we're here. How many people are we talking about? On board?"

"We have five thousand. Mostly women and cubs. Hundreds are injured, mostly burns, some other injuries. We are leaking atmosphere; we have hours at most before we start losing cubs because of lack of oxygen.

We can't maneuver. Our drives were already damaged; opening the Eye completely finished them."

"I'm getting there as fast as I can."

"I don't understand. I can't see your ship on our scans."

"No ship, *Ark of Cubs*. It's just me."

"What? I don't understand."

"Give it a few minutes, you'll see."

He switched his comms to a closed channel with Wistful.

"Wistful, can you confirm that this ship is unarmed?"

"It has light defensive weaponry, of a grade sufficient to ward off meteorites and perhaps armed shuttles. No more than that. It appears to be a repurposed cargo vessel."

"Copy that. One other thing, do our Ursans know about this ship?"

"I am waiting for Wei Li to arrive before I notify them."

"Huh. I'm going to assume these refugees are from the same side of their conflict, but someone should verify before we let them on board."

"Yes, Rohan. I've thought of that."

"Of course. Sorry, just thinking out loud, really."

"It's fine, Rohan. You should begin decelerating now."

"Thanks." He refocused his Power to reduce his velocity. It made no sense to reach the refugee ship only to blow by it and take ten minutes to return.

He switched back to open comms.

"Rohan of Wistful, another ship of our cousins went through the Eye about nine days ago. Did it arrive? Are our people safe? Are they alive?"

"That ship was full of your people?"

"Yes. Captain <unintelligible roar> is my cousin."

The Hybrid shrugged, mentally, and took a chance. "They're safe and on our station. I'm sure they'll be very excited to hear you have come through."

The Ursan sighed forcefully, an exhale loud enough to be audible over comms. "Oh, that's good. Let them know we made it. We evacuated Korulskan colony and hid in the planet's rings. We were running out of food and water, but saw the Eye open. That's when we realized the key would work and made a dash for it."

Rohan continued decelerating. He could see the wormhole, outlined in his display, and a dot in front of it that outlines labeled as the Ursan ship.

"The good news is, *Ark of Cubs*, our atmospheric and dietary requirements are similar. You'll be safe on Wistful."

"That is good. How is it that your words are unfamiliar, yet I can understand you, Rohan of Wistful?"

"That's hard to explain. When you arrive, you'll all need to learn Drachna so you can talk to everybody else. The other Ursans are already picking it up."

"I see." A pause. "I am sure we have much to learn. We haven't thought much beyond surviving the day. We didn't really believe we would see another sunrise."

"We'll take good care of you, don't worry."

"Then we are forever in your debt, Rohan of Wistful."

Rohan chuckled to himself. "No debt, *Ark of Cubs*. This is my job. If you feel the need to repay me, we can get drunk and eat fish together. For now, just find a point on the ship that I can use as an anchor. Something that I can pull without structurally damaging the ship."

"Are you saying that you're going to pull us by hand toward the station?"

"Her name is Wistful, and yes, I am. You should be able to see me flying toward you soon."

Wei Li's voice broke in on a closed channel. "Rohan, we are contacting the Ursans on Wistful to confirm this story."

"Do you want me to wait to bring them in or stall them? If they're telling the truth, delay could be pretty bad."

"Bring them in as fast as you can. We have visual confirmation of atmospheric loss. Wistful doesn't want innocent lives sacrificed to caution here."

"Copy."

Rohan was three-quarters of the way across the Toth system, moving toward the wormhole at tremendous velocity. He was slowing as rapidly as he could, shedding speed every second.

The wormhole was close enough to be visible, a bright circle ringed in stone. He knew where the Ursan ship was only because it was outlined in his heads-up display.

Wistful's voice broke over his comms.

"Tow Chief, there's something else coming through the wormhole."

Wei Li interjected. "It's got drives, it's moving and closing on *Ark of Cubs*. Hold on, it's broadcasting."

A stern male voice spoke Ursan over the open channel. "*Ark of Cubs*, this is *Millennial Inquisition*. Make your final prayers to your false gods, we are ending your heresy here and now."

Rohan muttered, "Rudra's braids."

The captain of *Ark of Cubs* was yelling. "Please stop! We are mostly females and cubs! They're innocent! You don't have to do this! We'll never come back!"

"The gods will know that you escaped. We must end this now."

"Please help! We're taking fire. Our armor is already weakened. Drives are non-functional. We're defenseless!"

Wei Li spoke to Rohan. "Ursula confirmed these are her cousins. She believed the colony destroyed, with no survivors. The story from *Ark of Cubs* is plausible. Repeat, story is plausible, bring that ship home."

Ark of Cubs was still broadcasting shouts over the open channel. "If anyone can hear me, please help. If they want my life, and the lives of my officers, we offer them. But please make them spare the cubs! We have hundreds of infants on board who can't even speak yet!"

Another voice from *Millennial Inquisition* came. "Nobody cares about you heretics. We'll wipe you out and the galaxy will be a better place for it."

Rohan was muttering. He didn't even know if he was broadcasting. "No-no-no." He switched the vector of his *push*, accelerating again, determined to reach the new ship before it could cause more casualties.

"We are taking damage! Light damage sustained from long-range weapons. We cannot handle much more of this. May the gods have mercy on us in the next life."

Wei Li. "Two more contacts emerging from the wormhole. Repeat, two more ships emerging."

Ursula growled. "Let us go to them! Please! We must to help!"

Wei Li again. "Get back. I have told you that you can take your ship out. This is an open—" The audio from Wistful cut abruptly.

Ark of Cubs: "Two more attack vessels came through! They are closing rapidly. We cannot maneuver, repeat, we cannot maneuver. Defenses are minimal. We are unarmed. Please, we have mostly young females and cubs aboard, we cannot defend ourselves."

Rohan flew with his left fist outstretched, his right hand pinned to his side. He *pushed* himself to accelerate at a greater and greater rate.

His Power bubbled up, his Hybrid anger and rage whispering around its edges.

"Major hit! Losing hull integrity. We're engaging drives, we can't control our movement but perhaps tumbling will buy us some time."

Millennial Inquisition again. "Tumbling will not help you. Your heresy will end, finally. Hold your cubs and pray that your gods tend you on the other side."

Rohan shouted. "*Millennial Inquisition*, my name is Rohan. You don't know me but if you don't turn around right now, I'm going to kill every single sentient being on your ship."

Three barks of laughter came over the comms. "There isn't a ship within two planetary orbits of us. Who the hell is this? If you're trying to scare me, you're going to have to do a better job than that."

Power surged through the Hybrid. His acceleration grew. "You're about to find out, and you're not going to like it. Turn around. If you don't, I'm going to destroy all of you, then fly through that wormhole and start working on your kin. When I'm done, nobody will be left to remember your names."

More chatter over the comms. "We're taking fire! Hull integrity dropping in rear sections! We're on fire now!"

Rohan set a blinding pace. The wormhole loomed large in his field of vision, and the four ships on his side of the spatial distortion were becoming visible.

His heads-up display had the four ships outlined.

He took aim at *Millennial Inquisition*, the ship closest to *Ark of Cubs*.

"*Millennial Inquisition.* Turn around now."

The Ursan attack vessel grew at a dizzying rate as Rohan continued to accelerate into the ship. It was almost identical to Ursula's ship; a large silver teardrop with rounded bulges at the front and back where the bootstrap drives jutted out past the hull.

A background voice was audible over *Millennial Inquisition*'s broadcast. "Sir, missile approaching."

"Shoot it down. Shoot it down!"

Projectiles converged on Rohan as he flew. A quick exertion of his Power split the stream, deflecting the shells around his path.

"*Millennial Inquisition,* last chance."

"Forget him, destroy that cargo ship! All of you, fire on that ship! Kill the heretics!"

"Captain, negative on missile intercept! Still incoming!"

"What? What in the spawning beds of hell could have survived that? Anti-ballistics, full spread."

"Yes, Captain."

Rohan pulled more Power through and into his body, driving it with his rage.

Another barrage of projectiles and energy weapons took an intercept course toward Rohan.

He split them like the prow of a ship breaking ocean waves.

"Missile is still accelerating, sir."

Rohan surged over and past the cargo vessel. It was huge, about half the size of *Insatiable*, and with a similar blocky, rectangular shape. There were perforations and scorch marks peppering its hull and visible puffs of air leaking from a variety of places along its length.

Just past *Ark of Cubs*, Rohan saw the three attack vessels, one in front and two others flanking and behind it.

He flashed by the cargo vessel and closed the gap between it and the first attack ship. Another salvo of projectiles rushed toward him, split apart by his Power and passing harmlessly into space.

Rohan tensed his body and folded his arms in front of his head. He peeked between his forearms, sighting on the ship, then on the space between its front bootstrap drives, then on the window that opened onto its flight deck.

He collided with the nearly impervious material of the front window. Their relative velocity was so high that the energy released by his impact vaporized the window and superheated the gases inside the bridge.

Rohan caught an instantaneous glimpse of surprised Ursan faces just before the sailors on the flight deck exploded into a thick cloud of boiling blood and roasted meat.

The Hybrid's momentum carried him deeper into the ship. He redirected himself as best as he could, using his Power to twist and turn through the ship, letting the heaviest structural members of its frame deflect him into a jagged course through its core.

Most of his kinetic energy was absorbed by the time he burst through the aft bootstrap drive in a plume of twisting metal and flame.

Millennial Inquisition had been knocked backward by the impact, so the other two attack ships were passing it on their way to *Ark of Cubs*.

Rohan's body ached from the impacts, his shoulders sore to the bone, even as Power flooded through him, bringing fresh energy for the fight.

The attack ship was breaking apart, expanding gases from its wrecked fusion generators pushing at sections of hull clinging to one another by threads of steel. Furry bodies fell out into space, blood spraying from eyes and ears as they decompressed. Munitions all around the ship continued to detonate, unable to withstand the heat generated by Rohan's impact, further disintegrating the large vessel.

Small shuttles, lifeboats from the look of them, burst out of the ship in a cloud.

Rohan yelled again, oblivious to how it would sound over the comms. He spun toward *Ark of Cubs* and the two remaining attack vessels.

Voices came from *Ark of Cubs*. "One of the ships just stopped! But the other two are closing. We're in range of primary cannons now! We're going to break apart!"

Rohan yelled. "No no no!"

Wei Li's voice reported over the open channel. "*Millennial Inquisition* is disabled."

Ursula's voice followed, hollow, as she spoke in the background of the microphone. "Disabled is not word. Is destroyed. Only enough life pods for maybe half of crew."

"Confirmed. Two remaining ships on attack vector to *Ark of Cubs*. Nothing further is coming through the wormhole. Yet."

Like a hammer blow from a god, Rohan's anger and Power slammed into him again, driving him toward *Ark of Cubs*.

Thick cannon nozzles were extruding from the hulls of both ships, pointed at *Ark of Cubs*. Rohan *drove* himself until his eyes ran with tears of blood.

The cannons warped and flexed with the force of the projectiles they fired at the crippled cargo ship.

He stretched his arms out and *pushed*, streams of Power spreading out and deflecting the fired projectiles away from *Ark of Cubs*. He trembled with the effort, drained by the sheer mass of the ordnance he was moving, and by the sharp angle of deflection he needed to create so they would miss the huge refugee ship.

"Rohan, the attack vessels are arming primary energy cannons. Those beams will be harder to deflect."

Some kind of prayer was coming from *Ark of Cubs*, Ursan voices chanting together.

Rohan was between *Ark of Cubs* and the two attack vessels. He spun, his back to the refugee ship, and deflected another wave of physical ordnance out into space.

There was no more chatter over open channels from the attacking ships.

Rohan saw the energy cannons extend from the front of the two attack vessels. He braced.

Beams of superheated plasma lanced out from each ship. Rohan reached out with his Power and *pushed*.

The beams bent, but barely.

A quick glance told Rohan he wasn't doing enough.

He *pushed* harder.

The plasma arced down into the cargo ship, twin blinding pillars of fire. They struck into the very tail end of the ship, vaporizing the structure where they hit.

"No no no."

Rohan abandoned his efforts.

He *pushed* all his strength into one of the two beams, deflecting it entirely away from *Ark of Cubs*.

Then he flew into the other.

The energy burned into his chest, searing through his uniform, then through skin and fascia and muscle. The Hybrid's entire body lit up in agony for a moment that felt like a lifetime. Then another. And another.

Before the energy could punch through his ribs and into his heart Rohan had to let go of his deflection and use his Power to save himself. He deflected the second beam away from his chest, the pain redoubling as the energy pulsed out into space.

Both beams were finished, the projectors drained and recharging.

He turned and saw that the huge refugee ship was still floating, still mostly intact.

He turned to face the attack vessels, his blood and fluids boiling out into the vacuum of space. His wrists, elbows, and shoulders resisted any attempt to move, traumatized by the impact they'd absorbed when he struck *Millennial Inquisition*. Every breath was agony.

Prayers continued over the comms.

Wei Li updated him. "Captain Ursula and her crew are on their way, Rohan, but they are too far to reach you in time to be of help." Her voice was flat, professional.

He didn't answer.

Rohan faced the two remaining ships and roared his defiance, his Hybrid rage fully flowing through his body. It beat back the pain in his shoulders, the ache in his elbows. The oozing pores of his chest narrowed and sealed.

He spread his arms and legs out wide and willed himself into a barrier between the refugees and their murderers.

The attack ships paused. The gun nozzles remained dormant.

Bays opened on the sides of both ships, black dots expanding into wide-open holes. Out of each hole poured an array of pointed silver objects.

Armed and armored shuttles, they reminded him of Earth jets, with stubby wings for atmospheric maneuvering.

The streams of fighters, hundreds in total, arced out from each ship, then bent in a synchronized motion, turning toward *Ark of Cubs*.

As they closed, the shuttles spread out, leaving their tight formation behind and forming a huge cloud of attack vectors.

Rohan flew out to meet the fleet of small ships. He reached out with his Power toward one, *feeling* his way through the dead ship. Without a driving intelligence it could not resist his probe. He found the fusion generator and *twisted* its casing, tearing it apart and venting the superheated gas throughout the inside of the fighter.

The Ursan pilot inside the fighter died instantly. The ship exploded moments later as the superheated hydrogen ignited its explosive ordnance.

He *reached* out to another ship and repeated. It exploded noiselessly in the hard vacuum of space.

Meanwhile, fighter after fighter twisted into a strafing run on *Ark of Cubs*, dumping payloads of explosives into the relatively motionless and defenseless ship.

Rohan tore through the swarms of fighters.

He destroyed other fighters by *reaching* into their guts and tearing apart their generator casing or setting off some of their munitions with a shockwave.

Another fighter approached him on a collision course. Rather than avoiding, he turned into it and crashed through its window. He quickly smashed the faceplate on the surprised pilot's suit and let him die of decompression.

Rohan turned and saw lines of fighters tearing holes in *Ark of Cubs*. The wreckages of the ones he'd destroyed made barely a dent in the fleet.

He screamed wordlessly.

"Rohan, you probably know this: while the winged shuttles are armed, the spherical ships that escaped *Millennial Inquisition* are lifeboats.

They're unarmed and have minimal maneuvering. Just life support, simple comms, and a hull."

A new voice. Marion Stone was on Wistful's flight deck. "Wormhole is still open. Negative on radiation or energy release."

Wistful broke in. "*Ark of Cubs* will not survive this."

Wei Li spoke again. "*Ark of Cubs*, if you can get to lifeboats we may be able to save you."

They wouldn't understand. Rohan pulled back his rage enough to spit out some words. "*Ark of Cubs*, get to lifeboats. I'll save whoever I can."

The prayer chant stopped and the captain answered. "We only had a few lifeboats and they're damaged beyond repair. This ship is a cargo vessel, it's designed for a skeleton crew. We will not survive. Thank you for trying. It was good to have hope, if only for a short while. We will remember you in the next life."

Rohan shouted again. He grabbed a fighter by its wing and turned it into a tight circle, hard and sharp enough to render the pilot unconscious. He spun again and slammed the ship into another fighter.

The blast as their munitions detonated threw him toward one of the large attack vessels.

The ship was turning. Behind it Rohan saw the wormhole, a disk cut into space, an alien star system in view on the other side.

With a shout he tore through the bubbles holding the ship's drives.

"Rohan, what are you doing?"

He didn't answer.

He flew to the second ship and disabled its drives, then went back to the fighters.

A fighter slammed into him from behind. Lights flashed in his eyes and his spine strained with the impact.

He twisted in place and grabbed fistfuls of metal on the fighter's nose. With a shout he pulled a strip of hull away from it, destroying the ship.

More fighters veered off course and headed toward him.

A quick glance showed *Ark of Cubs* breaking into parts. The ship split in two, the halves falling away from each other like glaciers breaking off an ice sheet, enormous masses drifting slowly apart.

Air boiled out of the ship as it lost atmospheric integrity.

Rohan dodged an incoming fighter; the next one almost speared him in the chest.

Suddenly the fighters were coming at him in waves, redirecting their attention from the doomed refugee ship.

He coughed, softly, inside his mask. Blood flecked the inside of the diamond.

He smiled.

Space was packed with missiles fired at the Hybrid. Instead of simply deflecting them, he redirected the streams into other ships.

Another fighter tried to ram him. He dodged, but just barely, and grabbed its wing.

With a heave, he turned it at a right angle into another fighter.

He destroyed ten more fighters before they turned tail and flew away from him, giving him room and time to recover.

The prayers, and all other broadcasts from *Ark of Cubs*, had ceased.

32

Broken Point

U rsula was talking over the open channel, alternating Ursan and Drachna, her voice thick and husky.

"Survivors of *Ark of Cubs*, please respond. We are attempting to reach your location. Survivors, please respond. Tow Chief Rohan, please respond. We are getting to you as quickly as we can."

Rohan turned and flew toward *Ark of Cubs*.

The ship was disintegrating, huge sections of metal drifting apart, driven by exploding shells and superheated gases escaping from damaged generators. Space around the hulk was hazy, with a thin expanding cloud of vented atmosphere.

Rohan closed on the ship, eyes scanning the wreckage for intact sections or lifeboats he could rescue.

He found none.

He flew between the largest pieces. Corpses floated in space, their furry features distorted by decompression. Streams of blood and viscera arced across his path.

One chamber was nearly intact; just a single wall ripped away. Rohan closed on it, eyes dashing over the cribs containing Ursan cubs, their mouths frozen in their last desperate gasps for air.

The Hybrid screamed. And again.

Wei Li again. "Rohan, are you injured? What's happening? Get out of there, Rohan. You can't save them now. You did your best."

He tapped his cheek to turn off his microphone.

He tapped again, higher up, to turn on his camera.

His facemask broadcast everything he saw on an open low-power tachyon band. Wistful had repeaters in place set to automatically relay the imagery, so anyone in the system could see what he was seeing.

Wei Li muttered a curse. "By the Fists of the Twelve. . . ." Her voice tailed off.

Then Ursula.

"Rohan, respond. We come to help. Soon." She shouted something in Ursan, away from the microphone, talking to her crew. "By the gods. . . ."

Rohan screamed again, louder. He pulled and teased at his rage, stoking it, images of dead cubs dancing across his mind.

His Hybrid Power built and swelled, its edges licking at his body like flecks of surf on a beach. It *pushed* out from him, positive pressure against the world. Floating puffs of gas drifted away. Debris, from slabs of hull to pieces of lost furniture to full corpses and floating cargo containers, all moved away from him. Even the major sections of the ship vectored off, leaving the Hybrid alone in the empty center of the disaster.

Rohan shot away from the empty bubble he had created, heading directly for the wormhole.

A stream of fighters was already moving toward the open wormhole and the relative safety of their home system.

Rohan passed them, disabling their drives from afar until he reached the first in line.

He ripped the canopy off that fighter and, with a savage slash of his hand, decapitated the pilot.

Wei Li spoke. "Rohan, I can *feel* your anger from here. This is not . . . Please, Rohan. Come back."

The former Imperial lance primary faced the oncoming flight of drifting fighters. He flew from one to the next, peeling each open like a can of sardines and dismembering the pilots.

Ursula spoke. "Please, friend Rohan."

He grunted with each kill, a bark of rage brought up from the pit of his belly.

The fighters stopped advancing.

He headed toward the attack ships. Fighters were entering the ship through the open bay doors.

He followed them through.

Ursan crews were meeting the landing fighters, helping pilots disembark and locking the fighters into place.

Rohan stalked through the crowd, killing with sharp swipes of his hands.

Within moments the bay was ankle deep with clotting blood.

He continued on into the ship.

Some Ursans burst out around corners or from behind hidden doors, wielding guns or makeshift weapons. One came at him with a pair of cutlasses held in its massive paws.

Rohan slew them all.

He found the captain on the bridge, sitting in his command chair, his eyes glassy with shock, surrounded by a ring of his toughest, most able soldiers.

They roared their savage defiance.

Within seconds their roars had turned to screams. Then silence.

Ursula was speaking over his comms. "We are almost there, Rohan. We take prisoners, hold trials, maybe. Punishments will be given. Just a few minutes more."

He found the medical bay. Killed the injured. Killed the cowering medics.

He looked around. He was the last breathing thing on the ship. He was also lost.

Ha. Lost. That's funny.

With a shout he picked a direction and flew, tearing through floors and hull as he exited.

Once in space again he oriented on the last attack ship.

Someone was shouting in Ursan. "We surrender! Please, we surrender! We are at your mercy."

Rohan floated over to the ship's airlock. It cycled open.

"We surrender. You have defeated us. I have never . . . What are you? Are you a god? A devil? Of the Ones Who Came Before?"

The inner door opened. Five Ursans were arrayed in front of the door, kneeling on the cold metal floor.

Rohan tore off their arms and legs.

His video feed was still working.

Ursula made a strange sound, a choked-off yell. "Oh, Rohan, this is not for the good."

It took fifteen minutes more for the Hybrid to exterminate every living creature on the second attack vessel.

His Power had peaked. It started to ebb, to relax its hold on his mind, his spirit, his feelings.

He shook his head. Remembered the cubs. Fought the image into the forefront of his thoughts.

He left the ship. There were lifeboats still afloat.

As Ursula's ship approached, Rohan tapped his comm open again. "Stay back." His voice was hoarse and strange.

"Rohan, we will take these prisoners. We will see justice done."

"No. Stay back or you're next."

The ship rotated in space, turning its back to him, and halted its forward motion.

The wormhole started to change, twisting in upon itself, winking shut, returning to its dormant mirror-like state.

The lifeboats had the most rudimentary of drives. By the time Rohan destroyed the first one, they'd been moving away from the battle for some time.

The rage softened and slowed. The anger settled like a tide, leaving his mind cold and exposed.

He tore apart another lifeboat.

Pain lanced through his chest where the energy weapons had burned through him. The ache returned to the joints in his upper body. His fingers were in agony, traumatized by the forces needed to rip through steel plating.

His clothes were saturated in blood and body fluids, his long dark hair matted and caked with unspeakable things.

He came upon the last lifeboat. He peeled it open. The two Ursans inside stared at him with naked fear on their large bear faces.

They didn't even struggle as he snapped each of their necks with a quick jerk of his hand.

Rohan kicked away from the wreckage and drifted in space.

The area around him was clearing as debris and wrecked ships drifted apart, spreading across that corner of the system.

As the anger receded, it left exhaustion in its wake. He was too tired to move, too tired to think. Too tired to even feel. A numbness stole across his consciousness.

He let himself go limp and drift.

He wondered how long it would take for Toth's gravity to pull him in to Wistful's orbit.

Will someone pick me up? Maybe Wistful will send a shuttle.

His eyes were heavy. Surely it couldn't hurt to rest them for a bit.

The stars twinkled. Heavy objects drifted all around, a slow drift of chaos as hulls and bodies and pieces of equipment moved away on their independent trajectories.

The anger was finally gone, satisfied.

He missed his bed. Suddenly he wished he could talk to his mother. Was she still angry at him for leaving? Did she resent him?

His sleep, thankfully, was dreamless.

· · · ● · ● · · ·

When Rohan opened his eyes he was floating in a tank of viscous liquid.

It was a familiar sensation. He looked around, quickly found a nozzle nearly poking into his face. He sipped sweet fluid from it.

"Welcome back." Wei Li was standing across from him.

"Thanks." He swallowed. "How long was I out?"

She shrugged her muscular but slender shoulders. "Not long. A few hours."

"This is . . . where?"

"Central med bay. On Wistful." Her eyes didn't leave his face.

He swallowed again.

The room was similar to the one he'd recovered in after fighting Garren just a couple of days earlier. Spacious, well lit, white, very sterile.

The major difference was the regen tank in which he was floating. Large enough to submerge an Ursan standing up straight, it was filled with a high-tech liquid that promoted healing. Some secret mix of nutrients, stem cells, and a cocktail of growth factors.

Every Imperial warship had one for its Hybrids. It was the quickest way to return an injured lance to active duty.

"I didn't know Wistful had a regen tank on board."

Wei Li shrugged. "You haven't needed it before."

"No, I guess not."

"And I have been told to ask you to avoid needing it again in the future. The healing gel is apparently both expensive and difficult to come by."

He was naked inside the tank, a harness covering his groin more to recover waste than to protect his modesty, but serving both purposes.

He clicked his jaw. His comm unit had been removed. He had no mask. "No comms?"

Wei Li shook her head. "Doctor's orders."

"Ah."

He floated in the tank as his memories of the battle against the Ursans bubbled up through his consciousness.

Without the anger to shield him, the horror of what he had done struck him like a blow to the chest.

"Oh, god. I . . ."

Wei Li's gaze did not waver.

Rohan swallowed, flooded by a desperate, anxious desire to leave the tank, to move away, to run, to fly as fast as he could.

Wei Li cleared her throat. "You must stay in the tank for now. Doctor's orders. Please restrain yourself because I am unable to do so."

He struggled to calm himself. He let out a long, slow breath, held his empty lungs, filled them again.

"I will." He barely choked out the words.

She stared at him for another minute.

"You are in distress."

He swallowed hard. "I'm pretty sure what I did yesterday would qualify as war crimes in most civilized places."

Wei Li shrugged, lines of muscle and scale moving on her neck with the motion. "I am no legal scholar but I would guess that to be the case."

"That doesn't really make me feel better."

"I believe I have asked this before, but do you think it is my job to help you feel better?"

"I suppose not. But you're my friend, right?"

"Ah. You wish for me to talk to you as your friend, and not simply as security chief?"

"Isn't that why you're standing here? To be my friend?"

"Actually no. I am standing here because Shayjh assassins have been trying to kill you while you were injured and unconscious, making this place . . . not secure. And I am, as you know—"

"Security chief. Sorry, I didn't realize."

"As I said, you were unconscious at the time. If you wish for me to speak as your friend, I will. My first question is, do you believe you did the wrong thing yesterday? Do you wish you had acted differently?"

He paused and thought. "I really should have stopped when they surrendered."

"That is what most people would say. And yet you did not."

"No. I . . . I don't know. I don't want to make excuses."

"Yet there were some extenuating circumstances. You had just witnessed, from a close vantage point, war crimes committed on innocent victims."

"Yeah. Not really an excuse, though."

"I didn't say it was."

"Rudra's braids, how freaked out is everybody else about this? Do the Ursans all hate me?"

Wei Li paused. "I cannot speak for 'all' of anything. But speaking generally, you are not currently hated. I believe that everyone who viewed the footage understands on some level why you reacted as you did. In fact, there is a group of Ursans outside your room, guarding you against further assassination attempts, at the risk of their own lives."

Rohan twitched inside his tank, pushing small waves across the fluid's surface. "I don't want that. I don't want them here."

"Life is not always about what you want. As I believe you are aware."

"I came to this station so I wouldn't be in these situations anymore. And now it's happening again. I need the Power, and when I bring it, the anger comes along. Like a nasty hitchhiker."

"I do not know this term. But I would like to share something with you. Some advice."

"Go for it."

"You have a very particular gift. It happens to be a gift for violence. You could change your life in such a way that you are not called upon to use that gift again. You could retire to a secluded mountaintop, raise herd animals in isolation. That way you would not be a danger to anyone. But you would also be of little use to anyone."

"Are you saying I shouldn't feel bad about what happened? Because I do more good than harm?"

"That is definitely not what I am saying. If you didn't feel bad about it you would probably be well on your way to becoming an actual monster."

"That's what I thought. So . . . what do I do? Just go on about my life knowing that I'm a big bundle of theonite just waiting to go off?"

"I am not interested in coddling you through a bout of existential self-doubt, Rohan. You are fully aware that there are steps you can take now to gain better control of the anger that comes with your Power. You are also fully aware that none of those measures are guaranteed to be effective.

"You're going to have to decide for yourself whether it is worth it to you to remain engaged with the world, knowing you might lose control again in the future, or if you should . . . not.

"And you'll have to accept that your friends and acquaintances will be making similar calculations. Some may choose to stay away from you, and that is their right. But so far that has not happened, and for that you should be grateful."

"That was a good speech, Wei Li."

"Not one of my best, but if you found it helpful, I am glad."

"Were you serious about Shayjh assassins coming after me?"

She nodded. "Two so far. Doctor Simivar sustained mild injuries with the first attack."

"Oh, damn. I'm sorry."

"The corpse soldiers are very good at evading detection. Shayjh personal stealth technology is just as advanced as their ship tech."

"Two so far. Are more on the way?"

"I do not believe you are in imminent danger. Wistful and I reconfigured her internal sensors to sample the air for various Shayjh-specific biomarkers."

"I didn't know she could do that."

"It is a computationally expensive task, so she only does it with cause. Which there now is."

"Does that cover the whole station?"

"No, only the central core. We'll have warning if any Shayjh enter this section. Out on the arms we're on our own."

"Okay. Well, that's a lot better than nothing."

"Indeed."

"Do you think that corpse soldier was on board Wistful before? Or was it a new arrival?"

"I am not certain, but I suspect it was newly arrived. I doubt the Shayjh have maintained a warehouse full of frozen bodies on Wistful just in case they should someday need them."

"So presumably it came by shuttle. Any chance you can track that shuttle? With the new active sensors? The way we talked about the other day?"

She nodded. "Wistful is already running the calculations. I should have something soon. You're not going anywhere right now, so a few hours won't make any difference."

He felt a knot in his back unraveling. If he could find the Shayjh mother ship he could at least do something good for Tamaralinth.

"Thanks, Wei Li. I owe you one."

"I believe your counting skills are inadequate. But we do not need to keep score."

He laughed, coughing softly with the effort.

The door cycled open. Through it he glimpsed a crowd of heavily armed Ursans, waiting quietly for a chance to do something.

Doctor Simivar ducked her head as she came through the door so her twisting horns would clear the frame. Her left arm was in a white sling.

She walked to the regen tank, tapping on a screen built into the side of the tank and nodding. "How are you feeling, Rohan? Any pain? Unusual sensations? Difficulty breathing?"

He shook his head. "I can't feel my chest. But my breathing seems fine. More importantly, how are you?"

She shook her head. "It is nothing. If I had your metabolism I would be healed already."

She tapped at the screen, switching data streams. "Luckily for you, I've been researching Hybrid medicine since your last visit, and we were able to manufacture some painkilling agents that should prove effective."

"Thank you."

"You should know that you were quite badly injured."

"How bad?"

"Let's just say that the burns went *through* your torso. The skin on your back was blackened."

He whistled softly. "It seemed like a good idea at the time. Maybe it wasn't."

"Yes. Well. It's my job to fix you up, not to tell you how to handle yourself in combat. But it would be unwise to leave the tank right now. In fact, you should stay here through the night, at a minimum."

He sighed. "Would it make a difference if I said how much I dislike sleeping in these things?"

"No, it would not."

"Okay."

"It is possible that if you rush your recovery. you could sustain permanent damage to your heart or lungs. Not likely, but possible. Please stay in the tank." She turned her head to him. Her solid yellow eyes seemed to look into his. "Any gaps in your memory?"

He thought. "I don't remember coming here. Was I unconscious the whole time?"

"What is the last thing you remember?"

"Passing out after destroying the last lifeboat. Kind of near the wormhole. I don't remember getting cleaned up or taken on board any ships."

"You passed out, so that is to be expected. The Ursans cleaned you up and brought you here."

"Then no memory gaps."

"Headache? Dizziness?"

He shook his head. "Not really."

"You are still badly injured and showing significant agitation. I need you to relax. Since there are no signs of brain trauma I am comfortable increasing your medication dosage. You're going to feel very . . . let's say, altered. Drink as much as you can, even if you don't feel thirsty."

He turned his head, took the nozzle in his mouth, and took a long sip.

The doctor tapped a few commands into the tank, dispensing stronger medications to her patient.

Doctor Simivar looked at Wei Li. "Please encourage him to follow instructions and stay in the tank and try to relax. He really needs the rest. I doubt a single other humanoid on this station would have survived those burns."

Wei Li spread her hands apart. "You believe he listens to me? But I will try."

"Thank you, Chief. And you, please listen. You can have your comm and helmet back. But don't go anywhere."

"What if there's some new emergency?"

"Then somebody else will have to deal with it." Doctor Simivar looked at Wei Li again. "We still on for cards tomorrow?"

Wei Li smiled. "Yes. I wouldn't miss it. I believe Ursula, the captain of the Ursan ship, would like to join us."

"That sounds great. I've never beaten an Ursan in cards before. I'll double the food order."

"Better to triple it."

The doctor laughed, her sharp incisors flashing in the harsh light of the medical bay. Then she turned and left.

Rohan looked at his friend. "I was serious when I said that what I did should be considered war crimes. On Earth they'd put me on trial."

"Wistful has not asked me to put you under arrest."

"Will she?"

Wei Li shrugged. "I would not expect that. This system is her jurisdiction, and she is very old. Her sense of justice does not match your people's."

"Do you think she should?"

The security chief paused. "I am not a judge. Perhaps for a reason. I would have been strongly inclined to execute those soldiers, had you captured them. The fact that you killed them yourself does not upset me as much as perhaps it should."

"There would have been a trial first, though."

"Yes. And so there should have been. I do not agree with what you did. But I do not hate you for it, and I am not willing to go so far as pushing Wistful to have you arrested for it."

Rohan sighed. "Speaking of people with a reason to hate me. Is Garren still in the med unit?"

Wei Li nodded. "He is. I believe he is recovering, but I haven't checked up on him today."

"What time is it?"

"Three."

They passed some time in silence, Rohan floating in his tank while Wei Li watched over him.

He sighed. "Wow, those meds are strong. I feel like I just drank a barrel of whiskey. Would you get my mask? Or my comm link? Or both? So I can check my messages. Somebody might be trying to reach me."

"Such a male. Always assuming you are the center of attention, that if you are out of touch for a little while everybody else will fall apart. If you promise to stay in place I will get your mask."

"Deal."

The security chief kept her side of the bargain.

A message from Tamara was at the top of his queue. He tapped so quickly to read it he almost dropped the mask into the tank.

"Tamara sent me a message."

"Is this surprising? You are in a relationship, are you not? The entire station is aware of what happened this morning, I imagine she is concerned for you."

"We, well, it's complicated. I guess we're on a break right now."

"I understand. By which I mean that I absolutely do not understand, but I have no desire for further information regarding your romantic foibles. At least not today."

"Sure. She just asks if I'm okay. How should I answer? How's this: 'Other than my chest hair I'm fine. You'll have to come over and check that out for yourself.'"

"I believe that is too suggestive for a couple that is, as you say, on a break."

"Yeah, you're right. Delete that. 'Most of the damage was to my chest hair, not anything important.'"

"If she valued your chest hair, as I believe you indicated she did, this would be overly dismissive of her concerns. You might as well say the attack has rendered you impotent."

"Okay, not what I wanted. Deleting that one. Maybe I'm not cut out for cute or funny today. Let me try this: 'I'm mostly all right; recovering quickly. I'll talk to you tomorrow.'"

"Finally, a sensible message written by a male. I shall gamble heavily tonight, for clearly this is a time when the most unlikely events are likely."

"You know, you don't have to lay it on so thick."

"I do not have to. I do, however, enjoy it."

"Are you going to stay here all night?"

"I have nothing else pressing to handle."

"Okay. Did the Ursans want to talk to me? Or are they just going to wait in the other room?"

She shook her head. "They have not expressed any desire to speak with you. Do you want to talk to them?"

He shivered. "What the hell would I say?"

"I was asking, not suggesting."

He swallowed and let out a long breath. "Sorry."

"No apology needed. On a separate note, do you have some plan to deal with the Shayjh? Or should I plan to remain as your bodyguard for the indeterminate future?"

"If you can get me the rough location of the mothership, I can scare them off."

"Really? Just like that?"

"I fought a war against the Shayjh in the Zahad system. I learned a lot. Give me some credit. Plus, you know, if I'm most of the way to being a monster, might as well use it to my benefit."

"Well, then. I will have the tracking data ready for you in a few hours."

"Okay. As soon as I get out of this tank I'm going to go handle them."

"You lead a strange life, my friend Rohan."

"I do, don't I?"

33

Things are Still Nails

R ohan woke to darkness.

"Lights, soft." He was floating? Why was he floating?

As the room filled with a soft glow he remembered his circumstances.

"Sorry to wake you, Rohan. We had a small situation." The door was cycling shut behind Wei Li.

"It's okay. What's going on?"

"Another corpse soldier was sent here to kill you. I had to stop it."

"Oh, wow. Thanks. What time is it?"

"It's three."

"That can't be. It was three the last time I asked you."

"That was afternoon. This is morning."

"Oh. Right. Sorry, I'm not thinking straight yet."

"Get some sleep. I'm watching."

"Have you been here the whole time?"

"Yes. As I said, get some sleep."

"Oh. Thank you."

"You are welcome, Rohan."

He drifted off.

The next time he woke up the lights were brighter. Wei Li was still standing guard over him, and Doctor Simivar was tapping at a screen on the side of the tank with her undamaged arm.

He stretched his arms, creating ripples in the fluid.

"Good morning, Tow Chief. How are you feeling today?"

"Better than I expected. Is it morning?"

"Yes, you slept through the night. Your chest seems to be healing nicely."

"I feel good. I can't believe I slept so much."

"You've been an excellent patient. And I gave you exceptional drugs. I'm ready to release you whenever you're ready."

"Cool."

"Do you need help disengaging from the tank?"

He shook his head. "I've done this before."

He worked himself free of the harness and climbed out of the tank. A hydrophilic field at the top of the tank restrained the fluid, leaving him dry as he slid down the outside. A fresh uniform was waiting for him, folded neatly over his mask and comm link.

"Wei Li, just out of curiosity, are you expecting more Ursan warships to come through the wormhole? Now that they know how to open it?"

"No. Ursula and Ang have a plan to stop the incursions."

"Are they going through? Continue their war? Wistful will let them?"

"Actually, they're going to open the wormhole and send back the ships you destroyed. All of them."

"Oh. I guess that's going to be a deterrent."

"Yes. They also intend to maintain an active patrol of the area. To be quite frank, I doubt they'll need it. Once those ships go back I find it hard to believe that anyone on the other side will be eager to come here."

"You're probably right." He finished dressing and stuck his comm link to the skin behind his ear.

She paused. "Rohan, this is my day off. If you need anything, please let me know."

He thought. "Thanks. I think I can take care of this on my own."

"Very well. If you change your mind, you know how to reach me."

"I do. And thanks again, Wei Li."

"You would have done the same for me."

"I would have, but you'd never know if it was to protect you or just to get a peek at you all wet and naked."

She smiled and shook her head. "I would know." She turned and left the room.

Doctor Simivar smiled at him. "Please don't rush to see me again, Rohan. Or if you do, make it a social call."

"Will do, Doc. Thanks for patching me up. And sorry about the arm."

He went to the door while she reset her equipment.

He took a deep breath, braced himself, and opened the door. The next room over was crowded, a group of Ursans and a few Rogesh standing about. All were heavily armed.

"Hey."

They turned in unison. Rohan recognized one Rogesh, Ben Stone's assistant, the angry student whose life he'd saved on Toth 3. Haditz. He saw the Ursan officer Ang had teased for being gay.

He wasn't sure of the others.

They stood quietly and watched him.

He sighed. "Thank you all very much for watching out for me. I'm good now. You can go get some sleep or whatever. Really, I appreciate it."

One-by-one they walked to him and touched him. A pat on the back, a hand put on his shoulder for a moment. A young Ursan male squeezed Rohan's shoulder hard, his eyes somber. Another Ursan, a female, hugged him. None spoke.

When they were done Rohan was alone in the room.

He looked into his mask and checked the time and his messages.

Tollan had left a message asking Rohan to meet him.

Were the suits ready?

Nothing from Tamara. He was mostly relieved.

A message had come from Wei Li, sent during the night, with a set of coordinates. No explanation. He smiled; it wasn't a pleasant smile.

Soon.

He checked the station's most popular news feeds. Footage of his battle with the farside Ursans was in heavy rotation. He quickly set up filters so he would see none of it.

He was craving real food. It was still early.

"Personal. Is Pop's open yet?"

"Yes, Rohan. Pop's House of Breakfast opened seven minutes ago."

"Excellent."

He walked over to the café. Foot traffic was still light at that hour. Pop's only had a pair of customers. Rohan headed straight for his usual table.

Pop saw him out of one of his outer eyes. He turned away from his customer and walked to intercept Rohan.

Rohan stopped in his tracks.

Pop stood close. "I'm sorry, Rohan, but we can't serve you today."

Rohan swallowed. He should have realized. It was what he deserved. "What's up, Pop?"

Pop shifted from foot to foot. His face was expressionless but his hands were fidgeting with his tablet. "I'm sorry. Someone came by and suggested in the strongest terms that we not do business with you anymore. Until you can get it sorted out. I'm just a waiter, Rohan."

"Someone?" Who cared enough about the dead Ursans to threaten Pop? *Is this something else?* "Wait, was this someone tall and pale and humanoid?"

Pop nodded, his orange-and-black diamond-shaped scales glittering with reflected light as he moved. "A Shayjh. If I could help you, I would, but this is out of my depth."

"No, forget it. You're doing the right thing. I'll go. I mean, I'll fix this, then come back. You'll owe me a double portion of eggs."

"Sure thing, Tow Chief. Sure thing."

Rohan turned to leave. The older man put a hand on his forearm to stop him. "Are you going to be all right? The Shayjh are scary people."

Rohan looked at him. "You should worry about the Shayjh."

Pop pulled his hand back and nodded. He returned to his customers.

Rohan breathed in sharply, then let it out slowly. Held his lungs empty for a long count.

He found a food counter where the server didn't know him and got a glass of tea and a meal made of rice mashed up with tubers and seasoning, all served wrapped in a tangy blue leaf.

He ate. The food was what he'd needed: heavy and satisfying and spicy enough to leave a light burn in his mouth.

There were two hours to kill before Tollan's opened. He considered taking on the Shayjh first, but decided it would be rude if they killed him and he missed his appointment.

Instead, he walked out to the southern arm.

A certain Lukhor boy was playing in the concourse. "Hey, Rinth."

The boy looked up. "Hi, Rohan."

"How you doing?"

He shrugged. "Okay, I guess. Hold on, I'll get the disc thing."

"Frisbee. It's a frisbee."

"Sure."

Rohan lay down in the grass. It tickled the back of his neck. He stared up at the clear roof, Toth 3 hanging as always above him. He tried to relax into the grass. It didn't work.

Rinth came out after just a couple of minutes.

They played frisbee for a while in silence.

Rinth spoke first. "Hey, didn't you get hurt the other day?"

Rohan nodded. "A little. All better now. Doctor put me back together."

"Oh. Good. She couldn't fix your wardrobe?"

"Actually, I ordered new clothes. I'm meeting with the tailor as soon as he opens."

"Good."

"How's your mom doing?"

Rinth shrugged. "She's fine. Normal."

"Good."

A voice called Rinth's name. "That's my aunt; I have to go."

Rohan tossed him the frisbee one last time. "I'll see you later, Rinth. Have a good night of school."

"I will; we're visiting art museums today. I mean, virtually, but I like art."

"Yeah? I was never any good at art."

"You can still learn. You just have to try real hard."

"Maybe tomorrow. Today, I have stuff to do."

"Yeah, get new clothes. 'Bye!"

"'Bye, Rinth!"

A Lukhor woman was standing at the edge of the promenade, looking at Rohan. She was wrapped in a colorful length of fabric, her skin bright green.

For a moment Rohan considered introducing himself, make small talk. Then he turned and walked out along the promenade.

The station was, to all appearances, normal. No signs of the battle he'd just fought or the Ursans he'd killed. No impact on the regular people going about their business.

He wasn't sure how that made him feel. Why should the lives of the station residents have been affected? Why should they be doing anything different? He fought so people like these could go about their happy normal lives. Why would it bother him when they did exactly that?

He pulled his hood over his face and walked.

He found a barber shop. Sat in an elevated chair and pulled back his Power so the barber could neaten up his hair and beard.

He got another glass of tea from a different cart. It was too sweet, but he drank it anyway.

He was waiting in front of Tollan's Things when the light out front switched from Closed to Open. Rohan waited a few extra minutes. It seemed rude to barge in the minute the shop opened.

The corridor was empty, as it almost always was. Tollan's Things was not in a high traffic location.

The door chimed when Rohan pushed it open. Tollan sat behind the counter, as usual.

Rohan noticed how pointy the man's ears were. He looked almost human. Rohan had never figured out his species.

"Hey, Tollan."

"Tow Chief Second Class Rohan."

"That's me. A couple more years like this and I might make First Class."

Tollan grunted noncommittally.

Rohan cleared his throat. "You wanted to see me?"

"Yeah. Have a seat." There was a chair in front of the counter. Rohan didn't remember the chair being there before.

Rohan sat.

Tollan hit a few keys on his keyboard. Then he stood and came around the counter to stand in front of the Hybrid.

"You know what I'm going to say?"

Rohan shrugged. "That my suits are ready?"

"You know that's not it. Though they might be ready tonight."

"Crap. Okay, let me try again. You had a visit from a Shayjh? Maybe he suggested that you stop doing business with me if you're interested in a long and high-quality life?"

"Got it on the second try."

"You could have just texted."

"I don't particularly like being threatened. I wanted to look you in the eye to talk this out."

Rohan scratched at his newly trimmed beard. "Look, don't sweat it, okay? I'm going to deal with the Shayjh. Either I'll get them to call this off or they'll kill me. Either way you're not in the middle, okay?"

Tollan stared hard at Rohan for a minute. "You have a very direct way of dealing with things, don't you?"

"You ever know a subtle Hybrid?"

"Not many. Still, good to see the curse is good for something, in the right hands."

"The curse?"

Tollan hesitated, then nodded. "Sorry. That's what my people call the Power of the il'Drach."

Rohan paused. "You think it's a curse?"

"Don't you?"

"I guess it hasn't made me a better person. There are certainly five thousand dead Ursan soldiers floating out by the wormhole who'd agree."

"Yes, well, Shayjh aren't Ursans."

"Look, I'm sorry you got caught up in this. You okay?"

The older man shrugged. "He just threatened. And I have ways of taking care of myself."

"Okay. You keep working on those suits. I'll make sure you get paid even if I wind up dead."

Tollan snorted. "I'm not worried about my fee. I just don't want to see you get hurt."

"That's sweet. But you should be worrying about . . . Never mind. Just finish the suits. I'll take care of things."

The old man nodded. "You need help with this?"

Rohan shook his head. "Thanks, but no, I've got it. In fact, you already helped."

"How you figure?"

"Hearing from you and Pop kind of pissed me off. I think now I'm in the right place to deal with this. Mentally."

"All right, then. First suit will be ready for pickup by close of business today, one way or another."

"Great. Take care."

"You, too, Tow Chief. And try not to die; it would be a waste of some very fine clothing."

"I'll try. No promises."

Rohan left the store, then left the building. He tapped his comm. "Wistful."

A short pause. "Yes, Rohan?"

"I'm taking the day off. I have to deal with the Shayjh."

"Of course, Rohan. I did not anticipate you working today, in any case."

"Good. Also, I'm leaving the station."

There was a pause. "Rohan, do you mean temporarily leaving?"

"Oh, yeah, sorry. For a few hours. I'll be back if I survive. I don't have anywhere else to go, really."

"Yes, Rohan. Best of luck. And please be careful, you have sustained significant injuries this week."

"I'll be careful. Thank you, Wistful."

He walked to the nearest airlock. Was there something else he should do before visiting the Shayjh? He'd been reacting to immediate situations for so long, he'd forgotten what it was like to prepare.

He stood by the airlock, mulling things over internally, for a full minute.

He sealed his mask to his face and stepped into the airlock. Tapped the controls to open it.

The inner door sealed shut and the air was pumped out. Warning lights flared and changed from green to red. The outer door slid open.

He flew out into space.

"Personal. Open the message from Wei Li, I think it's dated this morning. Plot vectors to those coordinates."

"Acknowledged."

He flew a leisurely line across the station, taking in the lights glittering through the diamond exterior. Shuttles were flying back and forth, all at low speeds this close to Wistful.

"Music."

A medley of Bollywood dance hits hummed through his comm system.

"I need to make a trip to Earth just to get some more music."

"Note recorded."

"Delete that, I was talking to myself."

"Deleted."

Glowing lines swooped across the interior of his mask, directing him to the coordinates Wei Li had given him.

He started flying.

Shayjh were known for their stealth technology, but there was no way they could keep a full-sized ship anywhere close to Wistful without it being detected. So Rohan knew it had to be out near the dark edges of the system where she didn't keep a close watch on things.

"I should have brought a sandwich."

"I do not understand that command."

"Never mind. Talking to myself again."

The subroutine running his comm system didn't respond.

As he flew he pulled up maps of orbiting objects near the area the shuttle had come from.

Wistful may not actively scan the far reaches of the system, but Rohan was sure that everything in it larger than a shuttle had been mapped millennia before he was born.

"Let's assume this ship is hiding behind a medium-sized rock. Say, one at least as large as a typical Imperial cruiser. Filter out anything smaller."

"Filter executed."

"Great. Now show me trajectories. Take out the first seven listings, and the eleventh. Those are all too close."

"Done."

He studied and selected on his mask while gaining speed.

By the time he was thinking about slowing down he'd narrowed his targets to a handful of objects.

"I definitely should have brought a sandwich. I'm starving."

The subroutine didn't acknowledge. It was learning to distinguish when he was talking to himself.

"Plot quickest course to come to rest relative to objects A, C, D, K, and Q. Those are the most likely hits."

"Acknowledged. Plotting."

It was past lunchtime before he approached the first asteroid.

He circled the rock, checking craters and gaps in the surface. Nothing.

"Delete object A. Take me to the next target."

Two hours later, Rohan was orbiting a rock about the size of Earth's moon. It had substantial ice deposits and enough heavy metals to cast a good-sized shadow on casual scans.

"This looks promising."

The mask didn't answer.

He flew close to the moon's surface, slowing down to avoid accidental impacts with its mountains and crater ridges.

He *felt* the ship before he could see her, a dark presence hovering over the moon.

Rohan slowed while still out of line of sight from the ship. He landed on the rocky surface of a crater and climbed up to its edge and peeked over the ridge.

The ship loomed in his sight.

The body was a long, thin crescent, a new moon or an unstrung bow, curving back and away from the prow. Seven, long, rectangular sections jutted directly backward, parallel to one another, spaced at irregular intervals and of different lengths, like arrows ready for firing.

That design is familiar.

The ship emitted no light, had no windows or ports exposed to the outside. It hung in place, its bootstrap drives offsetting the moon's small gravitational force to keep it at relative rest on the far side, away from Wistful.

It gave no sign of being aware of his presence. He was too far for a typical empath to sense him, at least not while he remained calm.

It didn't take long for his anger to well up, bringing with it a wave of Power that washed away his hunger, his fatigue, and the lingering aftereffects of the previous day's battle.

A questioning tendril of spirit flared out from the ship. It was beneath the level of language, conveying both alarm and curiosity.

Rohan's eyes narrowed as he focused on a spot about halfway along one of the rear sections.

Right there.

"Open short-range channel. Low power. Tight band."

"Acknowledged. Open."

He kicked himself up and forward, *driving* his body directly toward a spot in front of his target with a heavy punch of acceleration.

"Hail Shayjh vessel. This is The Griffin."

The ship immediately turned away, as if startled, and began accelerating out toward deep space. Rohan saw a rift opening in front of it, a small temporary wormhole typical of the kind that interstellar ships used to cross the vast distances between systems.

"This is *Last Breath*. Forgive me for not staying to trade pleasantries." Even a Shayjh stealth cruiser wouldn't be so impolite as to not introduce itself.

"You're not quick enough to get away. Tell your captain you have a visitor."

The ship lurched forward in fits, moving erratically to throw off the Hybrid's aim.

Last Breath was two kilometers short of the rift when Rohan tore into the base of one of the large rectangular sections.

With a scream of tearing metal and exploding gases Rohan was inside the ship.

He planted his feet in a storeroom lined with heavy steel shelves. Whatever was on them was burning, the bright flames dying down as he watched.

Alarms rang.

Fifty meters forward of where I wanted to be.

Automated hull repair had started, closing the hole he had punched through the thick armored shell of the ship. The wind of escaping air died down.

"Your captain want to talk to me now, *Last Breath*?"

Rohan stalked to the back door of the storeroom and kicked it off its hinges.

The next room was larger and filled with Shayjh soldiers.

Rohan smiled. He'd been guiding himself from memory, hoping the basic layout of the ship matched other similar ships he'd fought in Zahad. So far it had lined up perfectly.

"Corpse soldiers! A matching set. I'm torn between telling you that this is a good try and being offended. You think eight zombies will slow down an il'Drach Hybrid? A Lance Primary? Even a retired one?"

Rohan attacked.

34

Already Dead

The eight soldiers were identical, clones from a common original. They had been brought to life and inhabited by his spirit long enough to imprint basic language and combat skills in their nervous system, then carefully killed.

The corpse soldiers had advantages over living soldiers. Being dead, they had no consciousness of their own. They could follow simple instructions or be directed by a Powered individual nearby. They had no fear, no conscience, no hesitation.

Being dead, they also didn't suffer from the weaknesses that come with a sense of self-preservation. They ignored pain. They could voluntarily contract their muscles at maximum power, throw every punch with heroic effort.

Which made them supernaturally strong, supernaturally fast, and supernaturally tough.

Rohan took down the first soldier, a savage low kick leaving it on the ground with both legs shattered.

He made the second one a quadriplegic with an efficient twist of his wrist.

A new voice spoke over comms. "Who are you? What do you want? We have no conflict with the Empire."

"I've already introduced myself. The question at hand is: Who you are, sir?"

Rohan crushed the ribcages of the next two, turning away as they knelt on the floor taking in wet, frothy breaths.

"This is Captain Elbaran Artikes of the Shayjh cruiser *Last Breath*. Why are you attacking us?"

"Attacking? This is just the way I start a conversation. An introduction. Say, just curious, I know another Shayjh. Adjudicator Magdon Krahl. Have you met him?"

"You're The Griffin?" The captain's voice seemed to have developed the smallest tremor.

"At your service. Well, not so much. The Griffin, yes. You can call me the Scourge. I haven't fought corpse soldiers like this since Zahad."

Captain Elbaran swallowed, loudly enough to be audible over the audio channel. "How is this happening?"

The remaining soldiers pointed rifles at the Hybrid.

Rohan monster-walked forward: a deep step to the right, then to the left, then to the right again, moving too erratically for the next soldier to target.

Stiff fingers to the throat took down another solider. Three left.

"We have no quarrel with the Scourge. We don't!"

"Your Adjudicator does. I told him who I was; he seemed to think I had lost my touch, gotten soft."

"Magdon Krahl?"

Three moves later and Rohan was the only thing still moving in the storeroom.

"What did he do? What did he do?"

The room had no aft exit.

"Magdon Krahl threatened me. He threatened the guy who makes the best breakfast in this sector. And my tailor. He told me he thought I was soft, that I wasn't someone to fear anymore."

With a wave of his hand, without turning, Rohan extended his Power and peeled back the steel of the room's rear wall.

"What do you want?"

The hallway beyond was empty.

A living Shayjh soldier stood in the next corridor; twin daggers in his hands.

"I'm just trying to have a conversation here. Do you think I'm soft? Maybe you could have a talk with your pal Magdon Krahl."

Rohan tilted his head to the side and looked at the living Shayjh out of the corner of his eye.

The man charged.

Rohan ducked and picked up a heavy steel plate that had torn loose somewhere in the fight.

He spun back, away from the Shayjh's first attack. Then he continued the spin, gaining speed, the square-meter steel plate held out from his body to gain momentum.

Its arc finished at the Shayjh's waist.

It barely slowed as it cut through his body and split him in two.

Rohan hopped over the corpse and walked deeper into the ship. He was looking for something specific.

"If the Adjudicator overstepped, that can be corrected. This is not necessary."

"I disagree. I think this is totally necessary. Are you questioning my judgment?"

He walked to the end of the hall. The doors there had been sealed shut.

He jammed his fingers into the line that bisected the doorway and forced the door open.

The room beyond was vast, a hundred meters long and packed with tanks that resembled smaller, cramped versions of the Wistful med bay regen tank. The bodies inside were prone and packed tight.

"What do you hope to accomplish? This is madness. You are trespassing on a holy place!"

"Holy for you, but to me, eh, not so much. Now let me tell you a story."

There were a handful of unarmed Shayjh in the room who scrambled to stay out of his way.

Rohan walked back and forth until he found a familiar looking panel. "I was badly outnumbered when I was sent to Zahad. That's a longer story, but let's just say I was meant to fail. There were too many Shayjh, too many war clones, lots of forbidden technology in every corner of the system. It was a death trap.

"So I had to get creative. Learn about my enemy. The typical Hybrid set of tactics weren't going to work. You know, punch the other guy until he falls down. If he gets back up, punch him harder."

He tapped at a few symbols on the panel and then threw a switch.

"I could have gone out in a blaze of berserker glory, but that's never really been my life goal. So I found a small ship. Captured it. Kept the techs alive."

Lights sprang to life over a bank of tanks. A hum of pumps whirring into life started.

"You know, the techs? Little guys, scurrying around? Do they teach you to scurry in Tech school? Is it a class? Maybe an elective? They're the ones who never get cloned, never get reincarnated. The guys who keep the tanks working. Turns out, they know a ton of stuff. And it took less effort than you'd think to get them to start sharing."

One-by-one the lids on the tanks sprang open. Naked Shayjh sat up in each, their eyes wide open.

The captain's voice shook. "Why are you doing this? Why are you defiling the clone room?"

"I learned quite a bit about the different clones, the different tanks, the different procedures. See, I know that most of the clones don't have explosives in them. I mean, you wouldn't want your own regular corpse soldiers to blow up when they're killed, wiping out the whole platoon, right? It's just the high-level ones, like the Adjudicator.

"And I know that you don't arm the explosives until the clones are woken up. Because you don't want some clone dying in its tank, then detonating and taking the rest of the clones, and the whole ship, with it, do you?"

"No, we don't. What's your point?"

Rohan pointed at one cowering against the near wall. "You. I'm not going to hurt you. Well, not directly. But tell your captain what I just did."

The Shayjh swallowed. He tapped his own comm and spoke in a shaky voice. "Sir, he woke up all the clones in Alpha row."

"Where is he now?"

"Sir, he's standing in front of the switch to wake up Gamma row."

Rohan continued. "Here's the loophole. Once they're awake, it doesn't matter if they were woken up by override or if someone like Magdon Krahl's spirit actually moved into one. They're up. And the explosives are armed.

"And I happen to know from experience that when they're packed together like this, once you kill one of them, the detonation kills all the ones around it. Then they explode. And so on."

"This is madness! You'll die as well!"

"Hey, come on, give me some credit. I mean, sure, maybe I will. But I'm pretty tough. I survived a point-blank detonation just a few days ago. And, even if I'm wrong, I'm willing to take that chance."

"Are you insane?"

"That's not the question. The question is, am I or am I not willing to destroy this ship, even if it means risking my life? And surely, if you doubt me, there must be an empath or ten on board who can tell you if I'm bluffing."

"I ask again. What do you want?"

"Now we're talking. I want to talk about Magdon Krahl."

"You want his life?"

"No, nothing dramatic like that. I'm trying to get over the revenge habit. No, it's about his contract."

"What?"

"Magdon Krahl is fulfilling a contract with a certain person. Eldarinth Lastex, First Citizen of Lukhor, hired him to keep his daughter from dating any inappropriate people."

"You're kidding. This is about a girl?"

"Hey, watch yourself. She's a great girl."

"What, then? You want to be exempt from the contract? Done."

"Not exactly. I want the whole thing canceled."

"What do you mean?"

"None of you interfere in Tamara Lastex's love life, ever again. Period."

"It's not just about you?"

Rohan sighed. "I wish it were. It's actually kind of ironic. You can come to the station and buy me a round of Sein Amber and I'll tell you the whole story. If you want. Hell, I'll buy you the round, it's the least I can do considering how much damage I just did to poor old *Last Breath*."

"That's all you want?"

"Yeah. To be fair, the Adjudicator should have voided the contract as soon as he found out who I was."

"Yes. He should have."

"Do we have a deal or do I start killing these clones?"

"If you kill the clones the ship will be destroyed."

"Not my primary intention here, but I'm okay with that."

"If the ship is destroyed I'll die. There will be nobody left in the system to put a leash on the Adjudicator."

Rohan paused. "'You're saying my threat isn't enough?"

"I'm saying The Griffin is famous for being ruthless *and* smart. Too smart to think this will work."

He looked around the room. "Get out." He pointed at the techs.

They jumped to obey.

"Captain, why don't you come in here for a private chat."

"Killing me won't get you anywhere."

"'Private chat' isn't a euphemism. I really want to talk, but if your techs or the ship hears what I have to say, you're all dead."

"I don't understand."

"Doesn't matter. What have you got to lose?"

The techs finished leaving. A tall Shayjh, well over two meters, walked into the room.

Rohan looked up. "*Last Breath*. You want to shut down internal sensors in this room."

The ship answered. "You're not in my chain of command."

The captain shook his head. "Do what he says."

"Yes, sir."

The Shayjh approached Rohan, eyes narrowed as he looked down at the Hybrid.

"What do you want to tell me?"

Rohan sighed. "Call off the Adjudicator, promise me what I asked for, and I fly away and never come back."

"Those contracts are important both financially and to our reputation. Why would I do that?"

"If you don't, things will get nasty."

The Shayjh captain didn't respond.

Rohan nodded. "Okay, fine. I'm going to elaborate on my last story, okay?"

The Shayjh shrugged.

"There I was, fighting my way across Zahad system. Tearing through warships, colonies, and, most interestingly, research stations. We both know that most Hybrids would go in, destroy everything, leave without a backward glance. But I'm kind of defective, you know? I have a curious streak. One of those stations was working on experimental corpse soldier projects."

No reaction from the captain.

"They were using Hybrids."

The captain staggered back, bracing against an instrument panel to stay upright.

"Didn't hear about that, did you? They didn't clone any, not as far as I can tell, but they were using Hybrid tissues to enhance their corpse soldiers."

"They were heretics. They've paid for their misdeeds. The true Shayjh would never dare—"

"Oh, we both know you'd dare if you thought you could get away with it. But you know you can't."

"What are you saying?"

"Funny thing is, I never gave a full report of everything I found in Zahad. I was kind of pissed at the time. Like I said, I was sent there to fail. I had no desire to see the Shayjh suffer, so I kept my mouth shut. However, if I hear that the Shayjh are continuing to harass the lovely Tamaralinth Lastex of Lukhor, I might find myself so irritated that I accidentally forward a few private files to il'Drach Fleet Intelligence."

"The il'Drach—"

"Come on. If they even suspect that I'm telling the truth they'll sterilize every Shayjh planet and colony in the sector, then hunt down every Shayjh ship and outpost. They will end your species."

"You would do this for a woman? Doom an entire people? End a culture?"

Rohan met the captain's gaze with hard eyes. "I've destroyed more for less."

The captain swallowed. "We will withdraw from the contract."

"Your word as a captain?"

"Yes. Magdon Krahl will not bother you again."

"Me, or anybody else associated with Tamara Lastex."

"Agreed."

"I think this should go without saying, but make sure to call off your assassins while you're at it. I don't want to have to come back out here."

"You won't. Wait, before you go. Is it true? The story?"

"Does it matter?"

"I would like to know."

"Yeah, it's true. Those heretics risked every Shayjh life in the galaxy with that research. If I had been anybody else, you'd be dead already."

The captain nodded.

Rohan followed fluorescent green marks to a waiting airlock; checked the seal on his mask and exited the ship.

"Personal. Plot a course back to Wistful."

"Acknowledged."

While his course back was being plotted, he flew around to the front of the ship.

"*Last Breath*."

"Yes?"

"Sorry for the commotion. And the attack. I didn't have much choice."

"Yes, sir."

"You can brag about surviving a fight with the Scourge of Zahad now."

"I do not think I will be doing any such thing."

"Well, it's up to you."

Lines came to life in his mask, vectors to follow to bring him home. He turned to face into the system and accelerated.

"I really should have brought a sandwich. Estimated flight time?"

"Ninety minutes at current acceleration."

He was tired.

Nice to stop the Shayjh without having to kill them all. Next time, remember to bring a snack and call it a victory for the new, improved, not-Griffin-anymore.

"Personal. Connect me to the Ton'ga Shell."

There was a long pause. He was connected to Wistful by a low energy tachyon stream, which was nearly instantaneous at insystem distances, so the lag must have been caused by waiting for an actual person at the restaurant to respond to the comms.

"Ton'ga Shell."

"Hi, this is Tow Chief Second Class Rohan. Book the private room for tomorrow morning, say eight o'clock. Me and one guest."

"The private room is for special customers only, sir. I'll have to check."

"No, don't check. I wasn't requesting, I was informing."

"Um . . . sir? That's not the way we—"

"Ask my close personal friend, Adjudicator Magdon Krahl, if it's a good idea to argue with me. I can wait, but for every minute you take before answering I'm going to expect a commensurate increase in groveling tomorrow."

Another voice responded quickly. "So sorry, sir, please forgive our host, he's still being trained. We would be delighted to have the private room ready for you and a guest tomorrow morning at eight."

"Great, thanks very much. I'll see you tomorrow."

"Very good, sir."

Rohan closed the channel and flew in silence for a while.

"Personal. Message to Wei Li. Call me back if you're free, no rush. End."

"Sent."

Wistful was still too far to be visible, but he had a glorious view of the stars. His job rarely took him that far out into the system.

"Rohan?"

"Security Chief. How are you?"

"I believe you should be answering that question first."

"True. I took care of the Shayjh. Only killed a handful."

"Are you all right?"

He thought. "Hungry. And still on edge. Nothing a good meal and a night's sleep won't fix."

"Do you want me to send a shuttle to pick you up?"

"No, thanks. I think I'm faster flying on my own."

"Is there a mess to clean up?"

"No. And good news, no more Shayjh assassins. I have their word."

"That is good news. It seems all your issues have been resolved."

"I wish you were right."

"Have I missed something?"

"I have to talk things out with Tamara. Still nervous about how that's going to go."

"I will not give you any advice. You may feel free to update me after the fact."

He laughed. "Will do. Thanks, Rohan out."

He closed the channel.

"Record audio. Begin. Tamara, it's Rohan. I guess you knew that already, before the message played. Not the point. Sorry, I'm a little scattered right now.

"The point, let me get there. I hope we can talk about some things. I mean face-to-face, not over a comm channel. I can explain everything that's been going on, and at least some of it is stuff that you need to hear. So I hope you'll meet me for dinner. My breakfast, your dinner. I have a table at Ton'ga Shell at eight. In the morning. Let me know, because if you can't meet me I guess I should cancel the reservation and come up with a new plan.

"Anyway, say hi to Rinth for me. And your sister. We sort of met. Just waved at each other across the promenade, but that's like meeting. I'm sorry things were so crazy the last few days. I can't promise that everything is okay or fixed, but I promise I'll explain.

"I hope you're good, I hope your shift is going well. I'll talk to you later. 'Bye.

"End. Send to Tamara."

"Acknowledged."

His stomach rumbled. He turned on his music and thought more about sandwiches as he flew down to Wistful.

35

Breaking Hearts

An alarm chimed.

Rohan sat up in bed. "Off. Lights dim."

He stretched carefully, testing his skin and joints where he'd been burned and injured over the previous few days. There was some pain, but nothing worth worrying about.

A decade as an Imperial lance had taught him a lot about healing. At least physical healing.

Rohan got up and showered. He dressed carefully.

A suit had been delivered to his quarters, as promised, the day before. Forest green and deep reddish brown, the cut was generic but somehow reminded Rohan of something an Indian groom would wear. The fabric was so soft Rohan took several extra minutes just running his hands over it.

He looked in the mirror. The cut flattered him as much as anything he'd ever worn, accentuating his broad shoulders and trim waist.

He felt as much a superhero as he ever had in five years wearing spandex and a cape.

The suit came with a matching satchel that hung at his hip, big enough for his mask with room to spare.

He took extra time brushing out his hair and beard. Checked his breath.

He looked over his messages again. Reread the one Tamara had sent mid-shift, late the night before.

He was to pick her up at her apartment, at a quarter to eight. He was nervous. He didn't know exactly why. He was sure he knew why.

At seven-thirty he was out the door, then navigating the heavy foot traffic outside to reach Tamara's building.

Rohan saw her first, waiting outside the building. She was draped in cloth, a long stretch of red fabric with stripes of white, silver, gold, pink, and coral. Her hair was pinned back with gold jewelry, her ears, neck, and forehead adorned with more ornate pieces.

She was wearing more makeup than usual, her eyes highlighted by a dark circle around each, then lighter colors in concentric patterns. Her flawless green skin was subtly enhanced from cheekbone to lip.

His heart sank heavily into his stomach. He reminded himself that he had met her only two weeks earlier.

I shouldn't care this much.

She smiled, hesitantly, as he emerged from the crowd and approached.

He knew his face was grim, but he couldn't muster a smile. "You look . . . breathtaking. Beautiful."

Her smile broadened, showing perfect white teeth between dark green lips. "I cannot tell if that pleases or displeases you. Should I have made less effort? Dressed, as you say, casual?"

He shook his head. "No, you're perfect. Fully perfect. Absolutely perfect." He stood staring at her.

"Shall we go?"

"Yes, of course. I got us the private room. We can talk, and you can ask me anything you want."

"Anything?"

"Yes. But in private."

"And how did you arrange this private room at this most exclusive restaurant on a tow chief's income?"

His lips finally allowed him a tight smile. "You know, when I came to Wistful, I was committed to living like a normal person. Wake up, work eight hours, have a beer, go to sleep. I didn't want special privileges or responsibilities."

"You say this with very deliberate use of the past tense."

He stepped to her. She stood still, giving him the initiative, to lean in for a kiss or not.

He didn't. Instead, he took her elbow and gestured down the avenue. They walked together, his hand inside her arm.

"The last couple of weeks I've been asked, several times, to do things that don't come with the job description of tow chief."

"That is true."

"So I figured, if I'm going to do the job of a lance, I might as well enjoy at least some of the perks of the job."

"Am I such a perk?"

"No, I'm sorry. That's . . . not what I meant. At all. I meant, perks like, you know, a seat at the table at any restaurant I want to eat at."

"Ah."

"Not all the time. Just today. I kind of sound like an asshole when I say it out loud like that."

"I did not say that, Rohan."

"I won't keep doing it. Just today."

They walked toward Wistful's center.

She shrugged, her sari lifting slightly as she did. He glanced over and caught a quick flash of cleavage. It didn't make things any easier.

"I am not one to begrudge you some liberties, Rohan. You have done much good these past weeks. You deserve some reward."

"That's sweet. I mean, I can pay for the room. I'm kind of rich."

"Are you?"

"Well, not compared to your family. But I was a lance primary for a decade. That's a lot of income, and I didn't get to spend very much of it."

"You were? A . . . lance primary? That is a very advanced rank, is it not?"

He shrugged. "Highest rank for a Hybrid. I don't know, it's not that I'm proud of what I did for the Empire."

"I infer that there is an unsaid portion of that sentiment."

"Well, I was never the strongest or fastest or most powerful Hybrid. Not even close. So I took a lot of pride in being a good lance. At the same time, I wasn't too proud of what I had to *do* to be a lance, so it's . . . complicated."

"I see."

"I'm sorry, I'm babbling about myself."

"That is fine. I like to hear about you. Perhaps not all the time. On occasions." She was smiling again, and he couldn't help but respond in kind.

"Well, you know men, we can talk about ourselves all day."

"Yes. And before I forget, let me say that you too are looking quite handsome today. Your clothing would not be out of place even on Lukhor."

"Thank you."

"On Lukhor, for someone of the lower classes, with limited finances, I mean."

"Well, you can't say I didn't try."

"I am teasing you, Rohan. It is a lovely suit."

He smiled again.

They passed through Wistful's center section, the corridors busy with workers.

"How have you been? The past few days?"

She shook her head quickly. "Busy. Fine. Rinth is well. That is my first priority. Work has been busy but good."

"What does it mean when work is good?"

She laughed. "Too hard or too much work and I enjoy it less. Too little or too easy and I enjoy it less. There is a lovely place in the middle where I am most happy."

"I get it. Here, this is the place."

"I have been here before, actually."

"Really? I want to ask who you were with, but I kind of don't."

"Please, you silly man. It was with my sister's family. But you well know I have dated other men before you. It is nothing for you to be concerned about."

"I know. Irrational male jealousy. I try to avoid it, but once in a while . . ."

They stepped up to the front desk. The host looked them over quizzically.

Rohan cleared his throat. "Back room. Two."

The man looked at his tablet, his brow furrowed, then his eyebrows shot up. "I apologize for the delay, sir. Right this way." He gestured toward the back.

Rohan looked at Tamara. "See? Perks."

She smiled.

They followed the host to the back room.

Wait staff came and delivered water and assorted breads and rolls. Menus were handed out and read.

"How about the tasting menu? Chef's choices? With the wine pairings?"

"Of course."

Rohan handed the menus to the waiter, who nodded. "Of course, sir. I'll be back shortly with the first course."

Rohan's feelings of unease were mounting. He was running out of ways to procrastinate.

Tamara split a small roll in half and spread something over it. There was no butter; the spread was a blended vegetable, something like avocado but with a more delicate flavor.

"This meeting does not meet my expectations."

"What do you mean?"

"I believed there were two possibilities. Either you are breaking up with me, or you wish to continue this relationship. If the first, I would think it would be quicker, and you would not have bothered with the new suit."

"If you thought I might break up with you, why go to so much effort to get dolled up?"

"To punish you, of course. Don't take it personally."

"Ah."

"Yet your behavior is very tentative for a man who wishes to continue. So I am perplexed."

Rohan took a gulp of his expensive wine, barely noticing its exquisite flavor and balance.

"I thought you might want me to break up with you."

"And why is that, dear Rohan?"

"I mean, after . . . the other day. I kind of lost it."

She shrugged. "I will not pretend your actions do not give me pause, but they are not the entirety of you. I am willing to hear you out."

"Yeah. I'm not sure where to start."

The first course arrived, the wait staff whisking food into the private room with brisk efficiency.

Empty glasses and cleared plates were removed just as quickly.

"Normally, I would advise starting at the beginning, but I think in your current frame of mind you'd tell me stories about your infancy. I may not have the patience for that today."

"No, not the very beginning. I'm sorry, I'm not good at this. Let me start with where the issues with us, as a couple, began. Okay, a few days ago, five, I think, I had a visitor."

"A visitor? An old lover? Your wife?"

"No, nothing like that. God, no. It had to do with you."

Tamara's eyes narrowed angrily. "Is this about my sister? Or her husband? Because, if so—"

Rohan held up his hands. "No, no. I don't think so. Not them. It has to do with your father."

The second course arrived, delicately flavored soups served in beautiful ceramic bowls. Later, Rohan would wish he could remember how they tasted.

Tamara's face had paled to a light green. She sipped at her soup and continued. "My father came to see you? He was here?"

"No, no. Not that. It's more like he sent someone to see me."

Her eyes narrowed. She finished her soup, sipped her wine, ate another bite of bread. "Go on."

Rohan sighed. His stomach was tight, a hard ball of metal. It was turning out to be the finest meal he hadn't enjoyed.

"Do you know anything about the Shayjh?"

Her eyes flared angrily. "I do. They are agents used for the most vile and despicable purposes by the wealthy of Lukhor."

"Ah. Well." Rohan thought hard.

The next course arrived, an appetizer. Something creamy on something crunchy. The waiter explained it all but the words passed right through both.

Rohan continued when the waiter had left. "I don't know. I don't know if I should tell you this. Let me say that differently. I don't want to tell you this, because I think it will hurt you, but it's something I think you need to know."

"Rohan, I am a grown woman, a mother, and a self-sufficient being. You should begin to worry less about protecting me and more about explaining yourself. If you know what is good for you."

He swallowed. "Right. Your father has certain expectations about the sort of person he wants you to, I don't know, date?"

"As do all fathers, as far as I am aware."

"Right. But he's First Citizen of Lukhor. Which I assume means he's a really big deal, I actually haven't looked that up."

"It does."

"So your father didn't just disapprove of me from afar. He sent a Shayjh Adjudicator to tell me to stay away from you."

She stared at him with wide eyes. "This happened? To you?"

Rohan nodded. "In this room. Five days ago, lunchtime."

"A Shayjh Adjudicator warned you to stay away from me? Stay away in the sense of romance?"

"Yes. And, just to be clear, he explicitly said he was hired by your father. That wasn't just a guess on my part."

She sat back in her chair. "Rohan, these Shayjh are very dangerous people."

"So am I. I mean, yes, I know."

"And that is why you stayed away from me?"

"It is. They threatened me, but also my friends and other innocent people. I needed some time to figure out how to fix things."

"Oh. Ah."

"I'm sorry, Tamara. Maybe I should have told you, but I wanted to figure out the safest way to handle them. So nobody got hurt. I mean, so only the people who *deserve* it got hurt. And I figured, a couple of days of uncertainty might not be great for you, but it's not the kind of bad that happens when you're on the wrong side of an Adjudicator."

"No, of course it is not. You did the right thing, I think. Perhaps. Wait, what are we doing here? What is this?"

"I'm not done with the story."

They were served more wine, then a light salad. The freshest herbs from hydroponics, exquisitely dressed in the oil of a seed Rohan had never heard of.

The room cleared again.

"Rohan, you were threatened by a Shayjh Adjudicator. Sent by my father. What are we doing here?"

Rohan swallowed. "It took a few days for me to work things out, that's all. That's what I've been doing."

"What do you mean 'work things out'? Write your will?"

"Tamara, I'm not just a regular tow chief. I was a lance primary. For a long time. Remember when I said I was good at my old job? Maybe not proud of it, but good at it?"

Her eyes widened further, her pupils darting back and forth as she tried to process everything he was telling her.

"What are you saying?"

"I went up to the Shayjh war cruiser and had a chat with their captain. They won't be bothering you anymore."

"You scared off a Shayjh war cruiser? And forced an Adjudicator to abandon his contract with my father?"

"Yes, that's what I'm trying to say. Yesterday morning. Everything . . . it all took time. I'm sorry."

"I do not believe that you owe me an apology for this, dear Rohan."

"I . . . don't know. I feel bad, so I say I'm sorry. I'm not sure I handled it right. Maybe I should have told you right away."

The fish course arrived, chunky portions of a shellfish Rohan had never seen.

They ate the exquisite, buttery meat, and drank a light delicate wine.

"You are saying that the Shayjh will no longer interfere in our relationship?"

"Yes. No. I mean yes, but more than that. I convinced them to renounce the contract. The whole contract."

"Please repeat that."

"Tamara, your father didn't hire the Shayjh to keep *me* away from you. He hired them to keep *anybody* he didn't like away from you."

"Oh." Her eyes widened again.

"It's an old contract."

"Oh."

"Which is now void. No Shayjh will interfere with you again. In fact, I'm pretty sure, knowing them the way I do, they'll keep an eye on you and make sure nobody else bothers you. Ever again. Because they know they really don't want me coming back for another visit."

"Are you truly that terrifying, Rohan?"

He finished his fish. "Yeah. I am. Ask the Ursans."

They sat quietly. The meat course arrived, with a new wine.

"Rohan, my mind is spinning like a cyclone right now. You have been living with this for days. Tell me, please, what you are thinking. What I think you are thinking."

He bit into the meat. He couldn't taste it at all. "I think your husband, Rinth's father, had the same kind of meeting as I did. I think they threatened him, threatened his family, his friends. Except, of course, he's just a regular guy, not one of the dozen people in the galaxy who aren't afraid of the Shayjh."

She paled further. "He is . . . a normal man. Maybe a good man, maybe a bad man, but no warrior."

"Knowing what I know, I would guess the Shayjh threatened to, I don't know, have his family tortured to death? And let's be honest, he would have been horrifically stupid to ignore that."

"You think so?"

"Tamara, I really like you. I mean, I really, really like you."

"That is nice to hear."

"You're gorgeous, funny, kind. Gorgeous. I've known you for less than two weeks and I'm completely sure I could happily spend the rest of my life with you. And wake up ecstatic every single day."

"That is a lot to take in. I do like you, as well."

"Look. I don't know for sure, but I'm pretty confident your ex-husband was driven away. And he was driven away by something that no normal person is equipped to deal with. I'd probably tell him he did the right thing by walking out on you."

She swallowed. "Perhaps."

"I hope with all my heart that you don't love him anymore. But I also know that you deserve to know why he left. And maybe that makes you think about things again."

Dessert came, served with a mocha liqueur, a station specialty.

"You say the Shayjh have voided this contract?"

"They won't bother you again."

"Because you demanded it?"

"I can be very persuasive. You're free, basically."

"Rohan. Dear Rohan. You did not simply demand they leave *you* alone?"

He sighed. "Please don't remind me. I can't tell you how badly I regret the way I handled this."

"You don't. You couldn't. You freed me, knowing that it is another who might benefit. You never had to tell me."

Rohan ate the dessert, not tasting it.

"I was being selfish. If I had done any differently, I wouldn't have enjoyed one moment with you. I would have thought, every day, that you should be with your ex."

"Selfish. I do not agree, my sweet Rohan."

"Don't spread that around, you'll ruin my reputation."

She laughed. "Rohan, I care for you. Quite a bit."

"Good. I'll have you know my chest hair is starting to grow back."

"I would care for you even if every hair on your body were burned away, never to return."

"I'm not sure I believe you, but that's sweet."

"I must think about this."

He sighed. "I know."

"This is why you hesitated."

"Yes." His voice was somber, his heart heavy.

She sighed. "I do not know, Rohan. I loved Rinth's father. He abandoned us, without explanation. Without cause, for all that I knew. For that, I could not forgive him."

"And yet."

"And yet now I know that there might have been cause. I have to think about that. This casts new light on old events."

"I know. I expected that."

"I'm sorry, Rohan."

"It's not . . . not your fault. Maybe not mine, either, though, right? Stuff happens."

"Yes. I must think, and . . . I must think."

"I know. Take your time."

"I care about you, Rohan. Ten years ago I would have thought that was enough, that it meant more than everything. But . . ."

"I know."

They sat in silence for a while.

"How was the food?"

She smiled. "It was delicious. I think. One day I'll come back when I'm in the frame of mind to actually taste it."

He laughed. "That's just what I was thinking."

They finished eating and sat while the table was cleared.

"Rohan."

"Yes?"

"You're a good man, Rohan."

He shook his head. "Let's not get carried away, there's plenty of contradictory evidence. Let's just say I do the right thing on occasion and not push it any further."

She laughed and played with her napkin, folding it, then unfolding.

He'd never felt awkward with her before. The Hybrid stood. "I'll save us both and say goodbye. You have to think, so by all means, think, then let me know."

She stood and nodded to him from the other side of the table. "I will think and let you know."

"Don't take *too* long. I have a delicate constitution. I'm not sure I can handle the stress."

"Have you known me to be indecisive, Tow Chief Rohan?"

He shook his head and smiled. "Never that."

"Very well."

"Say hi to Rinth for me."

She rushed over to him and wrapped her arms around his torso in a fierce hug.

He touched her back, lightly, with both hands. More contact than that would have just made things harder.

She left the room.

Rohan gave her a couple of minutes' head start. He finished a glass of water and ate a half a roll that had survived the meal. Then he walked out.

He brushed past the host checking to make sure his meal had met expectations and headed up the promenade.

"Wistful."

"Yes, Tow Chief?"

"Any work this morning?"

"Yes. A typical workload."

"Great. Let me change into work clothes and head out. Maybe twenty minutes."

"That will be fine."

36

Back to Work

He glanced through his messages while he walked.

Some financial updates came through. Some of his investments had lost a good bit of their value a couple of days before, then suddenly rebounded.

Shayjh shenanigans.

A lunch invitation from Benjamin Stone. He accepted.

The Stones are probably leaving soon.

The Ursans were organizing a public wrestling tournament, some traditional art form of their culture. He was invited to be a celebrity judge. He chuckled as he accepted.

Doctor Simivar had sent him a medical care follow up.

He completed it as he walked, repeating "Yes," "No," "Not very often," "Very often," and "Never" in response to the series of standardized questions.

He didn't remember getting as much paperwork from the Imperial Fleet doctors.

He reached his room and gently removed the suit, carefully folding it before placing it into the custom bag. He hung it in his closet, glad to finally have a piece of clothing worthy of an actual hanger and not made to be shoved into the back of a drawer.

He slipped on his uniform, then slipped himself out the airlock.

"Time to go to work."

The tightness across his shoulders unraveled, knot by knot, as he maneuvered each incoming ship into its berth on Wistful.

He felt, for the first time in days, that he was close to returning to the peaceful, boring life he'd lived before the wormhole first opened. He doubted Tamara would continue to be part of his life, but eventually he'd manage to date again, if he wanted to. He was no longer a teenager; didn't believe in soulmates anymore.

A luxury transport full of Tolone'an tourists finished sealing to Wistful's eastern arm and Rohan's morning shift was finished.

He found the café where the professor wanted to meet him. It was new to him, serving Tolone'an cuisine. Rohan had mixed memories of Tolone'an food, but he would try it.

He sat on a bench outside the café and waited for Ben Stone to arrive.

"Rohan!" The professor called to him from across a grassy square.

Rohan turned to see the taller man waving and hurrying over.

Dressed in a simple but well-tailored jacket and pants, the professor was wearing *Insatiable*'s standard gray with a white shirt. His hair and eyebrows were as voluminous and bushy as ever.

Rohan stood and waited for him. They shook hands.

"How are you? I'm afraid we brought you more trouble than we intended."

The Hybrid shrugged. "Not my finest hour, but not my worst, either, which is a pretty sad commentary on my life."

"Well, I'm here if you want to talk. I understand if you don't. But I'd be sympathetic, as much as anyone. We got comfortable with the idea of vigilante justice a long time ago."

"Thanks, I'll remember that. How are you? And your wife? Is this a goodbye lunch?"

The professor's eyebrows rose in surprise. "Goodbye? Why no, no. Come, let's sit, we can talk."

They went into the café and took a table. Menus were displayed on screens built into the table.

"Try the . . . number five. I can't pronounce any of this."

Rohan shrugged. "I'll take the five. I don't remember Tolone'a for the food."

"You? Oh, of course. Oh, sorry. This was quite insensitive of me."

The Hybrid shook his head. "No, it's fine. I kind of hope they don't know who I am, though." He tilted his head toward the kitchen. "They'll clear their tentacles in my food."

"I don't think they resent you as much as that."

"Your friend Garren felt otherwise."

The professor shrugged. "Garren has a lot of anger. I do not believe he's representative of Tolone'ans. I could be wrong, though. Do you want to go somewhere else?"

"No, we can stay. It's just lunch. Worst case, it's terrible and I will have learned a valuable lesson."

"Yes, quite."

They tapped out orders on the keypad. The professor waved a credit chip over a scanner to pay for the meal.

"So you aren't leaving? Or you are, but not yet? What's going on?"

Doctor Stone smiled. "Things are still up in the air, but Marion and I would both like to stay here for an extended time."

"Really? What happened?"

"Nothing specific. I can do my work here as well as anywhere, and to be honest, I like this station. We've been at Academy for a long time, I've enjoyed the change of pace. And we have some unfortunate memories back home which I've been glad to escape."

"I can imagine. What about your wife?"

"She's on the fence. She wants to stay, but only if Wistful gives her permission to do more testing on the wormholes."

Rohan's eyes opened wide in surprise. "What do you mean?"

"Well, there are five wormholes in this system. We now know how to activate one of them. We've only done it from this side once, but it's been repeated twice from the other side with no sign of degradation or dangerous emissions."

"Sure. Unless you count Ursan battleships as dangerous emissions."

"I'm sure Marion doesn't. In fact, we are going to open that wormhole again later today. Oh, don't worry, Wistful gave full permission."

"I'm not protesting."

"Of course. Providing that goes well, Marion has a number of theories as to a general method for unlocking the wormholes."

"You mean she thinks she can open the other four?"

"Exactly! Well, not exactly. She has some mathematical models that yield sets of sequences to try to use."

"Nobody has ever tried that before?"

Doctor Stone shook his head. "Nobody even had any idea that alternating gravity pulses would have any effect on the wormhole, let alone that a very specific and unnatural sequence would be needed. Don't forget, reversible artificial gravity is a relatively recent development in this sector. Mechanicals that can generate push and pull gravity fields in rapid succession are new."

"So nobody had any idea what to throw at the wormhole to open it until the Ursans came through and said they knew all along."

"That is basically correct. It's mostly hypothetical, of course. It's possible that the other wormholes are activated in completely different ways."

"But that's not what you think."

The professor snapped his fingers. "It's not! Occam's Razor and all that. We have every reason to think they were all built by the same people, it stands to reason that the keys would behave in similar ways. It's not proof, but it's not merely wishful thinking, either."

Their food was brought to the table, fish and plants from deep waters, cooked over open flames. It was all briny but flavorful.

Rohan was impressed. "This isn't bad at all."

"Right? This station has truly wonderful cuisine. It's hard to appreciate until you arrive just how big and diverse this place is."

"Two million sentients can't be wrong."

"We should get that printed on shirts!"

They laughed together and ate.

Rohan swallowed a lump of shellfish. "So your wife wants to stay here and continue her wormhole research?"

"Yes. If Wistful refuses, we'll leave. I'm confident she's done pushing her luck as far as that goes. But given permission, I think we'll be looking to stay."

"Stay on *Insatiable* or move onto the station?"

"That depends on what the Empire says. They might want their science vessel back. Of course, they might want her here so they can keep an eye on us if we do manage to open any wormholes."

Rohan scratched his head. "I'd be glad if you could stay. I don't have an abundance of friends, if you know what I mean. It's also been nice to practice my English."

"Agreed. Actually, if I do end up here long term, I thought we might swing by the old blue ball and pay it a visit."

Rohan sighed. "Let me think about that. I haven't been back to Earth in years. I'm not completely sure I want to go back."

"Absolutely, think about it. Just an idea. All very tentative. I'm getting old, getting the itch to see home again, maybe for the last time."

Rohan snorted. "You've got a lot of years left in you."

"Yes, but they're looking like busy years. Not a lot of vacation time."

"That, I believe."

"Speaking of work, there's one thing the others asked me to run by you."

"Oh, boy. Should I have had something stronger to drink before hearing this?"

The professor looked down sheepishly. "I don't think so. Ursula and my wife would appreciate a favor. They'd have asked you themselves, but they heard I was meeting you and . . ."

"Sure. What is it?"

"Would you mind escorting the Ursan ship when they open the wormhole and toss the dead ships through? The wormhole will only be open briefly, they think, so it's unlikely anything will come this way. But just in case."

The Hybrid sighed. "If Wistful gives me the time off, I can do it."

"Splendid! I'll tell them when we're done. Before I let you go, though, how are things with your lady friend?"

Rohan sighed. "I'm ninety percent sure we're done. I really liked her, too."

"I am sorry, Rohan. As I seem to repeatedly say, I am here if you want to talk."

"Thanks. Not today. I just want to get back to my normal life for a while, you know? Work, sleep, breakfast at Pop's. I had a nice little routine worked out, and then all hell broke loose. Starting with the Ursans, I guess."

"I understand." He stood. "I will let the others know what you said."

"Great, thanks. And thanks for lunch."

"Thank you for joining me! Now I believe we must both get back to work."

Rohan shook the older man's hand. They left the café together, then separated at the promenade.

Rohan wandered the station aimlessly for a while, picking up a dessert at one stall lining the avenue. It was a sweet dough, squeezed in lines into hot oil and fried. It reminded him of jalebi.

He had a sudden urge to take the professor up on his offer of a trip back to Earth.

What would I say to anyone after a decade away?

Messages interrupted his reverie.

Wistful granted him time off.

Wei Li asked him to be on the Ursan ship by late afternoon to accompany them to the vicinity of the Ursan wormhole.

Ursula sent him her deepest thanks.

Ang sent even deeper thanks.

Nothing from Tamara. Not that he'd been expecting a response yet, especially since it was the middle of her sleep cycle.

That didn't stop him from checking his filters twice to make sure he wasn't accidentally blocking her messages.

With a sigh, Rohan went back to his quarters.

He queued up some landscape footage he'd saved, beautiful scenery from a planet he'd never been to. Blue trees with purple leaves. Pale pink oceans.

He fell asleep to the view.

· · • • • • • · · ·

R ohan was still clearing the sleep from his head when he met the
    Ursans on their ship, docked in place in its berth on Wistful.

A young officer who bowed a few more times than was strictly necessary
led Rohan from the entrance to the bridge, where Ang and Ursula and a
few of the other officers were going over some charts.

"Hey, guys."

They all turned. "Brother Rohan!" Ang swept him up in a hug.

Ursula patted Rohan's back. "It is good for you to join us, War Chief
Rohan."

"The ship looks great."

Ursula and the engineers nodded. "Wistful's repair crews are excellent.
Ship feels empty with such small crew."

Rohan nodded and stepped to the side of the room. They had work to
do that didn't involve him.

Ang joined him. "How are your wounds, Brother Rohan?"

Rohan touched his hand to his chest. "Just a bit tender. Another couple
of days and I'll be back to normal."

Ang nodded. "It is amazing, this regen tank that you have. Save many
lives, I think."

"It helps. I also heal quickly. Part of the legacy. Being a Hybrid."

"Yes. Listen, please. I did not ask for you to be here. I did not think we
should bother you."

"It's okay."

"Well, I wished to so say."

"Sure."

"Yet here you are. If you could watch over the thing, just be present, all
will feel better. Comforted."

Rohan nodded. "I get it. Really, it's fine. How about this: Let me ride
onboard until we get close. I'll get out before Doctor Stone starts messing
with the wormhole, keep an eye on things. Sound good?"

"Yes, sound good. Thank you, Rohan."

They found a bench built into a back wall and sat down.

Rohan turned to Ang. "They don't need you to plan?"

Ang shrugged. "Is all vectors and intercept algorithms. Fastest way to collect ships. Is math. Ang not so much for math."

"Yeah, me neither."

"Most of work done before by shuttle and other ships. Lifeboat wrecks are collected already. We just have to get big pieces, ready them for tossing through Eye."

"Got it. How is everything else going?"

Ang shrugged his massive shoulders, nearly knocking Rohan off the bench. "We are adjusting. It is not easy, this life, but better than alternative."

Rohan grunted. "I guess so."

They waited and watched while the bridge crew finished their preparations.

Ursula turned to Rohan. "If you would?"

He looked at her blankly, then jumped up. "Of course, sorry! I'm not thinking straight today."

"Is fine. Please, we are ready."

He exited the ship. Wistful gave him clearance and he towed the Ursans out to the buoy-marked perimeter. Once they were clear of the no-fly zone, Rohan re-entered through the airlock and made his way back to his seat. The ship accelerated smoothly toward the wormhole.

Young Ursans served tea and biscuits to everyone on the bridge. They wouldn't make eye contact with Rohan. He wasn't sure if it was deference or fear.

At roughly the halfway point the Hybrid took a walk around the ship. The musky smell had been cleared away and it gleamed, as spotless and clean as any Imperial warship.

Everywhere he went he found quiet Ursans, eyes lowered.

As he neared the bridge, he heard loud voices and commotion. When he stepped through the door they quieted.

Fear or deference. He wasn't sure it made a difference.

With a sigh he took his seat. He turned to Ang. "Let me know when I should exit to cover things."

"I will, Brother Rohan."

The Ursan ship approached the wormhole.

Rohan overheard Ursula and the communications officer contacting the shuttle carrying Doctor Stone and her assistants.

Some signal passed between the officers and Ang. The big war chief turned to Rohan. "It is time, Brother. We will take you back when it's done."

Rohan sighed. "Actually, I'll fly back on my own. I could use the space. Ha. Bad pun, sorry."

Ang shook his head. "Never apologize for pun to Ang. I will see you in future. Soon, I hope. For better things."

"Yeah, better things. I'll stick around until the wormhole, the Eye, is closed."

"Thank you, Brother Rohan. We are again in debt of yours."

Rohan slapped the big Ursan on the shoulder. "You can buy me an ale, we'll call it even. Right now let's just get this thing done."

The Hybrid traced the now-familiar route to the airlock and left the ship.

None of the enemy warships were intact, but someone had collected them into heaps, jamming them together in huge balls of scrap and gore. For a moment Rohan wondered how they had got the pieces to stay together, but he quickly decided he didn't care. Didn't want to know.

He took a position a short distance away and drifted, waiting.

The work went quicker than Rohan expected. The Ursan ship let out four shuttles, and the five vehicles coordinated their efforts to wrangle all the wreckage into a small space.

They worked with Doctor Stone over an open channel to get the wreckage moving toward the wormhole before she opened it. *Insatiable*'s shuttle took a position close to the wormhole. As the mass of wreckage bore down on the shuttle's position, it engaged its forward gravity emitters.

Rohan tensed, expecting something to go wrong. He was ready to fly in and move the shuttle out of the path of the wreckage if they couldn't manage on their own.

His fear was unwarranted.

The wormhole opened, the surface of that huge mirror falling away onto a very alien system.

Insatiable's shuttle immediately skipped out of the path of the Ursan warship wreckage.

Transmissions were coming through the wormhole, Ursan voices raised in a jumble of demands and communications. A combination of threats, demanding questions directed at the dead Ursans, and confused chatter.

The wreckage went through the Eye. The chatter increased.

Rohan and the friendly Ursan warship hovered near the eye, ready to intercept anything with the lack of wisdom to come through.

Moment by moment the chatter died down as whoever was watching on the other side understood what they were seeing.

Insatiable's shuttle moved in to close the Eye.

Comm traffic died down completely. The enemy Ursans were silent.

The Eye dialed shut, twisting in onto itself, leaving behind the reflective surface of the dormant wormhole.

Somber acknowledgements and congratulations went out over the comms between the Ursans and the professor. Rohan watched as the shuttles entered the Ursan warship through large black ports on its sides.

He waved as the ship pivoted in place and started moving toward Wistful.

Rohan stretched, pushing his arms and legs out wide, loosening himself in that way he could only ever manage in zero gravity.

Then he tumbled in place, pointing himself back toward Wistful, and started to fly.

"Personal. Dance music."

His songs played as he worked his way insystem, the wormhole behind him.

His path took him close to Toth 5 and its moon. He turned to look at the moon's surface, wondering if the crater he and Jaroux had made was visible from orbit.

A bright red flash shot across his field of vision, followed by darkness.

· · · ● · ● ● · · ·

R ohan woke, his breathing labored by the pressure that squeezed him spread-eagled and face down over a black metallic dome.

The stars blurred past in his peripheral vision.

His head ached in the back, that annoying familiar post-concussion feeling. He could taste blood in his mouth. His own.

He worked his hands, trying to get a grip on the dome.

The ship relaxed its hold on him. He separated from it by a meter, then the pressure returned.

Rohan was slammed into the dome again. His breath hissed through his teeth and he saw a new field of stars as his face bounced off the hull.

It was the stealth ship; Jaroux's ship, or another of the same model.

He tore into the metal with his fingers, scoring ruts into the hull but failing to do appreciable damage.

The ship had disabled the safeguards on its forward bootstrap drive. The gravitational field it used to maneuver was active past the hull, pulling Rohan in toward it.

It was an old trick, but rarely used. It put terrible strain on the ship's generators. Creating an open gravitational field consumed a terrific amount of energy.

He worked handholds into the armor plating and was ready to pull himself free when the ship drove him into a solid object.

The moon of Toth 5.

The ship released just as his spine impacted the lunar surface. His head snapped back into the rock, another brain trauma to add to his troubles.

He tried to speak, to say something. He couldn't take in any air.

Through blurry vision he saw the ship retreat ten meters, then hover above him.

A hatch opened at the top, disgorging three figures.

Rohan settled back. The moment the first figure left the stealth ship he could *feel* the heavy atmosphere; the aura signature of another Hybrid. Followed by another. Then a third.

All three were on a level with Jaroux. These had serious Power, Lance Primary levels of Power. And they were familiar.

The Dwarf was first. Just shy of a meter and a half tall, a full meter wide, skin like stone. He and Rohan had been friends, once upon a time.

A Darianite followed The Dwarf out of the stealth ship. She wore a half mask, covering just her nose and mouth, her large reflective eyes naked to the vacuum. Her skin was so black he couldn't make out her features, but she seemed familiar.

Rex followed the Darianite out into space.

Rohan knew Rex well, but he would never say they were friends. The bigger, stronger Hybrid had always been an inadvertent caricature of himself, a badly written high school bully who split his time evenly between sucking up to the more popular kids and tearing down anyone lower in the social order. The fact that, unlike most bullies, he was legitimately, brutally strong did little to make him more likable.

Rohan choked out some words. "Hey, guys."

Rex flew down into Rohan, driving a knee into the smaller man's gut. Rohan pulled his arms down, trying to shield himself, but even through his crossed elbows the force knocked his breath away.

The Dwarf and the Darianite swooped in from the sides, completing the pincer. They grabbed his arms and hauled him to his feet.

Rex snapped Rohan's head back with a fearsome jab.

The ground beneath Rohan's feet, solid lunar bedrock, liquefied under him. He sank down to his knees. The two Hybrids holding his arms had no trouble with their own footing.

The Dwarf's Powers had always been potent when he bothered to apply them intelligently.

The stone solidified.

Rohan felt a pulse of Power from The Dwarf and his weight suddenly multiplied.

The gravity of the moon doubled, quadrupled. Soon his head alone was exerting at least fifty kilos of pressure on his neck. Then a hundred. Two hundred.

His Power flared up, anger stirring in his belly, but it was taking all of his strength to maintain the structural integrity of his own spine.

Rex loomed over him. The other two held his arms, partially to restrain him and partially to keep him upright.

Rex smiled, a grim, violent show of teeth that stayed far away from his eyes.

"Griffin. We just heard a story about you."

37

Just After the Prologue

Why am I sitting? Why does my head hurt so much?
Recollection trickled in as the dam between him and the recent past cracked and burst. With a gasp he whipped his head back and forth, his heart performing a speed-metal solo in his chest.

"Oh, good. See, I didn't break him. Not completely." Rex's voice.

Rohan forced his breathing to slow. The helmet could only keep up with so much hyperventilating.

"Rex."

"Oh, good, you can still speak." Rex's voice was snide and oily, his best attempt at sounding like a villainous mastermind from a cheap holodrama.

Rohan looked around. His legs were embedded in the lunar stone up to his knees, and his arms disappeared into it just below his elbows. The stone had been pulled up to form a chair, almost like a throne, its surface glassy and smooth. A hallmark of The Dwarf's Power.

Clear Eyes and The Dwarf were flanking him, but no longer holding on. Rex, as before, faced him, looking down from a great height.

Rohan eyed Rex warily, anticipating more violence.

The big man laughed. "Oh, don't worry. I'm done hitting you for now. We want you to have enough energy to try to escape again. It's such fun when you try to escape."

Rohan swallowed. "On my best day I'd have a pretty slim chance of fighting my way past any one of you. Against three? I know when I'm beaten. I won't try to escape again."

"Good, good. Let's get on with things, shall we, Griffin? There were questions to be answered."

"Call me Rohan. I'm not The Griffin anymore."

"Rohan, The Griffin, Scourge of Zahad, Conqueror of Tolone'a. So many names. I'm sure you'd like us to forget what you are, what you did, along with some of those names. But I assure you that won't happen."

The bigger man's anger was palpable, an aura almost visible to the normal eye.

"You can call me whatever you want. But as far as questions, here's one. Why do you want to kill me so badly?"

Rex shook his head. "We didn't. Oh, sure, everyone thought it was strange, the way you left the service, ran off to this place. But even Hybrids burn out, lose their nerve. It wasn't impossible. Then a raw recruit comes crawling back to us with a wild story about what ended the Rebellion. *Who* ended it. And, well . . ."

"Ah. Jaroux talked."

"Yes. Not exactly an impressive intellect, but that also means he doesn't have enough imagination to make up a story like that, does he?"

"I guess not."

"You did quite a number on him. He won't walk straight for two months. Docs had to tear him apart so they could put his legs back together the right way."

"I'll send him a get-well card."

"No, you won't. As Clear Eyes pointed out, you aren't ever going to be anywhere that's not the surface of this moon, ever again."

Rohan sighed and shook his head. *This is probably overdue.*

Rex continued. "Are you going to beg? Plead for your life?"

Rohan shrugged. "Would it help? Make a difference?"

"Probably not. But I'd still like to see you try."

Clear Eyes clicked her tongue, a sharp crack over the comms. "We are going to kill you regardless, but I want to know why you betrayed us."

"You think I betrayed you?"

"You have admitted that you ended the Rebellion."

"I did. Did any of you ever stop to wonder why I did that?"

Rex was trembling visibly with his anger. "I did. I wondered why any of us would betray the Rebellion. And when I heard it was you, oh, how I questioned it. Doubted. *Especially* you."

The Dwarf shook his head. "How could you, Griffin? Hyperion was your mentor. After what the Fathers did to him . . ."

Rohan snorted. "Your greatest strength is always your greatest weakness."

Clear Eyes suddenly redoubled her focus on him, pinning him in place with her gaze. "What do you mean? Where did you hear that?"

"It's a Darianite saying, isn't it? For us . . . what is the one thing we're trained to do? What's the highest value?"

The others responded in unison, like the well-trained former cadets they were. "Action."

"Exactly. We're trained to act. To act without hesitation. And you know what? It works. When you're fast enough, strong enough, just doing *something* is usually a pretty effective strategy. More often than not, you can overwhelm your enemy before they can do anything to stop you."

The Dwarf sighed. "What's your point, Griffin?"

"The point is that if you can't or won't hesitate, won't pause, that means you don't have time to think. We were all taught to *do* before we think. Or *instead* of thinking."

The Dwarf's face was expressionless. "And you're different? You thought about things, decided to betray the Hybrids? End our hopes for freedom?"

"There was no hope! There was never any hope! That's the part you guys haven't thought through."

Rex grabbed him by the front of his jumpsuit and shook violently. "Of course there was hope! *We* are the strength of the il'Drach! The Fathers cannot stand before us, you know this! We've followed them for centuries, doing their bidding, desperate for their approval, their love, a place of honor in their society. Desperate for family. All this time, we were their strength. All we needed was unity!"

The giant had tears streaking the inside of his mask.

Rohan's headache intensified with the shaking. "What if you're wrong, Rex?"

"How am I wrong? Tell me, how? I am tired of your half-baked insinuations."

"I am not trying to stall you, Rex. I'm trying to get you to understand. Listen to yourself. We're the strength of the il'Drach. Any one of us is stronger than any five of the Fathers, right?"

"Yes! We are. You know it."

"So you think your Rebellion was going to succeed? Because we're stronger than the Fathers? Does that mean we're stronger than the il'Drach? Clear Eyes, quick, what is he forgetting? What variable in this equation is our dear giant friend Rex ignoring?"

She answered as if it were a riddle. "The . . . Mothers?"

Rex let go of the smaller man.

Rohan laughed, letting his head flop to his chest. "Thank you, Clear Eyes. I always thought you were the smart one."

The Dwarf shook his head. "I don't understand what you are trying to say."

"I'm trying to say that the Rebellion was doomed. I ended it in the cleanest way I could. Oh, I tried talking to the Triad, tried to explain, but they didn't believe me. They were just like you guys. So convinced of their power."

The Dwarf stared at him. "So you killed them."

Rohan stared back. "I did. Because if I hadn't, we all would have died. All the Hybrids. And god only knows who else as collateral damage."

Rex shook his head. "What are you talking about? How? What nonsense are you spewing?"

Rohan tilted his head, pointing the top of it at Clear Eyes. "She just told you."

"What Mothers? A female il'Drach has not been seen off their homeworld in . . . ever? Thousands of years?"

"That is true. What conclusion do you, my old friend, Rex, draw from that fact? Do you conclude that there are no Mothers? That the il'Drach are all male?"

The giant's brow furrowed. "No. Of course not. There are young males, they must . . ."

"We know they aren't clones, you can't clone them. Or us. They must be born somehow, right? Surely not many, they're a tiny population, not very fertile, but still. They must have females, right?"

Clear Eyes slapped Rohan's shoulder. "What are you trying to tell us, Griffin?"

"You ever wonder why we're so much stronger than the Fathers? Only half il'Drach, we have orders of magnitude more Power. Everything except fertility."

She grunted at him. "Why will you not reach the point?"

"Oh, *excuse* me for trying to make you understand. Wake you up."

Rex was shaking his head. "He has nothing for us. He is stalling. We should kill him."

The Dwarf shook his own head, as hairless as Clear Eyes' but colored like white marble, complete with veins of blue and brown snaking over his flesh. "He's not stalling. This is how he always is. We should listen."

Rohan sped up his speech. He wanted, needed, them to understand. "I'm trying to explain. I *want* to explain. Look, the il'Drach Power, it flows through time, through bloodlines. Across generations. Think of it as a ghost, haunting the family tree. Every so often, it blossoms, comes to full fruition. In us. But why? Why in us?"

They stared, no answers to offer.

"Think about it. The Power only manifests, like, fully manifests, in a dead end."

They stared at him.

"We're not infertile because we have Powers; we have Powers because we're infertile. We're mules, right? il'Drach can't make fertile offspring with any known species in the sector. *Anywhere* in known space. The best they get is us, half-breeds. But each one of us is a generational dead end. We're viable, healthy, whatever, but we can't have babies. That's why the Power flares in us."

Rex was looking at him with wide eyes. "How do you know this?"

Rohan shrugged. "My *father* told me. He's weird, for an il'Drach. Picked my mother for her brains. Trained me to think from an early age. It's why I never fit in, right?"

Clear Eyes shook her head. "What does this have to do with the Mothers?"

"You know enough to figure it out. But fine, I'll explain: The Fathers are always off somewhere trying to reproduce, right? They're not very fertile, but you know, they find a planet, screw everything that's even remotely female in the hopes of producing a Hybrid. They keep this up for a few hundred years, returning every so often to Drach, maybe do some politicking, then back out trying to breed. Until they die."

She nodded. "That is the way of the Fathers. Serving the Empire."

Rohan snorted. "Sure. Serving the Empire. They worship their fertility. Every last one of them is screwing around nonstop until their last breath is drawn. Where are the Mothers?"

"On the homeworld. On Drach."

"Yeah. Why? Why don't they ever leave?"

All three shrugged.

"Clear Eyes, are mammalian females fertile their entire lives? Typically."

"No. Most go through . . . menopause."

Rohan chuckled. "Yeah. The balance of power in the sector, in the galaxy, ultimately comes down to menopause."

Rex shook his head. "I don't understand."

"Of course you don't. Look, Rex, as strong as you are, it's because of two things. Your Power is only present *at all* because you're part il'Drach. The reason it comes out *in full* is because you're not fertile.

"The Fathers are full il'Drach but fertile. That holds back their Power. They can only use a tiny piece of it. But the females are full-blooded il'Drach. For most of their lives, they're fertile, as strong as the males, which is stronger than a typical humanoid, but nothing like us. But then, one day, their hormones shift, their uterus does whatever the hell happens to women at that age, and suddenly they've become a biological dead end."

The Dwarf stepped back. "You're saying the Mothers have Power? Like us?"

"No, not like us. They're *full-blooded* il'Drach."

"But, then . . . then why do they need us?"

Rohan shook his head. "Their Power is too strong. Come on, you three have all gone into berserker rages, haven't you? The Power takes over, the rage takes over, you wake up two days later and everything around you is dead. Friend, foe, animate, inanimate, doesn't matter. Am I wrong?"

Nobody answered.

"What do you think happens when the Power is twice as strong? Or five times as strong? They didn't come to me and say, gee, Rohan, be a good sport and kill your friends, pretty please. My father took me to Drach."

The three leaned forward. Rex spoke. "You've been to Drach?"

Rohan nodded. "I was taken through the wormhole at the Academy. It leads to a separate system, with another wormhole. Both heavily defended. On the other side . . . it's a planet, nothing special. At least, not as far as I can tell. Big station in orbit. World full of il'Drach. Plenty of other species, you know, doing the actual work. I get the feeling they're permanent residents. Their children and grandchildren will be servants forever.

"The females can reach menopause at any age, it seems. Once they turn, everything changes. The Power comes in a rush, and it drives some of them insane. For those, that means dying in berserker rages that can take out entire cities.

"The ones who *don't* go insane are on a knife's edge for the rest of their lives. They sit in Zen gardens, arrange flowers, meditate four hours a day. Anything to maintain control. And the men, all the men, are terrified of those women. The Matrons, they call them.

"I met some. I felt their Power, dripping off them like water when you get up out of a bath. You can believe me or not believe me, but the Matrons scared me a whole lot more than the three of you.

"They don't leave Drach because once they start fighting they have a nasty tendency to destroy entire planets. You know what people think of Hybrids? That we destroy civilizations? The Matrons actually have.

"And if the Rebellion had gone on much longer, if it had been a little more successful, if I hadn't stopped it, the il'Drach were going to set the Matrons loose."

He sat back and breathed. His left elbow was swelling painfully inside its rocky prison. His right knee had been damaged somewhere along the way.

Worst of all was his head, aching and hollow in the back. He wondered if his skull was fractured.

Rex slowly shook his massive head. "That is a great story, Griffin. Super creative. I can't tell you how impressed I am. But it's not going to save you."

Rohan let his head hang to his chest again. "You don't believe me."

The Dwarf cleared his throat. "It's all too . . . fantastic. I don't know, Griffin."

Clear Eyes nodded her agreement. "You should have come to us. We could have found a way."

Rohan shrugged, his head rocking on his chest. "I tried. They wouldn't listen. Just like you won't listen. But that's okay."

Rex reached down and lifted Rohan's head, looked into his eyes. "What do you mean it's okay?"

Rohan refused to support himself, let his weight rest on Rex's hand. "I guess I always thought it would come to this. It's fine. Kill me, I'll be dead. Case closed. I'll die with a clear conscience, knowing I did what I thought was right. It was bound to happen sooner or later. I don't have a ton to live for, anyway. I can't lead a normal boring life, if I've learned nothing else the past couple of weeks, it's that."

Rex's eyes flared angrily. "Another trick? You think we'll take pity on you? Poor Griffin, gave his life to save the rest of us?"

"If you're going to kill me, go ahead. I don't have to care how you feel about anything anymore. It's not my problem."

"You think we'll feel guilty? You'll have your revenge that way? We'll be haunted by our old friend Griffin, who we killed unjustly?"

Clear Eyes reached out and put a hand on Rex's arm.

He shook her off.

Rohan shook his head. "You're giving me too much credit, Rex. I'm just . . . I'm tired. My head hurts. I don't want to argue anymore."

"You know what? After what you did, I don't think dying is punishment enough."

The Dwarf took a half step back. "What are you talking about, Rex? That's not what we agreed to."

"What, you're going soft on me, Dwarf? Look, he doesn't care about his own life. But he *has* to pay. We have to make a lesson out of him. Something for others to remember. So next time, people think twice before betraying the Hybrids of il'Drach. Something they tell stories about."

Clear Eyes had her attention fully on the big man. "What are you talking about, Rex?"

He let go of Rohan's head and stepped back. "I say we kill him. Then we go to that station down there, what's her name, and go to work on his friends. The people who care about him. Those animals he rescued, I bet he feels good about them. Let's kill them. All of them. Hell, let's destroy the station."

"The Fathers will not like that we—"

"To hell with the Fathers and what they like or don't like! You know I'm right! That's the whole point. Why even kill him, even get revenge, if we just turn around and go back to sniveling under their boots?"

Rohan wanted to sleep. So badly to sleep. "Please, please don't. They had nothing to do with this. Nobody on that station even knew I had anything to do with the Rebellion, in any way."

"Why shouldn't I, Griffin? What bargaining chip do you have? I want to do this for my people. So Hybrids remember for generations. And the next time we *can* rebel, The Griffin of that future era will think twice about betraying his comrades."

Rohan shook his head. "Please don't do this. It won't help."

Rex laughed. "It's not up to you anymore, Rohan. You should have thought about consequences before you took out the Triad."

Rohan thought. "I can give you something."

"You have nothing to give. Unless you mean begging and pleading?"

The Dwarf shook his head. "Maybe he does have something. Let him talk, Rex."

Clear Eyes stepped closer to the big man, as if ready to get between him and Rohan. "Let him speak."

Rex nodded. "Fine. Griffin, what do you have to offer me?"

"You already know."

Rex slapped him, a quick backhand that pulsed a fresh wave of agony through Rohan's skull. "No games, Griffin. Tell me."

"I know the way to Drach. It's heavily defended, I don't think you could break through. But maybe, in a few generations . . . If you want to beat the Fathers, you'll have to get there."

Rex paused. "That is a tempting offer. What do you want for it?"

Rohan swallowed. "Your word. All three of you. On your honor, you leave this system after I'm done. No retaliation against anyone else here because of me."

"You're not even bargaining for your life?"

Rohan shook his head. "Would you offer it? Besides, if you let me go, the Fathers could always send an empath to interrogate me, find out what I told you. No, you can't let me live. You have to kill me. Incinerate my brain, so the Shayjh don't get any answers, either."

The Dwarf rumbled. "It's more than we expected."

Clear Eyes nodded. "I agree. It's something concrete, Rex. Worth more than a story about revenge."

Rex shook his head. "I don't like it. It could be a lie. We won't know if the directions are true until we try them, and that won't be within our lifetimes. It could be a trap."

38

It's a Trap

Rohan laughed. "It's not a trap, Rex. I'm on your side here. I want you to win. After what happened to Hyperion, I *need* the il'Drach to fall."

"I wish I could believe that."

"Look, I'll—we have an expression on Earth: 'I'll sweeten the pot.' I can give you something more. Something concrete."

"What are you talking about?"

"I kind of want to say you already know, but I'm not in the mood to get hit again. I can give you something concrete, something tangible, that answers more of your questions and gives your descendants a fighting chance against the Fathers."

"What do you mean? What questions?"

"You had more questions for me, didn't you? Like, how did I take out the Triad? Come on, you've all fought me. You knew them. Don't you wonder how I not only killed them, but managed to walk away in one piece?"

Clear Eyes focused back on Rohan. "I want to know. I care about how you defeated the Triad more than I do about why."

Rohan looked up at Rex, who nodded. "If it's some stupid answer like you poisoned their drinks or infected them with some Earth virus the deal is off."

Rohan shook his head. "No, nothing like that. The Fathers sent me to end the Rebellion. They gave me a tool to do it with."

The Dwarf perked up. "What kind of tool?"

"A weapon. A weapon of Power. It's old, older than Wistful, older than the Empire."

"And what, we're supposed to show mercy on you because you tell us a story about a weapon?"

Rohan chuckled. "Not a story. I'll give it to you."

"You still have it?"

He nodded. "I convinced them it was lost, destroyed in the battle. I hid it. I can give it to you."

The three Hybrids looked at one another. Rex turned to The Dwarf. "Is what he's saying even possible?"

The Dwarf nodded. "Such things definitely exist. My people—my mother's people—have a hammer that can make whoever holds it as strong as a Hybrid. Summons lightning from the sky. That won't work for one of us, but there's no reason I know of why similar weapons couldn't be made that are attuned to Hybrids."

Clear Eyes nodded. "We have to try. If it is a lie, then he has broken the deal, and we may take your revenge, Rex. If the weapon is true, then we take it and never return to this system."

Rohan sagged again. They would either agree, or not. It was out of his hands. The safety of the people he cared about was out of his hands.

There was a long silence.

Rex broke it. "Griffin, I will take your deal. You show us this weapon. If it is real, we kill you and go. On my honor as a Hybrid and a lance primary I swear it."

The Dwarf and Clear Eyes echoed his words.

Where Rohan had been hoping for a feeling of relief, instead he felt renewed tension.

"I accept. You'll have to take me to the hiding place."

Rex nodded. "No games, Griffin. Tell us where to go."

"It's on Toth 3."

The Dwarf stood up straighter. "Aren't there some kind of dangerous animals on Toth 3?"

Rex waved at him dismissively. "They're animals. We're Hybrids. They should be worried about us. Come on, let's take *Void's Shadow* to the planet and get this weapon."

The heavy gravity squeezing Rohan into the stone eased and abated. The stone liquefied and poured off his hands and arms, the three Hybrids forming a cordon around him to prevent any escape attempt.

He didn't bother. He couldn't put even his moon weight on his left leg, so he floated with them, taking care to move slowly so they wouldn't overreact.

They directed him to the ship.

"Are we leaving this place?" The ship sounded young.

Rohan looked at it. "*Void's Shadow*, isn't it? I thought I told you not to come back here."

The ship answered. "I'm sorry, sir. I didn't have a choice."

Rohan nodded.

The ship's personnel hatch opened. Rex and Rohan entered the airlock first.

For a minute Rex and Rohan were alone inside the ship. It was the perfect moment for Rohan to overpower the bigger man and flee with the ship. Rohan looked up and saw Rex eagerly anticipating the attempt.

He let himself go limp.

Soon all four were inside.

They barely fit inside the cockpit. The instrumentation was shiny and new, all made with a design aesthetic unfamiliar to Rohan.

Rex tapped Rohan's shoulder. "Tell him where to take us."

Rohan nodded. "*Void's Shadow*, can you bring up a map of Toth 3?"

"Yes."

A moment later they were looking at a projection of the surface.

Rohan pointed at a small island close to the middle of the planet's largest ocean.

"There. Take us there. Once we've landed I can walk you to the exact spot."

Rex nodded. "*Void's Shadow*, do it. Smooth and quiet, I don't want the station noticing us."

"Yes, sir."

The ship rose up off the moon's surface. With a twist it pivoted away from Toth 5 and began a long arc toward Wistful and the planet beyond.

The pain in Rohan's head grew as they got closer to Wistful.

The Dwarf nudged him. "Don't sleep. If you die from brain hemorrhage before we get the weapon we won't be able to stop Rex."

Rex smiled down at them. "He's right."

Rohan nodded and fought to stay awake.

Clear Eyes looked at Rohan. "What sort of weapon is it?"

Rohan shrugged. "You'll see it soon enough."

Her eyes narrowed. "And you can tell me now. Or is this trip to the planet some kind of trap? Or stalling tactic?"

He sighed. "They're bracers."

"Bracers?"

"Yeah, bracers. Part of a suit of armor, they cover your forearms."

"What do they do?"

"More than I figured out how to use. For starters, a reservoir of Power. But that's not the best part."

She didn't respond, staring at him with her huge, reflective eyes until he continued.

"They let you manipulate time."

"You mean time travel? Go back in time? That's—"

He was shaking his head. "I wouldn't say that. I mean, I guess it's possible, but I couldn't do it. All I got was time manipulation. Make time move slower or faster."

"How is that helpful?"

"I used it to slow down time for *me*. With that, I could basically move as fast as I wanted to."

She nodded. "That sounds impressive. And useful."

"It takes energy, so there's a limit to how much you can use it, but you can be infinitely fast. Or make your opponent infinitely slow."

She settled back in her seat.

Rohan did, too. He thought about Tamara, letting the pain of that relationship keep him conscious.

The four Hybrids mostly sat in silence as *Void's Shadow* whisked them through space toward the lush green surface of Toth 3.

For Rohan the trip passed slowly. It hurt to breathe and something in his chest wasn't right, because he could taste blood in his mouth when he coughed.

He would have worked himself into a rage, bringing forth a surge of Hybrid Power, and fixed some of the damage, except the three other Hybrids in the ship would likely take poorly to that action and kill him.

"So, *Void's Shadow*."

"Yes, Griffin?"

"Your bosses back home won't be mad you decided to take these three on this little tour?"

"No, sir. I was reported destroyed by Jaroux as punishment for my failure. I no longer have a home."

"Well. That sucks. I'm sorry."

"Not your fault, sir. I did fail."

"You didn't fail, *Void's Shadow*. You were beaten."

Rex snapped at them. "Quiet."

"Sorry."

They passed Wistful in her glittering, diamond-coated glory. Soon Toth 3 was growing fat and lush in the viewscreen.

Rex grunted. "Nice planet. It's unpopulated because of the animals?"

Rohan nodded. "Big animals. Very dangerous."

Rex snorted. "Weaklings. We would make a settlement and surround it with a sea of blood if the natives didn't like it."

Rohan didn't argue.

Their view shifted from mostly black sky with a blue-green dot in the center, to a large blue circle, to vast ocean filling their screen, obscured here and there by white streaks of cloud cover.

Void's Shadow made small adjustments as they went. She slowed appreciably as they neared the atmosphere, obviously not accustomed to high-speed maneuvering inside a gaseous layer.

Rohan was perched at the edge of his seat, studying the screen, when Clear Eyes spoke.

"I see it. Right there." She pointed.

Rohan nodded. It was as he remembered.

The island itself soon dominated the screen. An extinct volcano in the middle, covered with trees and shrubbery. Black sand beaches.

Any other time it would have been beautiful.

Rohan searched, comparing the view to his memory.

"Do you see that little inlet? There's an extra-wide beach there. It's rocky, but probably the best place to land."

Rex grunted, "*Void's Shadow*, do what he says."

"Yes, sir. Landing."

The stealth ship settled into the sand. The hatch opened.

The Dwarf and Clear Eyes used the airlock first, Rex and Rohan right behind them. The four assembled on the beach.

Following Rohan's lead, they took off their facemasks. The air was delicious compared to canned shipside air.

Rohan floated. His leg wouldn't support him.

Rex stared at the smaller man. "Well?"

Time to amp them up.

Rohan looked at the larger man. "You sure we can't just have a dance battle, call it a day? This has to end in violence? We can still walk away from this."

Rex flashed forward and slapped him. Rohan recoiled from the shot.

Rohan looked at The Dwarf and Clear Eyes. "You're going to let him get away with this? Let this buffoon make all your decisions for you? Did both of you have your pride extracted? Some surgery gone wrong? Come on, Clear Eyes, they used to say you have quite a set of balls. For a woman."

She leaned forward, about to hit him, but restrained herself. "Take us to the weapon."

He looked at The Dwarf. "We were friends once. Drinking buddies. You betray that so easily? I've saved your life in battle. On Tolone'a. You know this is wrong. Against your code. You're just going to go along with it?"

The Dwarf shook himself. "Shut up, Griffin."

"'Shut up'? Don't you get it? I saved all of you morons. You're too stubborn to admit how stupid you've been. The Rebellion. You idiots were doomed from the beginning. I killed three to save the rest of you. If you'd had any chance of winning I'd have been in the front lines, right with the Triad, not a coward like you three."

Rohan could feel their anger building like a red fog covering the beach.

Rex closed on him. "Coward?"

"Yes, coward. Three of you to take me out? Where's the honor in that? Sneak attack using a stolen stealth ship? What are you guys, Shayjh? This isn't how Hybrids fight, hiding in the shadows. Quick, name one historic battle, one story, a single legend where the Hybrids outnumbered their enemy. Oh, sorry, you can't."

Rex punched him in the belly. Rohan sank to the sand, vomiting freely on the beach.

Rex lifted both hands overhead and brought them down across Rohan's upper back, flattening the smaller man to the sand.

"I said shut up! Take us to this weapon! Or I'll kill you here on the sand, and—"

"What is that?" Clear Eyes had stepped away from them and was facing the water.

The Dwarf looked at her. "What?"

"You don't feel that?"

Rex paused.

The Dwarf shook his head. "Neither of us are as *sensitive* as you. What is it?"

"Something . . . large. Huge. Something powerful."

"Where?"

She pointed south. "There." She paused, then pivoted. "No, there."

Rex shook his head. "What are you blathering about? There's nothing on this planet but us and a few—"

Clear Eyes was running down the beach, toward the water.

The wind struck her first, a thudding shockwave of displaced air that knocked her stumbling back toward the other three.

Right behind it came the flying kaiju.

It was smaller than the decipedes, five meters long with a ten-meter wingspan. Its wings hung from massively muscled arms, large claws jutting forward about halfway along the leading edge.

The beast was reptilian, red scales with rows of feathers running down its body. The head was long and tapered, two eyes facing the front, along a pointed jaw. A pterodactyl's nightmare cousin.

Clear Eyes punched the thing square in the nose.

It opened its mouth and bit her arm off at the elbow.

She screamed in rage, slipped to the side, and flew up to strike at the creature's eye.

Rex shouted. "What is that?"

The Dwarf rushed to her side.

A second kaiju dropped onto the short, marble-skinned man, driving him into the ground and tearing long furrows of blood into his back.

The reptile hopped backward and a sudden surge of gravity slapped it to the sand.

Clear Eyes drove her intact arm into the first kaiju's eye, digging in as deep as her wrist with a squelch. It twisted its head away, then snapped back and grabbed her by the legs.

It tore and twisted, dislocating her hips.

As she shrieked in agony Rex dove down to the beach to reach her.

Rohan whispered under his breath, keeping the anger down, keeping his rage suppressed, sealing the il'Drach Power that ached to answer this new threat.

Calm, calm.

He inhaled quickly and deeply; let the breath out slowly, slowly, held his empty lungs until the oxygen hunger threatened to overwhelm him. Said his mantra, quietly, quietly. Chanting it.

The Dwarf was screaming in defiance, his black blood tracking lines down his legs and out onto the sand.

Rex had delivered a terrific blow to the first kaiju. One of its arms hung limply from its shoulder. With the other hand it whipped Clear Eyes into the ground, crunching sounds coming from her body with every impact.

A third and fourth kaiju were closing on Rex. He struck one in the face while another raked talons along the back of his legs.

Blood trails sprouted on the enormous Hybrid. He spun to face the one that had hurt him and received a slash across his chest.

Rohan lay in the sand and breathed. He forced his arms to relax, then his legs, willing himself to sink into the ground. He watched the scene through dull, half-lidded eyes, knowing that at any moment the kaiju might turn on him.

They didn't.

The other three Hybrids were summoning up their Power, energy pouring into and through them and forming a miasma over the beach. Rohan could feel the strength and the anger and the rage echoing in his chest.

Rex slammed his fist down on one reptile's foot, breaking bones with a snap that Rohan could feel through the sand.

Clear Eyes stood, her Power reinforcing crushed bones, blood spurting from the stump of her left arm. She moved forward in a dash, tearing flesh from the throat of the kaiju that had maimed her.

The Dwarf spread his arms wide and spread a field of gravity alteration, pinning two other kaiju to the sand with their own weight.

Rohan repeated his mantra and relaxed into the beach. He watched the savage combat and thought about drinks with umbrellas in them and cool breezes and dozing to the sound of waves gently breaking.

The creature that Rex had injured lifted its head and let out an ear-piercing shriek. Another hopped over and met a tremendous punch from the Hybrid that stopped it cold. A third bit down, catching his shoulder in its frontmost teeth, and tore a huge chunk of meat out of him.

Rohan watched the eye that Clear Eyes had damaged close and heal, the kaiju regenerating faster than she could hurt it. It slashed at the female, slicing almost through her lower leg. The Darianite stumbled to the ground, her foot hanging from her body by a few shreds of tissue.

One reptile flopped forward onto The Dwarf, stunning him with its weight and bringing him to the ground. The two he had pinned with his gravitational control swarmed forward, one biting off one of his arms, the other taking a chunk out of his side.

Rex slugged another flyer in the snout, but two others buffeted him to the ground with wide swings of their huge wings.

The tall Hybrid tried to stand, but they knocked him down. Sand was blown away in huge arcing waves until he was squirming on exposed bedrock while they continued to slam him down.

Two of the reptiles cut into The Dwarf, dismembering him joint by joint. He screamed his overwhelming pain and agony, and Rohan remembered his old friend, remembered getting drunk together their first night on Tolone'a, remembered the crazy plan they'd hatched to end the war.

Rex stood again, and again was knocked down into the bedrock. One of the kaiju hopped closer and extended one long talon from its foot and stabbed through his back and into the stone beneath.

A kaiju slashed through Clear Eyes' remaining leg, severing it completely at the knee. She crawled toward Rex, dragging herself with her one remaining arm, leaving a blood trail in the sand.

The Dwarf let out a final strangled cry as a kaiju sliced through his neck. His head rolled free, his flat, cold eyes staring at Rohan as it came to a stop on the beach.

Rex writhed and squirmed in place but couldn't free himself. The kaiju twisted its talon and the Hybrid's legs went limp, his spine obviously severed.

Rohan remembered when Rex had convinced him to try Andervarian cod for the first time.

The kaiju Clear Eyes had wounded bit off the Darianite's head, its teeth crunching loudly on her skull.

Another sliced through Rex's upper body, separating both arms and his head from the piece already pinned to the rock.

Suddenly all was quiet except for the sound of water rushing into the hollow where Rex's corpse lay.

One-by-one the monsters hopped over to edge of the water, stood tall, and let out a shriek loud and piercing enough to drive fresh spikes of pain through Rohan's head.

Rohan waited until he could wait no longer. He pressed himself to his knees, slowly, bracing for a reaction from the monsters.

They ignored him.

He crawled, unwilling to risk exerting his Power. His right knee throbbed terribly with every moment of pressure, his left arm barely able to support his weight. Within two meters he gave up supporting his weight on his left hand, dropping to the ruined elbow.

One of the kaiju took off from the beach, a small tornado of sand formed by the powerful draft of its wings, stinging Rohan's eyes.

He blinked back tears and continued his slow crawl toward *Void's Shadow*, leaving a trickle trail of blood behind him.

He reached the ship. A bubble of sadness welled up in his chest. He couldn't reach the airlock.

Stupid way to die, after all that.

To his surprise, the ship rolled over in place. It presented a hatch for Rohan to use. He sighed and reached for the edge of the hatch. He pulled himself into the ship. He rolled into a reclining command chair, panting heavily.

"Hello, sir."

"Hello, *Void's Shadow*. My name is Rohan."

"Yes, sir."

"Thank you for picking me up."

"Yes, sir. I owe you for coming back here after I said I wouldn't."

"That's okay, *Void's Shadow*. Can you do me another favor? If you don't mind?"

"Yes, sir?"

"Can you take me home? To Wistful?"

"Is that all, sir?"

"Well, that's what I really need at this moment. You're welcome to stick around after, if you'd like to. You're free to leave if you want."

"You mean that, sir? I can stay? Or leave?"

"Yeah. Drop me off at Wistful; we'll call it even. If you want to stay, I'm sure we can find you a berth and some useful things to do. And if you don't, I'll give you a cookie and send you on your way."

"I don't eat cookies, sir."

"I know. It was just . . . sorry. Please take me back, I don't want to leave a messy corpse in here."

"There's an emergency regen tank to your left, sir. It should fix the worst of the damage in an hour or so. If you'd like to use it. I can get you back in less time than that."

"Oh, that's great. Thank you. Thanks very much."

He crawled into the regen tank, a coffin-sized container of clear gel, and fell asleep.

Epilogue

R ohan sat in lotus position across from Rinth, whose slender green limbs had found the posture with envious ease.

"Okay, good. Now breathe out again. Hold that. Think about that spot, but in *my* body. Focus on it. Can you *feel* it?"

They were near the center of a quiet field of grass in the promenade by Rinth's house. They had played frisbee for a while before Rohan gave in to the boy's demands.

The boy shook his head slowly, then paused. Suddenly he bolted to his feet. "I felt it! I did, I did!"

Rohan smiled. "Great, that's awesome. You're a quick learner. Look for the same spot inside yourself. It won't be as easy to spot, but you'll get there."

"Does that mean I can fly now?"

"No, sorry, buddy. It means you're on step one of a long process. At step, I don't know, five hundred or something maybe you'll be able to do some levitation."

"Really?"

"Definitely. It's a lot of hard work, though. You might get bored and stop."

"I won't! Well, I might. I do get bored of things. Especially if they're hard."

Rohan shrugged. "That's okay. I'll help if you want to learn, and if you decide you don't want to anymore, you can stop."

"Thanks."

Rohan paused. "Look, I wanted to thank you for loaning me Squishy."

"What about it?"

"It was nice to hold onto Squishy for a few days, but I think he belongs with you again. I'm old, I don't need him as much." Rohan reached into a small bag at his side and pulled out the octopus plush.

Rinth took the toy. "Are you sure?"

"Yeah. I think you should save him for another grownup who's having a tough time."

"Okay, I'll do that."

Tamara walked across the field toward them.

She wore her work jumpsuit and had no makeup on. Her long hair was tied back in a tight ponytail and she had a couple of grease smudges on one cheek.

Rohan stood quickly, his heart in his throat.

"Rinth."

"Yes, Mom?"

"Go inside and wash up. I'd like to talk to Rohan alone. Okay?"

"Oh, Mom. I was just about to start flying."

"No whining. You can see him another day, maybe. Now go wash."

"Yes, Mom."

The boy stood. "'Bye, Rohan. Thanks."

"Sure thing, buddy. Take it easy."

They stood next to one another, not touching, and watched the boy trudge across the field and into the house.

Tamara looked at the Hybrid. "I hear you had another adventure."

He scratched his head. "Hopefully, the last for a long time. This was a crazy couple of weeks."

"Yes. I suppose in many ways."

"Yes." He watched her, desperate to know what she would say, certain that he already did.

"Rohan . . ."

"Yes?"

"I feel this is very unfair to you, and for that I am very sorry."

He shrugged. "My mother always told me life isn't fair."

"It isn't. I owe you a great deal for what you've done for me. For us."

"It was . . . You're welcome."

"I spoke with Rinth's father."

"Did you."

"Yes. And he . . . denied it at first, but he eventually confirmed your thoughts. Our thoughts. Our suspicions. About what happened between us."

"Ah. Good. I'd feel pretty stupid if, you know, I had been wrong."

"Yes. And I'm not sure if it's the right thing to do, or if it is even possible, but I feel we have to try again. To be a family. For Rinth's sake. For my own as well, a little."

Rohan shrugged. "Sure, I get it."

"Perhaps you and I can be friends?"

Rohan shrugged again. "I'd rather not. I don't think I can handle that."

"I understand."

"At least not now. Maybe not ever."

"Oh. I see. Yes, that's smart. Makes sense."

"Can I be Rinth's friend? If you don't mind?"

"Yes, that would be good. I would be glad of that."

"Great. Well, best of luck." He turned, ready to walk away.

She caught his arm. "Rohan."

He turned to her. "Yes?"

"I really am sorry."

He smiled at her, or at least attempted to. "Don't be, Tamara. It's not your fault. Just, I don't know, be happy. I'll go and try to do the same."

"Yes, I hope you are happy, Rohan."

"I'm going to go. I'm having breakfast with some friends."

"Yes. Take care."

"You, too."

She let go of his arm, and he walked away.

Both professors Stone were at Pop's House of Breakfast, along with Wei Li, Ang, and Ursula.

They waved as Rohan approached.

He limped to a seat. His knee would need a little more time to heal. "Someone please tell me things are going to quiet down."

Marion Stone shrugged. "We're ready to open another wormhole. God only knows what's on the other side. So, I wouldn't bet on it."

He groaned. "At least I can get some eggs and face things on a full stomach."

They called Pop over and ordered.

The others talked. Wei Li was asking the Ursans if any of their young wanted jobs in security. Her department had openings.

Ben Stone looked at Rohan. "You sent me a message about the kaiju? Something you found out?"

"I tested your hypothesis. Sort of. You remember your idea that the kaiju are empathic?"

The professor nodded. "So far I haven't been able to rule it out, but I can't support it well, either. Hard to test by instrument."

"I had the idea that they are, but they only sense, or only respond to, anger. Maybe not anger, but fighting spirit? Combative feelings? Something like that? It's the feeling that seems to fuel Hybrid Powers."

"Which would explain why they don't immediately react to just any intelligent life forms, but only after some delay."

"That's what I was thinking. Until now. Now let's say I found corroborating evidence."

"Hm. Perhaps when people tried to settle the planet things went fine until someone got into an argument. And in the aftermath, nobody put together what happened because they didn't think to look into that. Or there was nobody left to put anything together."

"Something like that. The other day I had five flyers within three meters of me, and they left me completely alone while I stayed calm. That's the ironic story of my recent life, eh? After always losing it, this time I manage to survive only because I kept my temper."

"Should I ask why you had five flyers within three meters of you? Or will I regret knowing?"

Rohan chuckled. "A little karma came after me. Toth 3 saved me from it."

"Well, Tow Chief Rohan, understanding the kaiju, that is a wonderful discovery. Might not be useful, but it's fascinating."

Wei Li spoke across the table. "He is not tow chief any longer, Professor. He is Captain Rohan now."

The professor raised bushy eyebrows at his friend. "Oh?"

Rohan shook his head. "She's not serious."

Wei Li's vertically slit eyes flashed at him. "I am most serious. You are now the owner of a living ship. She says you are her captain. Therefore, captain you are."

Ursula slapped him on the back. "Congratulations to yourself, Rohan. Is my favorite rank, captain."

He laughed. "I tell you what, call me captain whenever we're on board *Void's Shadow*. Which will be almost never, because you guys can't fit on her."

Marion Stone looked at him. "May I take a look at her tech? I've never seen such advanced stealth capabilities on a ship. Hiding inside another ship."

Rohan shrugged. "It's not up to me. Ask her yourself."

Ben Stone smiled and wrapped an arm around his friend. "You, Rohan of Earth, are one of the nicest people I've had the pleasure to meet in a long time. I am truly glad to call you friend."

"Nicest Hybrid, you mean."

"No, I meant what I said."

The rest of them cheered softly, mugs of hot coffee raised in salute.

Rohan sipped his coffee and relaxed, half listening to the buzz of conversation.

Wei Li was beefing up security because traffic through Wistful was increasing dramatically. Lots of companies thought the wormholes presented commercial opportunities.

The Empire had assigned *Insatiable* to Wistful indefinitely, to assist the professors as they saw fit.

The Ursans would settle on Wistful and help in the exploration efforts. There was also some talk of the station acquiring warships and building a system navy, crewed by the Ursans.

His comm chimed. "Priority message from Drach."

His belly sank. "From whom?"

"It is unsigned. Shall I analyze contents to determine authorship?"

"No. Just read it to me."

The unit behind his ear read his father's words in Wistful's voice.

"Son,

"I have to admit I thought you had lost your mind, quitting the Fleet and retiring to that backwater station, but you've done me proud.

"Sending that idiot back to Drach with his tail between his legs to draw out the most prominent rebels? Bold move, son. I wouldn't have advised taking on three at once like that. But you did it.

"You'll enjoy that scout ship, too. She's all yours now; I bet she'll come in handy.

"Sorry things didn't work out with the Lukhor female. It was a good try; her father's resources could have been useful.

"I'm digging up all I can on that station and its purpose. I'll get back to you when I have something concrete. You stay there, keep building your power base. Those big mammals you rescued could form the core of a nice army.

"We'll make you emperor yet!

"With pride.

"End message."

Rohan sighed. *He never stops.*

The comm pinged him. "Respond to message?"

"Block that address. I don't want to hear more from him."

"Yes, sir."

The comm chimed again.

"I said block—"

"Rohan." The voice differed from his personal comm unit.

"Ah, sorry, thought you were someone else. Wistful, how do you handle it when someone approves of you, but only when they completely misunderstand everything you do?"

"I have never had that experience."

"No, of course not. Never mind."

"I have a question of my own."

"Of course, Wistful. Anything."

"The mantra you whisper. To calm yourself. I am curious."

He laughed and sipped his drink. "It's something my friend Spiral's father used to say. You know what the Fathers teach us to say?"

"I believe I do."

"'Be strong.' That's the mantra. That's what we meditate to. Spiral's dad, he was kind of crazy, more than kind of. But the thing he'd always say to Spiral was, 'Be nice.'"

"That is your mantra? 'Be nice'? Not, for example, 'Be good'?"

"Yeah. Once you try to do the right thing, the moral thing, you find all sorts of ways to justify whatever. Oh, this action here is cruel, but it's for the greater good, so it's right. But you can't argue with nice."

"That is a lovely thing to meditate on, Rohan."

"Thank you. It's why I'm here, you know. You're a legend across the sector, the ancient independent space station Wistful. During Fleet training, we're all taught not to mess with you, that you're off limits. You have a third of the interstellar trade in this sector going through your docks. But the thing I always noticed was that you're so . . . so nice. Two million sentients on board and nobody goes hungry, everyone gets medical care. They think you're cold because you're an AI and you don't talk to most people, but it's not true, is it? You care about these people."

"I am very old, Rohan. And perhaps more alien than you realize."

"Nah. Not buying it. But I'll keep your secret safe. Just don't tell anyone that your tow chief has a soft heart."

"I will keep your secret as well, Tow Chief Second Class Rohan. I might even consider promoting you to First Class in a little while."

"That sounds lovely, Wistful. Really lovely."

Rohan finished his coffee and took in the group seated around his table, smiling and joking with each other.

Things weren't back to where they had been two weeks ago, but the new normal wasn't looking bad at all.

THE END

The *Hybrid Helix* continues in *Return of The Griffin*

About the Author

If you enjoyed this book, please rate and review it on the platform of your choice. Then visit jcmberne.com and sign up for the Book Berne-ing newsletter. We promise not to spam you, but we will send you media reviews, blog posts, updates on forthcoming books, and a free short story. Follow JCM Berne on Facebook or Instagram for more puns, reviews, and the occasional travel photo.

JCM Berne has reached middle age without outgrowing the notion that superheroes are cool. Code monkey by day, by night he slaves over a hot keyboard to prove that superhero stories can be engaging and funny without being dark or silly.

Printed in Great Britain
by Amazon

86370407R00231